P9-DGG-430

GRAND CENTRAL
PUBLISHING

LARGE
PRINT

RAVES FOR
JAMES PATTERSON

"Patterson knows where our deepest fears are buried... There's no stopping his imagination."
—*New York Times Book Review*

"James Patterson writes his thrillers as if he were building roller coasters."
—Associated Press

"No one gets this big without natural storytelling talent—which is what James Patterson has, in spades."
—Lee Child, #1 *New York Times* bestselling author of the Jack Reacher series

"James Patterson knows how to sell thrills and suspense in clear, unwavering prose."
—*People*

THE
NINTH MONTH

JAMES PATTERSON
AND RICHARD DiLALLO

GRAND CENTRAL
PUBLISHING

LARGE PRINT

Copyright © 2022 by James Patterson

Grand Central Publishing
Hachette Book Group
1290 Avenue of the Americas, New York, NY 10104
grandcentralpublishing.com
twitter.com/grandcentralpub

First Edition: August 2022

Grand Central Publishing is a division of Hachette Book Group, Inc. The Grand Central Publishing name and logo are trademarks of Hachette Book Group, Inc.

The publisher is not responsible for websites (or their content) that are not owned by the publisher.

The Hachette Speakers Bureau provides a wide range of authors for speaking events. To find out more, go to hachettespeakersbureau.com or call (866) 376-6591.

ISBN 978-1-5387-5300-2 (trade paperback) / 978-1-5387-2439-2 (large-print paperback) / 978-1-5387-2081-3 (ebook)

Library of Congress Control Number 2022939865

Printed in the United States of America

LSC-C

Printing 1, 2022

CHAPTER

1

SHE IS NERVOUS. SHE IS LATE. She is pregnant. And at the moment she is trying to run—bobbing and weaving—through the rush-hour crowds in Times Square.

Betsey Brown prides herself on her intelligence and efficiency, but both those talents seem to have left her in the lurch.

Betsey, a top-notch surgical nurse at Renwick Hospital, has just finished six hours assisting at a liver transplant procedure. Just when she thought that the operation was about to wrap, just when she thought that she'd be able to make her appointment with NYPD Detective Joel Tierney, a problem shot up, literally shot up:

During the reattachment of the bile ducts one of the adjacent blood vessels began hemorrhaging. It was Betsey Brown who saw the bleeding and quickly handed the necessary clamp to the head surgeon. Betsey didn't mind that the doctor didn't thank her for…ohhh…saving a patient's life. Betsey just wanted to get out of the OR.

A half hour later, mission accomplished. Operation successful. Betsey threw her coat over her bloody hospital scrubs and ran. Now, in her last trimester of pregnancy, her ankles are swollen, her back is burning, and she really, really, really has to pee.

Breathless, sweating, hurting, Betsey falls into a chair in Tierney's office. Tierney is chowing down on a cold piece of pizza, and he appears slightly amused at the sight of his former high school friend Betsey Brown trying to catch her breath and massage her ankles at the same time.

"We still have taxis here in New York, Betsey. Next time, you should take one," he says. Despite Tierney's stab at wit, Betsey's almost restored her breathing to normal.

"I'm here because I need your help," she says. "We need to talk."

"Okay," says Tierney as he looks directly

at Betsey's belly. "Start talking. But talk fast. Because you look like you're ready to pop."

"Could you be any more annoying and cheesy?" Betsey says.

"Didn't mean to be. I apologize. You know me."

"I sure do," she says.

Tierney drops his pizza crust in his wastebasket.

"Listen, Joel. This is really important."

Tierney nods.

"Okay. Give me the story. What's your problem?" he asks.

"It's not my problem . . . well, it is sort of . . . but it's not about me . . . or us . . . Not to worry. And Frankie and the kids are fine. It has to do with a friend."

Tierney's eyes narrow, and then he speaks.

"Let me take a wild guess." He pauses and then says, "It has something to do with your friend Emily."

"How'd you know?"

"I'm a detective. Remember? Instincts?"

"Yeah, but, that's still pretty amazing."

"You can't have forgotten that you called me when she had her break-in," he says.

"And you showed up right away," says Betsey.

"Just saying. We ran all the info, Detective Scofield talked to the building staff, a few neighbors. We got nothing. So if you're here to complain, then..."

"You're right. It is about Emily. But it's worse, a lot worse," says Betsey.

"Hit me with it," says Tierney.

"Emily's gone missing."

"How long?"

"Four days. Four days that I know of," says Betsey.

Tierney stands up and leans across the desk.

"Four days! Why the hell did you wait four days? You must be as crazy as your missing friend is."

"I kept thinking that she was going to show up," says Betsey. A pause. Then Betsey speaks with extreme concern in her voice: "I didn't tell you this before...but Emily thinks that someone has been following her. Do you think it could be that guy?"

"No. I think Emily took a cruise ship to Antarctica. I think aliens came and captured her. For Chrissake, Betsey, of course it could be the guy she *thought* was following her. Does she have any idea who the guy is?"

"Maybe," says Betsey.

"Maybe?"

"Well, it could be this guy Mike. She used to buy drugs from him." Then Betsey adds, "In the old days, when she was using. But anyway. She's not even sure the guy is the dealer. Emily isn't in the greatest shape."

Tierney shakes his head. "Why the hell did you hold off telling me?"

"I'm sorry, Joel."

"Do me a favor, Bets. If I'm ever missing, get in touch with NYPD before they find my body rotting in an alley in Jersey City."

Betsey bites her lower lip and says, "Look, Joel. I should have, but I didn't. And now the situation is what it is…"

"And the situation is screwed up."

Betsey finds her courage and talks.

"Will you come with me to Emily's apartment? She gave me a key to the place last month when… You remember. That's when she said she thought someone was following her… and that's when…"

Tierney presses one button on his phone.

Thirty seconds later, Betsey is shaking hands with Detective Kalisha Scofield, whom she met once before when she and Joel came over to Betsey's to investigate a possible break-in. AD Scofield is tall, she's big, and she's clearly all business.

When Betsey says, "Good to see you again," Scofield simply nods. No smile.

"We're going to do an emergency enter and search," says Tierney. "Possible MP."

Betsey's hands are shaking. Her brain is doing the crazy dance. *Why didn't I call this in earlier? Why didn't I at least call Joel earlier?*

Then movement. Lots of it. Scofield checks her phone. Joel stands up. They're getting ready to run.

"We'll call you, Bets," Tierney says.

"No way. I'm with you," says Betsey, trying to stand up as quickly and gracefully as she can. "And anyway, I've got the apartment key and the code, and the doorman knows me."

Then...car doors opening. Siren on.

Scofield drives the trio to Emily's building on the Lower East Side. The doorman has no problem letting them in. He recognizes Betsey.

Tierney pushes the key into the Schlage electronic lock.

Betsey gives him the punch-in code for the secondary lock: 0-9-9-1-7-0-1. The number is Emily's birth date in reverse, October 7, 1990.

Tierney pushes the door open. He quickly turns his head and pushes Betsey and Kalisha away from the door.

"Holy shit!" he yells. "Stand back! This goddamn smell alone could kill you."

MONTH ONE

NINE MONTHS EARLIER

CHAPTER

2

A WOODEN SIGN WITH faded red lettering hangs over the door at my favorite drinking spot. No, it's not Le Bernardin. No, it's not Eleven Madison Park. The sign for my favorite place simply says:

TED'S BAR AND GRILL

The "bar" part is certainly true.

Ted's is the perfect Lower East Side hangout: a million beautiful liquor bottles standing like a row of chorus girls behind the bartender, an only-in-New-York assortment of terminally hip downtown young folks, along with a just-enough amount of "old timers"—middle-aged bald guys wearing windbreakers, plus one or two middle-aged ladies in cotton print house-dresses. The ladies are putting down some Dewar's before they go home to catch *Wheel of Fortune.*

Yeah, Ted's is a wonderland of perfectly mixed cocktails *and* a long list of beers—from downscale chic Schlitz all the way to upscale chic Sam Adams Utopias.

Now, what about that word *grill,* which also hangs on the sign at Ted's? Well, yes, it has a kitchen, but, fair warning, you'd better like your pretzels cold and your burgers well-done.

But nobody really comes for the food. They come for the booze and the bar and, of course, for Ted's terrific attitude.

I like everything about Ted's. The location, 2nd Street, just above Houston Street. Coolest neighborhood in the world. (Yes, I said "the world.")

I like the cheap black-and-white linoleum floor tiles.

I like the sign that says PIANO IN REAR. And because Ted's has absolutely no piano, sometimes when I've had a bit too much to drink (which is not *that* often) "piano in rear" momentarily sounds like some perverse sexual direction.

I like the photo on the wall of Yankee pitcher Don Larsen being carried off the field after his perfect game in the 1956 World Series.

I like that Larsen's picture hangs next to a more recent photo: Lady Gaga and St. Vincent standing together out on Avenue B smoking a joint and sharing a slice of pizza.

Yet, as is usually the case, the thing that really makes Ted's so cool is Ted Burrows himself. When a guy has got a cute Paul Rudd kind of face along with the wiry muscles of a David Beckham, *and* he can mix a perfect peach daiquiri (Ted's secret? A dash of orange bitters plus a teaspoon of honey), you've got the best bar in Manhattan.

"Is it going to be a Diet Pepsi or a slightly more adult pleasure?" Ted asks me as he slaps a cocktail napkin on the bar. His smile is so adorable.

"In fact," he adds, "that sparkle in your eyes tells me you may have already had a pop or two before you settled down here, Peaches."

I should point out that Ted calls his regulars by their usual *drink*, not by the name on their birth certificates. My usual peach daiquiri means that I'm Peaches. There are a few other regulars who share the same joke—Margarita, Gin Straight Up, Perfect Manhattan, for example—and one or two who might want to change their drink orders. I'm talking to you, Moscow Mule. And you, Mr. Pink Lady.

"I haven't been any place but my office until now, one hand holding a phone, the other banging away at my laptop." I'm lying a bit here. I've actually been lounging around my apartment, drinking Diet Pepsi and gobbling ibuprofen. (I'll admit I'm still trying to fully recover from my wild and crazy Las Vegas trip last week.)

"Whatever you want me to believe, I'll believe," Ted says, and, okay, I'll admit it, as Ted shakes my peach daiquiri, I watch his butt for a few pleasantly satisfying seconds.

"You look very nice from the back," I say to him.

"You look very nice from the back *and* the front."

Flirtation between me and Ted, as always, is on. On the other hand, I am thinking that my flimsy, scoop-neck sundress, white with pink and red flowers, does look kind of adorable and, okay, sexy. (Maybe it's just eye-catching because I'm the only woman in New York today who's not dressed in black.)

Ted and I are pretty honest with each other. But not honest enough for me to tell him that he guessed right; I did do a teeny-tiny bit of drinking before I arrived at Ted's. I fueled up a bit at my favorite dive bar, the nearby Library on Avenue A. I guess I thought that a white wine spritzer in a quiet saloon wouldn't really count as drinking. Anyway, here I am.

Ted is pouring my peach drink into a large, chilled cocktail glass (I told you the place was perfect) when I feel a hand on my shoulder.

"Emily," says the voice that's attached to the hand. "Long time, no see."

I know that voice too well, and I'm really not in the mood to hear it right now.

CHAPTER

3

THAT VOICE BELONGS TO Mike Miller, and the phrase "long time no see" is Mike's idea of a clever conversation starter.

"If you consider yesterday a long time ago, Mike," I say, "then I guess it's true."

I don't exactly remember when and where I met Mike Miller. If I went to church on a regular basis, I'd say that church is where I met him, because Mike Miller has the face of an altar boy. He also has the fashion sense of an altar boy: button-down white shirt, blue blazer, baggy chinos, no socks, penny loafers. You've met this guy.

On the other hand, most altar boys don't

peddle drugs, and, although Mike claims to be an attorney with a degree from Harvard Law (I've never checked, but I should), selling coke and various other mind benders is really what Mike does best.

"How about a snow flurry to go with that drink, Emily?" he asks.

A girl has a better chance of scoring coke in New York City than she does of finding a seat on the subway. But coke is really not my thing. So, saying no isn't all that hard right at the moment.

"Not even a tiny taste?" Mike asks. "Half a line, on the house."

Then Ted jumps in. "Okay, Beefeater, your sales pitch is over. We sell booze, burgers, and pretzels here, nothing else."

Mike's smart enough not to mess with Ted. Mike holds up the palms of his hands to say, *I'm going. I'm going.* Then the creep begins walking toward the exit.

I finish my drink. Sweet and icy and fruity and tangy and smooth and...I look at my watch. The digital face says 11:46.

Oops. I forgot to mention. That's 11:46 a.m., as in 11:46 *in the morning.* I know I showered and did my makeup this morning. But I'm not remembering if I actually slept. My life and my schedule are relatively confusing.

Okay, maybe one more daiquiri. Ted makes them so well. But first… "Hey, Mike!" I yell.

Mike Miller stops just as he reaches the door. He turns around, looks at me. I nod, and Mike raises his eyebrows. He walks back over to me.

"I've changed my mind," I say. "There is something you can do for me."

"Emily, I would do anything for you. You know that."

"Actually, I do know that," I say. "I'm a little too lovable for my own good."

Mike is nodding and smiling. I'm not sure he got the joke.

"Okay. How may I help you, mademoiselle?" he asks.

"I've gotta get back to work. And I'm just not feeling it. Have you got an amphetamine in that vault?" I ask.

Mike's eyes widen.

"You've come to the right place, my lady," he says.

He reaches into the inside vest pocket of his

stupid blue blazer. Then he smiles and says, "Emily, I've got a lid-popper with your name on it. How many you need?"

"I *need* about forty of them. But I'll settle for just one."

CHAPTER

4

THE HUGE MOLLY THAT Mike Miller sells me must be the amphetamine version of a 7-Eleven Big Gulp. I swallow it, and a shudder goes through me. This feeling is nothing like the reds that I popped when I was at Princeton and had to stay awake to finish a term paper, nothing like the ones that got me through a few deadly boring dinner parties that my folks insisted I attend.

Now even with just one or two drinks inside me I feel myself going from buzz to blotto.

Ted pulls me a nice big glass of ginger ale with a splash of bitters. That's his way of saying that he knows what I'm going through. Okay. Good. I *do* have to get back to work, and I *do* have to deal with my irritating boss and my clients and my colleagues.

My straw and I are playing with the ice cubes in my ginger ale when I have a visitor. A woman—my age, my height, my hair color—stops at my spot. I think she's on her way to the ladies' room.

"Can I ask you a question?" she says.

"Nothing hard," I say. "No state capitals."

She pauses. She's confused. I don't blame her. So am I. Then she continues.

"I was just wondering. What's the name of that mascara you're wearing?"

Without even a second's pause, I say, "I have no idea, ma'am."

She smiles and says, "Come on. What is it?"

I consider telling her that I'm feeling so strange in my blurry little upper world that even if I knew the brand's name, I might not be able to enunciate the word. The lady walks away. I think I hear her mumble the word *bitch*. Too bad she thinks that; I'd have told her if I could only remember.

I look around the room. It's filling up with people. Lunch-break people. People in neat jeans, people with good haircuts. In other words, people with real jobs, people who care about those jobs.

The air is filled with the smell of broiling burgers and fries. One of Ted's bartenders, Aviva, has come on. Ted is mostly making cocktails. Aviva is mostly pulling Allagash White on tap.

Suddenly I'm feeling sleepy. The glass of ginger ale feels heavy, and I'm afraid that if I do manage to lift the glass, I won't be able to find my mouth. My instinct is to rest my head on the bar, like a first grader who stayed up too late the night before. I am, however, somewhat aware that Ted probably doesn't want anyone snoring on his bar.

In a moment I see Aviva standing before me. She doesn't look angry. She doesn't look happy. She simply looks...professional. Yeah, professional. That's the word. Why I decide to share this opinion with this annoyingly attractive bartender is a mystery to me. But things you think when you're a wee bit drunk are often a mystery. I speak.

"You look...you look like a real bartender, like a beautiful bartender in a movie or a TV show. Real professional. Like that girl on *Cheers*. The first girl. Shirley Long."

"I don't know that. Is that a movie?" Aviva asks.

"No," I say, in a voice that even I know is way too loud. "It's a TV show. You don't know *Cheers*?"

She does not answer my question. Instead she says, "Emily, how about you go to the back room and take a little nap. You rest, and I'll stay here and help Teddy."

I think I just want to say no, but instead I say, "Teddy? Teddy? When did you start calling him Teddy? I never heard anyone call him that."

For reasons that I can't explain (of course), I just want to leave the bar. I must get to the office. I really do have work. I have to return calls and texts and emails. I'm so very busy. And I'm so good at my job. And everyone likes working with me.

I look at the guy sitting next to me, a middle-aged guy, fifty maybe. He's dressed like a teenager from the fifties. Tight jeans and a white T-shirt and classic Stan Smith sneaks.

"I gotta get back to my office," I say to him.

"Uh-huh," he says. Aviva is watching me closely. Then the guy speaks to me.

"It's Shelley," he says.

"What?" I say.

I just discovered how to straighten my legs. I am convinced that I am finally standing up.

"The woman on *Cheers*. The actress, her name is Shelley Long. Not Shirley."

I don't mean to be rude, but I only have enough energy to say, "Oh…thanks."

No time for good-byes. I'm only slightly confused. I head toward the door. I've had this wonderful, glorious feeling a million times before. My boozed-up body decides its own direction. My brain is barely involved in my body's decisions. I am like a mechanical rag doll. I push the door open. It's not sunny out-side, but it sure as hell is bright. I fumble in my pocketbook for my sunglasses. I can't find them. Maybe I should go back. Maybe I left them in the bar. I turn. But my shoes simply do not move with my feet.

My left shoulder explodes with pain, and just as suddenly it shoots down my left arm. I think the pain might burst through my fingertips. I shake. With pain. With fear. My chest begins to throb with pain, as if some powerful person five times my weight is squeezing me hard from behind. These are symptoms of what? A stroke? A heart attack? Some neurologic catastrophe? Does it matter? One thing is certain, I know I'm going to die.

Again, I try to turn, and then I fall, a five-foot-six woman falling straight down on her face like a piece of wood. I am gone. I am out. I assume that I am dead.

CHAPTER

5

ONE OF MY EYES is working. The other eye sees nothing. I am in a bed somewhere.

This is not good.

Two men who are wearing powder-blue scrubs are standing over me. Three women, I think, are standing with the men. Maybe it's four women. Have I forgotten how to count? It is a great wall of powder blue. Nurses and doctors and all those eager little residents. Clearly, I'm in a hospital.

This is not good.

I tell myself, *Let's look on the bright side, Emily. At least one thing's for sure. You're not dead.* Put more accurately, as I can figure by the voices coming from around me: You're not dead *yet*.

MALE VOICE 1:   So, you've ruled out cardio?

MALE VOICE 2:   Yeah, sure. Unless we cut her open and see something we don't like. The echo is good. The first two ECGs are good. The echo confirmed it. The enzymes are all good. The ankle pulse is still very fast.

(I feel hands touching my ankles and legs. Then I hear people reading off a bunch of numbers and then responses.)

MALE VOICE 3:   Not terrible.
MALE VOICE 2:   Not great, either.

Damn, why did this third guy have to show up to contradict the other guy?

And damn, it turns out that he's the one my body decides to go with.

Suddenly there is a sharp pain in my chest, a pain so huge that I begin gagging. The back of my head throbs with pain. It feels as if I'm choking, really choking, a car tire is stuck in my throat, and the pain in my head will have to escape through my ears. I want to die, and I may just get my wish. Air. What the hell happened to my air?

Alarms and screeching sirens go off. It's just as I thought, that crappy little two-pronged plastic plug in my nose is totally useless. Somebody has read my mind. Somebody pulls it out.

> **MALE VOICE 2:**   (*yelling*) Give her a
> tube!
> **MALE VOICE 1:**   (*yelling louder*) No
> tube! It's got to be her heart. Fuck the
> cardio results. I'm betting it's the heart.

Then I hear a woman's voice. It is a calmer, more soothing voice. "Swab," she says almost softly. Then, only a little louder, she says, "Double swab." A moment later I feel a sharp stabbing pain just above my breastbone. Then I'm out.

The next time I am conscious—I don't know how much later—I hear the same woman's voice. Maybe it's a few seconds later, maybe a few hours, maybe weeks.

"Ma'am," the woman says. "It's all right. It

was your heart—it stopped for a moment but we got it going again. Dr. Calvelli is coordinating your recovery. He's great, one of our best. He'll be in to see you soon. Everything is going to be..."

My body begins shaking, and the pain that I had in my chest has made a mad rush to my back. I am not nauseated. I am not gagging. Is this what labor feels like? Is this what death feels like?

"Call it!" someone shouts.

A screeching alarm begins. A red light over my bed begins to flash. A voice on a loudspeaker: "Patient emergency! Patient emergency! Patient..."

CHAPTER

6

SURPRISE! THE NEXT DAY arrives, and I am still here.

I am actually a living, breathing part of the world. For all I know, I'm *barely* living and *barely* breathing, but here I am in a hospital bed. There are plastic tubes and noisy monitors connected to my arms and my neck. There is a persistent but small amount of pain in my chest. There is a woman in a sort of white pantsuit sitting in a visitor's chair. The woman in the white suit seems to be studying me as if I were a painting hanging in a museum.

"I see we are wide awake," the woman says.

Because she uses the plural pronoun *we,* I am sure that the woman is a nurse. In the next few minutes I learn that she is relentlessly sweet, kind, and cheerful. But her eyes are deep, strong. I'm smart enough to realize that she's going to be in charge of me, not the other way around. I will come to learn that this woman is the impossible combination of strength and sweetness, muscle and mercy.

"For someone who's been through what you've been through, you are looking excellent," she says as she straightens my top sheet and blanket.

There is no mirror nearby, so I don't know for certain how I look. But I'm pretty sure that the word *excellent* does not apply. Yet my sense is that this is a woman who is pretty much addicted to the truth. Then she speaks again.

"Now, before I prattle on and on, I'll introduce myself. I'm Betsey Brown. I'm a surgical nurse. If there's anything you need, just…"

But she won't be finishing her sentence. We both hear a man's voice, a voice that sounds both New York City tough yet nice-guy gentle.

"Sorry to interrupt you, but can I come in?"

Both the nurse and I look toward the doorway. Hmmm. I'm thinking that I truly must be alive, because this is one sweet-looking just-tall-enough short guy: longish dark hair, glasses in nerdy black frames, jeans, all topped off with a doctor's white coat.

"I'm Doctor Calvelli," he says. "And you are…" He doesn't know my name. He glances down at his iPad. "And you are Ms. Emily Atkinson, who, I could add, has miraculously survived a heart attack and a severe lung infection."

"Wow, I did both those things?" I say. Dr. Salvatore (it says so on his ID badge) Calvelli smiles at my little joke.

Dr. Calvelli (who in my mind has already become "Dr. Sal") looks at Betsey Brown and then says, "Is it my imagination or did I see you listed for renal TP this morning, Betsey?"

"I am so talented that I can be in two or three places at once," Nurse Brown says. Then she adds, "I'll say good-bye so you can talk to Ms. Atkinson privately."

"No, please stay," I say. "That way, when the doctor leaves and I can't remember anything he told me, I'll be able to ask you."

CHAPTER

7

MY BUDDY DR. SAL pulls up a chair, and my buddy Nurse Betsey stands at the foot of my bed.

But I can sense that although this scenario has all the trappings of a children's story (*Dr. Sal and Nurse Betsey Help Emily Get Better*), this is going to be something serious. My guess is confirmed as I watch the doctor's sweet little smile transform into a sort of blank-faced seriousness.

"So, Emily," he begins, "I'm the doctor who took care of you when they brought you in yesterday. And, to put it mildly, it was touch-and-go, as we say, from the moment you arrived...unconscious. To begin with, you were having a heart attack. You had a blockage in one artery and a thickening of the aorta wall. It was necess…"

I really think I'm being helpful when I interrupt and say, "My father and my grandfather both had bypass procedures, three arteries each…"

"Okay. Fine. That's helpful to know," he says, "but the tests show that your coronary problem—which could very well be hereditary—was exacerbated by alcohol and drugs."

My self-defense mechanism kicks right in.

"Like I said, it's got to be hereditary. But I'll be honest. I do have one or two drinks every day. I admit it, and I occasionally do some recreational weed. So there you go."

Calvelli is listening to me, but I can see he's not buying it. Or he doesn't care. Or (most likely) he's heard this song a million times before. Betsey Brown remains looking on, but she is looking on quite seriously. Calvelli continues.

"Our tests show that your blood alcohol was point-two-five. That's severe intoxication. Much higher than that, you might not still be alive and breathing."

And speaking of breathing, what Calvelli

says next is almost as frightening as the cardiac info.

"You also presented with a serious lung infection."

"Imagine that," I say, but, wow, this flirtatious-funny approach of mine is not working with Dr. Sal. If anything, my act may actually be pissing him off.

"Lung infection? It's a big bad day for me if I even share one Marlboro Light with a friend." There is a dead silence in the room. So I jump right in.

"I was at a nasty little party the other night. And you know the old saying, 'If you do coke or crack at a party, it's not really doing drugs.'"

"My instincts tell me that you know this is serious, Ms. Atkinson."

Why am I not listening? Why are the doctor's comments not registering for me? What the hell is wrong with me? Other than heart disease and a lung infection?

Calvelli stands up.

"I don't want to give a sermon. I'm a doctor, not a preacher. But the fact is, Ms. Atkinson, that there's the truth we tell ourselves and others, and then...well, there's the actual truth."

I say nothing, but, damn it, I feel my eyes welling with tears. Holding the tears back is making my chest hurt worse. And I know my hair is greasy. And I know I'm lying like a five-year-old.

I cannot keep the tears inside of me. I dab at my eyes with the top of the bedsheet. I do the best I can at taking a deep breath. Then I say, "Truth or not, what are we going to do about all this? The heart? The lung?"

Betsey walks from the front of my bed to the side of my bed. She takes my hand in hers.

"For the lung infection, all I can do right now is prescribe medication. I started you on a steroid regimen last night. But the best thing to be done is something only you can do."

Stand aside, Emily. Here it comes. I've read about it. I've thought about it. And, God knows, my friends have mentioned it a few times.

So I say it. "An alcohol recovery program. Great. Wonderful. I'll sign up today. Now. What about my heart? Bypass? Replacement? What?"

"We ballooned the worst artery last night. But in your condition, we have to postpone cardiac surgery. I've already discussed it with Dr. Mullen, head of cardiology."

"My condition? If I clean up my act a little, I'll be fine," I say. As gentle and charming as Dr. Calvelli is, I am becoming some awful combination of angry and sad. Ridiculous, I know, but that's how I'm feeling.

"Ms. Atkinson, listen to me. At the moment, we're somewhat limited in recommending both medication and surgical procedures for you." I must look a little confused, because then he adds, "due to your condition."

I know I'm woozy. But this is starting to not make any sense. Because of my heart condition? They can't do anything about my heart condition?

He and the nurse look at each other for a second. He takes a step closer to the bed.

"Something that invasive...at this point... well, there could be a risk to the fetus."

Say what? That's what I'm thinking. And while my shock and confusion don't seem to register with the doctor, they do with the nurse.

Betsey Brown leans in toward me and smiles gently. Then she speaks.

"Emily, you're pregnant."

I react like a dumb teenager.

"I can't be," I say. "I'd feel it. I'd know it."

I think this doctor has grown very tired of me. And why not? Hell. Even I've grown tired of me.

Calvelli takes a few steps toward the door. Then he speaks.

"It's very early, but your blood work has spoken. You are definitely pregnant."

CHAPTER

MY HOSPITAL ROOM IS filled with baskets of tulips and buckets of carnations and vases of white roses and sprays of lilacs. Work colleagues. Ted. My friend Quinn. The nurse who checked my vitals this morning said, "Smells like a rich man's funeral in here."

Cheerful way to start the day.

Although the room is filled with flowers, at my own request, the room has not been filled with visitors. Everyone's been told to stay away. I really like a lot of people (and I think that a lot of people return the feeling), but I don't have the energy or the interest to be "good old charming Emily." Plus, I've got to absorb...

the...surprise...the shock of my...What did the doctor say? *Condition?* I even have trouble thinking about the word...*pregnancy.*

Luckily, I've been assigned a really down-to-earth, no-bullshit ob-gyn, Dr. Jane Craven. Dr. Craven is the only person, other than Betsey Brown, whom I've spoken to several times here.

Twice Dr. Craven—in a matter-of-fact way—has brought up the subject of "termination." Once she said, "If you're considering termination, you're here in the hospital now, and the sooner is always the better." Another time she said, "I don't know where your mind is about terminating, but if you're not going to do it, the sooner we get started working on a healthier you, the better." Apparently, "The sooner the better" will be my mantra.

A person lying in a hospital bed can only watch so many hours of CNN. So there's plenty of time to think, to ponder, to worry, to fret.

I review the three men I've been with in the last month or so. I review them over and over and over. I'm certain that I would not care to live with any of them, no offense to three perfectly fine guys. And I certainly would not choose any of them to be the father of my—our—child. I consider Dr. Craven's advice that termination is wise, "the sooner the better."

At other times, of course, I consider the other side of the situation. I'm thirty-two years old, I've got money of my own, I'm not in love, I could easily be in love with a baby. Then I think...but as I'm thinking this time around a hospital orderly knocks on the door and wheels in a gardenia plant that's so large, they could use it in a production of *Jack and the Beanstalk*.

"Put it wherever you can find room," I say. And as the orderly is moving the plant to a place near the window, I hear Betsey Brown's voice.

"Jumpin' Jehoshaphat!" Betsey says as she enters the room. "You've got enough flowers in here to hold a wedding...or, for that matter, a funeral."

My response is simple. "That funeral joke must be going around the hospital. But here's the other thing...I can't believe I actually heard someone use the phrase 'Jumpin' Jehoshaphat.'"

"Well, you actually also hear folks say that in Matamoras, Pennsylvania, where I grew up," says Betsey. She is straightening and smoothing my bed linens.

The man who brought the towering gardenia plant gives Betsey and me a quick wave as
he heads toward the door.

"Thank you!" I shout after the guy in the
light-green scrubs the orderlies all wear, his blond
hair tied behind his head in a long ponytail.

I'm not sure that Betsey even sees the guy.
She's too busy talking. "Oh, my mom had a
whole catalog of old-fashioned sayings like
'Jumpin' Jehoshaphat.' She'd say, 'Mind your
own beeswax' or 'You're full of donkey dust.'
And my favorite was always, 'You kids'll be the
early death of me.'"

"And were you?" I ask.

"Were we what?"

"Were you the early death of her?"

"God. No. She's eighty years old now and lives
with my brother and sister-in-law and their four
kids over in Port Jervis. She does all the cooking,
the laundry—Jeff and Elyce both work—and
Mom still drives. So she picks up…"

Betsey stops talking for a moment. When
she begins to speak again, she places her hands
on her hips and says sarcastically, "I don't
believe for a second that you're at all interested

in hearing the autobiography of the Browns of Matamoras, Pennsylvania."

I already know a great deal about Betsey—two kids, a husband who's a New York City firefighter, a week each summer in the Adirondacks. But I'm hoping to extract some other information from Betsey.

"Well, I could lie and say that your life story is fascinating. But to tell the truth what I would be most interested in hearing is the inside scoop on Dr. Calvelli."

"Would that be the truth about him or the speculation?" Betsey says.

"I'll take both."

"The truth is that Dr. Calvelli is engaged. *But* Dr. Calvelli confided in Dr. Holden who told one of his residents who told me that Dr. Calvelli is not about to rush to the altar. I know that this is really high school gossip. But I thought I'd share it anyway. So if I were you I'd keep my hopes up, and I'd wear a smidge of makeup at all times while you're a patient here."

Betsey hands me my toothbrush and a cute little basin for me to spit into. As I brush my teeth she keeps talking.

"Have you had many visitors?" Betsey asks.

I now spit into that cute little basin. Betsey hands me some water. I take some of the water and spit again. Then I speak.

"No, not a one," I tell her. "But you know that's how I wanted it. I texted my folks to stay at whatever art auction in Munich they're at, and just in case they didn't choose to obey I told them that I was being transferred to a special care facility in Boston. As you know, that's a complete lie, but they'll find that out only if they decide to fly to Boston and look for me."

"You are an evil child," Betsey says.

"Listen, Betsey, the rotten apple doesn't fall far from the poisoned tree. Just because I present like a perfect person doesn't mean I'm not a scum-bucket deep down inside," I say.

Betsey is now checking my chart.

"I see you had an ultrasound this morning," she says.

"*Early* this morning," I say.

Betsey continues to read from the chart. Then she says, "Looks like everything on the sonogram is fine. And as soon as Dr. Craven comes by and says that you're okay, you're going to be discharged."

"Discharged?" I say, and I have alarm in my voice.

"I'm only reading what it says on this chart. It says that you can't leave without setting up appointments with Calvelli and Craven. And there's an addendum that says, 'patient decision pending elective procedure reco SA.'"

"What's a 'reco SA'?" I say, struggling with my emotions.

"It means 'suction-aspiration.' It means that that's what Dr. Craven is recommending. Now it may be early enough that she just..."

I burst into tears.

"I can't be discharged," I say. "I'm not ready to leave. I have to get organized, make decisions."

"When Dr. Craven comes around you can talk to her about your decisions," Betsey says. "I think the best thing right now would be for you to get some sleep." She glances at my chart on the screen, and with outrageous exaggeration she speaks. "Why, those awful radiology people got you up at ten a.m. for your ultrasound. Can you imagine that? That's practically the middle of the night. What an outrageous time."

I laugh at her sarcasm. The tears stop.

"Well, for me, ten o'clock is sort of really early," I say.

"I'm sure it is," Betsey says, and I respond.

"You must think I'm a spoiled brat, right?"

"I don't think any such thing," she says. "I think you're a woman who has been through a lot, is going through a lot, and may have even more to get through. That's what I think."

She takes my hand.

"I'm just not sure about this baby thing. The smart thing to do is..." and I'm looking for the word.

Then Betsey gives it to me, "To terminate."

"But I just can't bring myself to do that. Not just yet. Maybe I'm being selfish or stupid or... I don't know."

"Then don't do anything," Betsey says.

"Don't do anything?" I say. Is it possible that I never thought of that?

"Uh, yeah. You're three weeks pregnant. You've got time to decide."

"But Dr. Craven said I should think about what I want to do."

"Then think about it," Betsey says.

Why do I feel so stupid and happy at the very same time?

"Oh, Betsey. You can't imagine what I'm going through," I say.

"Oh, I think I can imagine it," Betsey says. "I'm pregnant, too."

"Congratulations!" I say.

"Yeah, this is the third, and then we're closing down the shop," Betsey says.

I've heard that expression before, but this time it makes me chuckle.

To have a baby? Not to have a baby? I'm calming down. I'll take my time deciding. But who am I kidding now? I do know which way I'm leaning.

CHAPTER

The Present

A CHOKING, DISGUSTING STENCH has formed a kind of invisible wall that forces Joel Tierney, Kalisha Scofield, and Betsey Brown to reflexively squint, gag, and turn away when Tierney fully opens the door to Emily's apartment.

"Oh, shit," Tierney says. His words are punctuated by his gulping, gagging, snorting noises. "We should get backup medical. Emergency waste handlers. We should wait out here before we hit this shit. That's the problem."

But Kalisha has something to say.

"The real problem is that this woman here is

not NYPD, and she shouldn't be going into the scene with us."

Tierney freezes, just for a second. Closes his eyes, opens them, then says, "Scofield, you and I will go in. Betsey, you wait out here until we…"

Betsey's response is just short of violent.

"Don't you understand? Don't you fucking get it? This is my friend! This my best friend! *She could be dead in there!*"

"Fuck it all!" Tierney shouts. "All three of us'll hit it."

Breathing through the handkerchief he holds against his mouth, Tierney takes a deep breath, then he steps into the apartment's elegant entrance hall—a small but expensive antique rug, a mahogany umbrella stand with two umbrellas and an ivory-tipped walking stick. A large white bowl sits on a skinny-legged, lacquered mahogany table; the bowl holds a few keys and a Cartier pen. Yes, the odor is sickening, but the hallway looks elegant, safe, fine.

Betsey, of course, knows this apartment, inside and out. Three thousand square feet that serve as testimony to Emily's exquisite taste and money.

Joel, Kalisha, and Betsey make their way through the hallway.

The air is rancid, but the neatness of the hall gives Betsey hope. So far so... "Holy shit!" yells Kalisha. "What the fuck happened here?"

Betsey immediately joins Kalisha in the living room.

Nothing but chaos. A gray sectional sofa is turned on its back, sofa cushions are tossed on the floor. Glassware and china have been pulled from their shelves. Broken. Shattered. Books and fireplace logs and porcelain bowls and Murano ashtrays and papers and magazines are scattered on the floor. Bottles of Absolut vodka and Wild Turkey bourbon have crash-landed on the stained Persian carpets.

Betsey glances behind the upturned couch. No dead woman.

Betsey remembers exactly when Emily showed her the new sofa just a few months ago.

"Yes, a Herman Miller sofa is stupidly extravagant, but once I fell for the Noguchi coffee table, I couldn't put a junky couch behind it."

Something beyond awful has happened here. A break-in? A murder? Betsey is certain that this was the death she always thought Emily might end up having—scary and cold and brutal.

The odor is beginning to overwhelm her. Betsey thinks that if she opens her mouth even for a second that she'll upchuck.

Betsey swallows hard. She speaks. "You remember the layout from the last time you were here."

Tierney is all business. "Kalisha, you and I will each take one of the big bedrooms. Betsey, you hang with Kalisha. Then we'll check the kitchen..."

"And there's also this little room off the kitchen," Betsey adds.

Tierney says, "Okay, thanks." Then he adds, "By the way, I'll handle the storage room off the dining room."

Betsey is confused, and asks, "Joel, how'd you know that there's a storage room off the dining room?"

"For God's sake, Bets. I can see it from here. The door is open. Okay. Let's get on it," says Tierney.

Betsey's eyes won't stop tearing up, a crappy combination of the fetid odor, her own anger, and her growing fear that somewhere in this apartment is Emily's dead body.

Tierney shouts—loud, no-nonsense, determined. "Get a picture of anything that is even remotely of interest, then check back with me. If you find a dead body..." he doesn't finish the sentence.

If you find a dead body? How can he be so matter-of-fact? Is this what cops are like?

"Okay," he says. "Let's get on it."

CHAPTER

10

BETSEY AND KALISHA WALK through the nightmare that is Emily's living room. Betsey thinks that it's like those old Westerns where the town sheriff would "deputize" some of the men when a crisis arose—from bank robberies to cattle rustling.

"Yeah, that's me. A deputy. I've been deputized," she mumbles to herself.

The awful smell is closing in on her. Kalisha enters the big primary bedroom and immediately starts clicking away at the damage and mess. Betsey stands frozen at the sight of broken mirrors and overturned bottles of Chanel and Creed. Emily's beautiful clothes are torn and piled up like the aftermath of a storm of silk and cashmere.

The thick, stomach-churning odor seems to have become stronger.

"I'll be right back," says Betsey.

"You stay with me, lady," says Kalisha.

"Like I said, right back," says Betsey, and she walks down the hallway to the kitchen, which is its own shocking hellhole. The doors of the giant Gaggenau refrigerator are wide open. The contents of the monster fridge are scattered over the floor. Ground turkey and stinking fish fillets have turned blue and green and black from days of rot. Milk and a smashed glass jar of fancy mayonnaise have created puddles. *At least we know where the smell is coming from,* she thinks—she hopes it's the *only* source of the odor.

Betsey passes through the kitchen quickly, as if propelled by some obsession. Suddenly she feels brave, not calm, but, yes, brave. She has a certain place in mind, a room in mind, a tiny place that might turn out to be a treasure trove of clues.

Next stop—the little room off the kitchen—a.k.a. the nursery.

She knows that this room was always in a

funny-crazy state of disarray, back when Emily used it as an office. A small glass-topped desk piled with papers and letters and file folders, an Apple laptop with a pink-and-green leather case. Stacks of books on the floor (everything from James Joyce to Joyce Carol Oates). Skyscrapers of magazines (everything from French *Vogue* to *Sukiya Living*).

Betsey pauses outside the room. Her hand freezes just for a moment as she reaches for the doorknob. She is not afraid of finding more filth and chaos. What she actually now feels is that this little out-of-the-way room would be the perfect place to stash a body.

Betsey opens the door. What she wasn't prepared for was the heartbreak she feels when she sees the room again.

CHAPTER

11

IT IS A BABY'S ROOM fit for a magazine photo shoot. It is a perfect symphony of bright yellows and pure whites. A wooden crib with a quilt that holds a big sun design in the middle, a mobile hanging above the crib—dangling yellow stars and white crescent moons. A wooden changing table with a tall stack of cloth diapers, baby powder in a Victorian shaker. Three of the room's walls are painted an Easter-egg yellow. The fourth wall is white.

Betsey feels a stab of pain as she looks around this room that holds so much promise for the future.

The only trace left of Emily's office is the small glass desk. It stands near the doorway, and on it rest two items: Emily's laptop in its crazy-color leather case, and a big book covered in yellow satin. The cover reads: *Baby's First Book*.

Betsey opens it. On the first page is printed:

MY NAME IS ... That space is left blank.

On the second page is printed:

MY MOMMY'S NAME IS ... Emily's elegant curvy signature is unmistakable.

Betsey turns to the next page.

MY DADDY'S NAME IS ... This space is blank.

Everything in the room feels sad to Betsey. This beautiful, perfect little room. This almost-destroyed apartment. But most of all the disappearance of Emily.

Betsey tries hard to put the pieces all together. But none of it makes any actual sense. Did the home invasion come from people who knew Emily? Friends or enemies? Possibly the father of the baby? Possibly the man who Emily thinks is following her? Someone hired by Emily's family, perhaps? A random intruder? But why was this precious nursery left untouched while the other rooms were so terribly trashed? Last time the apartment was broken into, this room was disturbed. Is it the work of a crazy person? And scariest, could Emily be that crazy person?

Betsey looks around the room again and again. Near the small glass desk are two framed Disney animation cels. One is Snow White talking with the dwarf Dopey. The other picture is Winnie-the-Pooh with an upturned pot of honey pouring down over his head.

"Oh, I know I'm a self-indulgent wacko, Bets, but I saw these two original Disney cels from some online auction, and I just had to bid on them. They were just too adorable to pass up."

Betsey smiles at the memory of the crazy indulgence of her missing friend.

Betsey moves closer to the two Disney animation cels. (Each one was a *$2,000* crazy indulgence.) What catches Betsey's eye, however, are the three small pieces of paper that are Scotch-taped to the wall near the Disney art. These pieces of paper measure no more than four by four inches. They have typed words on them. They are stuck haphazardly in a room that has been put together with precision. Betsey reads the words on the first piece of paper.

A baby is God's opinion that life
should go on.

Carl Sandburg

Next to this quotation is another, slightly
longer piece. Betsey reads it.

My mother said to me, "If you are
a soldier, you will become a general.
If you are a monk, you will become
the Pope." I was a painter, and I
became Picasso.

Picasso

Betsey wonders if these quotes are meant as
words of wisdom for the unborn infant. Or are
they words of hope for the mother-to-be?

There is one more piece of great writing
attached to the wall. For the baby? For Emily?
Or for Betsey?

There is nothing I would not do for
those who really are my friends. I
have no notion of loving people by
halves. It is not in my nature.

Jane Austen

This sweet room, these wise quotes, they remind Betsey of the other woman who hides within Emily—the smart woman, the kind woman, the sane woman.

But Betsey does not have much time to consider any of this. Suddenly a voice interrupts. Betsey looks toward the nursery doorway. Kalisha is standing there, and she doesn't look happy.

CHAPTER

12

BETSEY WATCHES AS KALISHA executes her own investigation of the beautiful little baby's room. Kalisha opens drawers that are empty and a closet that holds nothing but ten white satin–covered hangers. Emily hadn't replaced the clothes after the room's previous vandalism.

"By the way, I saw that the hurricane hit the kitchen as bad as the other rooms," says Kalisha. "I think we found the source of the smell." Then she adds, "Your best bud, Detective Tierney, and I did a thorough survey of the third bedroom. They were both as crapped up as everything else, but they turned up nothing. The detective is doing the storage room now.

Then he'll get a look at this perfect little baby's nest. I guarantee that this room'll even blow Detective Tierney's mind."

"Do you have any theory as to why this room wasn't destroyed?" Betsey asks. "You remember, last time the apartment was broken into, this room was tampered with."

Kalisha shrugs and says, "If I had a theory about that, ma'am, I would not keep it to myself."

Kalisha moves to the desk. She flips Emily's laptop open, then says, "I assume you already tried to get into this here machine."

Shit. Amateur oversight, Betsey thinks.

"Uh, no. I hadn't gotten around to that yet," she says.

Kalisha presses the On button, and in just a few seconds the machine sounds the familiar up-and-running *ding.*

On the aqua-colored screen is one item—a folder icon. The folder is labeled:

A KIND OF DIARY

Scofield double-clicks on the folder. A window pops up. Password required.

"We're going to need one to open this folder—and probably anything else that's on here," says Kalisha. "Let's just bring it back to NYPD Tech for that."

"No need. I think I know the password," Betsey says.

"Now *that's* a close friend," Kalisha says. "Most folks can't even remember their own."

"Emily was never too concerned about security and never changed her passwords." Betsey leans over and types DICKINSONBLUNTBRONTE.

Kalisha says, "I get it. All famous people named Emily."

Betsey hits Enter. A second later, Kalisha says, "Bingo. That works."

"What works?" It's Detective Tierney's voice.

He is standing at the door, looking around the room.

"How'd they miss this room?" Tierney asks.

Tierney is as calm as…well, as calm as an NYPD detective is supposed to be. Betsey thinks that he might be just too calm.

"Maybe whoever destroyed the rest of the place just didn't want to mess this one up," says Betsey.

"Unless they didn't know that this room was

even here," says Kalisha. "It looks like a closet from the outside."

Tierney doesn't even venture an opinion. After a few seconds of surveying the room he simply says, "Who the hell knows?"

Betsey and Kalisha update Tierney on their examination of this utterly pristine room—the empty closet, the empty drawers, the quotations on the wall, and then, most intriguing and maybe most helpful of all, the computer, luckily booted up and waiting for the three of them. Kalisha sits at the controls.

The newly opened BITS AND PIECES folder shows nothing but a few saved emails and a few Word documents that have been cut-and-pasted into place.

Kalisha begins scrolling. Betsey and Detective Tierney lean in and focus on the screen.

You're just not being fair. I told you I just wanted a drink. So you can't be angry cause I wouldn't eat that o-so-famous Minetta Tavern Black Label Burger. No. I was happy with my martini. So, be angry. But I know you won't stay that way. I know because later on was so nice for us. Love always, Emily.

The next piece. They all immediately notice that it feels like a diary entry.

I should tell Ruth that I think Im being followed. But its hard to trust anyone. Even Ruth. Maybe Betsey.

Betsey clarifies. "Ruth Mendelsohn is Emily's on-again-off-again shrink. I called Dr. Mendelsohn yesterday. She said nothing except that she hasn't heard from Emily in a while. I don't know, maybe patient confidentiality. Who knows?"

So its sort of like always Im alone. Im the crazy one. But someone is following me Im sure of that. Leon said someone was looking for me twice yesterday afternoon. But he didnt want to leave a message. You know how you can just tell someone is staring at you and then hes suddenly gone. I should tell Betsey.

"Leon is the doorman," Betsey says. Then another entry.

August 17. Ive got to do something about this guy. Betsey. Still a maybe. I think she'll believes me. If she doesn't trust me no one else will.

Betsey takes a few steps away from Tierney and Scofield. She hopes they won't see her starting to cry.

"I can't keep looking at this," Betsey says. "At least not now. I'll read it all later. Or you guys can fill me in. I just can't read anymore."

She leaves the room and heads back through the kitchen and back to the living room.

Kalisha and Joel are still reading.

Yes youre right. I am lonely, very lonely. and this morning in bed when you said we could go way beyond the sex thing into a place of commitment. Well, it just scared the hell out of me. Commitment is definitely not my thing. At least not right now. Somehow loneliness actually feels

better than getting involved with you.
Now that doesn't mean I don't love you.

Tierney and Scofield say nothing to each
other. The pieces of the puzzle are being found,
but they're not coming together. Next is another
diary piece. It is not dated.

There are so many people on the street
and I know one of them is coming after
me. The person is definitely a he. I know
I saw him. I can feel him outside of me
the same way I can feel the baby inside of
me. This is terrifying. And I cant do any
thing to make anything come together.
Well there is one thing and I could just
do it. Im not a brave woman. But maybe.
So many people.

Kalisha speaks. "Ready to move to the next
page, Detective?"

"I guess that we can come back to this," says
Tierney.

"You think that this could lead to something
here and now?" asks Kalisha.

But before Tierney can respond, they hear Betsey's voice. Yelling. Loud and urgent and frightened.

"Blood!" she yells. "There's a lot of blood in the guest bathroom!"

Tierney rushes from the room.

Before Kalisha joins her partner she notices for the first time a tiny memory flash drive protruding from the side of Emily's laptop. Maybe it's not important, but her detective instinct is telling her that it is.

She yanks it out and slips it into her pocket.

MONTH TWO

CHAPTER

13

THE BOOKS MOST PREGNANT women buy are *What to Expect When You're Expecting* or *Birth Without Fear*. What's your favorite pregnancy podcast? Who's your favorite pregnancy expert? The doula Dr. Elliot Berlin or the glamorous mommy Rosie Pope?

These are choices that I don't have to make. You see, I have my own personal medical expert, my BFF, Betsey Brown. She supplies the answer to any question I might have. I might not always like the answer, but she supplies it anyway.

EMILY: I don't think that one little glass of white wine at night is going to cause any harm.

BETSEY: No, it's a truly not-at-all-great idea. Because then you'll have two alcoholics—you and your baby. What's more, I'll report you to Dr. Craven.

Yesterday I made the mistake of bringing up exercise.

"You know," I say to Betsey, "I started running a long time ago, the one good thing I did for myself. In college, in working life, in spite of my partying, I always ran a few miles almost every other day. But recently...well, I stopped. Let's just say that it *interfered* with my lifestyle. And now that I'm pregnant I can't start doing it again."

"That's crazy," Betsey says. "You can keep running up until the day you give birth. Very healthy."

"I dunno, Bets. Running seems kinda dangerous to me."

"Well, you're wrong. Drinking is dangerous. Running is good. Ya know what? I have an eleven a.m. start at the hospital tomorrow. So

I'll take the bus to the six train, and I'll meet you at the reservoir. I'd like to start running."

"Great," I say. And part of me truly means it, and part of me doesn't mean it all.

When Betsey appears, she looks and acts like the enthusiastic coach of a girls' field hockey team: cut-off gray sweatpants, a Penn State T-shirt. Her red frayed baseball cap is worn backward. She looks like Charlie Brown. But I don't tell her that.

"G'morning," she says. "Let's get started."

"Whoa. Calm down, Wonder Woman," I say. Then I touch my stomach. I know I'm only pregnant a few weeks, but I swear that I can feel the bump. This makes me feel nervous and comforted at the same time.

"Running can't possibly be safe for the baby," I say, but Betsey doesn't even respond.

We run in silence for a while. Then we move to the upper track, the reservoir itself, and I'm running faster. Betsey is working to keep up with me.

"Talk about Wonder Woman," says Betsey.

"It's my orange juice and vodka diet," I say.

"That's not funny," says Betsey.

I'd forgotten how much I liked running. I

even liked it at Princeton. I was young enough then that I could party hard at night and run hard the next morning.

Right now I try to ignore my achy knees and my stiff lower back. For a while longer, Betsey and I run without speaking.

I consider sharing something that's been on my mind the past few weeks. It's probably nothing but a silly, paranoid, "pregnancy brain" delusion. But I've been having a faint suspicion that someone's been following me. Watching me. Stalking me.

Nuts, right?

I know.

I hope.

So instead, at the northern tip of the reservoir, I break the silence with a medical question.

"Betsey, how do you know if you have preeclampsia?"

"You swell up, and your blood pressure goes through the roof," she says.

"Could I have it?"

I can practically hear her eyes rolling.

"You could, but you don't," she says. "It usually happens around the sixth or seventh month."

"But it *could* happen."

"Anything *could* happen. You could get hit by a truck. You could be crowned the queen of England. You could take cha-cha lessons. You could…"

"Okay. Okay," I say.

We keep running.

"Okay, what if I have a miscarriage?" I say.

"What are your symptoms?" she asks. We slow down.

"I'm pregnant," I say.

"Pregnancy is a condition. It's not a symptom, Emily."

"Well, I know that. I just mean…"

"Have you had any bleeding or spotting or cramps?" she asks.

"No," I say. "But what if I do?" And before Betsey can answer I begin to cry. "Oh, shit," I say. "I'm so nervous and crazy and anxious and confused and…"

"And none of those things is a sign of anything bad. They're a sign of being normal."

We both stop running. Betsey puts her sweaty arms around my sweaty shoulders and squeezes me.

"Let me tell you," she says. "Let's just take

it one day at a time. Both of us. Stay calm and take care of yourself."

"One day at a time," I repeat. "That's the big maxim at AA."

"Why do you think I said it?"

As luck and chance would have it, a man and a very pregnant woman jog past us. They are jogging very slowly.

Betsey laughs and says, "She may give birth before she leaves the park."

"Oh, shit," I say. "Damn. I think I'm missing a meeting at my terrible, horrible, no good, very bad job." See? I already know some children's literature.

CHAPTER

14

DAVID ZINGERMAN WENT TO Dartmouth. He graduated summa cum laude with a double major in economics and modern art. And while he occasionally lands a job interview at places like Google and Yahoo!, he's not going anywhere. David seems content being my assistant at Dazzle, the very successful, very hip marketing agency where we work.

One of David's assignments—and it is an important one—is to meet me at the elevator when I arrive each morning (or on occasion, afternoon).

The procedure is simple. I text David when I leave my apartment. Then I text him again when I enter the lobby of the office building. He then waits for me to step off the elevator on the fifteenth floor. I arrive in the reception area, where I never get bored looking at the Hockney watercolor hanging over the gray leather sofa.

David then tells me anything I need to know—there's a pissed-off client in my office, there's a pissed-off CEO outside my office, there's a table available this afternoon at Frenchette.

Today, I'm experiencing my daily disgusting roiling stomach upset. Every day I blame it on some food I ate the previous night. And every day I say, "It's morning sickness, Emily. Have you heard the news? You're pregnant."

When I step off the elevator, I am delighted to see David waiting in his assigned spot. He looks a combination of angry and nervous.

"Where have you been?" he asks.

He doesn't even wait for me to lie. He says, "You had a meeting scheduled with Keith at nine o'clock."

"Well, can't Keith wait a little bit? I had important things to do. I'll explain it to him."

David shakes his head and doesn't even bother to ask what it is I've been doing.

Keith Hennessey is chairman and creative

director of Dazzle. The fact that he's thirty-five years old and looks like a hipster rock star helps make him one of the hottest talents in the crazy new digital world of modern advertising and PR. Keith is very nice and very talented, and that is a very unusual combination in the New York City world of social media.

From a personal point of view, I find the fact that Keith is willing to put up with most of my shenanigans—coming in late, leaving early, postponing assignments until the last minute—very comforting. Keith doesn't always exercise such patience with his people.

"Keith knows I'm a flake," I say. "He always forgives me." I also know that I'm looking pretty good: a black bomber jacket over a just-short-enough burgundy dress.

I'm not nervous. But I am nauseated. Hello, morning sickness. I am vaguely aware of following David past my office, down the corridor we all call the cement driveway, a long, gray hallway with a cement floor, cement-block walls, and a cement ceiling. I think I should really visit the bathroom, but when I mention this to David, he insists that Keith is really anxious to see me.

Thirty seconds later I'm seated in a very

uncomfortable recliner and Keith is saying, "Thanks for coming in, Emily."

"You're *thanking* me? Are you being sarcastic?" I ask. "Because I do have a simple explanation."

Keith speaks very gently, uncharacteristically gently.

"No, I'm not being sarcastic at all. I mean it."

Hmm. Maybe he's telling the truth. He is acting very serious, but it's a weird seriousness. He seems to have put away his hotshot communications guru act. He also seems a bit nervous as he taps one of his shiny black Ferragamo shoes against that cement floor.

A pause. A long pause. Then he leans forward and speaks.

"I guess we both realize that this meeting was inevitable," he says.

"Inevitable?" I ask. "We've had a million meetings. None of them has ever been, as you say, inevitable."

Now there really is a pause. Keith takes out his iPad. He taps a few buttons before looking at me directly.

"I chose not to have anyone from Human Resources present, but there's a protocol that requires me to be absolutely clear. So let me say it once. Emily, I'm going to have to let you go."

What did he just say? My mind doesn't go blank. But it certainly isn't functioning at full speed. Did Keith just fire me? Holy shit.

"Are you all right?" he says. Then he stands, and for a moment it looks as if he's going to move closer to me. Touch me. Try to comfort me perhaps.

Then Keith sees the confusion on my face. He sits down again, and silence fills the room. He speaks.

"I thought telling you myself would make the news less traumatic..."

Now it rings like a loud church bell in my head. I instinctively share my epiphany with Keith. My voice is filled with a breathless amazement.

"You're firing me? You're firing me?"

"Emily, please. I like you. Everyone around here feels the same. You're fun and charming and nice and funny and..."

I step in. "...and so you're firing me."

Keith is too cool to show that he might be worried about my reaction. I'm certainly not the first person at Dazzle who's been thrown out.

But I'm certainly the most "fun and charming and nice and funny" person to get tossed out.

"Go ahead," I say. "Tell me that I'm fired. Say, 'You're fired, Emily.'"

"Let's not do this. No one's going to win if…"

"No, that's not true. You've already won."

"Emily, listen. This conversation actually hurts me more than…"

"Don't say it!" I yell. "That's the dumbest expression in the world. Don't insult me. Don't insult yourself by saying it."

Then he stands up again and speaks quietly. "Emily, please. We simply cannot put up with you anymore, no matter how sharp you are."

There is a pause. Then he lowers his voice even more, but it remains perfectly audible.

"You've shown up drunk a few times. You've come in hungover a lot of times. You're unreliable. Blowing off today's meeting was just the last straw."

Then the cherry on the cake shows up. Keith says, "I'm going to miss you, but I've got to do this."

I want to scream. I want to tell Keith what he already knows. That I have pots full of money from my crazy parents, that men are always asking me out, that the salespeople at Bergdorf know me by name. What Keith doesn't know is that I'm going to have a wonderful little baby, and that everything is fine, everything is great. Light the candles. Pop the champagne.

And I still feel like...well, like...I guess *sad* is the word I'm looking for. Every heartbreak in my life—the colleges who turned me down, the guys who dropped me because I wouldn't buckle under and do things their way—it all comes back. And suddenly the private money and the great apartment and the new baby cannot compensate for what's happening here.

A drunk? A druggie? Unreliable? Please, give me a break. My nausea escalates until I can feel my throat tightening. Oh, no. I bend my head down and throw up on the cement floor.

I can barely speak. But before I leave, I say, "Sorry about that. I guess it's just my way of saying good-bye."

CHAPTER

15

I LEAVE KEITH'S OFFICE door open. I step out. To my happy amazement (and, I hope, to Keith's embarrassment) twenty or so of my colleagues—editors, writers, assistants—are standing there.

Suddenly this beautiful group of people begins applauding. A few of them move close to me, creating a sort of warm and safe...well, womb. Some embrace me. Louise, the IT person who handles all my wacky, urgent requests, along with our in-house photographer, the ever adorable Rod, both have tears in their eyes.

"It absolutely sucks that this is happening," says Louise. I gesture toward the open door behind me. I make a sort of the-boss-can-hear-you gesture. Louise responds simply, "I don't care if Hennessey hears me. This absolutely sucks."

I reflexively glance at the door, and I am surprised to see Keith standing there. He says, "Louise is right, Emily. This absolutely sucks."

There is the very pleasing murmur of crowd agreement, and I am brought to tears myself. In a life that's not always brimming with love and support, it is today, this moment, particularly terrific to be feeling a little bit loved.

Wait till Betsey hears this. She'll explode.

"I can't imagine this place without you, Emily," says my archrival and office nemesis, Olivia Hudson. I think she really means it. And if she doesn't mean it, I'm impressed by her ability to sound so incredibly sincere.

"You always kept me on my toes," Olivia says.

"And you always knocked me off my feet," I say.

"We made one another better at our jobs," she says. And she's correct. After that exchange, Olivia and I hug each other. I'm not sure either of us meant it honestly, but we did it, and just doing it made me feel good.

I shake my hair, pull it back behind my head like a model in a shampoo commercial. I rub the palms of my hands against my cheeks, not caring if I mess up my makeup.

"God," I say. "I feel like I'm accepting an award or I'm at my own retirement party... which in a way I guess I am...and I can't believe how much you guys care...but then, come on, it was only a matter of time before they showed me the door. I deserve it. I'm a screw-up and a crazy person and..."

Someone yells out, "The best people in the world are the crazy ones!"

"Maybe some of the time," I say, "but not all of the time. Let's face it, I kept asking for it again and again and again and again. And finally, my prayers have been answered."

Almost everyone laughs.

"There's just one other thing to say." I pause. And then I say it: "I love you all."

"We love you, too!" are the shouts that come back at me.

A few more hugs. A few more kisses. A few more tears.

And I know exactly what I'm going to do next. I'm going to go to the ladies' room and brush my teeth (morning sickness is such a drag). I'm going to fix my makeup. Then I'm going to visit my favorite place on earth, a place where no one would ever ask me to leave.

And besides, how bad could a single vodka martini be?

CHAPTER

16

THE ANSWER TO THE previous question about the martini?

Very bad.

My ob-gyn, the charming but stubborn Jane Craven, has a rule with all her patients: If you drink or do drugs, she has the option to drop you. Dr. Craven says in one of her "mom-to-be" email newsletters that even the smallest amount of alcohol or unapproved (by her) drugs can be harmful to the fetus.

So far, Dr. Craven hasn't caught on to me. Like I say, so far.

Of course, she's right. Who can argue with science? Dr. Craven could drop me as a patient.

And if Betsey finds out she could drop me as a friend. So I think. I consider. I...oh, look at that. My taxi has just pulled up in front of Ted's Bar and Grill.

Ted notices me immediately when I walk into the almost empty bar. He smiles and then glances at the clock on the back wall.

"Whoa! Look who's back on her feet! How are you feeling?" Ted asks.

"Well, it's not even noon and I'm back here, so how do you think?" I say. Not that that's an unusual time for me to be here.

"Since it's early, how about an Irish coffee? Hold the coffee," Ted says.

"Leave the comedy to the professionals, Ted," I say. "Stick to mixing martinis."

"Peach daiquiri, then?"

"No, this day feels like a gin martini, straight up."

"Okay," he says. "One martini, but just one."

Ted laughs and grabs that beautiful green bottle of Tanqueray and slips some ice cubes into a shaker. Ted and I are good friends, very good friends. On one or two occasions, we've been as friendly as two people can be.

Simply put, Ted is never without female

companionship. If you need further proof of that, you should see what I see at the other end of the bar: a very tall, very shapely brunette who can only be described as ravishing. Her breakfast is very different from the breakfast Ted is mixing for me. On the bar in front of her is a cup of coffee and a glass of orange juice. She is nibbling on an English muffin as if it were a boyfriend's ear.

I gesture in the direction of the girl who's eating breakfast. "Was there a pajama party last night that I wasn't invited to?" I ask Ted.

"There was. Your invitation must have blown off the front porch."

And so it goes, my conversation with Ted. My decision to come here to unwind was a smart one. I enjoy our part-gangster-movie-part-rom-com dialogue.

Ted is about to place the martini in front of me, but I hold up my hand in the classic gesture that says *Stop*.

"Can you put that-there beverage in a doggie bag? I think I'm going to try to stay clean today," I say.

"Yeah, right. And I'm going to flap my arms real fast and fly to the moon," he says. But he does remove the cocktail from my area.

Then I nod in the direction of the ravishing brunette and say, "I'll have what she's having, but hold the English muffin and the OJ."

And, damn it, I am going to try. I know the Twelve Steps from AA. I've been to a few meetings, not recently, but I've been. Now I close my eyes and think that the time has come—to be good to myself, to be good to my friends, but most of all to be good for the baby.

I literally am waking up to smell the coffee, the coffee that Ted is placing in front of me.

I retrieve my phone from my bag. I am sitting almost precisely opposite a sign that says TAKE YOUR PHONE CALLS OUTSIDE, PLEASE.

"Mind if I make a quick call?" I say to Ted.

"I don't care if you burn," he says.

"Wrong punchline," I say.

"I know," Ted says. "But it's the only one I had ready."

Now I say hello to Betsey.

"Emily, is everything okay?" she asks with the urgency you should display when the caller ID shows the name of your pregnant best friend.

"Couldn't be better," I answer. "Thanks for calling."

"You called me," Betsey says.

"Oh, I meant thanks for asking," I answer. Then, with true pleasure in my voice, I say, "I have some wonderful news to share with you." I don't even pause before I announce, "I got fired this morning."

"Oh, I'm sorry, Em."

"Don't be sorry. Keith isn't a bad guy. He did what I didn't have the nerve or the brains to do," I say. I think that I mean it. I really do.

I tell Betsey the same things I've been telling myself: It was a stupid job. I don't need the money. I could do something really great now—if I can just figure out what that something might be.

"But, Emily. The job is...was...your anchor. It's central to your life. And, other than me and some of your guy friends, it was your support group."

"Oh, please, Betsey. It was no support group. Plus, I don't need a support group. I've got you, and I've got my buddy Ted here and..."

"Is that where you are now? Ted's? Ted's Bar?" Betsey asks.

"Well, where do you think I am? The unemployment office?"

Suddenly a very sharp edge comes into Betsey's voice.

"Just cut your wiseass bullshit with me, Emily. I'm trying to help."

"Bets, stick with me. I'm at Ted's, but I'm not drinking."

"Emily, I'm no expert on how to stop drinking, but I don't think that the best place to try to quit is at a bar."

"Really. I'm really not drinking."

Betsey gives a very weak and unconvincing, "Uh-huh." Then she says, "An hour ago, you were running, doing something good for yourself. Now you're in a bar drinking."

Betsey cares for me in a way that nobody else has ever cared for me—with intelligence and heart. Nobody—my mother, my father, and a procession of boyfriends—never really gave a good goddamn about me. Betsey is smart. Betsey is good.

I decide to have fun with the situation. I say, "Oh, wow. Ouch. Just burned my tongue on this hot coffee. Ted, drop an ice cube in here, could you?"

"I'm warning you, Emily. As soon as I get off today, I'm coming over there to see what you're up to."

"Come on down, Betsey. I'll save you a seat at the bar."

"Damn, you are really impossible," she says, but it is the kind of "impossible" that might possibly be translated as "adorable."

"Why don't you come over and have dinner with me and Frank and the kids tonight?"

Betsey amazes me. She works nine to twelve hours in surgery, most of it mind-boggling precision transplant work. Then she stops at Key Food and picks up a chicken, works a miracle with the dead bird, and feeds a scrumptious meal to her family. Then...damn, I say about Betsey what my nanny used to say about me when I was a bratty little terror: "I get worn out just thinking about you."

"Lemme give you an 'absolute maybe,'" I say. "We can connect later, and I'll let you know for sure."

"Yeah," says Betsey, her voice full of skepticism. "You're not going to join us. I can tell."

"No, really, we'll see. Maybe."

I hear Betsey let out a deep breath. Then there's a pause. Then she speaks.

"Listen to me, Emily. You've got to be good.

You've got to behave. You've got to start some-where, and you've got to start now."

Of course I know that she's right, and, fuck it, I'm going to try.

But the *first* thing I've got to do is try to fig-ure out who the baby's father is. I know. I know. That sounds easy enough, but, let's say there's a bit of confusion.

I consider the three men I've been with in the last month or so. And, damn it, the one thing I'm sure of is that I wouldn't want any of them to be the father of my child.

Now, don't get me wrong, all three of them are pretty nice guys, pretty smart guys, and, when they want to be, pretty decent guys.

But as husbands? Fathers?

Not a great selection.

CHAPTER

17

THERE IS NOTHING QUITE so warm and cozy as an old-fashioned New York City saloon on the day you've been fired. Sitting at a bar, however, with only a cup of coffee is not much fun. I should really get out of here.

The ravishing brunette has left. My guess is that she's a model with a fashion shoot this afternoon, and she's got to...Oh, who cares? Time sure doesn't fly when you're at a bar without a friend and without a martini.

Ted, who is starting to look way too adorable in his snug-fitting Levi's and red-and-blue flannel shirt, asks if I need a refill.

I say, "I'm a one-cup girl. How about I switch over to club soda?"

"Go crazy," he says. "Have a Diet Coke."

And I do.

In the past hour, while I've been drinking and talking with Ted and Betsey, the bar has filled up with the lunch crowd. Ted's menu is helpfully brief: "Burgers, Pretzels, Booze."

Why don't I leave? Why don't I just leave?

Today I spot a typical group at the bar: three women who are clearly work colleagues, celebrating somebody's birthday with margaritas and cosmos. A postman is spending his lunch break with a bourbon and water. A sweet middle-aged couple, actually a little beyond middle age, are sharing two tall-neck bottles of Grolsch.

I cut my census-taking short when I suddenly feel two hands massaging my shoulders. It can only be the friendly neighborhood pusher, Mike Miller. I'd like to give the creep an elbow to his midsection, or even lower, but instead of hauling off, I try holding off.

"Well, it wouldn't be lunchtime at Ted's without Mike Miller," I say.

"Good to see you, Emily," he says, and steps around to face me. One thing I'm sure of: I'm not going to tell him about being fired.

Mike and I talk about such important topics as the predictably lousy Mets' season and the splendor of the fairly new Second Avenue subway.

Mike says, "Let me buy you a drink."

"I'm not sure that Ted is serving me," I say. "He's put me on Diet Coke."

"Teddy," Mike calls. "Did you really cut off our girl?"

"Not me. Emily asked for a Diet Coke. I serve what the customer calls for," Ted says.

"Lemme buy you a grown-up drink, Emily."

"I don't think so," I say. "I'm going to be a good kid today."

The absence of a drink and the presence of Mike is playing bad games with my head. It's not quite withdrawal, but it sure isn't fun.

"Why won't you do a guy a favor, Emily?" Mike says in his sickly, smarmy way. "Lemme buy you a drink."

"Just get the hell away from me, Mike," I say.

I speak loud enough that a few people nearby turn and look at Mike and me. I'm loud enough that Ted immediately joins us and speaks: "That's it, Mike. Leave her alone."

"Just trying to be a gentleman," Mike says. I turn away from him and walk to a small table for two. Mike walks to the other end of the bar, and Ted moves from behind the bar and stands at my little table.

"You okay, Emily?" he asks.

"I'll be better if you bring me a martini straight up with..."

Ted finishes my sentence. "With a glass of ice cubes on the side." Then he adds, "I'm not going to do it, Emily. You're trying to be good today."

"I changed my mind," I reply. "Remember what you just said. 'I serve what the customer calls for.' And I'm calling for a Tanqueray martini, straight up."

Ted shakes his head, and I watch him mix a very short martini that he pours into a very short glass.

I nurse my tiny drink ("Oh, look, a baby martini," Mike says when he passes by), and I end up sitting there for about an hour. I watch the people at the bar leave—singles, pairs, groups. It's like a series of very cool lap-dissolves in a movie.

Where'd Mike go? Where are the margarita ladies? I wonder where Ted's ravishing brunette went.

"Hey, sweetness," says Ted. I look up from my chair. My head practically revolves on my neck and shoulders. "I'm going to call you an Uber."

I don't protest. I couldn't even if I wanted to. The fact is that suddenly I don't have the energy to form words. My God. I've barely had a sip of alcohol. Hey, is there any such thing as a "contact drunk"? Do pregnant women ever get "afternoon sickness"? Whatever it is, I'm not feeling great.

I shake my head slowly and, using my wobbly arms for support, I manage to stand up. I'm not drunk. I know I'm not too bad. The baby? No, please, not the baby.

And then I'm thinking. *Would I rather have my second martini or have my first baby? What's wrong with me? Maybe this whole baby thing is just plain stupid. Maybe I shouldn't even have...* I'm holding on to the barstool. I begin walking toward the exit.

Maybe I was mistaken. Maybe Ted is actually throwing me out.

"I'm calling an Uber, Emily," Ted repeats as he follows me. But he gives up. He knows from previous times that it's better not to tangle with me "when I'm this way."

It's late in the day, not so late that it's dark outside. I try to stand up straight and walk.

I push my handbag up and over my shoulder with an unexpected burst of energy. It swings carelessly against my stomach, and I suddenly feel something happening there. Even I know it can't be the baby. At least I don't think it can be. But, hell, it's a kind of pinch, a kind of cramp, a punch? What the hell?

The street is crowded, and I'm not quite certain where I am. There's a classy mani/pedi salon, an old-fashioned shoe-repair place, a row of beautiful brownstones. Some of the brownstones are hung with elegant wooden shingles announcing professional offices: R. RYAN CRANE, ESQ., SUSAN SALOMON, ESQ., M. VOK-SHOOR, DDS.

And then another brownstone with a simple bronze shingle.

GREYSTONE WOMEN'S HEALTH

COMPLETE GYNECOLOGY AND CONSULTATION

I stop and study the sign for a moment. I touch the bump. Yep, there's a baby in here, and a daddy out there.

I read the sign over and over. "Consultation," I know, is code for "abortion consultation."

Life is filled with decisions, and almost every decision has a part in it that absolutely sucks.

CHAPTER

18

HALF AWAKE, HALF ASLEEP. Half aware, half unconscious. I am waking up. And, as is almost always the case, I am having a hard time of it. The sleep angel and the wake-up angel are having their usual tussle over me.

I have been dreaming, a dream I've had before. My father and I and the beach and a very early autumn morning. When I was a little girl, during summers in Southampton, my father woke me every day and made me join him for his morning swim. Seven a.m. He was relentless. His methods seemed just short of cruel. Clapping his hands, he would rip the covers off his little girl. Occasionally he would carry me down to the beach and drop me into the water. He thought it was all such fun. It was not.

The dream is interrupted by the sound of the lobby buzzer.

I glance at the dial of the bedside clock: 11:23. I am about to answer the buzz, just to stop the piercing sound, but then I feel a sharp pain in my lower abdomen. I bring my hand to the place of pain, and as I push against the painful spot I am suddenly painless. I bring my hand farther down and feel a significant wetness in my underwear. As I push the bedcovers from me I see that the sheet and underwear have the blood equivalent to the beginning of my period. But, hold on, lady. You're pregnant. I swing my legs over the side of the bed, and the sharp pains increase. Only now the pains have traveled to my abdomen and my back.

I realize that the buzzing has ended. I notice that the stomach and back pains are coming and going and coming and going. And then I hear a voice from outside the bedroom.

"Em, it's me. Betsey. It's Betsey."

Betsey appears at the open bedroom door.

"Why didn't you answer your phone?" she asks.

Then she quickly walks toward me and kneels at the side of the bed.

"What's the matter? Are you all right?"

"No. I'm not. I have a lot of spotting." I gesture to the spot on the bedsheets. I point to the area between my legs.

"Did you call anyone?" she says.

"No. I just woke up."

"Damn it. Didn't you hear the phone?"

"I guess not." The pains so far have not returned.

Betsey is helping me stand. My legs are sturdy, but I still feel sleepy. We are headed toward the bathroom.

"I stopped by Ted's, and he said you hadn't been there this morning. So I called your cell a few times. A few hundred times. Then when I stopped here the doorman said he hadn't seen you."

By now we are in the bathroom.

"Okay, we've got to get you cleaned up a little, and then we're going to get the hell over to Dr. Craven's office."

I start recounting my previous day to Betsey—the odd depression and elation of being fired, the time I spent at Ted's place, the walk down that elegant little street of brownstones, the different signs advertising lawyers and dentists and doctors... I stop talking. Betsey is gently washing me, brushing my hair, telling me to calm down.

"Oh, shit, Bets, what do you think is happening?"

"I don't know. Dr. Craven will tell us."

"Do you think it's going to be something bad?"

Betsey holds me firmly by the shoulders.

"Listen, it's going to be whatever it's going to be. It could be bad. It could be nothing. Let's just go and find out."

CHAPTER

19

JANE CRAVEN HAS FINISHED with her examination, and I'm sitting on the edge of the table, my legs dangling above the floor. I'm still wearing my paper gown, feeling vulnerable, scared. Betsey is sitting in the visitor's chair, and Dr. Craven is standing and typing at the very large computer that holds the lives and hopes and joys and disappointments of so many pregnant women. The doctor seems to be typing a lot. But I don't know if it is actually a lot. I steal glances at Betsey, and when our eyes meet she flutters her hand gently downward, signaling me to stay calm.

For obvious reasons, one of my mother's frequently used favorite phrases comes back to me.

"I'm more nervous than a turkey in November."
But I am, or at least I think I am. Or maybe not
nervous. Just nauseated, breathless, petrified.

I have a terrible feeling I know what Dr.
Craven is getting ready to tell me.

I'm wondering how she'll phrase it. Will she
do that useless setup of *I've got some bad news for
you*? Or will she dive right in? *Ms. Atkinson, I'm
sorry, but it looks like you've had a miscarriage.*
Maybe she'll use the other gentler, kinder expression, *I'm afraid your pregnancy is no longer viable.*

Finally, she turns around and looks directly
at me. There is no pregnant pause (forgive the
expression). I know Dr. Craven well enough now
to know that drama is not her usual approach to
things.

She speaks. "We've got to do an ultrasound
to be certain, but I'm pretty sure about what's
going on here. First of all, you are *not* having a
miscarriage. I have every reason to believe that
the fetus is doing well."

Betsey pulls her fist down through the air.
"Yes!" she says.

"So what's the story? Why the blood?" Suddenly I'm the sensible one, and Betsey is the
slightly crazy one.

"I think that your body was discharging an unfertilized egg," says Dr. Craven.

Betsey stands. "That means that you could have had..."

I hold up my hand, preventing Betsey from finishing her sentence. Unfamiliar as I am with pregnancy, I know that Betsey was about to say the word *twins*.

"And the egg that's all alone in there is all right?" I ask.

"Everything else is fine."

I understand this, and I know I should be pleased. No miscarriage. Yet I feel sad, very sad, perhaps as sad as I might have felt if I had suffered a miscarriage. I imagine the teeny-tiny egg. I imagine the baby that won't be. I imagine a stroller built especially for twins.

Am I crazy? Even when the news is essentially good, I end up being sad.

"And *I'm* all right? *I'm* okay?" I ask.

Now there is a real pause.

"No. *You* are not," she says.

Oh, shit. I guess I will have something to be sad about.

"What's the matter?" I ask.

Dr. Craven turns stern. She is not loud. She

is not unpleasant. She's merely stern, and stern is bad enough.

"Nothing's wrong with you that can't be cured by sobriety and generally proper living. Right now, you have the symptoms I see sometimes in homeless pregnant women. My heart breaks for them, and I do everything I can to help them. Life has given them a big pile of crap to deal with, but I... well, in your case, Ms. Atkinson, the limits of my understanding are strained."

She's on a tear, and she's not going to stop.

"I can tell by just looking at your eyes and seeing the color of your skin that you're still drinking. I don't have to wait for your blood test and your liver results and glucose levels. You're also not gaining weight. I don't know whether you're just not eating properly or whether you're ingesting party drugs or... Let's just try to get it together now."

Dr. Craven is clearly pissed off.

She stops talking and walks a few steps until she is standing in front of me. She takes my hand, but instead of addressing me she turns toward Betsey.

"If you're truly Ms. Atkinson's friend, Nurse Brown, you'll help her," Dr. Craven says.

"I know. I'll try," says Betsey.

"Betsey does try. She tries hard," I say. "I'm an asshole, and there's nothing she can do about it but remind me to clean up my stupid act."

"Then let's do it," says the doctor. "Like I've said, women with much bigger problems than yours get through this okay. If you don't...and I really don't mean to be nasty and alarmist... but frankly, you'll end up killing your baby."

I begin shaking my head up and down very quickly.

"I will do better. I swear I will. I know you and Betsey don't believe me, but I will."

"Good," says Dr. Craven. Then she adds, "The front desk will set up an ultrasound for this afternoon or tomorrow."

She turns to Betsey and says, "Thank you, Nurse." Then she turns to me and says, "I'll see you soon, for your next appointment."

Dr. Craven leaves, and I push off from the examining table. I step into my panties.

"Do you want me to wait outside while you get dressed?"

"No. It'll only take a second." And it is only a minute. I slip into my jeans and my sandals.

I pull my T-shirt over my head, and I'm ready to go.

The sadness about the unfertilized egg—something I crazily imagine as a lonely little yellow egg, an illustration in a little kid's book—hasn't left me.

I stand fully dressed. I adjust my T-shirt over my one and only barely-there bump.

"Ready to go, Em?" Betsey says.

"Yeah, all ready."

"I'm so happy for you," she says.

"Bets, I have to tell you something."

Betsey looks puzzled. Then she says, "What now?"

"Yesterday afternoon I took myself on a little walk. I was totally crazy and confused and maybe a little drunk, and...I almost got an abortion."

Betsey realizes that I'm not being dramatic.

She hugs me, holds me. She says, "Okay. Okay. Okay."

And before we leave to go home, I feel a need to say it one more time.

"I almost got an abortion."

CHAPTER

20

The Present

FRUSTRATION AND ANGER AND sorrow and confusion. How can all those feelings squeeze into the patrol car that Tierney and Kalisha and Betsey are driving back to the station?

"Scofield, contact Forensics and tell them to send a chem team to the Atkinson scene immediately."

Betsey is thinking, *Oh, dear God. Emily's apartment is now "The Atkinson Scene."*

Apparently Kalisha is not responding fast enough to Tierney's request.

"*Immediately* means immediately, and that

means right this goddamn minute. Do you understand that?" says the man in the driver's seat.

"Of course I do," is all that Kalisha says in response. Betsey, in the backseat, notices Kalisha's sneer. And that sneer says a lot more. Betsey is surprised...no, Betsey is amazed.

While Kalisha orders a medical-forensic team to the "Atkinson scene," Betsey dabs at her slightly teary eyes with a tissue, muffles her sorrow, and says, "So, what do we do now?"

"I'm sending Forensics. You just heard that. They'll do blood and print and DNA and every other goddamn workup that they always do," says Tierney. "Let me blunt. This is urgent, especially if Emily was murdered. Our best chance of finding leads is within the first twenty-four hours. After that, everything— any clues, any trails—usually turns ice cold."

"I see," says Betsey. She is not being sarcastic. She is simply numb.

More silence. Thirty seconds of silence. Finally, Tierney can't control his temper.

"Are you listening?"

Betsey speaks slowly, quietly. "Yes, of course

I'm listening." But there is one thing she does *not* understand. Why the hell does Tierney get so pissed off so often?

Oh, the hell with it. Whatever the reason behind his outbursts, Betsey doesn't think she has to listen to them if she doesn't want to.

"You guys can let me out here. I need a walk. It'll be good for me."

"No, a walk won't be good for you," says Tierney. His voice is suddenly warm and soothing. The anger has disappeared. He continues. "I'll drop you at Herald Square. That's where you get the F train, isn't it?"

Suddenly Detective Nasty-ass has turned back into Detective Nice Guy.

Tierney is wrong. It's not the F Train. It's the E train that she takes. And it doesn't leave out of Herald Square. It leaves out of Penn Station. And for Betsey... Oh, hell... she just wants to get away, get going, get home.

"Yes," Betsey says. "The F Train. Herald Square will be great."

"Good choice," Tierney says.

Tierney flips on his flashing lights, presses the siren button, and pulls up to Herald Square.

Moments before Betsey hops out, Tierney speaks to both her and Kalisha in a calm, confidential-sounding voice.

"Hey, one other thing, no one needs to know that we included a non-pro in our investigation."

CHAPTER

21

BACK AT THE 22ND Precinct House, Tierney and Kalisha meet in his ridiculously sloppy office.

It's piled with books that have nothing to do with police work—classic American novels like *The Scarlet Letter* and *Moby-Dick,* and four huge volumes about French Impressionist painting. A pile of old *Esquire* magazines, hundreds of CDs, and two Manhattan phone directories—one from 1973, the other from 1975. Stacks of police reports are on the floor. Photographs of World War II airplanes are on the walls.

For a moment Kalisha considers speaking and comparing Tierney's sloppy office to

Emily's horrifying apartment. Then she thinks better of it. Her only observation is, "I know that your brain is a lot better organized than this room. Thank God."

"Could be that you're right, Detective," Tierney says.

"Could be that I am," she says.

She's thinking also that the mood between her and her partner actually seems warm, pleasant... what some people might simply call normal.

Kalisha taps a button on her phone, then says, "Okay, let's grab our notes and fill out an MP report and a breaking-and-entering report. I can..." but she doesn't have time to finish.

"We're not filing anything except a Missing Person Silver," Tierney says loudly.

"Silver?" Kalisha says. She knows that while *Silver* is technically the code word for a missing person who's mentally impaired, it usually refers to a senior citizen, someone who's wandered off because of dementia or Alzheimer's disease or elder abuse.

"This isn't silver, sir. This is plain breaking, entering, destruction with a possible regular missing person attachment."

"Only if we say so," says Tierney.

"And this detective is saying so," says Scofield.

"And this *senior* detective has other ideas."

"Okay. What's the deal, *partner?*" asks Scofield. She says the word *partner* as if it were a nasty curse word.

"Look," Tierney says. "I want *us* to stay on top of this. Do you think that makes sense?"

Kalisha is almost never one to leave matters alone.

"I'm hearing you loud and clear," she says. "But I'm thinking what if another department— say Robbery, for example— could go in and find something…"

"There's nothing they can find that the three of us couldn't have found," says Tierney. "The follow-up team will bring in some lab guys for the blood in the bathroom. That'll be it."

Again, Kalisha returns the ball. "The *three* of us? You mean that you're including your nurse friend?"

"That's exactly what I mean," says Tierney. He closes his eyes.

There is a silence, a long silence. Tierney moves some papers on his desk. Kalisha goes to work on her phone

"Okay. Read me whatever notes you've taken," Tierney says. Then he adds, "Try to keep it under twenty pages or three hours. Whichever comes first."

Even Kalisha, the butt of the joke, has to smile. Then she starts to talk, referring to her electronic device most of the time.

"I'll save the preliminaries—the entrance and first observations—for last. If it's all right with you, I'll begin with my notes on the final discovery of assumed assault, the discovery of blood..." She pauses and says, "I've checked with the lab. They're moving ultrafast on the blood samples that the coroner dropped off for analysis."

Tierney nods. But Kalisha suspects that Tierney has drifted off into another world. She keeps talking.

"Significant blood found in second bathroom. Some moisture from blood on tile wall sample. Significant amount, measuring approximately thirty-one inches by twenty inches, dried on tile flooring. Broken glass on shower door may indicate..."

Joel Tierney sits quickly upright and speaks in a loud, almost enthusiastic voice. It's not his angry voice, but it certainly isn't calm.

"Hold it. This whole thing is a fucking red herring."

Kalisha twists her face and says, "A red what?"

"A red herring, a distraction, a misdirect," says Tierney. "Unless that blood comes back as Emily's..."

Then he stops and thinks out loud. "Shit, even if they identify it as Emily's blood the whole scene is still designed to mislead us."

Kalisha knots her eyebrows and purposely blinks her eyes.

"Excuse me, Detective," she says. "Your red herring idea is based on what?"

Tierney gives her a what-the-hell-do-you-think look and says, "On what? On instinct. On the instinct, the gut feeling I have that often turns out to be true."

Kalisha wants to roll her eyes, but wisely she does not. Instead she says, "Well, let's coordinate your instinct with whatever we learn from the lab's blood workup."

She's about to review more of her notes, hoping to get Tierney back on a less instinctual track. But suddenly the conversation is interrupted by an emergency alert on their phones.

The detectives tap on their devices and read.

FEMALE VICTIM. DEAD. MULTIPLE KNIFE WOUNDS. VICTIM APPROX 35 YOA. PREGNANT APPROX 8 MOS.

14 ST. MARKS PLACE. APT. 3. POLICE ON SCENE VIA 911.

A woman eight months pregnant, an apartment located close to Emily's apartment, a victim who's thirty-five years old . . . If the outcome is what they both fear, then Kalisha's meticulous notes and Tierney's legendary instincts aren't worth a bucket of spit.

CHAPTER

22

JOEL TIERNEY'S FIRST ASSIGNMENT years ago, as a tag-along detective, was Narcotics. Tierney was an "altar boy," the name given to young and young-looking rookies.

He watched but he wasn't allowed to participate. The first bust he ever witnessed was three men and two women at a Polish church street fair in the Bronx. The five of them were selling heroin in the church restroom as openly as the folks outside who were selling kielbasas and pierogis. Six officers surrounded the five suspects. The altar boy was so excited and uplifted that he slapped cuffs on one of the dealers.

This very rookie move led to Tierney's

baptism with two nicknames: Little Asshole and Kid Enthusiasm. The joke names were understandable, but the fact was that Tierney loved being a detective. And the higher-ups noticed.

One month later, Tierney was not only participating in drug busts, arrests, and investigations, he was also on call seven days a week.

Kid Enthusiasm never got tired. He turned into the detective that the others had to beat.

One year later, Tierney was transferred to Homicide. "Sort of a promotion," the precinct captain told Tierney. "The thing is, as I'm sure you've heard, it's tougher than shit." Then the captain added, "But you'll get used to it."

Tierney was delighted.

The captain turned out to be correct. Tierney actually did get used to it. At some point, he became essentially immune to the horrors of homicide work. The newborn twins who were suffocated in a green plastic garbage bag. The drug-addled teenage boy whose drug-addled girlfriend amputated the five fingers of the boy's right hand and left him to bleed out. The old man who put a bullet in his wife's brain because "we both suffered enough from her Alzheimer's."

Yes, he has more or less become used to it,

but this case...well, this case is a first for him. His friendship with Betsey puts him closer to her friend Emily. Even though Tierney didn't answer Kalisha's question—"You think it could be Emily?"—she knew the answer. And, of course, so did Tierney.

They continue driving across St. Marks Place, the street circus of tattoo parlors and pizza joints in the East Village.

They arrive at the crime scene, a heavily guarded and police-barricaded area. Tierney's been at places like this a few hundred times now.

POLICE LINE DO NOT CROSS POLICE LINE DO NOT CROSS POLICE LINE DO NOT CROSS.

An NYPD sergeant opens their car door and gives them a quick "Follow me, detectives. The team is at work. It's all pretty gruesome."

Tierney thinks, *So, what else is new?* but says, "Do we have an ID yet?"

"Not yet," says the sergeant. "There was no wallet or license. Victim had a phone. The IT guys just got here. They're working on cracking it. She had no computer or laptop or anything else on her."

Tierney nods, but all he can think is: *In a*

*minute we may actually have an ID. In a minute
I might be the guy who makes the ID.*

Tierney and Scofield now head down a short
hallway toward the room where the victim is.
Tierney glances into the small closet just outside the bedroom.

Kalisha's hands and arms are actually shak-
ing, and she is thinking, *Whose place is this?
Some guy? Some friend? Is this where that Emily
woman ended up? In a crappy cookie-cutter East
Village apartment? Betsey called her "charming."*
Charming, *yes, that's the word she used.*

"Did you get anything from that little closet
outside?" Tierney asks. An NYPD sergeant
responds.

"Nothing, empty, like the rest of the place.
There was just an old-fashioned broom in
there. That's it up against the wall, all wrapped
and tagged and ready to go."

"It's a *corn* broom," says Tierney.

"What?"

"It's a corn broom. That's what you call those
brooms that you swing, sorta sweep-sweep-sweep."

"Yessir," says the sergeant. "In any event,
like I said, we'll send the broom over to the lab,
along with some kitchen sink rags and some

Roach Motel traps. That's all we got. A roll of toilet paper, an empty can of Diet Pepsi."

"Well, check the closets again," says Tierney. The sergeant nods, and it's obvious to Kalisha that the sergeant is surprised that Tierney's so involved with the empty closet.

Then it suddenly comes to Kalisha. She realizes what's going on. She senses that what Tierney is doing is playing for time. Detective Joel Tierney simply does not want to continue in. He doesn't want to see the body. Kalisha stands back.

"Let me know if you find anything, especially from the *corn* broom," says Tierney.

"Of course, sir," says the sergeant. Then he adds, "Uh, the victim is in here."

"Yeah," says Tierney.

They take a few more steps, and the sergeant speaks again.

"Right through here."

"Yeah," says Tierney.

The sergeant continues. "This is a rough one, detective. Ugly. Really ugly. You'll see."

The usual cast of characters are at work: two police photographers, an assistant medical examiner, a coroner (the only team member who Tierney knows by name, Jonathan

Ramiro), and the assorted group of print-dusters and chem experts.

But Tierney and Scofield barely notice their police colleagues. They are, of course, immediately focused on the victim, who is lying on her back near the center of the room.

An assistant medical examiner and two police officers, both women, are kneeling near the body's feet. The sergeant's earlier description of "pretty gruesome" was ridiculously gentle.

I've never seen anything like it, Tierney thinks.

The victim's neck is deep purple. Strangled. The hands look broken. The skin on the arms, where it's not caked with blood, is covered with burn marks and dark bruises. A large pool of blood begins on the floor near the head and streams down to a trickle near the knees. The woman's head is tilted to the left, partially covered with bloody sprays of hair. Tierney slips on a pair of examining gloves. He squats down and gently moves the victim's head to the right. Frightening as it will be, he wants to get a full-frontal look at the victim's face. He moves to the other side of the victim. He crouches down near her head.

Then the most shocking observation. The

victim's face is so disfigured that the corpse is unrecognizable. Great globs of blood form a large red and yellow hole where once the nose was, cheekbones so cracked that the one eye that is not covered by blood seems tilted outward from its socket, the hair (blond once, perhaps?) is bathed in blood, the corners of the mouth are severed. The victim's upper torso has been covered in a coroner's cloth, but bright turquoise tights—spattered with blood—have been pulled down below the victim's knees.

So who is this woman? Who in hell can she be? Emily? Who?

But now he thinks for a split second: Turquoise? Turquoise tights. Emily would never ever wear turquoise anything. But who the hell knows. Everything that's happening is totally startling, totally perverse.

Kalisha slips on latex gloves. Then Kalisha points to the general area of the victim's stomach. All she says is "Look."

Kalisha Scofield and Joel Tierney see a sight they never want to see again.

The woman's pregnant womb has been slashed.

"We just got a fairly certain ID, Detective."

Tierney snaps at the officer. "For Chrissake, you can't have a *fairly* certain ID. You have an ID or you don't have an ID. You can't be *fairly* certain."

"Yes, sir," says the sergeant. "We *may* have an ID. We're not certain. We found a small purse in the access hall on the second floor. The only thing in it was this phone."

The officer holds a phone, which is sealed inside a plastic evidence bag. The phone itself is in a black-and-orange paisley case. Tierney considers this, hoping that Emily would never own such an ugly, goofy-looking phone case.

"What's the victim's name?" Kalisha asks.

The sergeant answers. "If it's who we think, her name is Caitlin Murphy. The report we got says she's thirty-three, single, an executive at MHD, some sort of internet ad agency. Two assistant MEs have brought what's left of the fetus to NYU Medical. DOA. They think that Ms. Murphy was seven or eight months into her pregnancy."

Tierney stands stricken. He is not excruciatingly unhappy. And yet...and yet he is happier than he expected to be. It's not Emily. Yet it's still a horror show. He stares at the victim's bloody belly.

Then Kalisha gives her opinion: "Everything about this case sucks."

"You think so?" Then he points to the phone that the sergeant is holding. "May I see that for a minute?"

"I really should hold it for the lab," says the sergeant. "I don't want to compromise the condition of the phone."

"Give me the fucking phone," says Tierney, who snatches it from the officer's grip.

Through the plastic bag, Tierney punches the button marked CONTACTS. Then he punches in the letters A-T-K. A name and a number appear.

The name is ATKINSON Emily.

"Sunuvabitch," Tierney says. "Caitlin Murphy. Emily Atkinson. These two women knew each other."

CHAPTER

23

IT'S ALMOST 9:30 P.M. when Scofield and Tierney leave the apartment where Caitlin Murphy was found. As they walk down the building's back service stairway, Tierney says, "I've got to make a quick phone call."

Kalisha understands immediately that this is some sort of courtesy code for "I want to make this phone call in private."

Kalisha says, "I'll grab the car then."

Five minutes later she drives up to the rear entrance of the building. Tierney sees her, just as he's ending his call. He slides into the passenger seat.

As Kalisha drives across St. Marks Place, she speaks.

"So, have you told your buddy Betsey about what went down here just now?"

"No way. Betsey doesn't know anything about it, and since nothing has come of it..."

Kalisha interrupts. "Emily was a contact in the victim's phone. That's *not* nothing."

"Until we find out more about the case, let's just keep it quiet. She's messed up enough about this whole thing."

Kalisha wants to say *Wait a second, Betsey did an investigation with us, Betsey is the one who instigated the entire search, but you won't tell her about this?* Instead, she says the ever-useful phrase, "Yes, sir."

"Anyway, you and I have an interview now."

"Now? Right now?" asks Kalisha.

"Right now. I had set it up for tomorrow morning, but I called her, and she's available now."

All Kalisha would really like to do is go home, crack open a Bass Ale, then get a good night's snooze. But she's not going to share that thought with her partner as he begins briefing her on the person they're about to interview.

"It's Emily's neighbor. They've lived next door to each other for about two years, and it sounds like they've had a few—the polite word is *tiffs*. The usual kind of stupid stuff. 'You play your music too loud.' 'You're always coming and going.' That sort of thing."

"How old is she?" Kalisha asks.

"You'll see her in a few minutes. I'd call her middle-aged. You'd probably call her old."

He looks down at his phone and continues talking.

"Her name is Mariana Micelli. Italian, I assume," Tierney says.

Kalisha stifles the urge to say, "Italian? Really? I never would have guessed." Instead, she says, "Okay, what's the deal with this woman?"

"Two officers spoke briefly with her after we investigated the destruction at Emily's apartment. They got the impression she might have more to say about her missing neighbor. So I thought we could give it a shot. On the other hand, both Betsey and Emily—I'm pretty sure—told me once that Emily and Micelli barely knew each other."

"So you don't know anything about her?" asks Kalisha.

"Well, I know what I know from a little deft googling."

"Is she some sort of zany old Italian mama with the hand gestures and the accent?"

"Actually, she's a professor at NYU. And quite elegant. One very interesting thing about her is the death of her much younger husband, Lorenzo Micelli. He was an art dealer in Turin, I think. Let me see." Tierney is clearly about to consult his phone.

"Put down the phone, Detective," says Kalisha. "Let's just assume it was Turin for now."

Tierney smiles and continues the story. "Anyway, Signor Micelli was very popular with the ladies. But one summer day, while he and the missus are summering on Lake Como, he shoots himself. No one knows why, it seems. Coulda been girlfriend trouble. Coulda been business problems. Coulda been…I dunno… Coulda been…"

Kalisha fills in the words. "Coulda been his wife who shot him. Is that what you're trying to say?"

"I guess," says Tierney. "But it was a while ago, and it was in Italy, and...who knows?"

When the two of them arrive at Mariana Micelli's apartment, it turns out that Joel Tierney is correct about the elegance of the interviewee. Mariana Micelli is no stock character from a TV spaghetti sauce commercial. This woman—perhaps sixty years old, with hair the color of spun gold—presents herself more like a Florentine countess.

When she greets them at the door, she does not bother to read their NYPD IDs, nor does she shake Tierney's hand when he offers it.

"Thank you for making the time for us, Professor Micelli."

She responds, "Detectives, if I may, there are two little things you must know before we begin our discussion."

"And those things are?" Tierney asks.

"The title I use is 'doctor,' not 'professor.' And my surname is properly pronounced 'Michelly,' not with the soft s as you spoke it, not 'Miselly.'"

"I'll keep that in mind, Doctor," says Tierney.

"Please do," she says. So far Dr. Micelli has not cracked even the touch of a smile.

Scofield and Tierney follow her into a

palatial living room. The high walls are covered in dark-green fabric. The furniture looks like authentic Louis XIV, heavy with gold leaf. An ornate crystal chandelier hangs from the center of the ceiling.

The three people sit. Dr. Micelli reaches toward the glass coffee table between them and pours a single cup of tea, for herself. She offers nothing to her guests.

"To begin," says Tierney. "How long have you known Emily Atkinson?"

"Approximately two years. I saw her the first day. The moving people were bringing in her furniture." She pauses, then adds, "Nothing of real quality, nothing of interest."

"And you and she spoke?"

"Yes. I graciously introduced myself. She told me her first name only, which I thought was far too familiar a gesture. But I ignored that. I wanted to be a good neighbor."

Another pause. Then Micelli says, "But that was not to be."

"What happened, Doctor?" Tierney asks.

"I told your colleagues who spoke to me earlier. This Atkinson woman and I are cut from a different cloth. I am devoted to learning and art

and the humanities. She seemed to be devoted
to men and alcohol and God knows what else.
My opinion, if you want it, is that she's killed
herself. I myself suffered the agony of the suicide of a loved one. My husband killed himself.
Suicide. Why do people do it? Only the good
Lord above knows."

Kalisha jumps in: "Is there anything else
you can tell us about your neighbor?"

Micelli takes a sip of her tea. Then she says,
"She seems to have had many male friends.
Why don't you ask them?"

"We are talking to anyone who might have
helpful information," says Kalisha.

"Men friends. This Atkinson woman seemed
to have mostly men friends. In fact, I wouldn't
be surprised..." But Micelli stops there.

"What would not have surprised you?" asks
Kalisha.

Micelli replaces her cup on its saucer. Then
Tierney speaks.

"Forgetting suicide for a moment, do you
have any other idea why Ms. Atkinson might
have gone missing?" Tierney says.

"Assuming she has not taken her own life,
then she's just run off to another place. The

reason? Women like that don't need a reason. They take off when it suits them. Their bags are always packed. She could be in Denmark now. Or she could be a few blocks away, taking a stroll by the East River. But most likely, as I've said…" Instead of finishing her sentence she holds an index finger to her temple and mimes shooting herself.

Tierney feels compelled to comment on Dr. Micelli's casual cynicism.

"You're really angry about your neighbor, aren't you?" he says.

"*Ascoltami,* Signor Policeman. She was not a good woman," says Micelli.

"How do you know?" Kalisha asks.

"Because I am wise."

"That's not a particularly helpful answer, Doctor," says Tierney.

"It is as much of an answer as I can supply."

It seems clear to the detectives that Micelli will not be elaborating on her opinion of Emily Atkinson.

Tierney takes one more shot at it.

"Is there anything else you'd like to say?"

Micelli looks annoyed. Then she sounds annoyed.

"No. I would just be repeating myself."

"One thing I'd like to know," says Kalisha, "is what course or courses you teach down at NYU."

Without waiting for even a moment, Mariana Micelli says, "Survey of African Culture."

Kalisha does not try to hide the surprise in her voice. "Did you just say, 'African Culture'? *You* teach a class about African culture?"

"Yes, it's quite popular. There's even a waiting list each semester. You see, I was born and raised in Ethiopia, and my family owned a number of tea plantations in Tanzania. So it's an area I'm quite familiar with."

"African culture. Will wonders never cease?" Kalisha says.

Micelli looks directly at Kalisha and speaks, "I often ask myself the same thing."

Scofield and Tierney stand. They leave their cards—"in case you can think of anything else that might prove helpful"—and say good-bye.

"You don't have to see us out," Tierney says.

"Very well," Dr. Micelli replies. "But there is one other thing I want to say."

The two detectives freeze in anticipation of what Micelli might tell them.

"And that is?" asks Kalisha.

"I must apologize for forgetting to serve you some of my father's perfectly beautiful tea. It was a remarkable first-flush Darjeeling."

Scofield and Tierney walk to the elevator. They do not speak as they travel down to the lobby. They do not speak as they walk to the car.

Kalisha breaks the silence. "Okay. Can I be the one who says it first?"

"Go right ahead," says Tierney.

"Here goes. Do you think that Mariana Micelli may have something to do with Emily Atkinson's disappearance?"

"Like Mariana Micelli said, 'Only the good Lord above knows.'"

Kalisha does not find his response satisfying.

"Okay, maybe Emily Atkinson *barely* knew Micelli. But it's pretty clear that Micelli knew a lot and thought a lot about Emily Atkinson. Don't you think?" says Kalisha.

"Only the good Lord above knows."

MONTH THREE

CHAPTER

24

I WAKE UP AT seven thirty this morning. Bang the cymbals. Start the parade. For me seven thirty is ridiculously early. And what has happened between seven thirty and now (eleven forty-five)? Nothing. Absolutely nothing. Very often noonish is the time I pour myself a crisp glass of chardonnay or cool off with a Coors Light. But not anymore. Not this lady. This is the new Emily. And I'm doing really well. I am very into taking care of the reborn me and my unborn baby.

It's as if I woke up from a dream, and reality slapped my face hard, very hard. It's simple. I got it. I got it. Dr. Craven's threats and Betsey's lectures have worked. I think. I hope. I've even subscribed to a Pregnancy Day-by-Day email. It's always one simple fact. Curiously today's fact is, "*Drink plenty of water, and avoid sugared soft drinks and alcohol.*" Oh, my God. They're watching me.

Somewhere in this apartment is *The Big Book* from AA as well as about ten copies of the twelve-step program. Okay, I've got to find these things, and the only way I can find them is to straighten up this place. It's a mess. I'll start with something easy, the kitchen, the dishwasher. Okay. I've made an important decision. I'll empty the dishwasher.

As I swallow my Lexapro and water, I think, *Emily, listen. A baby. Do you understand? You're going to have a baby.* Then I cry.

It's a big cry, a shake-your-head-back-and-forth kind of cry. I think about being a parent, and a person can't think about being a parent without thinking about their own parents. Betsey says that crying is therapeutic. I always think it's the first sign that a person should be institutionalized.

My mother and father never cried. And speaking of them, I haven't even told my parents that I'm pregnant. Not that I'm sure they'd even care. Or, just the opposite, they might care way more than they should. I know that they're back from Europe. They've sent texts and left about thirty voicemails. My mother even sent snail-mail on her Cartier summer-house stationery.

I hate to say it, but my "rich kid" story is not particularly unique. Liz and Lionel Atkinson fit the description of *rich*. I fit the description of *kid*. So here's how my story goes. (Don't try to stop me.)

When I was growing up, either my folks had absolutely no time for me, *or* they'd swoop in occasionally and be temporarily obsessed with me. First, they'd disappear. Then they'd reappear. Then...well, you get it.

And, because I was an only child, and because my father's inheritance left him free from the need to do any kind of real work, and because I was a meek, shy, chubby little clump of a child, I sometimes became Liz and Lionel's hobby.

My mother and I visited Golden Door or Canyon Ranch every few months; she would lose five pounds in a week. I would lose nothing but my self-esteem. When I was at Hotchkiss (that was my prep school) and failing both algebra and Latin, there was no need for a tutor. Liz was a wiz at math. Lionel was actually able to *speak* Latin. He would have made a great pope.

Three days later they were off to Moscow or Berlin or Kenya on an art-buying trip. Anyway... we've all got our stories, and I never tire of thinking of mine.

The tears stop as suddenly as they started. My hand moves down to my stomach. I'm sure I'm feeling something. It's there. He's there. She's there. My baby is there. It's all going to be good.

Right off the kitchen is the tiny adjoining maid's room. This is pretty much the room that symbolizes the Emily I Aspire to Be. I go in. Books that were bought and never read— books like *Eat, Pray, Love,* Michelle Obama's autobiography, *Becoming,* and *Dear Sugar.* Two Rosetta Stone CDs, one for Spanish, the other for Hebrew. Hmm. To use them, I guess I'd have to remove the cellophane wrapping. When I try to use my nearly new MacBook Air I can't remember the password to unlock it. I am poised to start crying once again.

So then I touch *the bump.* And I'm reluctant to say it, because it can't really be true that the touch is magical. But it is. You don't have to believe me, but it is. I look at this trash heap of an office and I see a nursery—a baby's room in pale yellow and the whitest white. That's where the crib will go. And over here where the dusty yoga mat is, a rocking chair. Then I reach down, and, of course, I touch *the bump*. I'm gonna straighten up. I've got some plans for this room.

I fill two clear plastic trash bags with junk.

Before I crack open a Diet Dr Pepper (yes, I know, diet soft drinks are nutritionally suspicious), I do something that always makes me feel good. I light two Jo Malone orange-blossom-scented candles. Then I head out to the service hall where trash and recycling are left for pickup. And then, well…Most people are perfectly capable of taking out the garbage without incident. It turns out that I'm not one of those people.

I take a few steps toward the service elevator. I seem to recall that this is the place to leave trash. All you need to do is buy an expensive co-op, pay an exorbitant maintenance, and—voilà!—your garbage disappears. I deposit my plastic bags at the elevator entrance. Then I hear a fairly loud, fairly unpleasant female voice.

"What exactly are you doing?" the voice says.

I'm startled. I spin around, dropping one of the plastic bags on the ground. It takes a moment until I recognize the stern-looking, older blond woman standing in front of me. Then I realize that it's my next-door neighbor, the ridiculously snooty Mariana Micelli. She really belongs in a cartoon.

This is not the first time Micelli has exploded at me. She seems to need the elevator when I need the elevator. She seems to need a taxi when the doorman is hailing me a taxi. This time she is wearing a mid-calf gray woolen skirt, a white silk shirt, and, in my opinion, a ridiculous amount of antique emerald jewelry.

"May I ask you, Ms. Atkinson? Has anyone ever told you about recycling? It's a somewhat new idea." Her voice is full of scorn.

"These are properly separated for recycling, *Dr.* Micelli," I say, with extra emphasis on the highfalutin title she insists on using.

"Forgive me," Micelli says, "but that appears to be a plastic cup peeking out of the sack full of paper."

Okay, she's right. I made a mistake. But, for God's sake, take it easy, lady. Why is she so involved with me and my freakin' recycling? I have wondered for the past year why this woman has taken such an extreme interest in my life, my comings and goings, my garbage. Yep, she always seems to be bumping into me accidentally when I'm coming into the lobby, when I'm saying good night to friends at my front door, now when I'm bringing out my garbage.

But apparently she's not finished with her criticism. She continues.

"I'm not surprised at your carelessness. I don't expect someone like you to be doing anything positive for the commonweal."

The commonweal?

What is with this crazy old lady? This is the longest conversation we've ever had.

I speak softly, but I know she can hear me when I say, "Give me a break, lady."

Micelli shakes her head in exaggerated sadness. She has the frightening sweetness, the hatred behind the smile of... of... Where have I seen this woman before? Then I remember, the horrid old movie my mother once made me watch, *Rosemary's Baby*. A woman full of curses and hatred.

"That's exactly the sort of language I'd have expected from someone like you," she says.

"What exactly is the matter with you?" I ask.

"No, my dear. The question is, what's the matter with you? What's the matter with men coming in and out of your apartment?"

"In and out of my apartment?" I say loudly, but Micelli is on a tear. She doesn't miss a beat.

"What's the matter with your personal hours? Coming in at five in the morning?"

She's the goddamn Gestapo!

"And what's the matter with you that you don't know that plastic and paper are supposed to be separated into different plastic bags?"

I try a different tactic. I look at her and speak softly, "I really don't care one little bit what you think. You're crazy."

But the crazy Dr. Micelli won't stop, and she's apparently determined to take one last shot.

"You shouldn't be allowed to have that baby!"

This last verbal grenade works spectacularly. When it explodes, I explode.

To my amazement, I pull back my right arm at the shoulder. I make a fist. And just as Speedy Stephanie taught me at Twentieth Street Shadow Box, I follow through with maximum speed toward Micelli's left eye. I purposely miss connecting, but the woman lets go a scream, and a somewhat unexpected, "You bitch, you bitch!"

I match the volume and intensity of her words.

"Listen. I'm warning you. Stay away from my baby. Just stay away from my baby!"

Yes, the witch in *Rosemary's Baby*. The witch who curses Rosemary's baby. Shit. Now I'm ashamed of myself. Just because Micelli is crazy doesn't mean that I have to be the same wicked way.

As I watch Micelli scurry back through her service entrance door I find myself wondering what's going on. With me, with my anger, with my baby.

I've just started my third month. I'm not even "showing" yet.

So, come to think of it: How does Micelli even know that I'm pregnant?

CHAPTER

25

WHEN I CALL BETSEY the next day, I say nothing about my encounter with crazy Dr. Micelli. Betsey has enough to think about. I say nothing about my ongoing fear that someone has been following me. But I do mention—as I probably do way too many times—my resolve to get in shape for the baby's arrival. And, as always, I can hear honest hope in her reaction.

"That's great, of course," she says. "Emily, let me ask. Have you considered, well, trying to get some help? Joining a group? It doesn't have to be AA. I told you a few weeks ago about Rational Recovery. That sounded pretty good to me, and there's a guy who..."

I interrupt. "I already have a therapist. This woman. Ruth. She's great. She's nice. She's smart."

"Okay, great," says Betsey.

"The only thing is...I keep canceling sessions. And when I do go, I lie a lot. And...I don't know. Maybe I'll get back into it."

There's silence on both Betsey's end and mine. Then she speaks.

"Shit," Betsey says. "I should just shut up and support you, not sound like Sister Mary Ignatius Holier Than Thou."

"That's okay," I say. "I deserve it. I've never been the most reliable at recovery. But I have a really good feeling about it this time." Betsey does not speak the next obvious sentence: *Yeah, you always do.*

It's clear to me, however, that this time Betsey is putting real faith in me. This feeling is verified when she says, "How would you feel about babysitting Bobby and Juliet this afternoon? My extraordinary, incredible husband scored two balcony seats for the *Hamilton* matinee today, and I was going to leave the kids with Frankie's sister in Brooklyn, but then she's got *her* twins, and..."

"Stop it!" I yell. "I love those kids."

One hour later, Betsey and Frankie and Bobby and Juliet are walking into my apartment.

Each one gives me a warm, prolonged hug. Betsey is pregnant, of course, but she isn't showing. She's duded up in designer jeans and a beige silk Tom Ford shirt that once belonged to me. Frankie—longish blond hair, tough slim gym body showing off in a denim shirt—is a perfect example of the guys in my prep school who my girlfriends called "cute." And speaking of cute, four-year-old twins Bobby and Juliet are the definitions of the word. Cookie commercial. Toy commercial. McDonald's commercial. Camera, speed, action.

Frankie and Betsey wrap up saying goodbye by distributing another flurry of hugs and kisses. And as soon as the parents leave, as if by magic, I turn into this very weird combination of Lady Gaga and My Little Pony.

"Backward Baby, Backward Baby!" Bobby yells.

"Great. So you remember the Backward Baby dance?" I say, and I clap my hands together as they both shake their heads wildly. I invented the dance a few weeks ago when I was visiting Betsey and Frankie. You start with music—say,

Post Malone or Cardi B—and we get down on the floor and walk backward on our arms and hands. When I yell "Fall down!" we all fall to the carpet and squirm about with our arms and legs in the air. As you might imagine, it's just a way to keep falling to the floor and jumping up again and again. Best of all, it's a dance that seems to let out all the craziness inside.

The only one who enjoys dancing Backward Baby more than Bobby and Juliet is me. Backward Baby eats up about fifteen minutes, a triumph of fun even though I never turned on any musical accompaniment.

Our next adventure is less successful—or more successful—depending on your point of view. On a previous babysitting occasion at my house we tried baking chocolate chip cookies. It was an unfortunate event. Given the meager baking supplies in my kitchen, we were forced to use some thawed eggnog I'd popped in the freezer after a Christmas party, and, even worse, something I thought was flour but was actually confectioner's sugar. Finally, since there were no chocolate chips, we used the contents of a two-year-old box of Frangos. The result was a baking sheet of mint-flavored chocolate syrup. (It was sloppy eating, but, man, it was delicious.)

This time around, our goal is to duplicate the previous disaster. We find the correct ingredients—milk, confectioner's sugar, Hershey's syrup, and, this time, a box of Jacques Torres chocolate truffles. Then, a sudden change of plans. As Juliet, Bobby, and I begin assembling a bowl and pan and all the ingredients, we make an executive decision. The hell with the confectioner's sugar, Hershey's syrup, and the low-fat milk. Let's just vacuum our way through the box of Jacques Torres chocolates.

So that's what we do, all washed down with Caffeine-Free Diet Coke. An hour later, the three of us are fast asleep on my super-soft king-sized bed.

By the way, Betsey and Frankie absolutely loved *Hamilton*. And I think that Bobby and Juliet really loved being with me. With little kids you never know for sure.

And I certainly loved the distraction. From my problems. From my future.

From whoever might be lurking outside, watching me.

CHAPTER

26

The Present

BETSEY KNOWS TED'S BAR and Grill, but it's not her favorite place to spend an afternoon.

But today, she's determined to do everything she can to help find Emily. Yes, everything, even if it means sitting at a bar, cross-examining Ted, and hoping that, at nine months, she's not about to go into labor.

From the get-go, it seems like Ted's information is going to be slim.

Betsey is anxious, grim, the far side of worried. But she's also determined. She believes that her determination is great, greater than anyone else's. Even Joel Tierney seems strangely resigned to the situation. "After all," he recently said to her, "Missing Persons and Homicide are doing all they can do."

Really? Betsey doesn't think so. Not at all.

Sure, Joel has told her that he and Kalisha have interviewed Emily's neighbor, and that they plan to speak with some of her friends and colleagues. But he also told her they're helping out on the Caitlin Murphy murder case. The brutal killing of that woman—about Emily's age, and pregnant, too—has been in the news a lot lately. And Betsey is worried that the homicide might steal the spotlight away from her missing best friend.

This concern, and the lack of any real police movement on the case, has jolted Betsey into action of her own. Her husband, Frankie, has begun calling her "our own little Nancy Drew." Yes, Betsey knows he means it as a joke to cheer her up. But she's told Frankie to stop, and since he loves her more than life itself, he stopped. Betsey knows that her husband is proud of her medical skills, but understandably skeptical of her police and detective talents.

The hell with that. Betsey has made the

decision to take on the case of Emily Atkinson's disappearance in one very specific way. She will interview any likely candidate—a friend, a coworker, a neighbor—who might know something about Emily. What she's actually hoping for is that she will eventually end up interviewing the father of Emily's baby. Ted is number one on her list.

"I don't even know when I saw her last," he says, drawing a big glass of seltzer for himself.

"Emily was your good friend. You don't know—even approximately—when you saw her last? Even if she hasn't been in, you haven't texted?"

Ted takes a big gulp of his seltzer water. He says nothing. He towel-polishes three beer mugs. He straightens the line-up of the cream liqueurs. Then he can think of nothing else to do to postpone a response.

He turns from the liqueur bottles and faces Betsey.

"Okay," he says, speaking in a clear, solid voice. "Of course I remember when Emily was in here. It was about a week or two ago. Early afternoon. She was really wobbly, and I couldn't figure out if it had something to do with being pregnant...I mean, what the hell do I know about pregnant women?"

Betsey gently shakes her head. She certainly agrees with Ted's statement.

"She asked for a seven and seven," Ted says. "Can you imagine? Pregnant, and she's asking for a 7 Up with rye whiskey?"

"I didn't know they even made 7 Up anymore," says Betsey. Then she says, "So, what did you do?"

"I told her no, of course."

"Did she go crazy?" Betsey asks.

"No. I thought she might start throwing things...but she didn't. She got real quiet, put her head on the bar. Then she picked up her head and shook it—just like you did a few seconds ago. Like she understood."

"Then?"

"Then I asked her if she wanted a taxi or an Uber or something, but she said no."

"So?"

"So, there was this young guy at one of the tables. He had a laptop and was banging away at it. Like I say, he was young. Maybe in college. I didn't card him, but I asked him if he was legal to drink."

"That's very trusting of you, and maybe just a little stupid. I can't imagine what the kid answered."

Ted smiles. But his smile vanishes quickly when he sees that Betsey is in no mood for humor.

"So the kid walks over to where Emily is sitting. I get a good look at him. He's handsome, I gotta say, but a kid, a runt, a college guy, most likely.

"Keep going."

Ted continues. "So, like I say, I can tell Emily's maybe flattered that this young guy is coming on to her. " 'I'd be quite glad to see you home, miss,' the kid says. 'See you home' is the nutso phrase he uses. What is this, *Bridgerton*? Anyway, that's when I jump in."

"Yeah?" says Betsey, straightening up on her barstool.

"So, I say, 'What's wrong with you, man? For one thing, this woman is pregnant. And you're trying to pick her up?'

"The kid says—very sincerely—'I'm trying to help her, sir. She obviously needs some help, not just your weak offer of hailing her a taxi.'

"I wanted to jump over the bar and paste

the kid to the wall, but, ya know, in a second or two, I figure that maybe he's right. I don't know. My mind is a little crazy. So Emily and the kid leave the bar. And then I start thinking, shit, maybe Emily and this kid really know each other."

"Do you think she had been drinking before this happened?" Betsey asks.

"No. I actually think she was sober. But I'm not sure."

The bizarre thought crosses Betsey's mind that maybe Emily and this kid knew each other, that he could even be the father...but no, no, no. That's too insane.

Ted lowers his head to his chest. When he picks up his head again a few seconds later his mouth is slightly twisted, his eyes wet with tears.

"I let her down," Ted says. "She could have gotten hurt. Maybe she did get hurt. You heard what happened to that Caitlin Murphy woman— pretty, successful, in advertising."

"I did," says Betsey.

"They found her dead, beat up. And she was pregnant, too. A cop who comes in here told me somebody bashed her face in."

He pauses and speaks again.

"Oh, shit. I *really* should have stopped Emily from leaving with that kid."

Betsey reaches across the bar and takes Ted's hand. When she tells Ted that he did nothing wrong, she means it. Emily was . . . or is still . . . a free spirit, on her own road to some sort of salvation or some sort of destruction. It could go either way. It could still go either way.

Betsey's mind jumps from the awful present time to the potentially awful future. Betsey is thinking that Emily now has two lives at stake—her own and her baby's.

Suddenly Ted lets go of Betsey's hand. He speaks loudly.

"I miss her, Betsey. I really, really miss her," he says.

"We all miss her, Ted," says Betsey.

"But I think I miss her more than most people."

Betsey thinks that Ted might be telling the truth.

CHAPTER

27

BETSEY SPENDS THE REMAINDER of her afternoon and much of her evening in semi–Wonder Woman mode. She assists with the second half of a kidney transplant for a three-month-old infant. She teaches a half-hour class in post–cardiac surgery procedure. During her very brief free time she texts with her children. And she also googles some names that she's found in Emily's address book.

She knows that she is becoming obsessed with finding her missing friend, and she decides that after her workday a return trip to Ted's Bar is in order. Maybe, just maybe, she'll run into someone there who could help her out.

Ted's Bar at 10:00 p.m. is a very different place than Ted's Bar in the afternoon. Ted's is one of those Lower East Side places that found the happy formula for attracting young hipsters, old-timers, and quite a few businesspeople, equally young and old, equally male and female. The jukebox reflects the place. Ariana Grande alternates with Tony Bennett.

Ted himself is one busy dude. He moves with intense speed. He's shaking drinks, mixing drinks, serving drinks, making change, scooping up tips, and making small talk with his guests. Betsey decides not to disrupt his pace.

Then things turn lucky for her. She notices Mike Miller standing at the far end of the bar. She recognizes Miller because once he stopped by Emily's apartment when Betsey was visiting, trying to get her to buy weed.

"Betsey!" Mike shouts as she approaches him. "Emily's best bud. I'd know you anywhere, Miss Nurse."

"That's *Mrs.* Nurse to you, Mike."

His response? "Give us a kiss, babe."

Without waiting for permission, Mike leans in and kisses Betsey on her cheek, dangerously close to her mouth.

Wow, Betsey thinks, *this guy is so easy to loathe.*

"Funny you should mention Emily," says Betsey. "I was wondering if you'd seen her lately."

"Before I answer, may I buy you a drink?" Mike asks.

Betsey figures that she should make nice with Mike if she wants info from him. She says, "Sure. I'll have a glass of chardonnay with one ice cube in it."

"That's a perfect description of you, Betsey. A sharp chick with a bit of ice."

She doesn't let on that she ordered wine simply to act friendly. She smiles and says, "Now, how about answering 'Have you seen Emily lately?'"

"I haven't. But you probably knew that. The word is that the beautiful Miss Atkinson is AWOL."

"I guess that is the case," says Betsey. "I'm trying to track her down."

Ted delivers the chardonnay and nods at Betsey. Mike passes the glass to Betsey, who does not say thank you.

"So," says Mike. "I also understand that the fair Emily is expecting a visit from the stork."

Betsey thinks she might actually throw up. Mike's idiotic expressions—Miss Nurse, a visit from the stork, a sharp chick, fair Emily— literally make her sick.

Betsey takes a pretend sip of wine. She is not certain that she is hiding the look of disgust on her face.

"Let me get right to the point, Mike."

"Please do."

"Did you have anything to do with the stork's visit?"

Mike throws his hands and arms in the air. He feigns shock at her suggestion.

"Me? Are you serious? Emily and I have a strictly professional relationship."

"You mean that all you ever do is sell her bennies and pot," says Betsey.

"That's right. And because she's a friend, I gave her a bargain rate. There's practically no mark-up on the weed. If I was selling other folks an ounce for $350, Emily got it for, say, $300. The wake-me-up pills were bonus gifts, too."

"What a guy," Betsey says. She just knows

that Mike is lying about the sale price. Emily never thinks much about money. She doesn't have to. Chances are if the retail rate for weed was $350 an ounce, Mike was holding Emily up for $400, maybe even $500.

"You are the holy apostle of drug dealers, Mike," Betsey says.

Mike loses his cool a bit. "Think whatever you want, but it's basic capitalism: I fill a consumer need. And to be honest, she isn't that great a customer. Wall Street guys and music folks, that's where the real money is. They're my hot consumers. The big bucks are in coke. And Em hardly ever reaches for the snow."

The nicknames, the cool attitude, they are making Betsey even sicker. But she forges ahead.

"So, let me ask. You don't ever sleep with your consumers?"

Betsey is becoming aggressive, and thinks that Emily told her more than once that she and Mike had an on-and-off romantic relationship. But who knows? Maybe not. Betsey is slightly confused. Emily knows so many people. And every one of them loves her. Even this scumbag.

"I'm a pretty easygoing guy, Nurse. But

you're getting a little too intense for me. No, I sold Emily medication. Maybe the bennies helped loosen her up and helped keep her up. But that was it. I never moved beyond simple package goods with my buddy Emily."

Betsey doesn't answer. A few seconds of silence.

Then Mike speaks.

"Do you need another ice cube in that?"

"I need an honest answer," Betsey says, "so stop being an asshole."

"You think I'm an asshole because I'm not giving you the answer you're hoping for. So listen. I'll clarify it for you . . ."

He pauses, and Betsey considers in those few moments that she might be wrong, that this jerk is telling the truth.

"Yes, of course, I did everything I could to get her on her back. I absolutely wanted to get her into bed with me. Nothing worked. Nothing. We never slept together."

Betsey just wants to leave Ted's Bar now. This interview is over. But, goddamnit, Betsey is bound and determined to find her friend.

Before she walks to the door Betsey places

her untouched glass of wine on the bar. She is angry, frustrated, yet she can't resist delivering her exit line.

"By the way, Mike, if you think I believe anything you just said, well, you're a lot dumber than you look."

CHAPTER

28

IT HAS BECOME BETSEY'S almost uncontrollable passion to find Emily and, while she's at it, to find out who is the father of Emily's baby. Betsey, by nature an optimist, knows that this is totally a minuscule needle in a colossal haystack. But she must do it.

Now that passion leads her to the quaint commuter village of Katonah, New York, in northern Westchester County. Betsey has been putting together a list. The list is entitled "The Men Most Likely," and it is comprised of twenty men's names, men who may have slept once, twice, or who-knows-how-many times with Emily.

The first name on "The Men Most Likely"

list is Quinn Langford Church. And yes, Quinn Langford Church looks and sounds just like his name. Exactly six feet, dusty blond hair, and as slim and fit as a man can be only from playing two hours of squash four times a week. Quinn Church called the NYPD, said he had once been a good friend of the missing person, Emily Atkinson, and offered to help in any way he could. Church spoke to Tierney. Tierney asked a few questions, but Tierney's instincts told him that this college friend of Emily's had nothing to add.

Ten years ago, in college, Quinn was Emily's best friend. Together they rented a house in Princeton. Between Quinn Church's and Emily Atkinson's money, their house on Allison Road could have been featured in *Architectural Digest*. Emily once told Betsey, "We furnished the place as if we were going to live there for the rest of our lives, not just four years of college."

Betsey has met Quinn once in New York City. They got along just fine. Two people with a mutual best friend. Good times. A few laughs.

When Betsey called Quinn and asked if she could meet with him, he graciously said that he could come into the city. ("My driver is on call twenty-four/seven.") No, Betsey said, "I could use a day in the country." Fact is that she has always been curious to discover why a single handsome man lived alone in a huge house in the country.

Three hundred acres. Tennis courts. Apple orchards. A two-hole golf course. Betsey hasn't even noticed the pool, cabanas, and stables when Quinn answers the door. He has that less-is-more costume that handsome guys know they can wear—Jockey brand white T-shirt and black Levi's, very scuffed-up Docksiders.

"Hey, I almost called you this morning," says Quinn, "and insisted that you stay in Manhattan and I'd meet you for lunch and..."

"No, this is an adventure for me," says Betsey. "Grand Central Station. The train ride up. The cab ride from Katonah station. And this place is incredible. Emily told me that your place was beautiful, but I wasn't expecting...I don't know... *Gone with the Wind.*"

She follows him down a long hallway. Ten huge, exquisite Berenice Abbott photographs cover much of the wall. On the left, just past the photographs, is an enormous room with quite high ceilings. Quinn pauses outside of it.

"I am happy to talk to you, Betsey. I would do anything to help you find Emily. But my life with her is, for the most part, history."

"I know," says Betsey. "But I've got to try."

Quinn gestures at nothing in particular as they enter the very big room.

"I won't bore you with a tour. But in the early 1800s this room was an actual ballroom. I only use it once a year for my Christmas party," he says. Betsey does not remember Emily ever mentioning a party, Christmas or otherwise.

"It's beautiful," says Betsey.

"Thanks," says Quinn. "I don't do much dancing, myself." Not a joke, just a fact. The guy is not exactly a funnyman.

So they sit on a small, uncomfortable sofa in a hotel-sized ballroom.

Small talk as Quinn pours coffee. Eventually he says, "Okay, you're here to talk about Emily, of course."

"Well, yes. I know that you two were really good friends," says Betsey.

"No, we weren't," says Quinn.

Betsey pulls back a bit. She looks startled.

"We were *best* friends," Quinn says. "I never had a friend like Emily before or since. I don't think I ever will. I mean that. Even if I get married. Even if I have children. I can never really love anyone the way I loved Emily. I could go on and on, but it would be all clichés—how we were soul mates, how we finished each other's sentences, how we had a kind of ESP..."

Betsey once read that the best way to conduct a great interview is to just keep quiet and let the interviewee keep talking. So that's what Betsey does for the next few minutes.

Finally, Betsey says, "You told Joel Tierney, the detective heading up this case, that you'd heard Emily had gone missing. Who told you that?"

"Well, first, I've got to say that this Joel Tierney didn't seem particularly interested in my phone call to him about Emily. It was an amazingly brief conversation. You're asking me something Tierney never asked me: How I found out that she was missing."

Betsey shrugs slightly, then says, "Okay. So how did you?"

"Well, I actually heard it from two totally different people: Roman Perez, one of the masseurs at my racquet club, and my father's friend Robert Feinberg. Feinberg's the guy who helped Fred Klingenstein run Wertheim and Company."

"A masseur and a billionaire," Betsey says. "That's quite a combination."

"Emily made friends everywhere," says Quinn. Betsey finds his comment funny, but she doesn't say so.

At that moment a woman enters. She is dressed exactly like Quinn—white T-shirt and black jeans. And like Quinn, the woman is dazzlingly good-looking—violet eyes, short, perfectly cut hair, a body that quite possibly sees a good deal of a squash court also.

"Can I get you anything?" she asks.

"No, thanks, Miriam," says Quinn. Betsey smiles at the beautiful woman, surprised that Quinn doesn't introduce them.

As soon as the woman picks up the empty cups and coffee service Betsey looks at Quinn and says, "May I ask? Who's she?"

"Just a friend. A good friend."

"As good a friend as Emily was?"

"Of course not."

"Yes, of course not," Betsey says. "That was stupid of me."

"Should I ask Miriam to fix us some lunch?"

Quinn says. He is as casual and charming and polite as a man can be.

"Oh, no, thanks. I had one of those disgusting ham-and-cheese croissants at Grand Central. I loved it."

Then Quinn stands, looks down at Betsey and suddenly starts to speak...sternly.

"Why don't you get to the questions you want to ask. Go ahead. Did I sleep with Emily all those years ago? Was she a friend with benefits? Did I sleep with her recently? Am I the father of her baby?"

Betsey stands also.

"And the answer to those questions is...?"

"You know what it is."

"No, not really, but I do think you're going to answer no."

"Yes, that's exactly what I'm going to answer, and that's exactly the truth. No."

"And it's just, well...I don't mean to be aggressive, but it's just unbelievable," says Betsey. "Two good-looking college kids, full of hormones and time and money and fun living under the same roof. Unless there's something you're leaving out, I just can't buy it. And as for now, I know—and you know I know—that the two of you have seen each other over the years since Princeton. Emily never hid that from me..."

"There was nothing to hide. Lunch, an occasional drink, if I was in the city for the odd freelance job for TV. I'm pretty good at the *Law & Order* and *CSI* genre."

"You must be good. Just look at this place," she says.

"No, my very erratic writing career doesn't support this place. My father and mother are my real income. That's how I can live this well."

Then, as if to prove Quinn Church's point, a white-silver classic car pulls up.

"Good Lord," says Betsey. "The only thing better-looking than that car is the chauffeur driving it."

Quinn laughs. Then tells Betsey more than she wants to know.

"It's a 1951 Jaguar Mark Five," he explains.

"It's beautiful," says Betsey. "I wish my husband were here to see it."

"I don't," says Quinn.

Betsey ignores the creepy comment and thanks him for his time.

CHAPTER

29

KALISHA SCOFIELD IS BINGEING. She watches three episodes of *Euphoria*. Then, despite her better judgment, she watches two episodes of *The Bachelorette*. It's been one very lousy day, and she's finally feeling *not* achy, *not* frazzled, *not* exhausted. She snaps off the television, goes to the kitchen, and takes a small bowl from the cabinet. Kalisha fills it with Trader Joe's nonfat plain yogurt and adds a carefully measured teaspoon of maple extract into the bowl, stirs, and sets the yogurt aside before she walks into her bathroom to run the hot bath she's been thinking about all day.

As the tub fills, Kalisha uncaps the bottle

of L'Occitane Verveine Foaming Bath. She is about to douse the steaming water with the beautiful brew when, even though completely alone, she yells out, "Oh, *shit*!"

She pauses, then continues in a staccato style, "*Shit, shit, shit, shit, shit,*" almost as if she were cheering a university basketball team.

She places the L'Occitane bottle on the bathtub edge and turns off the water. Then she rushes into the living room and opens her satchel. Reaching into the bottom of the bag—beyond her phone and official NYPD papers, beyond her ID, beyond the cuffs—she finds what she's looking for.

It is the flash drive that Kalisha had snatched from Emily Atkinson's laptop.

How the hell did I not remember this?

In her mind's ear she hears a pissed-off Joel Tierney.

What the hell possessed you to take a flash drive?

There's no good response.

That's crime scene evidence, Scofield.

Again, there's no good response.

She tries to create one. "Hey, I forgot. People forget. I'm a person." Well, that clearly sucks.

Kalisha opens her laptop and presses the

flash drive into the side of the machine. After a few seconds it connects. It seems to contain copies of the same text files she, Tierney, and Betsey had last seen when they were searching Emily's apartment. But this time, luckily, they're not password protected.

She opens one and scrolls to material that she hopes will be new and helpful to the case.

Kalisha notices that, unlike the Word files on Emily's computer, these are neatly composed, with ample margins and no misspellings. They seem to have been created carefully, thoughtfully. The first entry she reads has a bold heading.

IMPORTANT QUOTATION
The loneliest moment in someone's life is when they are watching
Their whole world fall apart,
And all they can do is stare blankly.

—unknown

That quote really sums up the feelings in my heart and soul and mind. And in my case, I also have a baby in my belly. Hey, there, bump. Are you lonely, too? Are you scared like your mom is scared? Don't be. I'll always be with you. You'll always be with me.

Kalisha scrolls down more.

My friends are good to me. Betsey especially. I haven't even known her for a year, and she treats me like a sister, a daughter, a best friend. But everything that needs to happen must come from me. Here is my favorite quote about friends.

TRULY GREAT FRIENDS ARE HARD TO FIND, DIFFICULT TO LEAVE, AND IMPOSSIBLE TO FORGET.

I can't remember who said that, but it describes me and Betsey. Perfectly. I've never met anyone like her. And if I have to leave her it will break both our hearts. Forgetting each other? That would be impossible. I have to stop thinking about it.

Kalisha scrolls down and discovers two blank pages. She scrolls down anxiously and then finds the following surprisingly cheerful entry.

Alex had an extra ticket to a Rangers game. His friend canceled. Never went anywhere but lunch with Alex. Ha! Sitting with a guy ten years younger than me at a hockey game. I insisted on paying for dinner after. Nothing else to report. Nothing more than a game and a steak. But, oh, I did feel a little happier. I guess. I think.

But as Kalisha continues to move through the document, the hockey game report turns out to be the exception to a very sad series of despairing entries. The next one is, for Kalisha, very troubling.

I've told people that someone is following me. I've told Betsey. I've told my shrink, Ruth. It's not that they don't believe me. They just don't REALLY believe me. But he was there today—at the corner near Whole Foods. I saw him strolling along Bleecker Street. I've got to do something about this. I've got to get away. But getting away may not be enough. I have memorized the line by some unknown person—probably some woman like me. I keep the line on a scrap of paper near me at all times. I use it to keep myself going.

Suicide doesn't end the chances of life getting worse.

It eliminates the possibility of it ever getting any better.

I guess.

But it's not the *most* troubling entry. What Kalisha reads next changes everything.

MONTH FOUR

CHAPTER

30

CAREFUL PLANNING IS NOT my strong suit. To be honest, I'm not quite sure what suit I'd select if I had to select a strong one. Is blow-drying your hair or sticking salt on a margarita glass a strong suit?

Anyway, the bump is showing ever so slightly, maybe so slightly that only I can see it. Can Betsey tell? "Maybe, maybe not," is her smart answer.

Fortunately, long ago some guy left a Burberry raincoat here at my place. Men's size medium. I'll belt it with a brown Armani scarf. Perfect.

I fill a small silver flask with vodka. (I said

small, and yes, at any AA meeting they would say I'm delusional, self-enabling, etc.)

All this preparation is important. I'm about to attend my parents' graveside funeral service up in western Connecticut, specifically, the charming town of Sharon.

Yes, that's right, Liz and Lionel are dead. Gone together.

A sort of accident. Nobody knows for sure.

How do I feel about their deaths? As for me, I don't know, and frankly, I feel nothing. Yes, I know, I know. "Well, after all, they were your parents," people will say. And I will not argue with those people. Yes, they were my parents, but that's all they were. "Well, they did supply you with a very nice upbringing." Yes, I know, I know, with luxuries they were generous, with love they were abominably stingy.

Whether they died in the tender arms of sweet senility or by an act of awful violence, it makes no difference. What did not die are my memories of the cold, loveless days and nights they brought to me. Those memories will never vanish.

Damn it. I thought I had planned my trip to the funeral so well. And I did, except...damn it again...the only thing I failed to do was set my alarm. So I overslept, and instead of waking up at 5:00 a.m., I woke up at nine. That gave me—before I showered, applied makeup, and got dressed—exactly one hour to make the two-hour drive to Sharon, Connecticut. I had to try.

It's amazing how precise my driving can be when I'm stone-cold sober. In fact, I make it to the cemetery just in time. The minister and the thirty or so people encircling the grave all turn to look at me when they hear my car screech to a halt.

So many people I know—some from New York, some from Sharon, some from South-ampton, everyone from my parents' world. My father's physiotherapist, my mother's dress-maker, a distant cousin. There are, of course, a few museum officials, well-dressed buzzards waiting to pounce on "the collection."

An elderly Black woman, Doris McCray, my parents' longtime housekeeper, walks toward me. We hug and kiss, and Doris says, "Your folks would be so happy that you came here to see them off. God bless you, Emmy."

All I say is, "Whatever you think, Doris. But I am so happy to see you."

I don't believe that either Liz or Lionel would care one bit about my being there. The little crowd parts to allow Doris and me a place up at the front. Two caskets, side by side.

"Welcome, Emily," Reverend Foster says. I nod my head and smile a very small smile. Then the clergyman says, "For those of you who don't already know her, this is Emily, the only child of the deceased."

Come on, I think. *Let's get on with this.* It's as if Reverend Foster knew exactly what I was thinking. He opens his black leather prayer book and speaks in a loud and serious voice.

"A reading from the book of Revelation. 'Therefore they are before the throne of God.... They shall hunger no more and God will wipe away every tear from their eyes.'"

Hmmm. A throne means a throne room. They'll like that. With the rest of the mourners I say amen. Doris places her frail arm around my shoulders, trying to comfort me, a daughter who is feeling no sorrow, no regret, no sadness. I see people in the group cast quick glances at me, and I straighten out my loose-fitting sky-blue shirt and navy-blue skirt. The minister speaks again.

"May their souls and all the souls of the dearly departed rest in peace."

Once again I rise to the occasion and join in the final "Amen."

Henry Kleinhenz, who has been my parents' attorney since before I was born, steps in next to Reverend Foster and says, "Thank you all for being here today. There will be a luncheon at RSVP, Liz and Lionel's favorite restaurant, and all are invited. See you soon."

I'm guessing that Kleinhenz's next step will be to speak to me. *Think quickly, Emily.* I can't *not* go to the funeral luncheon, but I plan to hold off on a conversation with him as long as I can. I hustle Doris over to my car, and we drive away before the crowd can disperse. I am actually looking forward to talking to Doris. She is as sharp and cynical as a late-night television host. And she is funny as hell.

We aren't even outside the cemetery gates when Doris says, "Well, I see that Henry Kleinhenz didn't waste any time getting your folks put down into the ground."

"The faster for him to start probating and dealing with the banks," I say.

"The faster he can start getting all those

Kleinhenz-Heller billable hours piling up to the sky," she says.

That's the only reference we make, even remotely, to the actual death of my parents. As we get closer to town, Doris says, "This fancy restaurant was your folks' favorite place. I used to say that your father sucked down so many ducklings with wild cherry sauce there that they should rename it Duckling à la Mr. A."

We pull into the small parking lot. Although I was first to leave the burial ceremony, I must have done something wrong. As Doris and I step out of my car, I can see friends and family already going inside.

I walk into the room where the luncheon is being served—a lavish buffet with smoked salmon and shrimp piled high, cold oysters on beds of chopped ice—and an immediate silence sweeps the room. I am thrown off guard, but, to my surprise, I handle the situation.

"As you were," I say with a smile. I hear my Aunt Dolly speak loudly, "It's just so good to see you, Emily."

I'm not sure everybody in the crowd agrees with Aunt Dolly, but her shout-out does change the room. The buzzy murmur of conversation returns.

"You and I should get some food," says Doris. "I'd bet my best shoes that you didn't have breakfast."

"You'd lose your shoes," I say. "I had an English muffin and a venti latte in the car."

I have no idea why I'm lying, to Doris of all people.

Quite suddenly there are two lines of people in the room. One line is for the buffet, and on the other line, the longer line, are people wanting to talk to me. I guess I've become the bizarre sort of mother of the bride.

My luck. The first person in line is the very pompous and annoying Dr. Hiram Salter and his wife. Dr. Salter is retired from his practice—gynecology-obstetrics—but he still lives in Sharon, and I, being just a little nervous and a lot crazy, am certain that...well, when I was a young teenager, I was certain that Dr. Salter could tell if you were pregnant just by looking into your eyes. Hell. Sometimes I thought he could tell if you had had sex or even masturbated or even thought about having sex or masturbating.

"I'm so sorry about Mr. and Mrs. Atkinson's death. Two extraordinary lives cut short too soon," he says. Then he looks me up and down quickly.

"You look as healthy as you looked the day I brought you into this world," he says. "Nice and big...but in a healthy way."

For only a moment I wait for him to ask, "Are you pregnant? You look pregnant." But apparently Dr. Salter has lost his magic sense. Better yet, Mrs. Salter smiles at me and then speaks to her husband.

"We'll be moving along, sweetness. I suspect Emily has lots of other people to talk to. So sorry for your loss."

The wafting scent of bubbling Swedish meatballs from the buffet table is beginning to nauseate me.

Don't throw up, Emily. Not at the funeral luncheon. Just hold on.

Next in line is Florence Packman, my parents' next-door neighbor in Southampton. (Of course, in that palatial world, "next door" could mean a half mile down the road.)

Mrs. Packman (yes, she was always called "missus" Packman) kisses me on both cheeks and immediately says, "I don't know how you'll cope with this tragedy, Emily. Your parents loved you so much."

I'm thinking, *Get ready for this, Emily. The bullshit and misinformation are going to be piled high.*

"I know. Thank you. Are you still in Southampton?" I ask.

"Yes, but of course it will never be the same again without Liz and Lionel."

"That's for certain," I say, and after I air-kiss Mrs. Packman and gently touch her shoulder, I find myself greeting Dr. Lawren Pierson. (Yes, his name is spelled Lawren and it is pronounced as it looks: Lauren.)

Dr. Pierson is one of the few people at the luncheon whom I am actually pleased to see. The only sign that he has grown older is the silver-handled cane he carries. Dr. Pierson was a dorm master at Hotchkiss, my nearby prep school. He was the English teacher who taught me to love the written word. What's more, he was provocative, exciting, and, for Hotchkiss, pretty controversial.

Controversial? More than once he'd said "*To Kill a Mockingbird* is overrated young-adult literature. If you want to read something grand that was produced by an American writer, I suggest Henry James's *The Aspern Papers*."

I had never heard of Henry James. And I'd certainly never heard of *The Aspern Papers*. I thought that perhaps an aspern was some kind of bird.

As for *Mockingbird*, I had just read it that summer, and I could not believe a book could be so beautiful and interesting and heartbreaking all at the same time. I thought it was the best book I'd ever read. By the way, I never shared my personal opinion with Dr. Pierson.

"I have been expecting great things from you, Emily. Is it possible that I missed them?" Dr. Pierson asks with a smile.

"Unless you saw my Cartier diamond bracelet promotion on TV at last year's Wimbledon, I'm afraid you'll have to wait a bit longer for something great," I say.

He is about to respond when I once again hear Aunt Dolly's voice.

Aunt Dolly, my father's younger sister, is cutting the line. Dolly has the same sense of privilege that my father had. Dr. Pierson says, "Well, I won't hog the conversation." But before he leaves me, he says, "I drove down here with an old friend of yours. I'll bring him over. I know he wants to talk with you."

As soon as Lawren Pierson steps away, Aunt Dolly begins talking.

"Now, Emily, I feel compelled to say something to you, something I couldn't say when your parents were alive. But I'm determined to say my piece today. We can talk here, or we can go someplace more private."

"But there are people waiting to..." I begin.

"They can continue to wait for a few minutes. I'm your closest relative, and I must get this out."

My aunt Dolly is a former nun, a former biologist, a rabid women's rights activist. What could she so urgently have to tell me?

She immediately figures out where her revelation should take place. It's a location I would not have picked, but Aunt Dolly's always in charge. We walk across the hall.

To the barroom.

CHAPTER

31

AUNT DOLLY HASN'T CHANGED a bit. Maybe that's good. Maybe that's not so good.

"You look like you've put on a few pounds, Emily," Aunt Dolly says as we sit down at our little table in the barroom. The room is empty except for Aunt Dolly, me, and a very bored bartender.

As I gently pat the bump under the table, I say, "That's what you wanted to talk about? That I look like I've put on a few pounds?"

My Aunt Dolly is not actually a nasty person, but like some people of her generation she doesn't quite understand the line between honesty and courtesy.

"No, of course not. Actually, you look good. Healthy. Heavier, yet it's flattering. But, of course, that's *not* what I wanted to talk about. May I?"

"Of course," I say.

"They treated you horribly," she says.

"Who?" I say, honestly.

"Those two we buried today. Your mother and father."

I quickly bury my true feelings.

"Aunt Dolly, listen. I'm not saying that you're wrong, but it's been quite a while since those two had anything to do with me. And besides, they had issues of their own."

"Issues? My ass. When you have a child, that child becomes your issue. Not running around the world trying to get your hands on a Warhol or a Kandinsky. Not attempting to become artists also..." She paused for a moment. Then added, "Especially if you're as *un*gifted as Lionel and Liz were."

"Well," I say. "Thanks for your support, but it's all over now."

"It's never over. Not really. I told them more than once that they mistreated you. Not that they ever cared what I thought or said."

Dolly now begins to roll with her anger.

"They'd smother you with nonsense when they were here—ballet lessons, cello lessons, riding lessons, French lessons—then they'd go off to Tokyo or Timbuktu for a month and leave you with Doris and all those tutors. It was dreadful."

What I want to say is *Tell me something I don't already know.*

Instead I say, "Aunt Dolly, I really need to go pee. And I need something cold to drink. And I need to think about what you've been saying. Okay?"

"Are you all right, Emily?" she asks. "I've been watching you since you and Doris got here. This is the third time you've gone to the bathroom."

"I think I have some sort of urinary infection."

"Stop right there, dear. Spare me the details."

If Aunt Dolly only knew the details.

I do what I have to do, and when I return, I see that Dolly is sipping a whiskey sour, and she has thoughtfully ordered me a vodka tonic.

"I'm actually not drinking these days," I say, hoping she believes my giant fib. Luckily, it seems like she does.

"How would I know that?" she says. I order a club soda with a slice of lime.

The bartender whisks away the vodka, and Aunt Dolly restarts her engine.

"Listen," the old lady says. "I want to take this terrible opportunity to say something."

"Don't hold back," I say. "Not that you ever would."

So she unloads.

"I have not forgotten how they both criticized you. Cruel. Your weight. Your hair. Your grades. I guess it's lucky that you didn't have many friends before you went off to Hotchkiss. Because they would have criticized them, too."

"Thanks for the memories," I say.

I want to laugh, but I don't have the energy for it. Dolly's speech simply reminds me how involved my parents were with art, with painting, but, most of all, with each other. Most couples love their children above all others, but with Liz and Lionel, they loved each other the most. Everyone else, including me, was incidental.

Art was their life. They had amassed one of the finest private art collections in the world. When the curators at MoMA needed to fill in a few gaps for a Lichtenstein retrospective, they borrowed four pieces from the Atkinson Collection. And Liz and Lionel themselves became painters...er, artists. Their work was terrible—derivative, corny, crude in its technique. But art was their life.

When I was eight years old my parents took me to Los Angeles with them, a rare treat. We had drinks with Richard Gere. ("He has an enviable collection," my father said.) We had dinner with David Hockney. ("No one can capture LA the way David can," my mother said.) But all I wanted to do was go to Universal Studios.

Enough of my lousy memories. I am becoming nauseated, and I'm wishing that I had kept the vodka tonic that Aunt Dolly ordered for me.

"In any event, I tell you this now, because I want you to know that I have always loved you. And I've already told that greasy attorney Henry Kleinhenz that if your mother and father didn't treat you right in their will, if they thought that museums and art schools are more important, then we will see Kleinhenz in court."

We?

We will see Kleinhenz in court?

Now I get it. It's about us.

Aunt Dolly wants to make certain that I'll

have the necessary money to keep her in the luxurious style she's gotten used to.

"Let's wait and see, Aunt Dolly," I say.

I am very tired. (Dr. Craven said that I would be.) What's more, for some reason, on the drive up, my nipples had begun feeling sore. (Oh, I guess the reason must be that I'm pregnant.) Worst of all, I'm still thinking about that vodka tonic.

Okay, just one. It's not going to kill me or the bump.

I excuse myself from Aunt Dolly and head to the bar.

CHAPTER

32

I KNEW I'D FIND you here," he says.

I'm standing at the bar waiting for my vodka tonic when I hear an unmistakably identifiable voice—earthy, nasal, happy. The voice of my old Hotchkiss classmate Greg Hayden.

I turn around and let out a tiny scream.

Yes, Greg Hayden. The nicest guy in our class. The tallest guy in our class. But most of all, the best writer in our class. According to the dean of community life, Greg and I were the brains and brawn of the biweekly *Hotchkiss Record*.

We hug each other. We stand back and look at each other. Greg's tie is loose, his shirt collar unbuttoned, his dark hair is in need of something—a haircut? A better barber? A conditioner? But age has been kind to him.

"My God," I say. "You still look like the gawky kid who's late for bio class."

"And you look like...well, you look...wonderful...beautiful..."

At this moment Aunt Dolly walks by with an exaggerated tiptoe.

"You two children look like you can use some time alone," she says. "I'll disappear."

"No. That's okay," Greg says.

"No. It's not okay," says Aunt Dolly, and she is out of the barroom.

Greg orders a glass of chardonnay. We sit at the same little table where Aunt Dolly lectured me on my inheritance. I get to work on my icy vodka drink.

"What are you doing here? I thought you were living in Cambridge," I say.

"I am, but I read the awful news about your folks, and I wanted to be here," he says. Then he reaches across the table and gently touches my hand.

Honestly, I don't ever remember Greg Hayden in my Hotchkiss days spending much time with Liz and Lionel, except maybe briefly at one or two of the rare visits they made to the school. Maybe I'm wrong; maybe I just don't remember. Greg could have come to the house in Sharon. Maybe he even came to New York. Maybe Southampton. Now I'm not sure of anything. I'm sweating, and I have to pee again, and I just finished drinking my vodka as if it were water. I gently pull my free hand away from Greg.

"Can you excuse me, just for a minute?" I say.

I have to get to the ladies' room quickly. I am feeling… What exactly am I feeling? I'm feeling like a woman who needs to urinate. I'm feeling like a woman who might vomit. I'm feeling like a woman who needs more alcohol. In the empty bathroom I remove the silver flask from my bag, then I take a very long slug.

When I return to the table, Greg, the nicest guy at school, stands up.

I am delighted that he's ordered me a fresh vodka tonic.

"You okay?" he asks.

"I'm fine," I say. "Sorry."

"You look a little, well, I think maybe a little… I think the word is *groggy*," he says.

"I think the word you're looking for is *queasy*," I say.

"Yes," he says. "That's the word."

"Remember, I was always great on rewrite," I say.

"You were always great on every possible level of writing. You could make the Prep School Tennis Invitational sound like the Wimbledon finals. Your fiction for the lit mag was incredible. God. I practically memorized your short story 'One Winter in Provence.'"

"Please, don't make me think about that awful, embarrassing story. It was so infantile."

"No, it was not. It was wonderful."

And then, as if he wants to prove *my* point, he quotes from the story itself:

"If you're in love, even your lover's imperfections are wonderful.

"'He's such a terrible slob. He's like a little boy. It's so adorable.'

"'She can't even make toast. I don't know why, but I find that incredibly sexy.'

"Then one day it all ends, and you can't remember ever being in love like that. So you think...If that was a mistake, if that wasn't real love, is everything just a rehearsal for real love?"

"My God, you really did memorize it," I say. My arms are glistening with sweat, and I can feel that my face is flushed. The nausea is increasing, and while Greg leans into the table I take another gulp of my drink.

There are all sorts of ways that AA meetings prepare you for times like this. The first is obviously to get up and walk away. The second involves... but it doesn't matter because my plan is to simply finish the remainder of my drink.

The combination of the two drinks from the bar, along with my big dip into my silver flask, is showing up in my burning eyes, my aching head. Now I have to focus on not slurring my words.

The hand. Here comes Greg's hand again.

"I've got to tell you the truth, Emily. The reason I came here today is that it seemed like an easy way to see you again. I loved you in school. I loved you all those times I came down to Princeton to visit you."

Although I'm shaky, I am astonished at what this blast out of my past is saying.

"Greg, that was a decade ago. You and I had absolutely nothing going on at Hotchkiss. And in college, well, sure, we slept together once or twice, but that was nothing. That was just, well, it was just sex. We even told each other that it was nothing."

A decade ago. A decade ago, for God's sake. But why does he look so familiar? Why does he feel so familiar? Where have we been? Where have I seen him?

Greg suddenly looks sad.

"Yeah, it was sex, but it wasn't *just* sex for me. You were everything to me. You were the whole package—smart and great-looking and sweet and really, really talented. Everybody, me included, expected great things from you—a book, a movie, a play."

The bartender brings me another drink. He must have instinctually figured that I was a keep-'em-coming sort of drinker.

"Greg, this is all news to me, and I don't mean to be mean or anything like that but, no, not now. That was a long, long time ago," I say.

"Not anymore. I've kept track of you, Emily. I've seen you in New York. I watched you at the bar at the Pierre. I watched you walking home from that other bar you always go to, Ted's.

I know you work at Dazzle. I've watched you running around the reservoir. Emily, listen to me. I want us to be what we were meant to be."

I feel a pit of dread forming in my stomach.

The man I'm afraid has been following me these past few weeks... is it Greg?

Part of me wants to confront him. Tell him to knock it off or I'll go to the police. But perhaps it is the magical strength of too much vodka that leads me to blurt instead, "Greg, this is really creeping me out."

" 'Creeping you out'? What's so creepy about it?"

"That you've been thinking about me for so long, that you've actually *followed* me around Manhattan. Now. You've come here. To my parents' funeral..."

I just want him to go away. If he doesn't leave, I will. But he doesn't budge. I can't tell whether his reddening face means he's angry or sorrowful or both. I know that I'll be wobbly when I stand up, but I have to. I finish my drink. With both of my hands placed flat on the table, I shove myself up and speak.

"I'm sorry," I say, but then I feel I should add, "Well, sort of sorry."

Now a look of pure fury comes over his face. He stands up.

"After all I've said. After all I've told you, this is how you act. I said that I love you, and you act like a bitch. Well, while we're both telling the truth about everything, let me tell you this. You panned out to be a nothing. Everybody expected you to set the goddamn world on fire. But look at you now. Nothing. Absolutely nothing. You're just a fucking mess. A rich mess, but still a mess."

I walk as fast as I can to the door. I turn down the hallway. I pass the room where the funeral luncheon is still going on.

The last voice I hear is Aunt Dolly's.

"Emily, please. There are people here you should be talking to."

CHAPTER

33

I SHOULD NOT BE driving. Even I know I should not be driving.

But I'm going to drive anyway.

Of course, I should not have been drinking, either.

I have to get away from the funeral luncheon. I have to get away from Aunt Dolly and her inheritance obsession and Dr. Pierson and his depressing memories.

But most of all I want to get away from Greg Hayden. Greg has done more than creep me out. He has frightened me. I'm not someone into psychoanalyzing others, but he sounds like a crazy man to me, the kind of crazy man who could go out and buy a gun to settle his feelings of unrequited love.

I stumble and slide into the driver's seat, and instead of fastening my seat belt, I pat my belly and say, *"Okay, little bump, Mommy's going to take us home."*

I imagine that the winding country back roads of northwestern Connecticut, the roads that will take me to the Taconic Parkway South, will be my biggest challenge. But for some reason these narrow streets are easy to handle. It's that curving, snaking, narrow, unpredictable, overused Taconic that turns out to be the bitch.

Damn it! Why does the guy in the entrance lane keep stopping and starting, hesitating? I could've rear-ended him four times. Merge, for God's sake.

I know I should snap my seat belt into place, but, hey, I've got to keep my eyes on the road now.

Okay, little guy or little gal, you're in for a bumpy ride.

"Bumpy" was not supposed to be a joke. I can be much funnier than a lame little pun like "bumpy" when I talk to my "bump."

You know that, little bump. You know that Mommy can be really funny.

For some reason the other cars all seem way too close together. But if I bear left, I'm going to hit the guardrail. If I move too far right, I'm going to go off the road.

Yes, I am shaky. No, I'm not drunk.

At least that's what I tell myself.

I keep assuming that my sadness and depression are because I just came from my mother's and father's memorial service. But my brain and my heart are a big jumble of feelings. The sadness comes from this ride, the memory of the hundreds of times that we drove back from Sharon to Manhattan, usually on Sunday nights. Walter, my father's driver, at the wheel. Liz and Lionel in the backseat. Me in between them. I hear my father's voice:

Well, I certainly don't think that seat belts make a difference. Seat belts are for sissies. And I'm using the word sissies. *That's right.*

What awful word does he want to use? How can he be so stupid *and* so wealthy at the same time? Only my mother knows.

Oh, for God's sake, Lionel. We should have waited until Monday morning to come back. I only told you that forty times. But, oh, no, you had to go and enroll Emily into that Monday morning art class. As if she has any chance of being an artist.

Lionel's thought?

For God's sake, Liz, the girl is only eight. We might as well try to find something she's good at.

I hate this parkway, and I hate the way I'm feeling. I'm like a human yo-yo. First, I'm very sleepy. Then very wide awake. I guess I'm thankful that they don't allow trucks on this parkway. The bump and I would have been crushed to death by now.

Don't you worry, little bump. Your mommy is watching out for you. I'll always watch out for you.

And I will. I absolutely will. That's one thing I won't mess up.

Then it happens, Lawren Pierson's voice from an hour or so earlier.

I have been expecting great things from you, Emily. Is it possible that I missed them?

I should have said, *No. You haven't missed them. I just haven't done them. I still have time. I still have time.*

Hey, little bump. Are you thirsty? Gotta stay hydrated. Mommy has to make sure we have enough to drink.

And, of course, there's just one thing left to drink. The flask. I know I left some delicious vodka in there when I took a gulp of it back at the restaurant.

Great. Now I'll just find the flask. I'll just feel around…and…and…there…got it.

Okay, it's going to take a magician to hold the wheel, hold the flask, and also unscrew the top of this lovely silver container.

But, bump. I can't risk it.

Suddenly the scraping, banging, scratching sound of my car against the guardrail overwhelms me. I reflexively turn hard to my left. This unleashes a brass-band-gone-crazy of honking horns. I rush to turn back to my lane, but overshoot it and manage to hit the guardrail once more. Because I'm without a seat belt, my head hits the steering wheel quickly, hard.

We're going to be okay, bump. We're going to be okay. Mommy will always take care of you.

I manage to straighten out and stay in my lane. I'm back on track. But everything else is wrong: Head aching. Vodka gone. Blurry vision. I pat the bump. I feel the taste of blood in my mouth. A car slows down so that it can drive exactly parallel to my own. The driver of the car honks. A teenage boy is in the driver's seat. Here it comes, I'm ready for it: "Asshole, idiot, fucking nutcase." I'm assuming that this will be accompanied by the middle finger.

But all the boy does is shake his head. The look is not anger; it's pity. He mouths some words. I don't understand what he's trying to say. Then he tries again. This time I get it.

"Be careful."

I pat my stomach.

Not to worry. Not to worry. That's right, bump. Mommy will always take care of you.

CHAPTER

34

IT'S A MIRACLE. IT really is.

At least it feels like a miracle to me. It's not funny. It's not crazy. I should not have arrived alive, but I did. And it makes me cry.

I make it safely down the East River Drive and actually make the turn off to 10th Street without crashing into anyone or anything. The bump and I are safe, but we are certainly not sound. I cannot drive another foot, another inch. To do so would be to challenge my incredible luck. I pull over and double park on First Avenue. I am at my parking garage, but I can't pull in. I must stop. I turn the car off, and grab the flask from the car floor. There's a tiny bit of vodka left. One slug. It's gone. It's sort of a celebration, right? But I'm still crying.

Then I hear the daytime parking attendant shouting.

"Miss A, are you okay? What happened to your car?"

I suddenly realize why he's so concerned. My passenger-side door must be awfully scratched and dented from scraping against the guardrail.

"Oh, that? Uh...it was a hit-and-run," I say. "Can you believe it?"

"How awful. Well, just leave it right there. I'll pull it into the garage."

"Wait just a sec. Let me get my things." I almost said, *Let me get my baby.*

"Take your time, Miss Atkinson!" he yells.

"You are very patient with me," I say. "Not everybody is."

"It's hard not to be nice to a lovely woman like you."

Then I suddenly think...Lucky...the attendant's name is Lucky. For some reason that makes me feel good. He's Lucky, so I'm lucky.

He opens the car door for me.

"I'll pull it into your usual space, Miss A," he says.

See, everything is fine. Mommy had a little accident, but everything is fine. Bump is good and healthy.

I pat my belly. I take my time getting out of the car. Then, once I'm out, I stand still in that way that drunks have when they're trying to pull themselves together.

I toss my head back. I straighten up. I take a few wobbly steps. Then I stop to watch Lucky drive my car through the garage entrance. A minute later he joins me on the sidewalk.

"Hey," he says. "You left your pocketbook in the car."

He hands it to me, and I say, "Thank you."

I remove my phone, then hand the heavy bag back to Lucky.

"Hold on to this, will ya?" I say. "I'm going for a walk. I'll get the bag when I get back."

CHAPTER

35

THE FIRST FEW YARDS of my walk involve a lot of stumbling and pausing and stumbling some more, but then I seem to get my bearings. If I have a fear (and most drunks are fearless) it is simply that I'll run into someone I know—a friend, an enemy, a buddy who might recognize me from a long-ago AA meeting.

I need a drink. But, in order to get a drink, I need a liquor store.

Damn it. Money. I don't have any. I don't have my wallet, either. Damn. Damn.

I must have left my bag in the car or the garage or someplace. Right? Yeah, that's it. Maybe Lucky's found it, and he's rifling through it right now, stealing from me. I should go back and get it, but I can't stop walking. What's more, Lucky is one of the nicest people I know. What's wrong with me? I'm surrounded by nice people—Lucky, Ted, Betsey, Frank—and I don't appreciate them. They support me, encourage me, and I just can't seem to handle it. Love? I was absent the day they taught that one.

I'm sort of near Ted's Bar and Grill, but I don't want Ted to see me like this. He'll just lose it and then tell Betsey and she'll be upset and…No, I'll just keep moving. Plus, Ted knows that I was at my parents' funeral, and he'll have a million questions. He's always asking me to talk about my childhood.

"C'mon, Em," he'll say. "Don't keep it all inside. You never talk about old ma and pa. That can't be healthy."

Yeah, okay, Ted, I think. *I'll talk about them. I'll talk about how relieved I was when I knew they wouldn't be around anymore.* Okay, a little sad, but mainly, relieved.

You see, Ted, if I talk about the past it'll just break my heart. Hell, it might even break your heart.

I'll tell you about how when I was eight years

old, and they took me to Barcelona with them for an art fair, and how they were going to go to dinner with some important dealer, and said, "You order room service, Emily, and watch TV. We won't be very late."

What's late? What's very late?

I'll tell you how they were gone for two days, that I was scared that they died or ran away, and I was left watching sitcoms in Spanish and ordering and explaining to the hotel manager who stopped by to see me that my parents were just "out, they'll be back," and how the creepy sunuvabitch manager touched my face and said that he would take care of me, and when he ran his fingers through my hair I pushed him away and locked myself in the bathroom.

Turns out, of course, that Liz and Lionel had a good reason to abandon me for two days. They "just had to go to Valencia to look at some wonderful Picasso ceramics. It was all very spur of the moment."

I sat on the bathroom floor and cried, and my father laughed, and my mother made some stupid face, and then my mother said, "Oh, for God's sake, Emily, don't be such a baby. It was a rare opportunity. We had to seize it, and anyway, you had a hotel suite and television and room service."

I keep walking, almost a slow trot. I might pass out, but I know I won't. I think my body is doing a fantabulous job of processing all the booze in my system. If I can ignore the headache and the perspiration, I'll be fine.

As I get close to Ted's place, I turn and walk south, in the opposite direction. My speed picks up.

I begin to run. It's not the first time that I've "run drunk," and I know I'm not the only person who's ever done it. Come to one of my AA meetings. There are plenty of us—runners, boxers, lacrosse players.

I run faster. The neighborhood begins to look familiar. The tenements of the Lower East Side begin turning into fancier buildings. Now I'm on a classy block. Brownstones. Iron gates, elegant signs of doctors and lawyers. One of the signs says:

GREYSTONE WOMEN'S HEALTH

COMPLETE GYNECOLOGY AND CONSULTATION

Yes. Of course. This is *that* block. This is *that* sign.

I've been here before.

CHAPTER

36

I WALK PAST THE medical office. Then I turn around and walk past it again. I stop and examine the sign, as if I expect more lettering to appear. Like, WELCOME, EMILY, or GO HOME AND THINK ABOUT IT, EMILY.

Then I do it. I have to do it. I walk up the stone steps and I walk into the clinic. I pat the bump. My eyes fill with tears.

I think we might be saying good-bye, little one.

I walk into the reception area. This elegant room—with ornamental molding and dark, highly polished wooden floors—was once probably some wealthy family's parlor.

A beautiful, short-haired, middle-aged Asian

woman sits at an ornate desk, the kind of desk that looks like fake French to me.

The woman asks the expected question, "How can I help you?"

Because I'm not quite certain what my answer should be, I remain silent for a few moments and take that time to survey the space. The reception room is a combination of styles—living room (elegant blue-and-white striped wallpaper), doctor's waiting room (black leather sofas with steel frames), *Elle, The New Yorker,* and *People* magazines (in neatly stacked small piles), and typical office (a very big PC at the reception desk, a printer). Even the signs that say: NO CELL PHONES, PLEASE and PAYMENT IS EXPECTED AT TIME OF VISIT are designed with typography meant to be gentle, soothing, warm.

There is no one in the room except me and the receptionist. She speaks again, no impatience in her voice.

"So, how can I help you?"

As I speak, I know that I sound ridiculous.

"Yes, you can help me if you want to," I say.

"Well, I certainly want to. *We* certainly want to."

Either she is one of the nicest people to ever

sit at a receptionist's desk or she is a natural performer. Maybe both. I know from experience that a person can be many things at once.

Then she says, "Do you have an appointment?"

"Well, I don't, but maybe I could have one," I say quickly.

"No problem, none at all. How about we talk for a little bit? Have a seat right here," she says as she gestures to a big brown leather chair facing her desk.

I look around the room nervously as I sit down.

"No one is scheduled here for the next thirty minutes. So we can have all the privacy you need."

I nod, and my face feels hot and my hands feel sweaty and I think I know why I'm sitting here in this chair in this office but I'm really not so sure and this receptionist has probably had the same conversation she's about to have with me with a few hundred other women and I wish I could have a drink, even a beer, yeah, a nice cold beer.

"Let's start with the most important question," says the woman. "Are you pregnant?"

I want to say, *Uh, well, duh. I'm not here for*

an ankle injury. But instead I say, "Yes, yes, I am pregnant."

It occurs to me now that this woman is so pleasant, so nice that a visitor could not possibly be mean to her.

"How far along are you?" she asks.

She's not writing anything down. Somehow that makes it feel more like a conversation between friends.

"About four months, I think."

"And who's your ob-gyn?"

"Dr. Craven," I say.

"Jane Craven?" she asks. Then she adds, "Dr. Craven is wonderful."

"Yes, she is. Wonderful, that is."

"I don't think we have a referral for you from Dr. Craven. Do we?"

She says this without consulting her computer. Has she memorized all the names of all the patients and their referrals?

"No," I say. "I was...well, I was just walking by and I saw the sign outside, and I saw it once before, and I know this sounds crazy, as if I saw a sign that was advertising a shoe sale or a new moisturizer, and..."

"Please, no reason to be embarrassed. That's

why they make signs. For shoe sales and for pregnancy advice."

Is this woman hypnotizing me? I am feeling so calm.

"Now, the next thing I need to know. What's your name?"

Simple enough, but suddenly the calm disappears, and I'm afraid to tell her my name. But I can't think of a fake name to give her. Oh, what's wrong with me.

"Emily," I say. "Emily Atkinson."

Now I wait for the inevitable. *Are you married? Are you and the father on good terms? Do you know who the father is? Have you spoken to any other person or group about termination? Are you crazy? Are you nervous? Are you stupid? Are you sure?*

But none of those questions explode at me. She speaks simply.

"Okay, Emily, my name is Margaret Lem, and when you have a moment—either here or at home—I'd like you to fill out this form."

She hands me an iPad.

"I...I can take this home with me, this iPad?" I ask.

"Certainly, but you'll have to return it," she says.

Trust. It's all about trust. I've been out of the city for a few hours and everything in it has changed.

I lean forward and speak quietly in this still-empty room.

"Look, Margaret. I want an abortion. I want one now...or as soon as possible," I say.

"We have a simple, careful procedure here, Emily, and you're going to be happy we have it. We'll make an appointment for you to come back and see one of our doctors or doctor assistants. You'll get a full evaluation, and we'll proceed with whatever it is you decide upon."

"Well, I've decided," I say.

I'm afraid that if I don't do it this minute that I'll never do it.

"You know, Emily, whatever you decide, an abortion is one of the safest surgical procedures in the United States. And we do everything we can to keep it that way."

"But you see..." I begin.

She holds up her hand. "Emily, please. Let's say you're correct, that you are in your fourth month. You still have about eight weeks left to terminate."

"No, you don't understand..."

"I do understand, and we can't move forward until we get some information from you, and we need important information from Dr. Craven. Then you'll have your examination and your consultation, and, Emily, there's something else stopping us right now."

"What's that something?" I ask.

Margaret Lem keeps her voice calm, as gentle as it's been during the entire discussion.

"I have a feeling that you've been drinking, and I think our people here will want to address that."

I see her comment as a weird opportunity to present myself as a totally screwed-up person. "You see," I say loudly. "I'm not meant to be a mother. I'm not meant to have a baby, to raise a child."

Then I touch the bump. I rub my belly as if I can actually bring peace and calm to the situation inside. Then I begin to cry.

Margaret reaches across her desk and takes my hand. She holds it just for a moment.

"Call or email Dr. Craven. Tell her that you've been here, and we'll set up an appointment."

"Thank you," I say. "I'll be back."

"Good," she says. I take the iPad. I smile at Margaret Lem. I head toward the door.

I'll be back. I'll be back. I'll be back.

I think.

CHAPTER

37

I SIT ON A BENCH in Tompkins Square Park. I watch the drug addicts sleeping on the lawn. I watch the nervy fat rats scurry over the addicts. I watch pairs of downtown hipsters—men and women, women and women, men and men, young and old—cuddle and kiss and hug and laugh and cry.

I watch for anyone suspicious who might be watching *me*.

Suddenly I have an overwhelming urge to talk to Betsey. If I don't tell someone about everything that's happened—the funeral, Greg the stalker, the treacherous drive back, the trip to the abortion clinic—I may just collapse.

I'm nervous as hell. I'm high as a kite. I'm a million miles away from the wagon I'm supposed to be on.

Don't be angry, little bump. I haven't done anything yet. We're still together.

Speed dial: Betsey.

"Where have you been?" she says. This is followed by the usual exclamations, the words I've heard a thousand times from a thousand people: "I left messages...Why didn't you call me back?...Are you all right?...This is so thoughtless...I was so worried..."

"I had to go to a funeral in Connecticut."

"Whose funeral?"

A perfectly reasonable question.

"Some people I knew."

"What people?"

"Just people, friends, sort of."

I could just tell her whose funeral I attended, but this is one of those things that...since I should have told Betsey when Liz and Lionel actually died...it seems strange to tell her now. Then there'd be explaining. Then she might become suspicious that I held back. Then Betsey mercifully changes the subject.

"Where are you now?" Betsey asks.

"On a bench in Tompkins Square Park. It's a beautiful day. A really beautiful day."

There is a pause. And now comes the evidence that there's no fooling Betsey.

"Emily, I've got to be at the hospital at eight o'clock. I don't have a lot of time to spare. So I've got a question."

"Shoot, Bets."

"Are you drunk?"

How the hell can she tell?

I don't answer.

"You are, aren't you?"

"Well, I was at this funeral. And I just had a half glass of white wine. That's all."

If I told her the truth about the amount of booze I consumed, Betsey would somehow transport herself through my phone, show up in Tompkins Square Park, and throttle me until I couldn't breathe.

"You. Are. A. Fucking. Asshole. Emily."

Then a deadly silence. Betsey's hung up. I press Redial.

Betsey greets me by saying, "Let me repeat myself. You are a fucking asshole. Your slurry pronunciation, your thick, loud voice. They both tell me that you had a lot more than a half a glass of white wine."

"You may be right," I say. "Now that I think of it, it might have been half a glass of red wine."

"Look, this bullshit is not funny. You know what I've said. If you decide to kill yourself, you'll also kill your baby."

I cry, and I try to hide the fact that I'm crying. I pat the bump. Then I gently massage it. Then I tell her.

"Bets, stay with me while I tell you something."

"What?"

"I just stopped by a medical office where they perform abortions."

"You went in? You talked to them?"

"Yes. I went in. I talked to them. And I thought about it. And they were very nice. I mean…the woman at the front desk was very nice…not judgmental at all…And, Bets, I would have done it, I think, if they had let me. But they make you get some sort of counseling, and they do some tests, and…and the woman at the desk said that she thought I had been drinking."

Betsey's voice changes quickly from anger to concern.

"Are you going back, Emily?"

A pause. A pause so long that Betsey repeats the question.

"Are you going back?"

"I'm not sure. What do you think, Bets?"

There's no answer, and I know Betsey well enough that she's not going to tell me what to do.

Finally, she speaks. "I just want you to do the right thing, Emily. That's all I want. That's all anyone wants for you."

"Let's face it. I'd be a terrible mother... Shit! I already *am* a terrible mother, and I haven't even given birth yet."

For some reason this last comment of mine elicits a bit of a chuckle out of Betsey.

"Oh, Emily," she says. "You are something else. You're not a terrible mother. You may be on your way to becoming a terrible mother. But you're a good person. You have kindness and humor and brains. Those are the things you need for being a mother."

I respond: "But what I don't have is

self-control and common sense. Hell, I don't even have a husband."

Another pause. A longer pause. Damn it. It's Betsey's turn to talk.

"Emily," she says, but she says it with a touch of accusation in her voice. The word comes out like "Em-a-leeee."

"What?"

Again, "Em-a-leeee."

Then she says, "I know all about Las Vegas and what happened there. Ted told me on Friday."

"Ted is lying. He's just lying. He knows that I went to Vegas…because I told him. But I didn't tell him who I went with. It sure wasn't him. He's lying to you, saying it was him."

"Why would he lie?" Betsey asks.

"Because…I don't know. I'm not sure. I think that it's his fantasy that we would get married. But the guy I did marry in Vegas… actually…he and I knew it was a stupid little joke. And we promised not to let on to anyone. The only person I ever told was Ted."

"You wouldn't tell anyone *that you got married.*"

"Listen," I say, "It was a stupid thing. It

was a couple months ago. We were in Vegas, and we both had drunk about a million Moscow mules. It was just a goof, a lark. We were wasted. And there are wedding chapels all over that crazy town. And we joked about it. And he dared me. And so... There was even a gift shop at the stupid little chapel where I bought a stupid little disposable veil. And that was that. We got married. I disposed of the veil. Then we disposed of the marriage."

"How, exactly?" asks Betsey.

"The next day, we were on our way back to the airport, and we stopped at the courthouse to get an annulment. It was so quick, we double-parked. We both signed a couple forms. I stayed in the car, my hubby ran in, dropped them off with the clerk, and that was it. Done. I was single again."

Betsey waits for me to say more, but I've told her everything I care to tell her. Or so I think. Then Betsey starts talking.

"I know you're not the first person to get married on a whim in Vegas, Emily. You're probably not the first to get it annulled the next day, either. But there is something I want to ask..."

"The answer is no. If the question is 'Is my *ex-husband* the father of my little bump?' the answer is no. No. No. No. No. No."

"How can you be…?" she asks.

"We were so drunk I don't think we even did the deed, I mean, to consummate the marriage. I know you're asking all this because you love me, Bets, because you care about me, but you've got to understand, it meant nothing. It's like I said, a goof, a lark, a dare."

"How about you and I meet before I get over to the hospital. We can have a cup of decaf. We can talk some more. We can…"

I begin to cry. It dawns on me that I've had nothing to eat all day.

"No, please, Bets. I love you, but I'm tired of talking. I've been talking all day, and I need to get a sandwich or something."

"Do yourself and the baby a favor, Emily. Have some seltzer water with your sandwich."

"Will do," I say. "Thanks, Bets. Thanks for being the friend I don't deserve. I'll talk to you tomorrow."

Suddenly Betsey speaks with urgency.

"Wait, there's one more thing before you hang up."

"What?"

"You never told me. Whose funeral did you go to today?"

"Nobody important. My mother and my father. A doubleheader. Gotta go. Talk soon."

I hang up. I turn off my phone.

CHAPTER

38

The Present

TIERNEY'S PHONE BEEPS. He glances at it and says to Kalisha, "It's Betsey."

"What's up?" he asks.

A few seconds of silence from Tierney, followed by a profound "Oh, shit." Then he adds, "Kalisha or I will talk to you later."

He hangs up and updates Kalisha. "Betsey went to see that guy, Emily's old friend from college, Quinn Temple."

"Not Temple, Detective Tierney. His name is Church. Quinn Church." She struggles not to laugh. Tierney is feeling some pressure, all right.

"Whatever," says Tierney. "Betsey said she got a lot of background, but she doesn't think there's anything for us to grab on to."

"So, look. No disrespect, but since you've got your lady friend, Miss Nurse, on the case, maybe we can move on." She quickly adds, "Don't bite my head off."

"I'm too tired to bite a head off, yours or anybody else's." Then he says, "We've got to keep digging into this connection between Emily and Caitlin Murphy. Maybe…"

Tierney's cell beeps again. So does Scofield's phone.

"What's all this?" says Tierney as they both look at their screens.

"I asked Missing Persons to send us their file on Nina Powell," says Kalisha. "You remember that case, right?"

"Of course," says Tierney. "It was a pretty big story for a while."

"The victim reminded me a little of Emily. And Caitlin Murphy, too. It's a long shot, but I figured it couldn't hurt to take a look. Maybe the three are related."

So Tierney and Kalisha review the case of Nina Powell, age thirty, who was reported missing about four months ago. Like Caitlin Murphy, Powell's apartment was also just a few blocks away from Emily's.

"Plus Murphy worked at an internet ad agency. And Powell's an SEO expert," says Kalisha.

"What the hell is an SEO expert?" asks Tierney.

"Search Engine Optimization expert. She makes sure that if someone googles 'High-powered NYPD detective,' your name shows up first."

Tierney chuckles, then thinks for a moment, his wheels turning.

"Is there any physical evidence yet linking the three victims? And similarities in the perp's MO?"

"Other than Emily being a contact in Caitlin's phone, nothing. Maybe that's just a coincidence. Maybe the cases aren't linked after all. Maybe they're—"

Tierney interrupts Kalisha by banging his desk as if his hand were a gavel.

"Bullshit. We've got three young women. Two missing. One dead. All early thirties. All lived on the Lower East Side. All worked in the same industry. Goddamn this city." He slams his hand again for emphasis. "You know what this means, Scofield?"

"What does it mean, sir?"

"It means we've got a pattern. And we're looking for one very sick guy."

CHAPTER

39

KALISHA DOES A DEEP DIVE into the life and times of Nina Powell.

Her Facebook page, her Instagram account, her mention in the *New York Times* Style section—they all show a beautiful woman with a totally natural smile. Nina Powell has a thousand freckles on her face, but on her they look simultaneously adorable and glamorous. She seems to favor white slacks and beige Dior shirts. A pair of sunglasses are almost always propped on top of her orangey-red hair.

But Nina Powell's great luck in life seems to go far beyond her good looks.

The two detectives find out easily and early that she grew up in a ritzy Chicago suburb (Lake Forest), went to a ritzy prep school (Lake Forest Academy), attended an academically demanding college (Swarthmore), and was engaged to a guy who could only be described as "a great catch" (Duncan Martin).

It was all going so great for Nina Powell. Until she disappeared.

Scofield and Tierney immediately reach out to Duncan for an interview. The fiancé is as handsome as his bride-to-be is beautiful. They were to be married three days before Christmas, he tells them—St. Thomas's Church on Fifth Avenue—and then a walk across the street to the University Club for the reception. He loves her "more than anyone on earth could love someone." That's how Duncan puts it.

As soon as the detectives leave his apartment, Scofield asks Tierney the usual and inevitable question.

"Do you think he's telling the truth?"

"The only time an investment banker might weep that long and that loud is when bond rates go down more than five percent." Tierney pauses for a moment, then says, "We're only about a five-minute walk from one of the neighborhood's hottest watering holes…"

Kalisha knows what he's talking about. "Ted's Bar and Grill?"

Tierney nods. As they walk the few blocks to the bar, Kalisha says, "You may not get this feeling anymore, Detective, but you know what? When someone goes missing, whether it's Emily or Nina, or when we were heading over to find Caitlin…I always get a sort of photo in my mind of them. I see them tied up and their mouths taped and their beautiful hair all greasy and messy. And I think of how scared they must be. And then I think that they might be dead already, lying in a kinda lake of blood. And I think how *really* frightened they must have been as they saw a knife coming at their neck or some scum touching them and laughing at them and then waving a gun and…"

"Stop it, Kalisha," Tierney says. He speaks loudly but not harshly. He wants to make an impact. "You can't concentrate on that shit. You've got to think about your job, your involvement. I had a boss who used to say, 'You gotta dance with the clues.'"

"I hear you, Detective. Your old boss is right. I know that. But how can you dance with the clues if those clues haven't shown up at the dance hall?"

By this time, they're standing outside Ted's Bar and Grill.

"You know, Detective Scofield, unless you're really thirsty, I don't think I want a drink anymore."

"Up to you, Chief. Up to you."

"Good," says Tierney. "Let's go find some more clues to dance with."

The two of them walk on.

CHAPTER

40

SHE DROPPED ME. SHE just cut me out of her life,"
says David Zingerman, Emily Atkinson's former assistant at Dazzle, the marketing firm
where she worked.

Tierney and Scofield are interviewing a few
of Emily's former colleagues. Tierney's plan is
to start with lower-level employees—like Emily's assistant—and work his way up to Keith
Hennessey, the chairman and creative director
who ultimately axed Emily.

"You never know who might know something," Tierney had said to Scofield.

Zingerman—handsome, charming, and wearing a Jaeger-LeCoultre wristwatch that costs

more than any car Tierney's ever owned—
seems genuinely shaken and sad by Emily's
disappearance.

"She always called me the most important person in her life. She'd refer to me as the
mother *and* father she never had. But once
Hennessey kicked her out of the office, Emily
kicked me out of her life."

"You never spoke to her after she was fired?"
Kalisha asks.

"Almost never. She called me the day after
she left...I think she was pretty hungover. She
wasn't slurring her words or anything, but she
was pretty tired-sounding. She wanted a file—
a paper file—from her desk. I'd never seen it
before. It was called Names and More Names."

"I assume you looked at that file before you
sent it to her," Tierney says.

"What good assistant wouldn't? But it was
nothing, really. At least I couldn't connect it to
anything. It was these random scraps of papers
with random words on them."

"What kind of words?"

"Like *summer, winter, autumn,* and another
one was like old-time actors like Rudolph Val-
entino and Cary Grant and...like...I don't

know. There was something like *Scotch and Soda* on one torn piece. I remember that. And another booze one. *Gin Rickey.* Then one was *David and Goliath.* Naturally I remember that one, because it had the name David on it."

Zingerman says he dropped the file off at Emily's apartment and that was the last time they spoke. Over the next few weeks, he tried calling her cell, but he always got her voicemail. Then her voicemail box became full, and Zingerman couldn't even leave a message. Emily never returned a single one of his calls.

"Maybe she was bitter," he suggests. "She had a lot to be bitter about."

Tierney is quick with the follow-up. "Bitter about what?"

"They kept giving her mixed signals, at least Keith did. Emily would do something great, innovative, nuts, and he'd shoot her a bonus... although she occasionally forgot to deposit the check...and a week later he'd be reaming her out for disappearing for two days."

"Did she *disappear* regularly?" asks Kalisha.

"Well, depends on what you call *regularly.* I almost always knew where she was. Sometimes she'd be someplace like the Spa at the Mandarin

Oriental Hotel to dry out a little. Other times she'd be at this place on Tenth Avenue, YAI— the Young Adult Institute—where she worked with these mentally challenged folks who needed a boost in moving on with life. Emily said it was all about self-advocacy. She was really into that YAI thing."

Tierney asks David Zingerman who else at Dazzle might have some insight into Emily Atkinson.

"When she felt like it, Emily was part this group called Team Crisis. They're the agency hotshots—two guys, two women...or one woman on the days Emily didn't make it into the office. I'll show you where they sit."

David leads them to a conference room with an engraved plaque on the door:

PRIVATE THINK TANK. DO NOT DISTURB.

Right beneath the plaque is a roughly hand-lettered piece of paper on which is scrawled:

SHIT HOLE. VISITORS WELCOME

David leads the detectives inside and makes some introductions. Two members of Team Crisis—Susan Marlow and Adam DeGiacomo—are seated at a marble conference table. Ricky Ranftle, another team member, David explains, is at New York-Presbyterian getting ready for heart bypass surgery tomorrow.

"It goes with the territory," Susan Marlow says. Then she quickly adds, "Joke. Just a joke. It's a wonderful job." But she does not smile.

Tierney says they're looking for some information on Emily Atkinson.

Susan Marlow asks, "What's up with Emily? She hasn't even worked here for a while."

Tierney replies, "She hasn't been *seen* anywhere for a while, either. We're gathering some background info from people who knew her, who might know something helpful."

Then, after giving that troubling news a few moments to sink in, he says, "What can you tell us about Emily Atkinson? Anything. Top of your head."

"Top of my head, I'd say Emily is one of the best in the business," says Adam.

Tierney is pretty sure that he's just seen Susan Marlow roll her eyes. He can't be certain. But he will be certain in a few moments, because Adam DeGiacomo wastes no time in piling up the praise for Emily's achievements in the cutthroat world of marketing.

"She just had a way to spin an idea. Like,

after a World Series, everybody would try to get the pitcher from the winning team to push a brand or a cause or something. Not Emily. She'd suggest the pitcher from the *losing* team. And, sunuvabitch, if she wasn't right. It was always more interesting."

Adam is only just beginning.

"But you can only do that sort of thing once or twice. Then everybody's doing it. The thing about marketing is that the old tried-and-true shit always works. But Emily always ran after something different. Em would never do Martha Stewart hawking stuff at Bloomingdale's. She'd never put a 'kills bathroom germs' aerosol on the side of garbage trucks. That sort of thing wasn't for Emily."

"No, she left that shit for us to do," says Susan Marlow. And anyone could tell she was not happy about it.

Adam has another Genius Emily story. He tells the detectives that one year—to encourage people to get flu shots—Emily persuaded the US Department of Health to offer free computer antivirus software to every New Yorker who got one. The theme was: "Protect your computer. Protect yourself."

"The folks were lining up around the block," Adam says.

"Adam has a gift for exaggeration," Susan says.

Adam just won't end his Emily stories. He actually stands up as he tells us how Emily spearheaded her most famous event. She had seen a wheelchair-bound woman stranded inside the 72nd Street Q train station because the station's elevator was out of order.

Here's the idea Emily hatched. On December 3, International People with Disabilities Day, a worldwide army of volunteers strung DO NOT ENTER tape across the exit stairs of every subway station throughout the world—from the T in Boston to BART in San Francisco.

"That meant that no one could leave the subway station. So everyone experienced what disabled people experience regularly, when the elevators and escalators aren't working. This stunt virtually stopped all underground transportation in the United States."

"I remember it," says Kalisha. "My mama called me in a panic, yelling. She was stuck for close to a half hour in a crowd underground at Rego Park."

Adam nods, then says, "The media coverage was extraordinary: TV news, internet news, Facebook, Twitter. Everywhere."

Susan merely taps away on her laptop. She pays no attention as Adam continues.

"Emily wanted everyone to know what it felt like to be a disabled passenger on the crappy underground transportation systems. No escalators. No elevators. I'll tell you, the next day a lot of transit boards were having meetings and figuring out how to fix their game."

Almost like a singing duo, Kalisha and Tierney say "Wow" at the same time.

Now Susan jumps in. "Let me tell you what Emily thought she was too important to do. She didn't do the coupons on the pizza boxes. She didn't write the boring podcast ads for shampoo or radial tires. There was no point in trying to find her when we needed a series of pop-up ads on a kids' website. We all knew where she was when she didn't come in. We'd call her. But she never picked up her cell when she was down at Ted's Bar and Grill."

"So you obviously don't share Adam's endorsement of Emily Atkinson," says Kalisha.

Susan is quick to answer.

"I don't. I really don't. Yes, she was good at her job. But *you're supposed to be* good at your job. And with Emily, you had to put up with all her *stuff.* The days off... I don't think she ever worked more than three days a week. And she drank. And whenever she felt down, or stressed, she'd relax with a little weed. And she used her assistant like a maid. And... oh, shit... I don't know. Maybe I'm just jealous. I just don't know. She was talented and actually pretty sweet and annoyingly pretty. But she required a lot of attention."

"Sometimes special people do," says Tierney. "The question you have to ask about those kinds of people is: Is she worth the trouble?"

"I think she was," says Adam. Then Susan speaks.

"But I guess Keith Hennessey didn't think so. He decided to fire her," says Susan. She sounds vaguely sympathetic, and then she adds, "But just wait and see. She'll land on her feet. People like Emily always do."

"Not always," says Tierney. "I guess we'll just wait and see."

CHAPTER

41

YOU DON'T SEEM TO REALIZE. This is not merely annoying. This is probable cause for an arrest. You are obstructing a police investigation."

Kalisha Scofield is speaking to Kathie McKirdy, one of two assistants to chairman and creative director Keith Hennessey. "I called you less than one hour ago and you assured me that Mr. Hennessey would be available to discuss Emily Atkinson."

"Like you say, that was an hour ago. Things change. I'm sorry," says the very pretty, very chilly Kathie. "I can't help that Mr. Hennessey was called away unexpectedly by a client."

"Who's the client?" says Tierney. "We'll meet Hennessey at the client's office."

"He didn't say which client it was," she says with no attitude improvement at all.

"That's true. Keith didn't say where he was going," says Charlie Bennett, the other assistant who sits at the desk next to Kathie's. This assistant is young and eager, as cordial as McKirdy is not. Tierney also cannot help but notice that every female assistant at Dazzle is drop-dead model-gorgeous, and every male assistant looks like a college student in rumpled chinos and a wrinkled light-blue shirt.

As Kalisha hands her card to McKirdy she says, "Please tell Mr. Hennessey that we need to see him very soon or..."

McKirdy interrupts. "I'll check his schedule."

Kalisha keeps talking, as if McKirdy had never even interrupted, "...or he'll be invited down to the station house for a discussion. So check his schedule very carefully."

"Thank you both," says Tierney to Kathie and Charlie.

"Thank *you* both," says the eager young man. McKirdy says nothing.

As they head toward the elevator, Tierney

smiles and says to Scofield, "That's quite a bit of smoke coming out of your ears, Detective."

"That woman had attitude that needed a good kick in the ass," says Kalisha.

"And I'm happy that you were getting ready to give it to her."

"Are we done with this place?" Kalisha asks.

"We're done, but we're going to make one more stop before we head back to headquarters."

Kalisha is about to ask where when they hear a man's voice in a sort of urgent whisper.

"Officers. Officers."

They both turn to see Charlie Bennett walking quickly toward them. Rumpled pants, wrinkled shirt, uncombed hair.

"It's not 'officers,'" says Kalisha. "It's 'detectives.'"

"Sorry, ma'am. Can I talk to you for a minute?"

"You can talk to us all day," says Tierney, "if it's about Emily Atkinson."

Bennett nods and gestures to a half-opened door. They follow him into an empty conference room.

Charlie Bennett is trying to control his nervousness by taking huge, deep breaths. He shuts his eyes for a few seconds and starts to talk.

"I want to tell you...I need to tell you that Emily was pregnant when she was fired."

Charlie pauses. He seems to be waiting for a reaction from the two detectives.

He doesn't get one. Tierney nods. Kalisha says nothing.

Charlie realizes that he's the bearer of old news.

"Anything else?" asks Kalisha.

"Okay. I really feel compelled to say this, but it has got to go under the you-didn't-hear-it-here rule."

"We'll abide by the rule until we *can't* abide by the rule," says Tierney.

Two deep breaths from the very nervous Charlie. Then he speaks.

"You guys obviously realize that Keith Hennessey left the office to avoid talking to you. But what you don't know is this: Keith Hennessey and Emily were having a really intense affair. It only lasted a couple of weeks. They were discreet about it. I don't even think Kathie knew. The only reason I know is that Hennessey had to have someone to cover for him and keep canceling meetings so they could...have sex in his office. Hennessey thought I was young and stupid and naïve. And he was right. I was! I am! When he told me that he'd kill me if anything leaked, I obeyed. But now…but now…it's pretty obvious that he fired Emily because he was tired of dealing with this. He was tired of sleeping with her. He was just plain tired. And then he found out that she was pregnant. And then she got fired. And…well, Emily is too good to have something like that happen to her."

To the detectives' absolute surprise, Charlie Bennett begins to cry. It is a full-fledged waterfall—sobbing, face in hands. The crying jag lasts an uncomfortable thirty seconds or so.

Kalisha reaches over and rests her hand on Charlie's shoulder. Both she and Tierney wait for him to stop. Eye-rubbing. Nose-blowing. Almost comical if it weren't so sad.

"We're not going to press you with more questions right now," says Tierney.

"Yeah, good. I got to get back to my cage," says Charlie.

Tierney nods. "I understand," he says.

Then it happens. Suddenly. Loudly.

An almost evil look invades Charlie's face. He rubs his hand across his face and speaks loudly. He is suddenly angry, livid.

"Shit!" he yells. "Who the hell am I kidding? I'm pretending to be holy and decent and that I care for Emily and her welfare, and I guess I do. But I'm telling you this not because I care so much about Emily. But because I hate Keith."

The detectives thank him. They'll be in touch. In a minute Charlie leaves the room. Then Kalisha Scofield and Joel Tierney head for the elevator. They do not speak to each other. They don't have to. They both know what the other is thinking.

Keith Hennessey might be the cause of Emily's pregnancy.

Keith Hennessey might be the cause of Emily's disappearance.

CHAPTER

42

AS KALISHA AND JOEL Tierney head toward Ted's Bar, Tierney says what he's already said three times.

"This could be a complete waste of time."

No response from Kalisha. She thinks it's a good idea. And she's not about to change her mind.

"Yep, could be a waste of time," Tierney says. Fourth time.

But Kalisha won't relent, and Tierney won't order her to. Kalisha has insisted that they visit Ted Burrows and ask some questions, and finally Tierney shrugs. "Okay, I guess," he says, and reluctantly files it in his It-Couldn't-Hurt list.

It's a lazy downtown afternoon as the two detectives stand at the far end of the bar. Kalisha is mildly surprised that Ted Burrows recognizes Joel Tierney.

"Greetings, Detective Tierney. Welcome to my humble saloon," he says.

"Thanks for remembering me," says Tierney.

"I not only remember *you*. I also remember your drink. Johnnie Walker with a splash of seltzer, not club soda."

"That is very impressive," says Kalisha.

Ted smiles as he speaks to her.

"I'll show you something even more impressive, ma'am. How'd you like it if I pour you a refreshing Bass Ale?"

"Holy shit," says Kalisha. "How'd you know that?"

"You were in here once about a year ago. You and an equally lovely friend. I don't recall her name. So I'll just refer to her as Vodka Tonic with a Twist."

"Amazing," says Kalisha. "My sister and I'd just come from a flea market. I can't believe…"

Tierney also says that both Ted's memory and Ted's smooth charm are pretty amazing, but he's also really anxious to get on with the interview, and he explains to Ted what the situation is with Emily. She's been missing for days. No notes. No clues.

"And we know that Emily spent a good amount of time right here where we're sitting," says Kalisha.

The two detectives watch the smile vanish from Ted's face. There is a pause as he takes time to quickly blot his face with a handful of cocktail napkins.

"Are you trying to suggest I had something to do with—"

"No one's suggesting anything," Tierney interrupts. "We're just chasing down every lead we can."

"And you're next on our list," Kalisha says. "Can you help us with anything?"

"Wish I could, Detectives, but you're wasting your time. I was on a ski trip in the Rockies all last week. Stayed at a resort called BlueSky Breckenridge. You can call them and check."

Another pause, and then a strong, quick string of words from Ted: "This is awful. Look. It's not a secret that Emily and I were friends, good friends, very good friends. Okay, yeah. We were as good as friends can be. That was a while ago. You know, sort of the old friends-with-benefits arrangement. But we stopped that long ago."

"How long ago?" asks Tierney.

"Not sure. Two months, three months. Six months, seven months," says Ted. "Anyway, it was long ago."

Kalisha: "You think two or three months is 'long ago'?"

"For me it is." Ted says these words with a cheeky grin on his face. He speaks as only a good-looking bartender can, no snark in his voice. Just the facts, ma'am. Then he seems to think it needs some explanation.

"Hey, like I said. Emily and I were friends, real friends. As you know, Emily spent a lot of time sitting on one of these barstools here."

Tierney gives a slight nod.

"I want to help," says Ted. "Please. What can I do?" His eyes are watery. He is leaning forward on the bar with both hands.

"Just tell us anything you know. Were you at her place recently?" says Kalisha.

"No, like I said, we stopped hooking up a while ago."

"Did you ever see her here with anyone unusual?" Kalisha asks.

"Never. She was always solo."

"Was she drinking a lot?"

"Maybe once in a while," Ted says. "I knew Emily was pregnant. I knew she shouldn't be drinking. Most nights or afternoons I could get her to settle for a ginger ale with a dash of bitters or a really weak white-wine spritzer. But other nights, well, like they say, *she persisted*."

Scofield and Tierney practice a studied silence with the hope that Ted Burrows will blurt out something meaningful.

"Last time I saw her was a couple weeks ago. She said the pregnancy thing was driving her crazy. A few months ago, she'd gotten so bored, she started a temp job at some real-estate place in Midtown. She called me on her second day to tell me about it. You know the one, the big one. Jones Day?"

"Jones Day is a law firm," says Kalisha. "Maybe you're thinking of Johnson and Mayes. They're the ones who sell those forty-million-dollar co-op apartments."

"Yeah," says Ted. "That's the one. Hell,

Emily must have been really bored or crazy or something to take a job with her baby due so soon. But then I heard from some guy, some old friend of hers, who comes in here, that she barely lasted a week at the real estate place. It figures. I mean, come on. She had pots of money. Her folks were really rich."

Suddenly Ted's eyes are filled with tears. He looks around the fairly empty barroom. Then he squints, and the tears seem to stop.

With sadness in his voice, he simply says, "Emily and I had some really fine times together. But then things changed." Ted pauses. Then he smiles and says, "Shit, I'm just sounding like a stupid old bartender."

"Stay strong, buddy," says Tierney.

"Thanks for your time, Ted," says Kalisha.

Ted turns away from them and faces the shelves of liquor. Scofield and Tierney leave their contact cards on the bar. As they head toward the exit, Tierney gives his partner a small nod. It seems to indicate an unspoken agreement between the two detectives. Both of them agree that Ted Burrows is probably telling the truth.

Outside, Kalisha says, "So what do you think?"

"I think we should go buy a co-op."

CHAPTER

43

DETECTIVES TIERNEY AND SCOFIELD are in the empty reception area of the ultra-swanky Johnson and Mayes Real Estate Agency. They are standing in front of a huge computer screen that sits at eye level on a smallish, red-speckled marble table.

"Where the hell is the receptionist?" asks Tierney.

"You're *looking* at the receptionist," says Scofield. "That's how it is now, Detective. A lot of these very fancy places have *virtual* receptionists."

"Nothing like a warm welcome. Virtual, my ass," says Tierney, tapping away at the keyboard. Then he says, "This goddamn machine won't let me continue if I don't enter the name of the agent I want to see," says Tierney.

"Lemme try," Kalisha says. And Tierney steps aside.

Within moments Kalisha has found and selected a prompt labeled *Paris,* and put her name down as *Louie.*

"Who the hell is Louie?"asks Tierney.

"It's a joke. A real-estate expression. It means 'Lookie Louie.' Lookie Louies are people who aren't going to buy anything. They just want to *look* at stuff. Wander through apartments and town houses and brownstones and just look."

At that moment a very pretty young woman appears. She was apparently cast to go with the spare surroundings. She is very tall, with chic bobbed hair and a perfectly cut, simple gray linen shift. She introduces herself without smiling, without extending her hand, without any warmth whatsoever.

"You're here to see me? I'm Paige Paris."

Kalisha can't resist.

"We're Joel Tierney and Kalisha Scofield. And we are detectives with the NYPD."

Paige Paris remains silent, no reaction on her face.

"We'd like to speak to someone about an employee or former employee here," Tierney says. "Emily Atkinson."

Paige Paris's hands shoot to her face. Her eyes widen.

"Emily. Oh, my God, did you find her? Do you know where she is? Is she all right? Is she okay? We're all so worried."

The woman's sudden explosion of emotion shocks Tierney and Kalisha.

"So, let me understand," says Tierney. "You people have known that Emily was missing?"

"Well, yes. Not *missing* missing, but she disappeared from here a few months back. Yes. She just disappeared one day. She used to sit right over here."

"Right here?" asks Kalisha. "And she's been replaced by a computer on a pedestal?"

"Not a pedestal, a *plinth*," says the woman, without a trace of sarcasm. "When Emily didn't show up, we called her and texted her a million times. No response. Then the next day, again, no Emily. I did most of the hunting around for her. I'm the most junior associate here, so I get all the crappy jobs. But everyone liked Emily so much, everyone was interested in helping find her, including the head of the company, Lydia Mayes. Ms. Mayes even spoke with the temp agency personally. Nobody there knew anything…So please, please, please, tell me what's up?"

As she's been speaking, Paige has punched in a number on her phone. Now she talks to the person at the other end.

"I'm in reception with two detectives. It's about Emily." Then she looks at Kalisha and Tierney. "So, where is she?"

"We don't know," says Tierney. "That's why we're here. We'd been told that she'd worked here. We wanted to ask some questions."

A handsome, thirtyish man in a black suit and open-collar black shirt joins them. He is almost immediately followed by a middle-aged woman with Paige's same haircut. The new woman wears a black dress, no jewelry.

There seems to be no time for introductions.

"What precisely did Emily do here? What was her job?" asks Kalisha.

"Well, she was hired as a temporary receptionist a few months ago," he says.

Paige jumps in, "But she did more than the usual receptionist tasks. Even though she was clearly pregnant, she had more energy than most people. She would field phone calls from prospective clients, edit outgoing emails. She even connected with an old classmate of hers from Hotchkiss and arranged for Ms. Mayes to take the husband and wife to look at a five-bedroom on Sutton Place."

The older woman speaks now, for the first time. "I'm bringing the couple back tomorrow morning to the co-op. I think they're going to buy it. It's more than twenty million, but with incredible views of the Fifty-Ninth Street Bridge and the East River."

The woman pauses and then says, "Oh, my apologies. I'm Lydia Mayes, the company founder. Please find our Emily."

"We are doing our best," says Tierney.

Lydia Mayes then says, "And when you find her, tell her this: If tomorrow's client buys the Sutton Place apartment, she'll receive a two-percent finder's commission."

Tierney and Kalisha are, of course, thinking the same thing: Money is just about the only problem that Emily does not have.

"Is there anything else you can think of that might help us?" asks Kalisha.

The lack of a response from any of the

Johnson and Mayes people is vaguely awkward. Then Paige Paris speaks.

"Well, there is one other thing. And I think we all noticed it. A lot. And that's the fact that Emily was pretty convinced that somebody, a man, was following her."

Lydia Mayes steps in to explain. "We posted a plainclothes security woman near the elevator. But Emily didn't seem to think that this mystery person was going to show up here. I think she felt safe here."

"But," says Paige, "she said she *didn't* feel safe on the street. Or in her home. She made that clear. She'd say things like 'I'm sure I'm just being crazy, but I just have this feeling that somebody is after me or following me or just being plain creepy.'"

Kalisha asks if any of the group thinks that this fear of strangers encouraged Emily to leave her job.

"Maybe," says the man in the black suit. "Emily seemed *extra* creeped out after she heard about that woman in her neighborhood… Nina something…"

Lydia Mayes corrects him. "The woman's name was Nina Powell."

"Right," says the man. "Emily didn't know her. Or she said she didn't know her, *but* she said that she felt like she knew her. And, of course, like you guys know, they still haven't found that poor woman, either."

Tierney nods. He tells them that both he and Kalisha are aware of that case, too. And that Emily and Nina's disappearances might be related.

Then Tierney says, "What amazes me is how open Emily was with all of you. She told you about all her worries, the man following her. It feels like even though she only worked here a few days, she became really good friends with all of you."

"There was just something about her that drew people to her," says Paige. "She was warm and funny and full of energy. She was always saying how happy she was to be pregnant. But then, sometimes, she was scared and quiet. And when she was like that, you just wanted to put your arms around her, take care of her."

Tierney nods. Then Lydia Mayes smiles at the two detectives and speaks.

"If there's nothing more, Detectives, we've got real estate to sell."

Lydia Mayes, Paige Paris, and the other man all head back into the office. Tierney and

Kalisha are alone again in the lobby. Alone except for the virtual receptionist.

"Speaking of real estate," Tierney says as he puts his phone to his ear, "I got a voicemail." He listens. He shakes his head. He hangs up. "Damnit."

"What is it?"

"That was Detective Fiddler from the Sharon, Connecticut, Police Department. Emily's folks lived up there before they died. They had a place in the Hamptons, too. I'd asked local PD to check them out, just in case. Both houses are dark and empty."

"In case what? Our perp abducted Emily from her apartment, and has her locked up in her parents' old house eighty miles away?"

"I figured it was worth a phone call. I knew it was a long shot."

Kalisha follows Tierney past the virtual receptionist and out the door.

"Sir, this whole damn case is a long shot."

MONTH FIVE

CHAPTER

44

I AM A WOMAN obsessed.

Did I say "obsessed?" Well, okay. That's a little too strong.

Betsey has told me that you can't really use the word *obsessed* unless you're referring to a true mental disorder. For example, if you actually stalk Taylor Swift, then you're obsessed. If you only listen to Taylor Swift singing "Lover" a hundred times a day, then you're just an idiot. You get it, don't you?

Right now, I'm walking to see Jane Craven, my ob-gyn. But I'm not thinking about the doctor's visit. I'm too busy looking at the screen on my phone, searching for information about

Nina Powell. I'm bumping carelessly into other pedestrians, and their angry comments don't really bug me.

"Hey, asshole, watch where you're going."

"You can't live without that thing?"

"Get off that goddamn phone."

Yeah, well, I can't get off it. I just received a Google Alert. The *New York Post* is reporting that Nina Powell may have just been spotted in a bar in a Detroit suburb.

Maybe I'm wrong, but news about Nina Powell is everywhere I look.

The missing girl's picture has been in *People* magazine. You can read regular updates on TMZ and *Enquirer* online. I've seen photos of Nina in high school, Nina in college, Nina in Madrid. I've seen photos of her fiancé, Jarrod. I see him playing rugby. I see him laughing. I see him crying. Shit. I see him on a skiff in New Zealand with a hot blond chick who is definitely not Nina.

I'm in front of the office building of my ob-gyn, Jane Craven.

I look up from the phone and look behind me, to my right, then my left. I look at the taxis driving past. Sometimes I think that I am being followed. Was Nina Powell being followed? The internet doesn't know. Or they're not saying.

Another Google Alert.

Before I enter my doctor's building I can't resist. I have to check the alert. It's Perez Hilton's gossip site. He usually knows what's going on. Perez has nothing new to add.

Wait. Another one. Okay. Just one more. This will be the last. I go to PopSugar. Nothing again. I'm going to be late for my appointment, but a final stab at Twitter. #MissingNina. More nothing.

As always, Dr. Craven's first move is to look me up and down, as if I'm a piece of sculpture. It's a way of looking that my parents always used when they actually were looking at sculpture or art installations or large canvases.

"You look okay, Emily, just okay. I've seen you looking better, and I've seen you looking worse," she says. "How are you feeling?"

"Not bad, I guess. A little anxious, maybe."

"Are you going to your AA meetings?"

How many times can I lie to this perfectly kind, very smart woman?

I guess I can do it one more time.

"I go to AA," I say. "But not as often as I should, I guess."

Dr. Craven drops her arms to her sides and sighs a big, dramatic sigh.

"Emily, we have a deal. You know the rules. Ninety meetings for the first ninety days."

"I go a lot," I quickly add. "Really, I do."

"Okay, let me get the question out of the way," Dr. Craven says. "Have you been keeping sober?"

Keeping sober. Some people use that expression. It sounds comfortable, old-fashioned. Like "keeping house" or "keeping a secret."

"Pretty much," I say.

Jane Craven is no pushover. Her reply is simple: "That's a completely unacceptable answer."

"But it's the truth. Would you rather I lie?"

Dr. Craven's eyes are pointed upward.

"No. I'd rather you be completely sober. We. Are. Not. Going. To. Have. This. Discussion. One. More. Time."

I nod.

"This is the last time I warn you. Either you get sober and stay sober or *I will not keep you as a patient any longer.*"

I nod again. Just like a stupid, embarrassed child. Which is kind of how I feel.

"I understand," I say.

"That's just it," Dr. Craven says. "I know you understand." She sighs again and says, "I need you to go over to pre-nate and get an ultrasound. I want a quick fix on how the fetus is growing. And I also…"

"But we agreed, no amnio," I say, my voice full of fear. "I don't want anyone piercing me and my baby with a needle and…"

Dr. Craven sighs yet again.

"It's only an ultrasound. We're not going in for amniotic fluid. I'll see how the fetus is grow-ing, and we'll probably be able to tell if it's going to be a male or a female. Now, let's get started. We'll see how your blood pressure is doing."

I'm tired. I'm sad. I should ask if it's hor-monal. I should tell her I've been to an abortion clinic. I should tell her everything. But I don't even have the strength to cry.

I turn away from her. I don't want to be examined. I don't want to have my blood pres-sure taken. I don't want my cervix poked at. I'm a goddamn nervous wreck.

So, God bless Dr. Craven. She seems to have radar that tells her exactly what I'm thinking. I'm expecting her to strap the blood pressure gauge around my arm. But instead she reaches toward me and takes both my hands in hers.

"Emily," she says. "The three people who most want this miracle to happen are right here in this room. Right now. You and your baby and me. Okay?"

"Okay," I say.

"So, look. I'll do my part of the job, and you do your part of the job. And that'll help the baby do their part of the job. But you must cooperate. Okay?"

"Of course," I say. "Of course. Of course. Of course."

Now she slips the blood pressure cuff around my arm. She pumps. She looks surprised. She speaks.

"Look at that. One-twenty over eighty. Perfect."

I smile.

"See? I'm already cooperating."

CHAPTER

45

THE ULTRASOUND TECHNICIAN LEANS over my naked belly, holding the kind of plastic bottle you find in diners, the kind that squirts ketchup or mustard.

"The jelly may be cold," she says with a soft giggle.

"You're not kidding," I say, but I am surprisingly calm. Where did this sudden sense of well-being come from? If my father were here, he'd simply say, *I guess that Craven woman just knocked some sense into you.*

Perhaps. But I've had endless amounts of sense knocked into me. It's the acting upon that sense that I have trouble with.

"Now, I will simply be smearing the jelly," says the technician. She does what she says, and she giggles some more.

"It actually feels good, Komal," I say. (The name tag on her pale green medical coat reads KOMAL PUJARI. And if someone wears a name tag, I always try to address them by name.)

"This will be a nothing of a procedure," she says. "Not to worry."

I cup my hands and hold my little bump. Then I speak to that bump.

"You hear that, Oscar? It's nothing. It won't hurt. We've done this before."

"You call your baby Oscar?" asks Ms. Pujari. "That is so sweet and funny."

I don't know where that name, Oscar, suddenly came from. I don't even know that my baby is a boy. Oscar. I don't even know anyone named Oscar. Oscar? Huh? Like the Academy Awards? I vaguely remember my mother wearing an Oscar de la Renta gown to a San Francisco gallery opening. But a baby name? Whatever happened to "bump"?

I adjust my brain to the new name quickly. Now it's easy for me to act casual. It's as if I've always called bump by the name Oscar.

I casually answer Komal's question.

"Yes. Whether it turns out to be a boy or a girl, I use the name Oscar."

Yes, she giggles again. I assume that Komal Pujari has had stranger conversations than this with some of her ultrasound patients.

Komal is now preoccupied. She adjusts knobs and buttons on the ultrasound machine with one hand while she moves the greasy something-or-other around my stomach.

"What's that thing you're moving on my belly called again?" I ask her.

Her tone of voice indicates that I have interrupted her.

"A transducer. Now just lie quietly. Don't move."

She adjusts the dials and knobs and buttons some more. She stops. From the corner of my eye I see her return the transducer to the monitor table, and I hear her on the phone.

"If you are available, patient Atkinson is in exam room four," I hear her say.

"What was that all about?" I ask.

"You must remain still, ma'am. It is important."

"Is something wrong?"

"The doctor will be here shortly."

"Tell me what's happening," I say, and now I don't care that I'm defying Komal by moving around.

"Let's take a look," comes Dr. Craven's voice.

"What were you doing?" I ask. "Waiting outside the door?"

"Just about. I was down the hall with a woman who delivered triplets. Now let's have a look."

Komal steps aside from the monitor, and Dr. Craven sits down. She moves her head closer to the screen. Then she moves her chair backward a few inches and looks at the screen as if she were looking at a painting at a gallery. I have a flash vision of my mother doing just that.

"Please tell me what's going on," I say, and this time I sit up on the examining table.

"I shall be across the hall," I hear Komal say.

Then, thankfully, joyfully, mercifully, Dr. Craven says, "Nothing is terribly wrong. Nothing that can't be taken care of. It's just that the fetus has not advanced...grown...as much as we'd like to see at this point."

"What happens now?" I say.

"What happens now is what I've told you. What happens now is that you never have another drink. Same goes for cigarettes. And cannabis.

Any drugs that I don't okay. You find an exercise class. I'll prescribe some vitamins, which will be the *only* pills you take. You will see one of the wonderful prenatal nutritionists we have here. And you'll lie down on this table two weeks from now, and everything will be fine. Okay?"

I do not cry. I do not yell. I do not feel sorry for myself.

I nod my head a few times. In a firm voice I say, "Okay." Then I add, "I mean it."

"I think you do, Emily. This time I think you do," says Dr. Craven.

She looks at the screen again, just a quick glance. Then she stands.

"One other thing," I say. "You referred to my baby as the fetus. But can you tell just from a sonogram if it's a boy or a girl?"

"Sometimes."

"This time?" I ask.

"It was easy with this one. Do you want to know?"

I nod my head *yes*.

"It's a boy."

Oscar!

CHAPTER

46

THE UNPLEASANT SMELL of really bad coffee.

Five rows of folding chairs.

A group of mostly strangers.

A few people know one another. Most do not.

Some smile. Some nod. Some, like me, just stare straight ahead.

Some people are wearing Prada. Some are in sweatshirts or T-shirts. A few have come from important CEO-type jobs. A few look like they live on the street.

Another AA meeting.

As one of the seemingly millions of helpful

AA sayings goes: "They come from Yale, and they come from jail."

"No smoking, Freddie," I hear from behind me. "You know that. It's really disrespectful."

"Sorry. Sorry. I forgot." That must be Freddie.

This meeting, at this location, at this time, comes highly recommended by Betsey. She asked around at her hospital. Her husband asked around at his fire station. She googled and phoned, and two days ago at Sarabeth's on Central Park South Betsey declared that "The AA meeting at St. Clement's on West Forty-Sixth Street is supposed to be one of the best in Manhattan."

I, being a professional pain in the ass, asked, "Does that mean that they have a great success rate? Or does it mean that a lot of cute single guys go there? Or does it mean that everyone goes out for drinks after the meeting?"

But Betsey was in no mood to fool around. She actually threatened to leave her turkey sandwich untouched if I didn't "start getting serious about this." For good luck she added, "This is your last chance, Emily. It really is."

Betsey and Dr. Craven are singing the same

song. For a moment I wonder if they've been in touch, if they've been discussing me. If this is some sort of emotional intervention.

"Please, Emily. Do it this time," Betsey said.

Yes. Yes. Yes. I know she's right. I know Dr. Craven is right. I know. I know. And yes, I'm going to do it this time. I'm going to do it starting now, right here at this meeting, right here at St. Clement's.

How can I be so sure that it will work this time? Because this time I brought a friend. I look down and talk to my belly. I whisper.

"Thanks for coming with me, Oscar. We're going to get through this together."

I am so lost in the world of my baby that I am surprised when I look up to see that someone is sitting in the chair next to me: an older man (around sixty perhaps), with a salt-and-pepper beard, wearing a dark-gray double-breasted suit. He half nods, half smiles at me.

"This is an open meeting, right?" he asks. That means that anyone can attend.

"I assume so," I say. (Please don't talk to me. I'm so nervous. I'm having a baby. If I don't keep sober, I'll lose the baby. I'll lose my friends. I'll lose my mind.)

"Is it a Big Book meeting?" he asks. A Big Book meeting means that the moderator will look to the Big Book, the four-hundred-page bible of Alcoholics Anonymous, for any topic that might come up.

"Yes, it is," I say.

I am thinking that maybe this guy is trying to flirt with me. When you've spent time on as many barstools as I have you develop a second instinct. But I am now also thinking two other things. First, I want to be alone in the crowd, alone with my Oscar. No talking. Just listening. Second—and where the hell is this thought coming from?—is this guy next to me the person who's been following me? I mean, come on, all he did was ask about the meeting. But still. Oh, shit. I know Greg confessed to following me, but did I imagine that? Sometimes when I drink I . . . But there's still someone out there. I know it. I don't think it's Greg. He's so tall, and I've been watching. I would have seen him.

I stand. I am going to move to another chair. I think for a moment that I will offer an excuse to the man—there's a draft on me, I've got to make a phone call, oh, there's my friend—but I merely stand and walk to an empty chair in the fifth and last row. I sit on the aisle. There's no one in the other seat beside me.

Yeah, we've moved, Oskie. We're in a whole new place. No one to bother us here. So Mommy can concentrate. Mommy can think. Mommy can get sober.

The talking begins. The confessions. The weeping. The laughing. Bits and pieces of the talking float through the air... "And my boyfriend actually encourages me to drink more. 'You were more fun when you were drunk,' he says..."

"So I went to the police station to ask them to help me find my car..."

"This is meeting number eighty-eight for me. Just two more to go..."

"But then when this meeting is over, that's when it's hard..."

Oh, man, sister, tell me about it. Tell me about the neon Bud signs at Ted's. Tell me about the extraordinary kick to the brain from that first sip of a Beefeater martini. The easy swallows of tequila sunrises.

"We've got our work cut out for us, Oscar."

Is my voice becoming too loud? Am I one of those annoying AA people?

The moderator, a gracious, pretty woman, is

reading from the Big Book. I know these passages. It is about supporting one another. Not just the sponsor, the personal buddy, the one you call any time for help and support. No, she's reading the part about always reaching out to one another.

But I'm not a reacher, unless, of course, I have alcohol in me. There's a crazy conundrum for you. Catch-22, Emily. Unless I'm a person who's drinking, I cannot be a person who is good. I've got to stop thinking this way. I've got to stop with the excuses.

I'm at a meeting, for God's sake. It feels good. The people here seem gentle. God knows I'm motivated. I should just stand up and talk. I hear my voice practicing in my head, *My name is Emily, and I am an... My name is Emily, and I am an...* No, wait. Even with the promise of anonymity I can't do it. I'll use another name. I practice some more, *My name is Laurie... My name is Ann... My name is Trudy...* But then I'd be lying, and this is about truth. And I'd be lying in front of Oscar.

By the time I drift out of my confusion, the moderator is reminding the group to go to the website. Fold the chairs and go to the website.

Clean the coffee machine and go to the website. I stand. I pat Oscar. I look toward the exit.

I see the man with the beard and gray suit is looking at me. He smiles. I'm on automatic; I smile back. Oh, shit. Will he think I'm inviting a conversation?

I walk out onto the crowded street. The Broadway theaters must be letting out. No available cabs. I should have arranged for a driver pickup. Across the street I see a window with a sign: PSYCHIC READING $5. (Who says there are no bargains in New York?) People—mostly tourists, I think—are on a short line to get into a family-style Italian restaurant. Next door to the Italian place is a Mexican saloon. There's a sign in the window: MARGARITAS $5. Only $5? Hey, they stole the psychic's idea.

Four people are taking a cigarette break outside the Mexican place. I'm keeping an eye out for a taxi when I realize that I recognize one of the guys smoking across the street.

It's Mike Miller, the ultimate asshole, the guy who peddles coke and weed and uppers at Ted's bar. Miller tosses a cigarette to the sidewalk. Every few seconds Miller glances at the church door where I've just exited.

I walk quickly toward Ninth Avenue. My legs hurt. I have to pee. I'm thinking that maybe Mike Miller has some customers on this block. I think maybe he was at my AA meeting, and I just didn't see him.

But you know what I really think? Of course you do.

There's no way I saw Mike Miller just now by accident. No way at all.

I think Mike Miller might be the person following me.

CHAPTER

47

I AM WORKING. I am working as a receptionist. I am working as a receptionist at a very prestigious real estate firm. I am loving it.

I know that some of us in AA replace our alcohol addiction with some other supposedly *safer* addiction. Like traveling. Or online shopping. For me, it is working. Working has always been something that made my heart beat faster. When I was sober (and occasionally when I was drunk or high), work was my passion.

A receptionist? Yes, it is perfect. Okay, it's not perfect, but it will fill the time. It will keep me sober. There's no way I could pick up and pack myself into another marketing or PR firm.

There's no way that I could connect myself to one of my late father's big-shot friends. I just want to do something where I can be busy, where people will be respectful toward me.

Okay, I'm a bit overqualified, but, hey, I'll be busy. I'll be occupied.

"The way you dress is important," says the HR man to me during my one and only interview. Obviously, it is important to everyone at Johnson and Mayes. Women in silk slacks, women with classic cropped haircuts. Handsome men with a few days' stubble. Men in black suits and thousand-dollar shoes but no socks.

Yes, I want to work at a place where the way you dress is important. Not because I love dressing up, but because it will be a component of staying sober.

"You are often the first face of the company brand," says the HR man.

Yes, that's what I will be. The first face.

"Will there be a problem with my so obviously being pregnant?" I ask during the interview.

The HR man may think this is a trick question, that I'm out to entrap him into stating a bias against pregnant women. His answer is perfect.

"On the contrary, pregnancy is very chic these days." I think he means this.

I begin on a Monday. I am efficient and sweet and smart. I know that I am as smart as the clients who walk toward my desk. I also know that I am wealthier than a good many of them. But only I know why none of that matters. I know that I am just ecstatic to be sober.

On my second day, Tuesday, I phone Ted. I tell him what I'm doing.

He says, "A receptionist?"

I make plans to see him at the Starbucks near his bar. We meet on my way home from that evening's AA meeting. I tell Ted about the people in my AA meetings. An eighty-year-old man sobbed because he has never been allowed to see his granddaughter. A woman had us on the floor laughing because she recalled being so drunk once that she forced her mother's best crystal glasses into the garbage disposal; she thought it was somehow connected to the dishwasher.

Ted tells me that I look good. He touches my hand and he worries that I won't be able to sleep when I order my second espresso.

On Wednesday I give a lead to one of the newest female associates who is desperate to make a first sale. (I heard that a friend of my late mother's from Southampton is searching for a pied-à-terre in Manhattan.)

Later that day—after arranging an apartment showing for my mother's friend—the associate places a gift-wrapped package of Jo Malone Wood Sage and Sea Salt fragrance on my desk. The accompanying card reads I DON'T KNOW WHAT I'D HAVE DONE WITHOUT YOU. I can't remember the last time someone wrote something like that to me. Probably never.

I'm turning into a force in the Manhattan real estate world.

A girl I knew from Hotchkiss married a hedge-funder. They seem to have billions of dollars. I call her and put her on to the owner of Johnson and Mayes. When the agency's owner, Lydia Mayes, invites me to accompany her and my fellow alum from prep school on a showing of the twenty-seven-million-dollar apartment, I decline.

"It's all in a day's work," I tell Lydia.

At five thirty the same Wednesday a male client—thirty-ish, handsome-ish, Mideastern-ish,—is leaving a meeting with one of our agents.

"I was wondering if I could ask you a favor," he says.

"Of course."

"I'm closing on an apartment tomorrow, a really nice place in West Chelsea, right on the Hudson."

"Congratulations," I say. "So what's the favor?"

"I have no one to celebrate with. My girlfriend is away on business. And I thought we could go for some champagne and possibly some dinner. You and me. And by the way, my name is Travis."

Ordinarily...but this is not ordinarily. I'm getting sober. I'm being sober. I am sober. Yes, ordinarily, Travis. But not right now.

"In case you hadn't noticed, I'm pregnant. No champagne for the baby. Good luck tomorrow."

He thanks me, and I go to my AA meeting.

The same grandfather from the other evening weeps again. A woman who doesn't look old enough to even be a mother tells the group that she, too, is a "discarded" grandparent. A discarded grandmother?

The use of the word *discarded* troubles me. Then the woman says, "I deserve to be discarded. I used. I really used. I couldn't be trusted. I would have discarded me."

I call an Uber and go home. I call Betsey. First on her cell. When she doesn't pick up, I try her at home.

"Bets is at work tonight," says Frankie. "She's in the OR. They had some kidney or liver thing going on, and they called her. She's going to be a while. I'm on kid patrol."

"Do you need company?" I ask.

"No. But thanks. Once I get them down, I'm going to take a shower and go to bed myself."

I tell Frank that his plan sounds absolutely perfect. We say good night, and I eat half of yesterday's sandwich, turkey on toast. Then I select tomorrow's wardrobe. After all, "the way you dress is important." Tomorrow I will be wearing a subdued Missoni skirt with a very pale-blue shirt.

I fall asleep with Seth Meyers. Seth is a perfect companion, a gentleman.

When I wake up tomorrow morning, all will be well. I have my lovely job and my Missoni skirt. I'll smell of Jo Malone's Wood Sage and Sea Salt cologne.

I sleep the sleep of the sober.

I'm fine, and then I wake up, shaking slightly.

And everything is wrong. Whatever made me think that I could be normal?

I have no desire to sit up in bed, to get out of bed.

I'm just too sad to move. I'm not sick. I'm merely sober.

I can't even summon the energy to call Johnson and Mayes and say *I'm sorry. Something's come up. I can't come in today.*

CHAPTER

48

NOT ONLY DO I not go in. But I don't go back. Ever.

I'll just stay in my apartment. My plan is to never go out. Except perhaps to have my baby. I'll see.

I have locked myself indoors for four days, and, frankly, it seems perfectly reasonable. Having never gone crazy before, having never had a nervous breakdown before, I'm not sure that this is what's happening.

FreshDirect delivers apples and bananas and oatmeal. My appetite longings are perfect for pregnancy—salmon and cheese and coffee ice cream. FreshDirect delivers toilet paper and light bulbs and Essentia bottled water.

Bigelow Pharmacy sends my vitamins and a weekly supply of Dr. Hauschka Quince Day Cream.

I call Dr. Craven's office and leave a message that I've been feeling a little nauseated lately, a little extra tired, but nothing serious. Her assistant calls and tells me that the doctor says to rest for a few days, call her if there's any change. If we need to, I can do a video visit with a physician's assistant. Or, if I'm worried, "Just pop by. Dr. Craven will squeeze you in."

My only outside contact is an occasional phone conversation or text message with Betsey.

"Let's Zoom," she says. "I want to see what you look like."

"No."

"I'll change my OR assignment and come by with lunch…"

"No," I say again. Then I add, "You don't have to come by. I know you just want to check up on me. So, whether you want to believe me or not, here's the absolute truth. I'm not drinking anything but organic whole milk and mineral water."

"Really?"

"Really."

Really. I have not had a drink. I have not smoked weed. In the past four days.

Of course, I have not left my apartment, not taken a shower, not worn clothes, not slept for more than two or three hours at a time. In the past four days.

My hair is a greasy tangle, and I'm sitting naked on my bed. Just me and Oscar. I pat my belly. I try not to shake. I try not to cry.

Then I pull open my laptop and google Nina Powell.

Ever since I heard about this woman—who lived in my neighborhood, who was about my age, who worked in my industry, who has recently gone missing—the story has completely sucked me in.

But there's nothing new about her in the news. I go to Twitter: #WhereIsNina. Not much here, either. Just a few haters and trolls who say she probably deserved whatever happened to her. A few crazies who are sure she is part of a Russian plot, a right-wing plot, a left-wing plot, a political plot in Myanmar. Concerned people: Make sure the cops have checked the sewers, people live down there.

But the number of posts about her on

Twitter has significantly dwindled. There is rarely much news about her anymore, either. Nina Powell is slowly fading into the black hole of corroding old news. Nina Powell is being replaced by new #MeToo scandals, new #CatholicSexAbuse scandals.

Why has Nina's disappearance taken such a hold on me? I've seriously considered joining the reporters who wait outside her fiancé's apartment building. I've thought about hiring a private detective. Yes, I know I'm crazy, but craziness is a kind of psychic fuel. It keeps me going. It might even be the thing that's keeping me sober.

I rub my belly.

"This is where you're going to live, Oscar. Right now, your home is in my belly. But in a little bit your home will be right here. Here with your mommy."

But is a naked crazy woman, now a sort of wacky recluse, fit to be a mother?

"Of course I am. You think so, Oscar. Right now, I'm just resting. When you come out, we'll be plenty busy."

I should read. I should binge-watch *The*

Unbreakable Kimmy Schmidt. Betsey thought it was the best thing on television. But I don't.

Instead I keep thinking about Nina Powell.

I slip my right hand under my belly and notice a tiny pimple-like bump. A bump beneath the bump. I examine it. A bluish, very tiny dot an inch or so below my belly button.

I panic. What if it's cancer? I mean . . . What the hell else can it be? Will I be able to have radiation even though I'm pregnant? Will it actually even matter? Because clearly, I'm crazy.

I rest. I wake around 2:00 a.m. and am ravenously hungry. I walk naked to the kitchen to find that the refrigerator is equally naked. Well, there are two small containers next to the milk. But, come on, how much full-fat mango yogurt can one pregnant woman eat?

But this is inspiration. I won't wait until tomorrow to order FreshDirect. I won't call for delivery from the twenty-four-hour deli. I'll slip on some clothes—jeans, a big sweatshirt. I'll even brush on a bit of eye makeup and pile my greasy hair in a twist on the top of my head. I'll go out and buy some food. Like a normal person.

Since I know where all the bars and liquor stores are, I also know how to avoid them.

Good.

I'll walk slowly. It's always busy on the Lower East Side. Even at night.

Who knows? I may even run into Nina Powell.

CHAPTER

49

SURE. I KNOW THE CITY never sleeps. But this is ridiculous.

Seventh Street and Avenue A at two thirty in the morning looks like curtain time on Times Square. Although most of the bars and restaurants are still open, the streets are filled with lots of people. I find them annoyingly young, as if they were gloating in front of early-thirties me, these lovely young girls in tight jeans and tight T-shirts. These handsome young men with their rabbi-like beards and way-too-interesting Nike sneakers.

It barely matters, I think, that I actually put on eye makeup and fixed my hair. My own sneakers are authentic pink-green-and-white French bicycle shoes. My secondhand Burberry raincoat is belted tight around me, even though there isn't a cloud in the night sky. These fashion items were once so cool, and now they make me look like everyone's maiden aunt. Oh, shit. I'm turning into Aunt Dolly. No, I'm not. Not yet. No, I don't look like my aunt, but I also don't look like a hipster. I know. How do I know? Because as soon as I put on my Ferragamo sunglasses, a teenage girl walks past me and says, "Hey, lady, are you a fucking spy?"

As soon as the teenage girl passes, I remove my glasses and drop them into my bag. I unpin my hair and let it fall back down to my shoulders. Straggly and oily and hanging on careless strands, at least it looks like an *idea* for a hairstyle. I may look like a bum, but at least I don't look like a spy...or Aunt Dolly...or...hell. What's wrong with me?

It dawns on me that I have so rarely shopped for food in my neighborhood that I don't know where to go. Obviously not the corner falafel shops or the famous restaurants where waiters are stacking outdoor chairs and hosing down the pavement.

But the fear rushes through me.

With so many people on the street, one of them must be following me. Yes, of course. I expect my stalker to be male. But, of course, he might be a woman. I expect him to be shifty and balding and blandly unattractive. But he— or she—could be none of those things.

I'm standing outside a store that easily might have stood here since the late nineteenth century, when the Lower East Side was mostly tenements crammed with Eastern European immigrants. The red sign that hangs over the window where I stand says simply DELI. For some reason I have always liked name- less places, places that simply announce their category—SALOON, DRY CLEANER, CHINESE RESTAURANT. An older South Asian man is behind the counter. He is finishing up his cre- ation of a ham and Swiss cheese sandwich.

"Mustard or mayonnaise?" he says to the customer, a handsome fortyish man in a black suit and black shirt.

"A little of both, Pahal," says the man. "You know what I like."

The customer looks at me. He gives the tini- est of bows and smiles. He is not just handsome.

He is very handsome. Dark-haired, distinguished, with the now-typical scruffy beard. If he were an actor? I'm not sure. Robert Pattinson? Perhaps. Or just himself.

The handsome man leaves with his sandwich, and I tell Pahal that I would like a buttered bagel, a small container of coleslaw, and a Snapple Apple Juice.

When he hands me my order he says, "I am adding a gift for you and the baby." I see that in addition to my juice and bagel and coleslaw, there is also a small container of something brown.

"Lentils," he says. "In Pakistan a pregnant woman eats lentils three times a day. The lentils are filled with protein."

I thank him as I pay. When I walk out the door, I see that the handsome man with the ham sandwich is standing there.

The Handsome Man with the Ham Sandwich.
It sounds like the name of a children's book.

"Pahal gave you some lentils, I see," says the man.

"Yes, because I'm pregnant," and, of course, I am now thinking that this man is the one who has been following me. Why did he wait for me? Why is he dressed entirely in black? And then I speak. I speak without even planning to.

"What are you doing out here on the street so late?"

"I work near here," he says. But he does not tell me what he does. And something inside me tells me not to ask. "You know, Pahal keeps a few containers of lentils handy for people he thinks need them. Children with colds. Old folks on walkers. And, as you've seen, pregnant women."

Now I am thinking that there must be poison in the lentils. Yes, it's all part of the children's story, part of the crazy plot. But the craziest plots are sometimes true. Aren't they? One thing I know is that I will never eat the lentils.

"Unless you're on your way somewhere," says the man, "we can go right here into this park and eat our sandwiches...well, you can eat your bagel, and I can eat my ham and cheese."

We are across the street from Tompkins Square Park. When I was a little girl here, Tompkins was a dangerous, filthy place—with way too many drug dealers and way too many rats. People used the park as a toilet. No one I knew would ever go there. Now it is so brightly lit that it could be high noon.

"No," I say. "I've got to get home." I begin to walk away. I cross the street. I am next to the park. The man follows me.

"We never introduced ourselves," he says. "My name is Tommy... Tommy Powell."

I will not tell him my name. I will not eat the lentils. I just want to get away. But I find myself wide-eyed and wanting to ask him a question. And I do.

"Tommy Powell. Are you related to Nina Powell?"

He laughs a big strong laugh. "The missing woman? *That* Nina Powell? No. We're not related."

"Excuse me," I say. "Good night," and I walk away quickly.

I don't want to be with Tommy Powell. And I surely don't want the lentils. And what if the Pakistani guy and the handsome guy are teamed up?

I start running. I run faster. Nobody really notices me. No sight is odd at 2:30 a.m. in New York City. A pregnant lady in a raincoat running? These streets have seen far crazier.

"Emily! Emily!" I hear from behind me.

I keep running.

"Emily!" again.

I keep running.

After a few more yards I begin to feel light-headed and nauseated. I slow down. I lean against the side of a lamppost.

A man—maybe fifty years old, chubby—stops a few feet away. This guy is also out of breath. He looks around. He yells into the distance.

"Amy!" he yells. Then again, "Amy!"

Wait a second. I could have sworn he was just calling *my* name. Wasn't he?

He looks at me and speaks. It's as if he can read my mind.

"I was running with my dog. She got away. I'm looking for her. Her name is Amy. In case you were wondering."

I wave him off and sit down on the sidewalk. God only knows how many dogs and rats and humans have been at this spot before me.

The chubby guy yells into the dark morning, "Amy! Amy!"

Then he runs off.

CHAPTER

50

HOW MANY TIMES CAN a sweating, trembling, pregnant woman check the locks on her apartment doors when she is petrified and alone?

Give up? The answer is fifteen.

That's the amount of times that I have checked my front door and service entrance door since I've returned home from my impromptu 2:30 a.m. jog.

But checking the doors brings me no peace. Because I know that the person calling for Amy or Emily—or the person who probably abducted Nina Powell—can easily smash through my windows, drill a human-size hole through my ceiling, bribe a doorman, disguise himself as a delivery man, a policeman...I try to sit quietly in the center of a sofa in my very large and now very dark living room. That lasts for about thirty seconds. Time to check the locks.

Before I stand up from the sofa, I gently pat little Oscar inside me. As I quickly move to check the door locks, I hold my little belly, as if I am carrying a smallish melon.

I have to pee. I always have to pee. I touch Oscar. I pat him.

"We're fine. You wait and see. We're fine. Sometimes Mommy gets a little nervous, but Mommy is nervous for you. Mommy is nervous because she loves you."

Great. Now I'm telling lies to my unborn baby. I'm not nervous because I love him. So I quickly add, "Okay, fine, Mommy is a little nervous because she's a little scared."

A little? Christ. I'm *really* scared.

And I know it. I've read it. I've learned it. And this is it:

The worst kind of scared *in the world is not really knowing why you're scared.*

But I do know why. I think I'm being followed.

I do *not* think about drinking. But if I don't get a grip soon, I just might. And if I slip up or have a drink or take a pill or smoke a joint, then the Oscar I love will... The door. The front door that's so well locked.

There's a loud insistent banging on it.

Whoever is pounding on it has got past the doorman. Whoever is pounding the door is screaming something that sounds like the word *Emma* or *Amy* or *Emily*.

It's a man's voice, a voice I do not recognize. The voice explodes with anger. My instinct is to run from the entryway, but the little bit of wisdom in me tells me to check the lock yet again and not confront the maniac outside.

My other instinct is to pick up the intercom phone and talk to the doorman. I do that. But no one picks up. Goddamnit, there's always a doorman or backup doorman or a backup doorman to the backup doorman.

"Get the hell away!" I say to the quivering door.

I look through the peephole, but the peephole has been blocked.

"Open the fucking door," comes the maniac's voice.

I try the lobby again. I grab my pocketbook. I grab my phone.

"We have to talk!" comes the intruder's voice.

Suddenly another voice. A woman's voice. Loud and angry but not insane.

"Get out!" she yells. "Get out! My housekeeper is calling the police. They will be here momentarily."

This voice is unmistakable. It belongs to my elegantly awful neighbor, Mariana Micelli. The neighbor who usually hates me is now actually helping me.

I hear the man: "Go fuck yourself, you ugly old bitch."

I'm too scared to look through the peephole, but Dr. Micelli's intercession seems to have worked. The pounding stops. I might be hearing running steps down the hallway. The thud and click of my neighbor's door closing. The lock clicking.

I look at my phone. No messages. I return to the sofa, and my attention focuses on my baby, my Oscar. Oskie, Oscarino, Oscar-pie, Oscar-pumpkin.

I pat my bump, but I do not have the courage

to promise him my protection. I cannot form the words that I want him to hear: *I'll always take care of you, Oskie. You're safe with me.* I know it's not the truth. There is no one to take care of me. So how can I take care of someone else?

I consider never moving from this sofa. I consider having a shot of vodka with a splash of grapefruit juice. I consider calling Betsey.

Then my phone rings. The screen reads NO CALLER ID.

It must be the madman who was just outside my door.

I want to know who he is. I want to pick up.

So I do. But I am too frightened to even say hello.

The voice of Mariana Micelli comes back at me.

"Is there no end to the trash you bring into this building?"

"Dr. Micelli…" I begin, relieved it's only her, if uncertain how she got my number. But I will not have the chance to ask. I will not have the chance to say anything other than her name.

"I am composing a letter to the cooperative board. Your neighbors do not deserve to witness and share your disgusting lifestyle. What's more, I will have my attorneys look..."

I click off my phone.

I sit quietly. My hands and arms do not seem to be shaking so much. I am not thinking of the nightmare that has just passed—the chase, the madman at the door, the awful lady next door. Instead I am thinking of a stranger: Nina Powell.

How do I stop my life from ending up like hers?

I know what I should do right now.

And I know what I shouldn't do.

I wait. I think. Then I do what I shouldn't do.

I go to Ted's.

CHAPTER

51

I TAKE A SEAT at the bar. Ted sees me and approaches quickly. I smile at him, but he does not smile back.

"Let me put it to you in the clearest possible way, Emily. Four very simple words: *Get the hell out*," says Ted.

Well, this certainly isn't beginning well.

I should have known, of course. The moment Ted saw me walk in he began shaking his head from side to side. It was not one of those *Oh, you wacky girl, you* looks. It was a furious *What the hell is the matter with you?* or maybe *Why the hell are you in this bar?* look.

It's almost 3:30 a.m. on a Wednesday

morning. It's getting close to last call and the bar isn't crowded. But it's not empty; Ted has a devoted clientele. The place just feels great. I can attest that the Heinekens at Ted's taste frostier, the whiskey sours taste sharper, and most strangers quickly become friends.

Without another word, Ted slides a glass of seltzer toward me. He walks away and returns immediately to squeeze a piece of lime into my drink. This time he does actually speak to me.

"This is it," he says. "I can't be part of this, watch you do this in your...condition."

Okay, fine. If Ted doesn't want to talk to me, someone else in the room does. But it's not someone I want to share time with.

"Em-bo!" a voice yells. No one has ever called me Em-bo or anything like it, but the voice is easily recognizable. Meet Mike Miller. If there was any way that this was going to be a relaxing evening, the combination of nonalcoholic refreshment and Mike Miller just erased that possibility.

It's been a few days since I'd caught sight of Miller on my way out of the AA meeting. I was satisfied that Mike hadn't seen me also. Turns out I was wrong.

"I think I saw you coming out of St. Clement's the other day," he says. "Could that be?"

"Not sure about that, Mike. The other day was a long time ago."

"What brought you to church, Em-bo? Some sort of religious experience? A baptism? An exorcism?"

I am really not in the mood for Mike Miller. Actually, I'm not in the mood for anything or anyone. Not Ted, not Mariana Micelli, and certainly not Mike.

"Don't mess with me, Mike," I say. Loud enough that the big, fortyish looking guy on the other side of him looks over at us.

I don't stop talking.

"You know goddamn well that I was at a meeting, an AA meeting. So if you think that you're being cute, or if you think that you're sounding cute, I need to tell you that you're not remotely cute."

"Whoa," says Mike. "I'm not being a dickhead, Emily. I just was concerned. I mean, okay, you go to an AA meeting, and here and now I run into you at a bar. I was just interested in your welfare."

"Stop it, Mike," I say, and I'm thinking

that if I weren't so furious with Ted, I'd call him over and ask him to quickly remove Mike Miller from my area.

But I don't call Ted, and Mike is not about to stop.

"I can actually help you with this, Emily. Are you familiar with the expression *Cali-sober*?"

The fact is that I am familiar with the expression. It's come up once or twice at meetings. *Cali-sober* is essentially when you substitute weed for alcohol. It doesn't make any sense to me, but some people in AA are fans.

But I give Mike a different answer.

"No, I'm not familiar with the expression, and frankly I don't want to be educated about it right now."

It's as if Mike never heard me.

"Okay, *Cali* is obviously short for *California*." And Mike stops talking right there. It seems that somebody else's quite large hand has touched Mike's shoulder very firmly. That shoulder is accompanied by an equally firm voice.

"I think you're having a tough time communicating with this woman, dude," says the big, fortyish looking guy on the barstool next to Mike.

"Hey, man, get your fucking hand…" Mike starts to say, and then he thinks better of the tough guy approach. He wisely opts for the let's be buddies approach.

"Emily and I are friends," says Mike. And before either man can speak any further, I say, "Positively, absolutely wrong."

"There. You heard it," says the big guy, who now removes his hand from Mike Miller's shoulder. "Looks like there are a few seats at the other end of the bar."

The new guy is not threatening. He doesn't even sound tough. He's just…well, completely assertive.

"See you later, Em-bo," says Mike.

"What is with this Em-bo thing? What the hell is wrong with you?" I say to Mike as he stands up.

"I thought it was kinda cute," says Mike.

I say nothing. The big guy says nothing. Clearly, we both feel that there's been enough conversation. Mike takes off.

"And an enormous thank-you to you, sir," I say to my barroom hero.

"Nothing to it," he says.

"What if it turned out that he actually knew

karate or had a knife?" I say, only partially joking.

"That'd be bad," he says. "Because I don't know anything close to karate, and, what's more, I'm a big baby, a coward. But..." He pulls out something that looks like a wallet and I see a photo of him with the headline NEW YORK CITY POLICE DEPARTMENT.

"So you're a cop," I say.

"Actually, a detective."

I look at the ID more closely and read it aloud.

"Joel Martin Tierney."

Actually—and I'm not about to tell this strong, striking man—but I'm pretty sure I remember spotting him at Ted's bar before, maybe three or four times.

"And your name is?" he asks.

I panic. I say nothing. I don't know why I've panicked. I don't know why I say nothing. I take a big drink of seltzer, now wishing that it was a bucketful of vodka. When I take the glass away from my lips I smile, but I still say nothing.

"So, you don't want to tell me your name?" he says.

"No. Of course I'll tell you. I'll tell you my

name." He must think I'm the craziest woman in town.

"Amy," I say. "My name is Amy."

Maybe I am crazy. Amy. Why Amy? Why not the truth? Why did I pick the name from the breathless, screaming, running man on the street earlier tonight?

"What kind of work do you do, Amy?" he says. If he senses I lied about my name, he doesn't show it.

"At the moment...well, like they say in show business, I'm between engagements."

I don't want the conversation to veer off into the work direction, but I am feeling very comfortable talking to this guy. I'm liking him, for all the right reasons, for a change—pleasant, normal, warm.

"I've got to tell you, Detective. I'm in this place more frequently than I care to say. And I could swear I've spoken to you here. Is that possible?"

Like a true philosophical NYPD detective, he says, "Anything is possible."

Ted stops by and asks, "Refresh your Johnnie Walker, Detective?"

"Two's my limit, Teddy. You know that. Hit me with a Diet Coke and I'll be happy."

"Another seltzer and lime, Emily?" Ted asks me. He's being way too smug now, knowing that I'm not about to fight him for an alcoholic beverage with my new friend Joel Tierney sitting beside me.

"Thanks, Ted. Only this time let me have *two* twists of lime. But only if you think I deserve them."

After Ted brings our drinks, Joel says to me with a smile, "I thought your name was Emily?"

I stammer for a moment, then say, "It is. Sorry. I don't know why I told you it was Amy. I got nervous, I guess. To be honest, I've been feeling nervous a lot lately. Scared, too." I don't tell him about the maniac who screamed and pounded on my door earlier tonight. But I do start to say, "And this whole Nina Powell story…"

Just my luck.

It turns out that my new detective friend knows a thing or two about the Nina Powell missing persons case.

Joel tells me that not all the pertinent info has been released to the media. But he releases it to *me* when I explain to him that the case has me scared as hell.

"The latest theory Missing Persons is working

with is, there might some connection between the Powell woman and at least one of the Bronx organized crime groups," he says.

I pretend that I know precisely what "one of the Bronx organized crime groups" means. As if all my knowledge hadn't come from binge viewings of *The Sopranos.*·

I ask him if he thinks they're going to find the woman.

He answers with a shrug. The shrug seems sincere. The shrug seems like both the correct answer and the honest answer.

I mention again how frightened I am feeling these days. I tell him that occasionally the lobby in my building is left unattended. He tells me that I should have my attorney call the co-op board to register a complaint.

"Attorneys always get a co-op board's attention," he adds.

I tell him that I'm suddenly paranoid that an intruder might climb up my fire escape and break in through one of my windows. He tells me that I should ask the super to install burglar-proof steel struts and braces.

"So now I need to tell *you* something," I say. Then I hesitate.

He doesn't urge me to speak.

Then I say—with a tiny sheepish smile—"I'm pregnant."

All hearty and happy he says, "Well, good for you."

"Thanks," I say.

Still semi-joyful he says, "You know, I was sort of suspecting. Who's the lucky father?"

I explain quickly that there is none.

He says, "I see, a miracle baby."

"No," I say. "The father's not around."

"But your friends are around. And I'm your newest friend."

I share with him one more time how frightened I am these days. I tell him that I don't think the locks on my service entrance door are secure enough.

With a flirtatious raise of one eyebrow, he tells me that he'd be willing to come by right now and take a look.

CHAPTER

52

A TALL, GOOD-LOOKING DETECTIVE goes to the apartment of a woman whom he's just met. He's visiting to check the locks.

Okay. I know. I know. I'm not *that* naïve. It sounds like the beginning of a porn flick. I never understood the appeal of porn, but my housemate at Princeton, Quinn Church, was a connoisseur (code word for *addict*). What's more, I think I really believed that the lock agreement between Tierney and me was innocent. I don't think I was looking for anything more.

Okay. Who am I kidding?

I'm not sure that it's only sex that I'm hoping

for, although I can't dismiss that motive from my mind at all. But talking to Joel Tierney back at Ted's, I felt safe with him. I felt at peace with him. I thought that here was a guy who doesn't seem to mind that I'm pregnant or a recovering alcoholic or, I've got to admit it, someone who comes across as just a little bit eccentric (code word for *crazy*).

Tierney doesn't even try the knob or lock on the back service entrance. He just bends down toward the door, examines the lock for two seconds and says, "You've got a Kwikset 991 here. You can't get a better lock unless you know someone in US Army supply acquisition. You're okay. Safe at home."

"I'm just a lucky girl," I say.

"No, I'm a lucky guy."

And now it's that time. Okay, I've been here before, but each time feels new. A little bit of experience mixed with quite a bit of instinctive improv.

Joel looks at me, the tiniest curl to his lips, almost a smile, just a millimeter away from a smirk. The man keeps his eyes steady. Eyelids don't blink; he knows they're not blinking. This is when a woman tries to figure out the future of the night. Am I standing here with a good guy—a not-too-rough, not-too-gentle man who's looking for fun, for both himself and for me? Or am I about to encounter what we used to call a sex slob, a guy who's only interested in pouncing and running hard to his own finish line? Yes, there are slight variations on both these types, but these are the two general divisions—nice guy or asshole.

I am happy to announce that Joel Tierney turns out to belong to the former group.

Now, in my NYPD-approved safe apartment, he moves behind me and brings his lips to the side of my neck. He slips his arms over my shoulders and cups my breasts in his hands. Yeah, I know, a very traditional move, but it's a move I haven't experienced in quite a while.

He whispers, "I gotta tell you. I love pregnant women."

"What a great coincidence," I say. Then I add, "You should hang outside of places where they give natural childbirth courses."

"It's crossed my mind," he says.

"Ewww. Creepy," I say. But he knows I don't mean it. Tierney seems anything but creepy. The vibe here is *tender but likes action*.

We move to the bedroom, and it is there, as we begin tugging gently at each other's clothing, that I realize something: Not only has it been a while since I've made love, but it's been a while since I've made love *sober*. I'm not frightened, but I am, well, curious. The style. The pattern. The movement.

Tierney is just short of—I'll put it this way—athletic in bed. He certainly isn't a careless, selfish lover, but he also doesn't hold back.

Eventually we arrive at the point that's built up a little bit of anxiety inside me.

"I'm afraid for Oscar," I say.

Pause.

"Who's that?" he says.

"That's what I call the baby inside me."

He smiles.

"I told you, Emily. I've done this more than a few times with moms-to-be. It's not difficult... not at all. Do you want to get on top?"

"Whatever you think," I say.

"No, ma'am, whatever *you* think. Tell you what. We can try one or two different things."

"Sounds perfect," I say. He gently positions me on my back, and then it appears that he's going to lie on top of me.

"What about Oscar?" I say.

"He'll be fine."

Joel Tierney places his hands flat on the bed. His hands are very close to my shoulders. He extends his arms up and out. He looks like a guy who's about to do push-ups. And this is almost precisely what he does. Slow, careful, loving push-ups.

There is no need for us to try anything else.

CHAPTER

53

The Present

SOMETIMES—EVEN IF JUST FOR a fraction of a second—Betsey thinks that the bulge in her belly is not really the vibrant, healthy, growing fetus she is carrying, but a huge roiling accumulation of the anxiety and terror she is feeling for her missing friend, for the charming, crazy, lovely, crazy, beautiful, crazy Emily.

"I'm no doctor," says Betsey's husband, Frankie, "but always worrying like this, not sleeping, skipping meals—it can't be good for the baby."

"Well, I'll agree with the first part of what you said, Frankie. *You're no doctor.*"

He holds her close, but the gesture fails to calm her.

Then she pulls away from him and says what she's already said a dozen times. "The cops are not doing all that they can. It shouldn't be that hard."

But Betsey knows that she's kidding herself. She knows that people like Emily disappear from New York every day. Yeah, sometimes they end up on the beach at Coney Island or a cousin's house a block away. But so many of them are never heard from again. Wasn't there a story a few months ago about another thirtysomething woman in Emily's neighborhood who went missing and still hasn't been found? Nelly something? Nora? Nina? Betsey can't remember. But it makes her mad anyway.

Betsey continues, "Honestly, Frank, I know he's an old friend, but I don't like the way the detective assigned to her case is handling it. I kind of think his partner is a bitch, too."

Frankie quickly squints his eyes and opens them. His reaction to his wife's comment is one of genuine surprise.

"Bets, whoa. This isn't you, babe. Name-calling, nasty. Try to cool it all down."

"I can't!" she yells.

Betsey begins to sob. This time, the trip to Frankie's arms soothes her a bit.

She thinks of all she's done herself, all of it alone. The trips to see Emily's old boyfriends. Hanging out at Ted's bar. Talking to lowlife scum like Mike Miller. She's become a semi-expert on internet investigation. The Renwick Hospital security team even managed to get her a contact at the FBI.

But everything has come up cold. Like everything else she's tried. Like everyone else she's called.

Like...everyone except the one person she *hasn't* talked to yet.

But what the hell. Yeah, what the hell. This is as big an emergency as Betsey will ever have. She goes for it. And an hour later she's sitting in the consultation office of Dr. Jane Craven, Betsey's hospital colleague and, most important, Emily's ob-gyn.

Betsey knows what she's going to hear when she starts prodding the doctor: a lecture on confidentiality.

Unfortunately for Betsey, Dr. Craven does not disappoint.

"Everything about the doctor–patient relationship is confidential," says Dr. Craven. "Who knows that better than you?"

Betsey tries.

"But this is bigger than confidentiality or privacy or...this is Emily's life. This is an emergency."

"Don't try to turn me into some cold, hard, medical personnel asshole. Yes, of course this is an emergency. But I'm not about to spread information when it isn't going to help anything. The police are into it. Detectives have been by. I've had two discussions with the department chair about how to handle it."

Betsey looks down at her lap. Her shoulders shake. Jane Craven stands and quickly moves to kneel next to Betsey.

"Nurse Brown, please listen to me. Please believe me. You already know most of the information you want me to tell you. What I know you already know. What I know the police know. Emily was...is...a person who doesn't take great care of herself. She is trying to..."

Betsey nods. "She is. Emily is really trying." Betsey bites her lower lip as she shakes her head.

"I have no secret information. If I did, I'd let somebody know. Somehow, I'd let it out. But there are no names. No places. No X-rays. No nothing."

"It's just that I feel so goddamn helpless," says Betsey.

Dr. Craven nods. She speaks gently.

"Me, too, Nurse Brown. Me, too."

CHAPTER

54

BETSEY HAS BEEN HANGING around with doctors since she was in nursing school. They neither impress her nor intimidate her. But she does respect them. And right now, she understands that the meeting with Emily's doctor is over. No question about it.

Dr. Craven certainly did not deliver the home-run solution that Betsey had hoped for, yet Betsey feels that she is leaving the ob-gyn's office a little wiser.

She grabs some Kleenex from the box on the doctor's desk. She is somehow oddly pleased that Dr. Craven also takes a tissue for herself.

"I'm better. I'm okay. I'm sorry," says Betsey.

"Don't apologize. I really wish I knew something that could help."

A knock on the door, and the doctor's receptionist steps in and speaks.

"Two people to see you, Doctor."

"I'm about to leave for hospital rounds. Who is it?" asks Dr. Craven.

Quietly, almost shyly, the receptionist says, "Two NYPD detectives."

"They followed me. They followed me! I know it," Betsey says angrily.

Suddenly Kalisha Scofield and Joel Tierney come into the room.

The composure Betsey reached with Jane Craven completely disappears. "You tailed me, didn't you?" she says.

Kalisha gives Betsey the traditional *Are you a crazy lady or what?* look.

Joel Tierney speaks.

"Of course not," he says.

"Yeah," says Kalisha. "It's a coincidence. You know how they say New York City is really just another little town. Here's the proof."

The two detectives introduce themselves to Dr. Craven.

Betsey Brown is not about to leave. She listens carefully as the detectives tell Dr. Craven that they want to ask her some questions about Emily Atkinson.

The doctor says, "I have work to do. We may have to make another appointment. You sort of jumped in on me, and anyway..."

Dr. Craven pauses and shares a glance with Betsey.

"...as I've told Nurse Brown here, I respect patient confidentiality implicitly."

"Solving Missing Persons cases is something the NYPD respects, too," says Kalisha. Her tone is not disrespectful, but it's also not friendly. In fact, she speaks with a nod and a slight smile.

"I'm sure," says Jane Craven. She gestures to the two chairs in front of her desk. Then she says, "Nurse Brown, you can take my chair. I'll stand."

"No problem," says Betsey. "I'm fine to stand."

"Is Emily a particularly difficult patient?" asks Tierney.

"Difficult?" asks the doctor.

"Uncooperative. Obstinate," Tierney offers.

Kalisha decides to help the situation along.

"We all know that the victim has problems with addiction," she says. "So we're asking…"

"I understand what you're asking," says the doctor.

Betsey is unexpectedly distressed by Detective Scofield's use of the term *victim*.

Then Dr. Craven speaks.

"Yes, Ms. Atkinson has some problems with alcohol and recreational drugs. But you both seem to be aware of that. You just said, 'We all know that the victim has problems with addiction.'"

Betsey is dismayed that Dr. Craven is going to be as uninformative with the detectives as she had been with her. For the police to solve this, they're going to need every piece of information related to Emily.

"We just want your opinion," says Tierney. "Your *educated* opinion."

"My opinion," says Dr. Craven, "'educated' or otherwise, is the same as yours regarding the patient's addictive personality. The fact remains that she is getting help. She is trying."

"She did go to AA meetings," says Betsey.

Kalisha answers quickly, "Thank you. We already knew that."

"Just trying to help," says Betsey.

Dr. Craven speaks. "I think it best that we get this interview over as quickly as possible."

CHAPTER

55

"I'm going to be perfectly frank. It would be enormously helpful if the NYPD knew who the father of Emily Atkinson's baby is. Can you help us with that, Doctor?"

"No. I cannot," says Dr. Craven.

"You cannot? Is that the same as 'You *will* not'?" asks Tierney.

"Whether I won't or whether I can't doesn't affect my answer. I'm not going to tell you."

"Doctor, we're not here to play some stupid verbal tennis game with you..."

Dr. Craven interrupts and says firmly, "All

right then. I do not know who the father of Emily Atkinson's baby is."

"Thank you," says Kalisha.

"Regarding your patient's health. Can you help us with that?" asks Tierney.

"Perhaps. What's the question?"

Tierney wants to remain calm. He closes his eyes momentarily, then proceeds.

"Is the pregnancy impacting Emily's overall health? How is the baby doing? We just spoke about her addiction problems. How is the mother herself doing?"

"I think she was pretty much cooperating. Her numbers were good the last time she visited."

"So, she is in pretty good shape?" asks Kalisha.

"I didn't say that," says Dr. Craven. "As indicated, Emily was frail, nervous. She may have had psychological problems. I think she could have a successful pregnancy, a successful birth. The ultrasound showed a growing fetus. But... but... it's not a great situation to be in..."

Betsey cannot keep herself from jumping in.

"Although women in far worse shape than Emily have given birth to healthy babies," Betsey says.

"I agree with Nurse Brown," says Dr. Craven. Then the doctor stands and asks, "Is this over?"

There is a silence. Jane Craven is being difficult, stubborn. Tierney and Kalisha are disdainful of the doctor and Betsey. *But the thing is... damn it*, thinks Betsey. *The thing is... that Emily—healthy or unhealthy, stable or not stable—is missing.*

"One more thing," says Tierney. "Has Emily... in all the drama surrounding her pregnancy... has she ever considered an abortion?"

Betsey makes a not-so-subtle face. The question strikes her as a little strange. Invasive. And completely unrelated to her friend's disappearance.

"You'd have to ask *her*," says Dr. Craven, obvious irritation in her voice. "But I would imagine it might have crossed her mind."

"Well, thank you for your help, Doctor," says Kalisha.

"I've got to get going," says Dr. Craven. She grabs a white medical coat, slips into it. Then she pulls a stethoscope from the coat pocket.

As soon as Dr. Craven leaves the room, Tierney looks at Betsey and says, "What do you think, Bets? Was Craven telling the truth?"

Betsey speaks slowly.

"I think she was telling the truth, her truth, what she believes is the truth, but the fact is..." A pause.

"The fact is...?" says Kalisha, prodding her on.

"The fact is...the fact is..."

Betsey hesitates. She's thinking about Tierney's last question to Dr. Craven. There must have been a reason he asked it, right?

She doesn't want to betray her friend's confidence. But then again, she doesn't want to withhold any information that might help the detectives find her.

"The fact is," Betsey says, "Emily actually, seriously did consider getting an abortion."

56

THE RECEPTION AREA AT Greystone Women's Health Complete Gynecology and Consultation is empty except for one very elegant receptionist seated behind a desk.

The receptionist is a stunning Chinese woman wearing a long red silk dress. Around her neck dangles a medium-sized diamond solitaire. The detectives might be standing before a dance instructor, a fashion designer.

Kalisha and Tierney show their badges.

"I'm Detective Tierney. This is Detective Scofield."

"I'm Margaret Lem, our lead patient coordinator and"—she spreads her arms to indicate

the empty space—"apparently backup receptionist."

From a speaker hidden within the blue-and-
white striped walls comes a cello version of
"Starman."

"We'd like to see whoever's in charge of this
clinic," says Kalisha. "According to your website, that would be Dr. Cynthia Darlow."

"I am sorry. Dr. Darlow isn't here at the
moment. In fact, only one of our nurses and I
are here. We have no procedures or consulta-
tions scheduled for today. Possibly I can be of
help?"

The sweet smile on the receptionist's face
seems to be immovable.

Tierney holds his phone screen for Margaret Lem to see. It shows a picture of Emily
Atkinson they'd pulled off her public LinkedIn
profile.

Lem's smile neither broadens nor narrows,
but she does speak excitedly.

"Her. Oh, of course, I remember her. It was
a while ago. She asked to be taken on immediately as a patient, but we... well, *I*... said no. We
couldn't do that. She had to fill out the proper
forms, have a consultation, the whole thing. But

really...of course, we've done emergency procedures before...But I knew I couldn't send her in
to Dr. Darlow immediately. The truth is...The
patient, you see, was lovely, very sweet, but...
drunk as a fiddler's sow."

"So she left?" asks Tierney.

"And we never heard from her again," says
Lem. Then she quickly corrects herself and
says, "Well, we heard from her in a way. I had
given the woman...Emily...an iPad for filling
out her application. I told her she could return
it when she came back. She never came back,
but a few days later a courier dropped it off. No
return number or address or anything."

"And the application?" Tierney asks.

"Nothing. She didn't fill it out."

Kalisha and Tierney leave their cards. They
request—with some urgency—that Dr. Darlow
get in touch with them. Margaret Lem says that
Dr. Darlow won't be able to tell them anything
more, but she promises to pass on the message.

Outside the office Tierney says, "Well, there
was no useful info there."

"Except that we know for sure now that
Emily Atkinson was considering getting an
abortion," says Detective Scofield. "Maybe

that's connected to her disappearance. Maybe not. But we did learn one other thing about Emily's behavior on that day."

A pause hangs in the air.

"I know what you're going to say," says Tierney. His voice is playful.

"You do? Then tell me. What am I going to say?"

Tierney smiles.

"Emily was drunk as a fiddler's sow."

CHAPTER

57

USELESS INTERVIEWS AND RELUCTANT witnesses and worry and fear and no sun in the sky on this bright sunny day.

Tierney and Kalisha arc no closer to a lead than they were a week ago.

As they walk quickly toward Ted's Bar, tired and dejected, Tierncy tells his partner what his first boss, an old and overweight lieutenant, sometimes told him when they were investigating drug cases.

"The lieutenant had this thing he made up for tagging a situation. We'd get to a certain point in the investigation and he'd say something like, 'Well, that sure as shit was EASY.'

Or 'We're walking down EASY street now.' Or 'Talk about EASY. Man, that was just too EASY.'

"For this guy, EASY stood for Everyone's A Suspect, Yep. EASY happened when you got too much information, too many opinions. Interviewees would tell you stuff but it never fit together. The only thing it did was confuse you. And you end up with every person you talked to as a suspect. Yeah. It could be the girlfriend or the cab driver or the pimp or the dealer or the wife... EASY. That's what's happening to us right now."

Tierney was uncharacteristically worked up, just shy of angry. Kalisha was becoming a touch frightened. Tierney kept going.

"And that's where we are now. EASY. Look at it."

"I'm looking," says Kalisha. Then Tierney talks. Fast. Intense. He's vaguely aware that he is being propelled emotionally by the memory of *that* night with *that* pregnant woman. Damn it. He doesn't want to feel it. But, damn it, he does. And—one more *damn it*—he can work hard to get rid of that feeling. But he can't control it now. He rants on.

"Why the hell was Craven so snippy and bitchy? She wouldn't be the first MD who covered for a rich patient or a hospital error or thought the detectives were too stupid to understand medical info.

"And the woman at the abortion clinic. I'll tell you this. We're getting a CO tomorrow to go back there and examine their files, talk to former patients. That office looked like a place where you go to get your hair colored. This is serious shit. And she's not telling us anything. For all we know, Emily showed up there and ended up dying there! Okay, not likely, but not impossible."

Ted's Bar is now a mere block away. Tierney won't stop talking.

"Let's, for example, take a good look at Betsey. She's a gal I'd trust before I trust my mother. But what's the deal with her attitude? And, while I'm at it, what was the deal with that tension in there between her and you?"

Kalisha is about to explain her feelings. She has a few things she hasn't told her partner, but suddenly and wisely she decides to keep it all to herself. Tierney, she suspects, is on the edge of an explosion.

As he is just about to push open the entrance door to Ted's Bar, Tierney pauses. He looks at Kalisha and says, "And what about that fireman husband of Bets? What's his deal? Get him on our list. I want to talk to Frankie. The lieutenant was right. EASY. Everybody becomes a suspect, but there's no proof for anyone. Where's the lead? Where's the lead?"

They step into the bar, busy for a midafternoon.

"Hey!" shouts Ted from the other end of the bar. "My two favorite cops."

"Not cops. We're *detectives,* if you don't mind," says Tierney as they take their places at Ted's end of the bar. A joke? A laugh? Maybe.

"And what'll the two *detectives* have to drink?" asks Ted. "The usual?"

"Your memory continues to amaze us," says Kalisha.

"I thought you guys didn't drink when you're on duty."

"Hey, if you don't want the business, we can go elsewhere," says Kalisha, with a smile and a touch of anger.

Tierney clears the air. "Put your mind at ease, sir. We're not on duty right now."

"Coming right up," says Ted.

In less than fifteen seconds Ted sets down a Bass Ale for Kalisha and a Johnnie Walker with a splash of seltzer, not club soda, for Tierney.

As soon as Ted walks away from the pair, the detectives get back to business. Kalisha suggests that since this bar was Emily's favorite hangout, it might be a good idea to talk to some of the late-afternoon patrons. Tierney disagrees.

"C'mon. These folks are like us," he says. "They're here to relax, maybe get a soft buzz on."

"A soft buzz," Kalisha repeats. "That's a nice expression. That's exactly what a few drinks should do to you."

Ted is back.

"So, is there any news?" he asks.

Neither detective answers.

Ted clarifies his question. "You know what I'm asking. News about Emily."

"No," says Tierney.

"People here keep asking about her," says Ted. "She was a popular gal."

Kalisha hates the word *gal*.

"Popular?" asks Tierney.

"Yeah. Emily was fun. She was witty, pretty. Like I say, she was fun."

"Like you say...a popular gal," says Kalisha.

"Popular with everyone?" asks Tierney.

"Pretty much so. Okay, maybe a few people— including me—thought that when Emily got pregnant, she should have stopped drinking. Sometimes she wore me down and I caved and gave her what she wanted. One guy, some hedge funder asshole type, said I should stop serving her. He even threatened to report me to the New York State Liquor Authority. I told him that it was none of his...none of his..."

Ted turns away. He rubs his eyes. Then he turns back and faces the two detectives. He speaks.

"You know that I loved her," he says.

"We know that you slept with her," says Kalisha. There is something about Ted that Kalisha is feeling—a distance, a sense of deception. Tierney knows his partner well enough to know that Kalisha is not buying Ted's act.

"If you're thinking that I'm the dad, then you're thinking wrong," Ted says.

The two detectives say nothing. They're using the tried-and-usually-true system of waiting for the person to fill the silence with more information. Ted obliges.

"Sure. Emily and I slept together a few times. But by then she was already pregnant."

"How do you know?" asks Tierney

"Because she told me," says Ted.

"Oh, well, if she actually told you herself," says Kalisha, "Then I suppose it must be true."

Kalisha can barely hide the disgust on her face. She drains the rest of her beer in nearly one gulp, stands up, and walks out of the bar.

MONTHS SIX AND SEVEN

CHAPTER

58

SINCE MY PREGNANCY BEGAN, I've made all sorts of discoveries about myself. Maybe *re*discoveries is more accurate.

I've rediscovered how much I enjoy a quiet night at home in front of the TV.

I've rediscovered how hard it is for me to sleep when I'm not passed-out drunk.

But most of all, I've rediscovered my love of running.

That jog around the Central Park Reservoir with Betsey was the first time I'd laced up my sneakers in quite some time. Since then, I've kept it up. I've been logging at least a few miles every couple of days.

But that's nothing compared to how much I ran when I was younger.

When I was ten years old, my mother created a new favorite sentence: "If you don't watch what you eat, you'll have the same big butt that your Aunt Dolly has."

She must have used that sentence three hundred times until I (and my potentially big butt) left for boarding school three years later, and Princeton four years after that.

The first time she said it I didn't argue. I didn't cry. I simply took a pair of sweatpants from my closet, slipped them on over my "big butt," and started pounding the pavement.

Since then, I've run exhausted. I've run hungover. Yes, I've even run drunk.

And now I'm running under a whole new set of circumstances. I am running while I'm pregnant.

I just hope I never have to run away—from the mysterious stranger who I know in my gut is out there. Watching me. Following me.

Dr. Craven says, "Exercise is fine. It's good for you if you don't overdo it."

"No chance of that," I tell her with a grin.

Today I begin at Joe Coffee in the East

Village, where I get a small decaf cappuccino with an extra shot. Then I jog gently uptown, turn left on 14th Street and pick up speed. Is it easy to run when you're six months pregnant? For me it's surprisingly easy. Sure, my sports bra is up two sizes. Yes, per Betsey's advice, I wear a stomach band just below where Oscar rests. But my knees are holding up. My hips feel strong. And, oh yeah, one other thing: a big shout-out to Alcoholics Anonymous.

Since my recent sobriety I am suffering from insomnia. I read great big books. I watch great episodes of streaming TV (I highly recommend *Schitt's Creek* and *The Stranger*). Sometimes I nod off, and sometimes, like today, I can't manage to fall asleep.

So I am out on the street by 6:00 a.m.

I'm hoping that my stalker, whoever the bastard is, is still fast asleep.

This turns out to be both the best time and worst time to use the sidewalks for running. Best because the streets are less crowded. Worst because the people who are out are tucked away in their own little oblivious world. Some finance-type man or woman, in love with their phone, might turn a corner and slam right into me. The truck drivers unloading hundreds of cardboard cartons of shampoo and Snickers bars into the basement storage area of Duane Reade will not break their rhythm, another possible head-on collision. Add to that the people who sleep on subway grates, the dog walkers and the occasional piles of dog shit, the sleepy hookers looking for one final client. A single pregnant woman has a lot to contend with. And most of the time I can do it quite nicely.

But today is not one of those days.

As I pass the TD Bank on 23rd Street and Seventh Avenue, three teenagers—two boys and one girl—step out of the ATM lobby. One of the boys is bleeding profusely from his mouth. The girl and the other boy appear to be completely stunned or stoned or sick. They are quickly followed out by another young man— older, bigger, angrier. I've been around. I easily spot a drug deal gone bad.

I collide with the presumed dealer. He reaches into his pants and pulls out the world's largest, sharpest screwdriver. I fall to the sidewalk and manage to scrape both my wrists so that they're raw and bleeding.

"It's okay, Oscar," I say, and I roll over to my

side to protect my baby from the surrounding chaos. The dealer isn't out to hurt me, at least not yet. I see him rush to the teenage boy, and he begins wildly banging the boy's head with the blunt end of the screwdriver. Two pedestrians cross the street quickly to avoid the chaos of the fight.

But the sight that troubles me most is now a man wearing a black sweatshirt covered by what I think is a black down vest. He seems to have nothing to do with the drug group.

I sense that he's interested in something else or someone else, and that someone is me.

I'm still on the ground. The man in black—who I don't recognize, who I'm not sure I've ever seen before in my life—is a few yards away. I am in a state of confusion. He is standing perfectly still. At first, I thought the man was bald, but now I see that he's wearing a light tan woolen cap. I have trouble distinguishing his facial features. He looks bland. If he were a drawing, he would be drawn with short simple strokes.

The man occasionally glances at the drug people, but his eyes always look back toward me.

I lose interest in the teenagers and their

attacker. Instead I stand up (thankfully, with surprising ease). I rub my bloody wrists against the faded orange letters of my Princeton Crew T-shirt. Then I take off running as only a pregnant obsessive runner can.

As I travel uptown on Seventh Avenue, I frequently glance behind me, and—out of focus—I see the man in black is rushing to keep up with me. He is no slouch. He can catch up to me. Shit.

I reach the Dunkin' on 27th Street. It's open. I glance through the window. No customers waiting for donuts. I rush inside and run behind the counter. Then I go into the back room. The older woman behind the counter screams, "What's the matter?" I instinctively realize that she thinks I'm about to give birth among the bags of ground coffee and blueberry donuts stacked in the back room.

I see a rear door. I take it. I'm no better off than I was when I entered. I'm merely in a small alley behind the building.

The man in the black shirt and black vest is there waiting for me.

I turn right and run toward Sixth Avenue. I try to hold my belly steady. I don't want Oscar bouncing around during my crazy flight. I head down Sixth Avenue. Yes, the man in black is still following me, but he's not gaining on me. Now I think that his slowness might be a tactic. He's preserving his energy, waiting for me to lose mine.

At Union Square I consider hopping on the subway, but if I'm trapped in a subway car...I turn right on 17th Street.

Then I see an open door, the entrance to a very hip store that specializes in china and glassware. Surprisingly, they're open at this early hour. Clearly, I'm about to cause a disaster. I run inside, and miraculously I manage to avoid knocking over anything. The problem— other than two hip people shouting "What the fuck?" over and over—is that I see no way out except by using the same door I entered through. No choice. I go for it, and the guy in black is not there.

I keep moving west on 17th Street. Now I'm headed toward the Meatpacking District. Here the streets are wide and deserted. They are mostly cobblestone, awful for running.

"Stop running. Are you crazy? You're pregnant," a woman walking two dogs shouts at me. My wrists are still dripping bits of blood. I head past the Standard, the hotel on the High Line. Taxicabs are lined up. I run toward the very nearby Hudson River.

Lots of runners are on the path above the West Side Highway. I do not see the man in black. I'm not sure I ever saw him.

I slow down to a simple jog. I head downtown.

Yes, I'm safe.

For now. It's happened before. It most certainly will happen again.

CHAPTER

59

OF COURSE I KNEW about childbirth. But barely. Why would I?

Because I never planned on being pregnant, I'd never really thought much about how a woman gave birth. Sure. I had a few friends and a second cousin who had taken the Lamaze classes or had done natural childbirth. And not to be disrespectful to these women, when they described the event it just sounded like a great deal of counting and breathing and, in some cases, a lot of screaming and swearing. But, as you can imagine, my colleague-in-pregnancy, Betsey Brown, is a huge fan of the childbirth classes, and she was absolutely insistent that I go with her and Frankie to a Lamaze class.

While we wait for the class to start, she talks about her enthusiasm for natural childbirth. "Bobby and Juliet were a natural birth," she said, and the delivery was easy and joyful."

"Joyful, Bets? C'mon."

"Yes, joyful, Emily."

"So why are you going back to a bunch of Lamaze classes for this baby?" I asked.

"I think of it as a refresher course," she said. "Say you took Spanish in high school, and five years later you were going to Madrid and..."

"I get it," I said. "I don't need the metaphor to understand."

I told Betsey that my mother told me that she absolutely preferred a C-section to natural childbirth. I gave Betsey my mother's direct quote: "With a C-section, you go in like a lady."

Betsey laughed.

In any event, Betsey was not going to let me get away with a request to "bring on the painkillers and let's get this over with." No way, and that's why I'm sitting in the small and seedy-looking living room floor of an apartment on West 114th Street with four other couples that include Betsey and Frankie, of course, and a central-casting cross-section of New York City: Chrissie and Nicky, she's a beautiful investigative journalist, he's a beautiful ad guy; Chloe and Aaron, she's a former actress who works production on a TV show, and he narrates audiobooks; Eleanor and Lucy, Eleanor is the pregnant one.

Oh, and let me describe the one other person. This gal will be sharing Betsey's husband, Frankie, as a coach. This gal is a single mother-to-be; I heard she's a recovering alcoholic and drug user, well-off financially but a real mess emotionally, Ivy League grad but recently quit her last job and fired from the one before, totally paranoid about being followed by a man whom she hasn't really seen or identified, a person who... Oh, shit. Grow up, Emily. Get it together. This birth thing isn't all about you. It's all about Oscar.

"I wouldn't want to have lunch with any of these people," I say softly to Frankie.

He chuckles, but Betsey overheard me.

"We're not here to make friends," she whispers. "We're here because Lois Messenger is the best Lamaze teacher in Manhattan."

I think that she may also be the oldest Lamaze teacher in Manhattan. Short and chunky with a singularly unfriendly face. The last time I saw a face so stern was on my prep-school girls' lacrosse coach. ("Ten laps around the track, ladies, *or* when you throw up. Whichever comes first.")

The only thing I say to Betsey is, "Not to worry. I'm going to be the perfect student."

Betsey smiles and rolls her eyes. But I honestly mean it. If not now, when?

I think I've got my booze problems straightened out. I haven't swallowed a Xanax or an Ambien or even an Aleve in months. I'm clean and, goddamnit, I'm going to do this Lamaze class right.

Lois Messenger distributes a huge rubber ball to each of us. In some cases, the balls look as big as the pregnant women, women who are resting and pushing and leaning against the monster balls. Lois says that the balls are for relief of back pain and leg pain and tension in general. And, of course, with my usual bad attitude I think at first that the balls are stupid. Within a minute of using my gigantic yellow ball I decide that I want to take it home. The balls are not merely fun, but they do alleviate back pain, and this accomplishment alone brings a chorus of *ooh*s and *aah*s of relief from the women.

I listen carefully to how to discern between false labor (when the hospital sends you back home) and real labor (when they tell you that the miracle is beginning). I am, of course, certain that I will experience false labor and be sent back home in humiliation.

Betsey says that I'm crazy. "You'll know when it's happening, Em. Just remember five-one-one. Contractions come every *five* minutes, they last for *one* minute each, and they go on for *one* hour, then you're..."

Betsey is an expert. This same five-one-one rule will be mentioned later by Lois Messenger. Right now it feels like I care so much that I'll panic and something will go wrong. After all this alcohol recovery, after all this good luck, it could all turn sour.

"Okay, pregnant women on the floor!" shouts Lois.

And we are, on our backs, a living room landscape of five human haystacks. The men, and Lucy, kneel at the women's heads.

"Is everybody ready?" asks the teacher sternly. She doesn't wait for the group to answer. "Of course you're ready. You're pregnant. You can't *not* be ready."

The class goes on—a constant flurry of questions, concerns, and slightly upsetting phrases like *mucus plug*. By the time it ends we are all good pals, like a jury that's spent a long time in the jury room deciding a very tough criminal case. One pregnant woman even whips out her calendar to begin finding a mutually good date four months from now for "our reunion picnic in Central Park."

I am, as I've come to expect, a bundle of love and a bundle of nerves. I am delighted that I am with Betsey and Frankie. When the class ends, I am delighted that I am feeling so well. We gather up our leather bags and sweaters and sweatshirts.

"Look at Chrissie," Betsey says. "That silk coat must have cost a thousand bucks."

"Yeah," I say. "That silk coat is actually called a duster. I have a red print one that I got in Cambodia. It's…" Then I stop talking. I am watching the woman's handsome partner. He is slipping on and zipping up a black down vest.

Although I'm not certain, I think it looks exactly like the vest that was worn by the man following me when I was jogging. He has a cloth hat, a ski-cap sort of beanie. It's white, but it could be a really light tan. It could be.

"Emily," says Frankie. "You spaced out. You were going to say something about the coat you got in Cambodia?"

"Sorry," I say. "I'm tired. I'm not myself." Then, as a little joke, I say, "Thankfully."

"You're doing great," Betsey says.

"I'm just so nervous, scared. For me it's all about Oscar," I say, and of course I pat my belly.

"Look, this is my third baby, and I'm scared," says Betsey.

"She's telling the truth," adds Frankie. "For this third-time mommy it's all about Amy."

Frankie's comment snaps me out of my hazy, crazy mood.

"Amy. You're going to call her Amy?" I say.

"Well, I think we'll start with Amelia. Then we'll shorten it. Amy. Yes, Amy." She smiles. Her eyes sparkle. Her cheeks rise. She looks downright joyful.

You know you have a true friend, a friend you love, when you're happy just because your friend is happy.

We are out on 114th Street. We walk to Riverside Drive. Frankie hails a cab.

All is well. I hope.

CHAPTER

60

THE DRESS MADE ME do it.

I saw the navy-blue, empire-waist silk dress with the tiny white polka dots hanging in my closet. Until then I had no plan to do something super-dramatic.

But the dress, there it was. Perfect. Beautiful. The dress made *me* feel perfect and beautiful. When I first started showing, as they say, my wardrobe consisted of stretch-waist jeans and one pair of stretch-waist black cotton slacks.

But today my eye caught the blue silk, and it unleashed something very powerful inside of me. The thought of wearing it inspired me. That dress made me want to inform the father of my baby that he was indeed the father of my baby.

Emily, the time is now. Emily, you're going to take control.

This will require the total hair and makeup procedure: facial cleanser, toner, moisturizer, eye cream. Foundation, blush, mascara, and eyeliner. Wash hair, blow dry hair, wet hair, blow dry again. Shoes? Should a pregnant woman risk wearing medium-high Louboutin black patent-leather pumps? This pregnant woman certainly will.

Twenty minutes later these black patent leathers are stepping off the elevator at Dazzle, the marketing firm where I was once a superstar... until I got kicked out. I've never been stronger. Okay, that's not saying much, but I'm feeling a helluva lot better than the last time I was here.

Marty Fontana, Dazzle's in-house photo retoucher, is waiting for an elevator as I step out.

"My eyes must be deceiving me. Do I see the divine Miss A?" he screams.

"Back from the dead," I say. I kiss Marty on the cheek and walk the cement driveway that will bring me straight to Keith Hennessey's office.

Plenty of shouts of *Look who's back* and *Welcome home.*

The door to Keith's office is closed. But that doesn't matter to me. One of Keith's assistants, Charlie Bennett, and I have been pals since he started. So I say, "Don't even bother with the 'he's on the phone' or 'he's in a meeting' routine. I'm going in."

And I do.

Now, of course, the question is: How will Keith greet me?

Will he act like a jerk? Will he throw a stapler at me? Will he call security?

Astonishingly, he's super-nice to me.

Keith stands and shouts, "Emily, you're back!" As he rushes around his desk to hug me, I think for a split second that maybe being fired was all a dream, a sort of nightmare where this shithead of a guy and I had great business success and a great romantic (well, okay, sexual) fling together, and I was never really fired. The last seven or eight months of my life didn't really take place.

"Let's look at the mother-to-be, and yes…" he says. "The legends are right: A beautiful woman can be even more beautiful when she's pregnant. You're glowing. You're radiant. You're..."

"Put a lid on it, Keith," I say. "I don't know what your plan is, but I am absolutely certain that you are not that happy to see me."

Quite suddenly his mood changes. The smile leaves his face. He turns serious.

"What's up? You need to talk?" he says. Not nasty, just his version of sincere.

"I've got about a month and a half left to talk. That's when I'm having my baby."

He gestures to the black leather couch. We sit at opposite ends. I am determined to look graceful. So I sit gently, cross my legs (a bit of an effort).

"Aren't those Louboutins tough on your feet?" he says. Only Keith would notice my brand of shoes.

"I manage," I say. "In fact, I've been managing. Quite well."

"Yeah?" he says. And I can tell he knows way more than I would like him to know.

"Yeah," I say, as firmly as I can muster.

"Well, I have heard that you're off the sauce," he says.

"Are you having me followed?" I say.

"No, but just because they call it Alcoholics Anonymous doesn't mean that it's always anonymous. I've got other pals who go to meetings. And let's be honest. You are pretty well known in this town."

I say nothing. I consider leaving. But I'm here for a reason. A very, very, very important reason.

Keith moves closer to me. He takes my hand. He looks piercingly sincere.

"Congratulations on getting sober," he says.

Instead of thanking him, I say, "Listen, there's something we need to talk about."

"Yes," he says. "There is something important."

Then, without pausing, he says, "I need you to come back here. How about I crawl on my hands and knees and beg and plead?"

"How about you just stop acting so strange? Humble is not your strong suit," I say, just short of a shout. I'm confused and angry, maybe actually more confused. I stand, and I do it without holding on to the shoulder of the couch.

"Emily, look. I made a mistake. The place, the work, the people—they're just not the same without you. I've been trying to get up the courage to call you. Ask your old assistant David how many times I've discussed you with him."

"Not only do I not believe you, but even if I did believe you, I'm not interested in you or Dazzle or my stupid job. That's my life from yesterday. I'm here to discuss today. I'm here to discuss *this*."

I point to my stomach, to my Oscar. Yes, I am being outrageously melodramatic, but I honestly think the situation warrants it. Initially Keith looks puzzled.

"Yeah? Your baby?"

"Listen, Keith. When my baby was conceived you and I were seeing each other," I say.

As I expected, he laughs, a sneer in his voice.

"*Seeing* one another?" he says. "You mean when we were having sex on this couch every day?"

"Do the math, mister. My calendar says that those two weeks straight coincide with my becoming pregnant."

Keith laughs. It's not quite the infuriating laughter of a movie villain, but it is still filled with disdain and disgust.

"You've got the wrong baby daddy, Emily.

Really wrong. We could have had sex twenty times a day, and I still couldn't be the father. I had prostate cancer three years ago, and had my prostate removed. You remember that week I was supposed to be at tennis camp in Tucson? I was at the Cleveland Men's Clinic having a prostatectomy."

"I don't believe you!" I cannot say it loud enough.

His response is simple. "If you want a DNA test, I'm up for it."

Suddenly I do believe him.

Then he says, "I'm sort of sorry it isn't me, Emily. But I'm just a cowboy who only shoots blanks."

CHAPTER

61

WELL, THAT CERTAINLY SUCKED.

My conversation with Keith plays over and over in my head as I walk from the Dazzle offices back to my apartment.

The tipping point for me was Keith's offer to take a DNA test after the baby is born. I should take the sunuvabitch up on that offer. On the other hand, Keith would never have offered to do a DNA paternity test if he wasn't sure of the outcome. The whole event would be a waste of a perfectly good cotton swab.

It's midafternoon, and Madison Avenue is packed with people. They look like they're all in a cartoon race-walking contest. Tourists walk three across, disrupting the flowing, snaking paths of other pedestrians. Scaffolding seems to be erected on every other building. I think, just for a moment, *Shit. I don't care if a chunk of cement falls on my head.* Then I say, "Oh, my God. Sorry, Oscar." I don't care who hears me.

Daytime always scares me more than nighttime. I know that's crazy, counterintuitive. But a nighttime walk has smaller packs of people. The safety of streetlights is everywhere. At nighttime you're ready for a problem, so you don't walk down certain side streets. Nighttime is filled with delivery people and garbage trucks and taxis. Nighttime is good.

Daytime breeds many more bad opportunities. Daytime is packed, loaded with people. Smaller groups of humanity push and slither through larger groups. If someone grabs your purse or shoves you to the ground, you are barely noticed in the bustle of the sidewalk. Try outsmarting a taxi driver as you try to cross a street corner. They'd just as soon run you over, and I've seen that happen at least three times.

I am walking down Fifth Avenue, and I am as frightened as if I were walking through the back alleys of Baghdad. I come to La Perla.

Since I'm not in the market for a two-hundred-dollar lace thong, I pass by. A few blocks later, I come to Kwiat, the jewelry store where all the salespeople knew my mother by her first name. Since I am also not in the market for emerald earrings (my mother had a collection, as I recall) I plan to keep walking. But a man who might have been window-shopping at Kwiat suddenly turns toward me, his left shoulder missing my left shoulder by a mere inch or two.

"Pardon me, Em." Then he's gone. It takes about two seconds.

I swear I heard him say, "Pardon me, Em."

Em? I don't know this guy. I may not even have seen him clearly. I think he might have had a beard. But I don't know. I'm walking. I'm walking faster. I could not describe his clothing for you. Fancy duds? Jeans and a T-shirt? I keep walking, and my ankles are hurting, and I think I can feel Oscar bouncing. But I'm not sure. Why the hell am I unable to process sights and feelings and sounds? Please, as always, I need a bathroom.

Fifty-Ninth Street. I'm standing outside Sherry-Lehmann, the fanciest wine store in New York City.

Great. A place that sells booze.

I stand and stare at a bottle of Puligny-Montrachet as if that bottle were a Matisse hanging in a museum. Then I hear it again.

"Pardon me, Emily."

What the hell?

I look around. There's no one there. The voice seems to have just exploded randomly from out of a crowd, a bunch of people who happen to be outside Sherry-Lehmann at the same time as one another, at the same time as me. But they keep on walking, moving. And I'm still standing in front of the wine display. Then I turn uptown. So many faces. One man with a dark-brown beard that covers the entire lower half of his face. Another man, another beard, a hipster type, carefully groomed. His is a well-shaped rust-colored beard. It covers only his chin. Both men disappear as they walk quickly downtown. I wait a few minutes, examining the Italian reds and the pyramid of New Zealand Syrahs. Then I walk a few more blocks.

I wait for a green light at one of New York City's big crosstown streets, 57th. The light changes. The people move across the street like one big pack of wolves. When I look to my right, I see the man with the dark beard. He does not look at me. Yet how could he be only this far? After all, he began walking at least five minutes before I started walking.

I pick up speed, and the bearded man falls behind me.

An upscale luggage store.

A chocolate store.

A men's shoe store. A children's barber shop.

I look behind me, and I think I see the bearded man. But maybe I don't, and so what, the city is filled with bearded men. Doesn't everybody have a beard today? But I am frightened and sweaty. The logical question arises: Am I crazy?

I know that a drink would help. A bourbon Teddy spritz. Ted invented it. It's Wild Turkey bourbon with a splash of ginger ale, a shot of maple syrup, then club soda to the top of the glass. Divine refreshment with a tiny bit of buzz. I could head west and end up at the Sherry-Netherland or the Pierre. They both have beautiful bars.

Instead I decide to lose my stalker. I turn around and now head back downtown. I wait again for a green light at 57th Street. I cross. I am near 58th Street. I stop to look in a store window at beautiful, heavy Lalique crystal, like diamonds that have exploded into vases and glasses. I stare through the window into the Lalique showroom. I see a man on the other side of the window display. He is looking at a crystal pitcher shaped like a daisy.

At first, I think it is just another stranger. I look again. Then I think that I know him.

It might be Mike Miller. No, it must be Mike Miller. Wait a minute, Emily. No. Yes. Best guess. It could be Mike Miller.

And if it really is Mike Miller, then Mike has been growing a beard.

CHAPTER

62

I SHOULD NOT EAT so much ice cream, but I do. I should go to Oh Baby! pregnancy exercise classes, but I don't. I should never ever be sitting on a barstool at Ted's, but I am.

It's the late afternoon crowd, and because I've often been one of those late afternoon drinkers, I know them well: the folks who just couldn't stop at the third vodka Collins and so they decided not to go back to work. They're the folks who want to get an early start on their nighttime journey into whiskey oblivion. And, of course, some of them are the normal people, the people who can hold their liquor, the people who decided to stop by for a friendly little

Jack-and-ginger or white wine spritzer. One drink, maybe two. Never more.

I'm none of those people, and as I see Ted walking toward the far-end spot where I'm sitting, it's easy to tell that he's up for an argument. He's got that look that says, *I'm not serving any pregnant women, and if you need proof, read the sign on the wall that says I'm prohibited from doing so by state law.*

Then he smiles. He surprises me.

"Okay, Emily. Here's the deal: one drink, very weak, and then I'm closing you down."

Now it's my turn to surprise him.

"How about I stick to a glass of club soda with an orange juice chaser. But only if the orange juice is fresh squeezed."

"That's my girl," he says when he brings me my order. "That AA thing is doing the trick."

I hold the OJ vessel high and toast.

"To Oscar," I say.

"To Oscar," Ted repeats, then adds, "Whoever the hell he is."

I don't feel like explaining the Oscar-baby-thing to Ted. And I suddenly realize that I don't feel like being at a bar. No, it's not the temptation of alcohol (that will never disappear). It's just that I want to be home in my apartment. I have a craving for a big dish of strawberry Häagen-Dazs and a nap with Niall Horan doing "Put a Little Love on Me." (I'm not embarrassed to say that I'm addicted to the guy.)

I put a twenty-dollar bill on the bar, and then Ted and I segue into a routine we've done perhaps a thousand times.

"Your money is no good here," he says.

Now it's my turn, my line.

"Drop it in the basket when you go to church this Sunday. Tell the priest it's from me."

"He'll never believe me."

Ten minutes later my doorman is opening the door of my Uber, and I cannot wait to hear Niall strumming and singing and soothing my aching head.

I step into my apartment.

Then the unraveling begins. It starts small. It stays small. But it is creepy as hell.

I walk into the living room. Immediately on my right is the baby grand Steinway. It's a beautiful off-white color. I haven't played the piano since I was a child. But it is the perfect location for a few silver-framed photos: one of me and Aunt Dolly riding one long-ago winter down in

Wellington. One of me and Betsey's children, Juliet and Bobby, at an Italian street festival in Brooklyn. Two photographs of my mother and father, one in Palm Beach, the other in Palm Springs. "We love the palms," my mother used to say, thinking that it was a clever line.

I glance at the piano, and I see that the long-stemmed yellow tulips, the ones that were delivered only yesterday, are seriously drooping. I step closer to examine the near-dead flowers, and I notice—it would be impossible not to notice—that, close by, the two photographs of my parents are lying facedown on the piano.

I leave the tulips for later and walk through the living room to the hallway that leads to the kitchen and maid's room, the room that I transformed into a spectacular little nursery for Oscar. The huge framed Art Nouveau Cinzano poster is missing from the hallway wall. Once again, I can't help but notice its absence. I walk quickly into the big kitchen, and I see that someone has leaned the poster—all five-feet-by-three-feet of it—against the refrigerator.

I'm not quite sure what I'm feeling. More than confused. A little bit afraid.

I buzz down to the doorman.

"Have there been any deliveries to my apartment, Leon? Has anyone been let in?"

"No, ma'am. Not that I know of. It would be in the logbook. Let me see."

After no more than thirty seconds, the expected answer, "No, ma'am."

I walk into my bedroom. I don't remember leaving my underwear drawer open, but it is. Maybe I did leave it...but...I used to be able to sleep with the light on when I was passed out from drinking, but now I can't sleep with the light on. So why is my bed table lamp still lit? And why is the photo of my parents—the one where they're watching a football guy from a special viewing box with George and Barbara Bush—also turned facedown? And...and am I going crazy? And why...why have I never noticed that all the photos I have of my parents have something missing from them? Me.

I'm not crazy, damnit. I'm not. But I may become crazy once I take the few steps into the nursery, the room that's waiting for my baby.

I walk in, squinting my eyes as tightly as a five-year-old child about to cannonball into an icy swimming pool. When I open my eyes, the room looks...perfect. I scurry about, touching surfaces, checking the drawers, the mobile hanging over the crib. I sit on the little yellow bench. I sit among my newest friends—the stuffed animals. A rabbit, a SpongeBob, a Raggedy Ann, a Raggedy Andy, a tiger, a bear, a kangaroo.

I sit peacefully and look around the room. Oscar's room. Clean and pure and safe. Yes, safe. Safety is everything.

I must keep Oscar safe by keeping myself safe.

CHAPTER

63

The Present

BETSEY BROWN HAS BEEN pregnant before. Twins, in fact. Nine months of carrying around what eventually turned out to be thirteen pounds of baby—Bobby and Juliet. It was a breeze, a cinch, a walk in the park. At least that's how she remembers it. She was still assisting at transplant surgeries in her eighth month. In her ninth month she even hosted her own baby shower (pigs-in-blankets, ten mushroom quiches, and a chocolate cake that Betsey herself made).

"I've really never felt better," she told her husband, her mother, her friends. "I guess I just have good, strong peasant blood in me. Made to be a mother."

That was then. Now it's an extremely different story.

More than once she's yelled out to her husband, "I just want to have this baby. I just want to get her out of me. Amy! Amy! Amy! Where are you?"

Frank wisely says nothing and simply holds his wife's hand.

The backaches are excruciating. The heartburn is so fiery that for the first time she understands why sometimes heartburn is mistaken for an actual heart attack. Betsey now finds herself experiencing Braxton Hicks contractions—sometimes for an hour at a time—and remembers from when she was pregnant with the twins the familiar, painful, stomach-pounding misery.

And, finally, there are the hemorrhoids, the disgusting, burning, itching, popping-out, untreatable, unbearable hemorrhoids. It's not funny. Goddamnit. Hemorrhoids are not funny!

But the fact is, in spite of the annoyances and aches of her ninth month, Betsey is totally drowning in worry about Emily's disappearance. And now that she's not working—two

weeks off before her due date is compulsory—
she is determined to do something about finding Emily. No one else seems to care.

She knows that she has become a significant
nuisance to Joel Tierney.

"You shouldn't call him every day, babe,"
Frankie tells her.

"I'll call him every hour if I want to!" she
snaps at her husband. Then she quickly adds,
"I'm sorry, Frank. It's the hormones." But she
knows it's not the hormones. It's Emily—in a
forest, in a hotel, in a morgue, in a...Lying on
the sofa (of course, on her side), Betsey reviews
her earlier conversations—Ted, Mike Miller,
Quinn Church. They were no help. Damn it
all, if the father is someone in Betsey's circle, it
could be any guy. Emily's boss, Keith. Emily's
assistant, David. Oh, shit, in a million-to-one
shot, it could be Frankie. No, that's ridiculous; she's ashamed to even think it. It could be
Joel Tierney. That's equally ridiculous. He and
Emily barely know each other. But Betsey simply cannot help herself. In her mind, she finds
every man in America a suspect. But then...
also in her mind, she finds each of those men
completely innocent.

With a big help from her forearms and wrists, Betsey sits up on the sofa and reaches for her phone. She goes to Contacts and finds the name and number of Quinn Church.

A woman answers Church's phone.

"Hello?"

"Hi. I'm looking for Quinn Church. My name is Betsey Brown."

"Betsey, oh, my God, hi! It's me. Miriam. We met up here a while ago when you came to visit."

Betsey certainly remembers the very pretty Miriam, the sort of secretary-assistant-lover. A serious, uncommunicative woman, as Betsey recalls. Now, on the phone, Miriam is all bubbly charm.

"Quinn's not here. He's on set. He never has his phone with him when he's working. He doesn't want to be distracted. And I'm not allowed to give out the production office number to anyone."

Miriam laughs as if there's something funny about such a self-important rule.

"Listen, this is really important," Betsey says.

"He's really strict about the phone number thing. He's writing and directing an episode of *The Law's Prayer*. You know that show, right?"

Know it? Betsey thinks that half of America

knows it and has seen it, a fast-moving story of a liberal-priest-turned-attorney who grapples with every crime from terrorism to pedophilia to corporate blackmail.

"Is he in LA?" Betsey asks.

"Are you kidding? You don't get that gritty old New York cinematography anywhere but in gritty old New York. Quinny is holed up in a studio somewhere in Queens."

Quinny? Miriam calls him Quinny?

As Miriam rattles on about how sorry she is that she cannot allow Betsey to interrupt him during this creative period, Betsey is already tapping the keys on her laptop. She goes to IMDb, then searches for *The Law's Prayer,* and within a few seconds discovers its production office is located at Buttercup Studios, 22-45 24th Street in Queens.

Betsey says good-bye to Miriam, all the time thinking, *Just how dumb does that woman think I am? This was certainly not a case for Sherlock Holmes.*

Then Betsey calls an Uber.

CHAPTER

64

BUTTERCUP STUDIOS WAS ONCE a giant bakery turning out cinnamon buns and blueberry muffins and sandwich bread. Now it's a giant television studio turning out game shows, documentaries, and police dramas that need lots of New York City locations. Glamorous nightclubs. Seedy saloons. Breathtaking skyscrapers. Quaint brownstones.

When Betsey tells the receptionist that she's here to see Mr. Church, the woman barely looks up from scrolling through Instagram. "Okay," she says. "Try the writers' room in the back. If he's not there, he's in his office. If he's not there, then I'm out of suggestions."

The first door Betsey comes to is partially opened. She reads the sign:

WRITERS' ROOM

STUDIO 7A

LAW'S PRAYER

Betsey stands at the door and peers in. It's the Big Room. The Big Room is a unique combination of office and rec room. Huge paper pads hang on the walls; all of the pads have writing on them. She reads one page; it's some kind of list:

PRECINCT HOUSE
Lt. Gavenport smoking weed
Smoke argue with Nancy
Can we say shithead???
Interruptive DA, with intro to new ADA
Cell phone annoying sound
Gavenport briefs group
(need dialogue, Quinn)
Veronika meets attacker (maybe)

Betsey, about to have a Vesuvius of a heartburn attack from an ill-advised breakfast burrito with extra hot sauce and jalapeños and onions, stands at the doorway. No one seems to notice this very pregnant stranger, but Betsey certainly is studying the people sitting around the big glass table.

Seven people with seven laptops. Four men. Three women. They are old and young and good-looking and ugly and thin and fat. No one is dressed for business, not the way Betsey imagines business wardrobe to be. A T-shirt with the words: MISS YOU FOREVER, KOBE. A skinny older man sucks on an unpacked, unlighted pipe. A chubby older man has ten empty Dannon yogurt cups lined up like toy soldiers on the conference table. One middle-aged woman in a pink wraparound dress that could have come from either Kmart or Prada is surveying the craft catering table, which is groaning under its weight of sliced fruit and cold cuts and deviled eggs and miniature tortilla breakfast sandwiches and miniature brownies and miniature bagels and miniature scones. Someone has attached a Post-it Note to a one-dollar bill and placed it near the miniature food. The Post-it Note says "miniature salary." An exceptionally handsome African American guy with that prep-school look (Shetland sweater, Levi's jeans, penny loafers) is typing fast and furiously on his laptop.

Yes, no one seems to notice Betsey, until she burps. Wait, it's more than a burp. It's a belch. She shoots her hand up and covers her mouth, and every man and woman in the writers' room shifts positions to look at her.

The guy in the Kobe T-shirt speaks first: "Obstetrics is just down the hall to your right."

Betsey is surprised to find herself laughing. Then she speaks.

"I was told that I could find Quinn Church here."

"You might, but I don't think he's here," says the woman in pink. With that cue some of the group begin to perform—one guy looks under the conference table, another looks inside a yogurt cup.

The woman in pink says, "Quinn's not here, but we had to make sure. Sometimes he's here and we just don't know it."

"He's probably in his cube," says one of the other men.

Another one clarifies. "*Cube* means *cubicle,* which in Quinn's case means *office.*"

"Yeah," says the pudgy guy with the yogurt-cup lineup. "Quinn's supposed to be roughing out two scenes, but I'm betting that he's talking to his financial adviser."

"Come on," says the handsome, preppy-looking guy, standing up. "I'll take you over to Quinn's place."

Betsey follows him down the hall to a cube marked CHURCH-YARD.

Her guide leans over the halfway and announces her.

"You've got a visitor, Quinn. And if I were you, I'd call the commissary and tell 'em to start boiling water."

Quinn stands up quickly.

"Betsey! What the hell are you doing here?"

"I need to talk to you, Quinn."

"Yeah, sure, of course, right, but how'd you know how to find me?"

"I'm a very clever person."

"Yeah, I'm sure you are, but even so . . ."

Betsey is so clever that she can sense that something isn't quite right about Quinn Church. Gone is the solemn, composed guy she spoke with at his Katonah estate. This Quinn is nervous. He talks fast. His face is glowing with perspiration, and globs of sweat stain the armpits of his blue Oxford-cloth shirt.

"We need to talk some more about Emily," says Betsey. But as she speaks, Quinn looks away—first upward, then down to the floor. There is a pause.

"Did you hear me, Quinn? We've got to talk." The pause continues. Then he looks directly at Betsey. Suddenly he is grinning.

"Did you find Emily? Did you find her, Betsey? God, I hope the answer is yes. I really do. You know, I had drinks...well, not drinks...coffee...well, not even coffee. I had coffee. Emily had herbal tea. She loves that Masala chai shit. She looked pretty good. She was a little scared..."

"Stop it, Quinn. Stop talking," says Betsey loudly.

He stops immediately. Betsey thinks his behavior is fueled by some sort of drug, most likely coke, possibly bennies.

"You're using, Quinn. Aren't you?"

"Just a little. I've got a lot to do. I don't know why I took this writing job. They don't need me. And I sure as shit don't need them. But I've got nothing else really. So I figure..."

"I've got to talk to you, Quinn," says Betsey.

He nods far too many times.

"I'm going to start with this. When you were with Betsey, was she doing drugs also?"

"No. Not at all. No, really. That's not her now. I mean, I don't think it is. She's pregnant, you know. Like you." He roars with laughter.

"Quinn, she's still missing. Do you understand? Do you even give a shit? We have to find her. If you know anything. If you know who the father of the baby is...If you are the father...if you know anything...you've got to help."

Quinn stares at Betsey. His arms and hands are shaking.

"All I know is what she told me when she was drinking her goddamn herbal tea. All I know is that she was in Las Vegas. *That* she told me. *We were best friends, you know.* It was around the time she got pregnant. She was with this guy. Anyway...she and this guy got married."

This information is dramatic, provocative, and useless to Betsey. What Betsey needs to know is not just that Emily went to Las Vegas, but who she went to Las Vegas with. Who did she marry? Whose union did she annul?

"Who did she marry, Quinn? Do you remember his name?"

Quinn is calmer now. He still trembles, but Betsey thinks that he is settling down. He speaks softly.

"No. And it really broke my heart," he says.

And all at once Betsey is sure that it did break Quinn's heart. She remembers what he told her the first time they met. This very cool, wealthy, handsome guy has loved Emily since they were teenagers.

"Thanks, Quinn," Betsey says as she walks to the door.

"Please," he says. "Please let me know when you find her."

She should say *I will* or *Sure thing* or *Of course*.

Instead she simply says, "Take care."

CHAPTER

65

BETSEY BROWN IS ANGRY with Joel Tierney.

Kalisha Scofield is angry with Joel Tierney.

And Joel Tierney is angry that he didn't listen to his father and go to medical school.

Betsey has been bugging Tierney daily. By phone. By text. By email. "You haven't done enough," "You're giving up," "I'm the only one who gives a good goddamn about Emily."

None of those angry statements from Betsey is true. Joel does care, but he's come up with nothing, nothing from the crime labs in Manhattan and Queens, nothing from interviews with Dr. Craven, the staff at Betsey's building, the nasty next-door neighbor Mariana Micelli, colleagues at Dazzle… But with Betsey's furious urging, Joel has agreed to do a deep dive on four specific persons of interest—Ted Burrows, Quinn Church, Mike Miller, Keith Hennessey—in addition to, as Kalisha puts it, "just about any other man in America who might have breathed the same air as Emily Atkinson."

Yes, that's why Kalisha is so pissed off. The assignment has trickled down to her, to Kalisha who believes that this case is at a dead end, who also believes that Betsey Brown should mind her own business.

But she's doing what she's been asked to do. She knows Tierney's limit for complaints. It's pretty elastic, but, like even the toughest elastic, it'll break at some point.

"How're we doing over there, Kalisha?" Tierney calls to her from his seat at the other end of the table in the large conference room where they've been working.

"I'm on number three of the twenty-two names we've got here."

"Great," he says. "You should be finished by the end of…"

"Please stop right there, Detective. My energy slows down when I'm unhappy."

Tierney smiles and says, "Yes, ma'am."

"And speaking of the title *ma'am*, have you noticed anything unusual about this list I'm going through?"

"Unusual? No," says Tierney. "It's about as diverse as a list can be—rich guys, poor guys, old guys, young guys, white guys, Black guys."

"That's just it. Guys. Guys and more guys. Who's to say that it's not a woman who's messed with Emily Atkinson?"

"Well, dumb as I am about life, it would take a man to get her pregnant," says Tierney.

"Well, you must have been a bio major, Detective, because there very well may have been a woman or women who had a hand in whatever's happened to Emily. Somebody like that Italian witch who lives next door or one of the women who has hung out with some of the victim's friends, you know, some of her close friends, the druggies. What about that strange lady, Miriam, who was padding around when our beloved associate Betsey Brown went to visit the rich dude, Quinn Church?"

"Okay, Kalisha," says Tierney. "Just put 'em on your list. And thank you."

Kalisha was afraid that this would be

Tierney's reaction—more work, more analysis, more phone calls to DC and any city Emily might have traveled through. Yet, angry as Kalisha is, she only knows how to do her job one way. The right way. So she shakes her head and goes back to the computer.

But not for long. Within a few minutes she's calling to Tierney again.

"Do you remember this David Zingerman guy?" she says.

"Yeah. The kid who was Emily's secretary at her marketing firm."

Kalisha sighs loudly. "Her assistant, not her secretary. Could you please try to jump into the language of the twenty-first century?"

"I'm trying. I'm trying. Anyway, we talked to Zingerman twice. He loved her."

"Yeah," says Kalisha. "He told us about a lot of situations at the office—Emily and her boss, Emily and her coming in late and drunk and groggy. But he left something out."

"And that is?"

"Five years ago...which would be one year before he went to work at Dazzle, he was arrested for drug possession in Hanover, New Hampshire."

"Yeah, Hanover. That's where Dartmouth is, and that's where the Zingerman kid went to college. Case closed. What was the substance? Grass?"

"First of all, nobody has called it 'grass' since Nixon was president."

"Stop with the language lecture, Detective," Tierney says. "Move on."

"It wasn't weed or pot that he was busted for. He was selling high-grade cocaine cut with fentanyl. He had some fancy-ass lawyer from Boston who helped get him off."

"Okay. So Zingerman is not or was not the geeky-looking choirboy we thought he was. Case closed."

"Not quite. Here's the interesting part."

She reads from the screen. " 'Suspect Zingerman's bail was set by Justice Leo Delaney at one hundred thousand dollars. Bail posted in the name of Zingerman, David, by Atkinson, Emily, State of New York.' "

Tierney agrees that this is interesting. Very interesting. In fact, he says that he thinks it is really very fucking interesting. He also thinks that there may be a simple explanation. Conceivably, Emily Atkinson and David

Zingerman knew each other from another time and place. Kalisha checks, and, yes, Zingerman, like Emily, was raised in Manhattan. Yes, the two both went to the same prestigious prep school, Hotchkiss, although a decade apart. It's possible that their families knew each other.

When Tierney finishes reciting his list of possibilities, Kalisha speaks.

"And before you tell me to do it, I will make it my business to pay another visit and have another chat with Mr. Zingerman."

"That's my girl," says Tierney. And before Kalisha can speak again, Tierney says, "I mean, 'That's my excellent detective.'"

Tierney thinks he hears Kalisha whisper the word *asshole,* but she looks to be very busy with her computer.

They both work silently for another hour or so, taking time out only to order a chicken salad sandwich on whole-wheat toast for Kalisha, and a BLT with a side of fries for Joel.

When the desk officer telephones to tell them their order has arrived, Tierney volunteers to walk to the front to pick it up. His hand has almost touched the doorknob to leave when Kalisha speaks again.

"Remember how Ted Burrows, the world's most adorable bartender, told us he was skiing out in Colorado last week when Emily disappeared?"

Kalisha doesn't wait for Tierney to answer. She simply says, "BlueSky Breckenridge just faxed over some receipts. With Ted's name and credit card on them. Looks like he was telling us the truth."

Tierney shakes his head, disappointed and discouraged. "So he's got an alibi."

"Yep. Shit. We're no closer than we were yesterday. We don't know where Emily Atkinson is. We don't know who the father is. We don't know anything."

"Well, we do know one thing," says Tierney.

"What?"

"We know that Ted the bartender likes to ski."

"Go get the food, Tierney. Go get the food."

CHAPTER

66

BETSEY AND HER AUNT are close. Very close.

How close? The older woman is known as Aunt Gloria to her other nieces. But Betsey has a special name for tough-talking, down-to-earth, bighearted Gloria McCarthy. Betsey calls her Auntie Mama. Even when Betsey was in high school and Auntie Mama moved to Las Vegas—"It's my dream town, honey. A gal like me can have a good time being a croupier"— they spoke every day by phone. They're talking on the phone again today. But the circumstances are entirely different.

"Betsey, honey. You're calling your old aunt earlier than usual. What's going on, baby girl?"

"Guess where I'm calling from, Auntie Mama?"

"I'm no good at guessing this early before I've had my first coffee and cigarette," Gloria says. Betsey supplies the answer.

"McCarran."

"McCarran! As in the airport? What are you doing, lady? You can't be flying after the seventh month."

"My OB said it was all right," says Betsey as quickly and softly as she can. As always, Betsey is a terrible liar.

"Things are sure changing," Auntie Mama says.

"No. I'm out here on business. Sort of."

"What kind of business does a surgical nurse have in Vegas? Is Céline Dion having surgery?"

"I'll tell you all about it when I see you. But I'm going to need a little help from you."

"You need money?"

"No. I need someone to drive me around. And I need her to do it ASAP."

"Well, that'd be my pleasure. I don't have to start spinning the roulette wheel until eight tonight. I'll just guzzle me some coffee and pick you up. I'll phone you when I'm almost there."

An hour later Auntie Mama and Betsey Brown, fortified with Egg McMuffins and some beverages (Coke for Gloria, chocolate milk for Betsey), are riding Gloria's Honda Civic across Highway 95.

Betsey explains the situation to her aunt—Emily's condition, Emily's problems, Emily's disappearance. She explains how Emily had a quickie, spontaneous wedding at a Las Vegas wedding chapel. And although Betsey suspects who the groom is— Ted Burrows—she needs to find out for sure.

She's also hoping against all hope that she can stumble on something that'll give the whole investigation some direction.

"Honey, stumbling is never a good plan. Stumbling is only for birdbrains. Stumbling is something lucky that happens when you're doing something logical."

Betsey, hoping that Auntie Mama will not think her niece a birdbrain, tells her that she's mapped out, on Google, a route that will let them visit all the wedding chapels that—

But before Betsey can finish explaining, Gloria jumps in.

"Honey, keep your Google phone in your

fake Chanel purse. I know this town like I know my own house. I say we start down Las Vegas Boulevard, cross over to Fourth Street and hit the four or five most popular wedding places. Chances are pretty good that I even know some of the folks working in those chapels. And I need to warn you, they take their jobs real serious."

Betsey says, "Well, I don't think Emily and Ted or whoever she was here with was taking this whole wedding very seriously."

Gloria seems to be annoyed.

"Maybe so. But these are *real* weddings. These are *legal* weddings. You can't just run in, get married, and say it didn't happen. Never mind the orchestra on tape and the pictures of Elvis and Marilyn and Reba and Garth on the walls. These are very real weddings."

Maybe it's the dry heat seeping into the air-conditioned car. Maybe it's the pregnancy. Maybe it's the fact that Betsey's husband thinks this is dangerous for her and the baby. Maybe it's because Betsey easily figured out that while her aunt was glad to see her niece, she didn't expect...well, whatever. Betsey has to pee. Betsey hopes her nausea subsides. Betsey is scared.

Then Gloria speaks.

"Well, speaking of Elvis, we're coming up to the place that might as well be our first stop. It's a popular chapel. Maybe it's even *the most popular.*"

Gloria pulls into the driveway of a building that could be a high-end motel. But the neon sign over the churchlike entrance clarifies everything.

Graceland Wedding Chapel.
Prompt and beautiful ceremony.
Sale price. Today only. $177.

"Must be our lucky day," says Gloria. "Too bad we're not getting married."

So begins one of the strangest tours that Betsey Brown has ever taken.

She and her sassy-sweet aunt visit four chapels along Las Vegas Boulevard. It is an extraordinary education. By noon on a desert-dry day, Betsey learns the following:

Her aunt is correct. The people who run these chapels take themselves and their jobs quite seriously. They celebrate the fun and joy, and in some cases, because it is Las Vegas, the goofiness of the event. But the person officiating—even if the man is dressed like Elvis or the woman is done up with more makeup and bigger hair than RuPaul— reads the vows slowly and gravely.

The chapels themselves are so overdecorated and ugly that they have a certain kind of ostentatious beauty to them. Most of the places Gloria and Betsey visit have big photos of famous couples who decided to get married in Vegas: Angelina and Billy Bob, Demi and Bruce, Kelly Ripa and Mark Consuelos.

The chapels all take credit cards. The chapels that take cash want the money before the ceremony. If the couple hasn't brought "folks to stand up for them," a man or woman "in the office" will do the job for fifty dollars each.

At every chapel, Gloria does the explaining. ("We're trying to track down some information about this wonderful couple who eloped a little bit of time ago. Show 'em the photographs, honey.") Then Betsey holds out her phone and taps on a few photos of Emily. The chapel people, a man and a woman, initially seem to think that they remember the bride. But sooner or later they shake their heads no. At all four chapels the chapel officials go to their computers and look up the names Emily Atkinson and Theodore Burrows.

After finding nothing at the fourth chapel, Betsey tells Auntie Mama that she must make another bathroom stop really soon, that she must get something more nutritious than an Egg McMuffin for her and her unborn baby, and that maybe they both should just give up on this investigation.

"You're a crazy lady," Auntie Mama says. "You used all your air mileage and came out here to help a friend, and now you're throwing in the towel because you're hungry and you've got to pee?"

Betsey says nothing. Her stomach aches. Her back is stiff. And she thinks that her heart could begin breaking at any moment.

"Let's pull into one more chapel, honey, and, soon as we're done, I'll take you for a good steak-and-potato lunch at Golden Steer," says Auntie Mama.

Soon they're pulling into an entrance drive with a sign that says LUCKY LITTLE WEDDING CHAPEL.

Betsey looks at a huge electronic billboard with alternating photos of real brides and real grooms. Each couple is holding a placard that says WE GOT LUCKY IN LAS VEGAS.

The fact is, Gloria McCarthy and Betsey Brown did just get lucky in Las Vegas.

When Betsey flashes Emily's photo to Pete Rodriguez, the owner and minister of Lucky Little Wedding Chapel, he nods and says, "I do remember that lady, matter of fact. She was nice enough. Sweet. Charming. Maybe a little drunk. But not so drunk as I wouldn't marry them."

"So they actually did get married?" Betsey asks.

"Yes, ma'am. This is not a joke. This place is a real chapel, with real marriage licenses, and real people who want to get married."

"I see," says Betsey. "And if those real people want to get a real annulment, how quickly could they do it?"

"As fast as state law allows, I'd imagine. Now as far as this wedding goes, I do remember that the groom wasn't the nicest guy I'd ever met. I think he told the bride that it'd be best to use *her* credit card. Let me check."

He consults his computer at the reception desk.

"January. February...here we go. Here's the receipt. It's what we call a Cherish Ceremony. Not the most expensive package, but very nice indeed. Five hundred fifty dollars. The name is Emily Mary Atkinson. Five hundred ninety-six dollars and nine cents total, with Nevada state tax."

The chapel minister turns the computer screen to face the two women. Betsey sees the marriage license. Emily's address. The address of Ted's Bar and Grill.

"Whose names are these? Margaret Lloyd and Peter Deacon. It says that they were the witnesses."

A pause.

"Well, those are the *names* of the witnesses. But sometimes we just put the names down and ignore the formality."

Betsey asks if there's anything else on that computer about Emily and Ted.

No.

Betsey asks if there are photographs of the event.

No.

Can he print out the three or four pages of the file?

No.

Can he remember anything else about the event?

"Well, we do an awful lot of weddings out here. So it's pretty much a miracle that we even got this far. But thinking about it now, there is one thing I was thinking before, during, and after the ceremony."

"What was that?" asks Gloria.

"The bride was very nice, very pretty. I honestly think she could've done a lot better than the jerk she married."

So now Betsey knows that Ted told her the truth.

He and Emily did get married.

But there is something odd about everything.

Why did Emily insist that it *wasn't* Ted who she married on that funny, crazy day at the Lucky Little Wedding Chapel in Las Vegas?

CHAPTER

67

SOMEWHERE BENEATH THAT MOUNTAIN of Nature Valley wrappers and crushed cans of Diet Coke lies the head of Kalisha Scofield," says Joel Tierney.

Big mistake. Almost forty-eight straight hours of Kalisha trying to uncover some clue, some scent, some piece of evidence that might send them toward a hint of how to find Emily Atkinson. The conference room table is a mess. And Kalisha is not happy.

"I'd pick my words very carefully," says Kalisha, without looking away from her laptop. "The next time I go to the bathroom I may just not come back."

Hmmm. Tierney realizes that he's on thin ice.

"Holy Mother!" says Kalisha. She doesn't quite scream it, but it sure registers with Tierney. "Get over here. I think we may have an actual lead."

Tierney thinks of all the files and Google searches and websites and police reports and school transcripts and police blotter chronicles Kalisha has gone through. He knows that she's delved into the background of Emily's masseurs, tennis teachers, her prep-school friends, her college professors, her uncles and cousins and dry cleaners and dentists and emergency room nurses and… "Get over here, Detective. Move your ass."

Tierney knows it must be shocking. Kalisha Scofield would never speak to her partner this way. Tierney moves his ass.

Kalisha keeps talking.

"It's about that guy Mike Miller," Kalisha says. She's actually clapping her hands. Tierney can't stand that degree of enthusiasm.

"Mike Miller, big catch," says Tierney. "We know he was her drug dealer. We know he was tagged twice by the local narcs."

"Yeah. But here's something we didn't know," says Kalisha, as Tierney crouches down to see her computer screen.

CITY OF LIVERPOOL
CONSTABULARY INDICTMENT
25 JANUARY 2008

"Liverpool? How in hell did Liverpool information show up?" asks Tierney.

"It's our only lucky break, sir. I was inputting Syracuse, New York, police reports—Mike Miller went to college at Syracuse University; I've been looking at all towns in and around people's alma maters—and then I got this from Liverpool, England. It's a mistake. But it's a great fucking mistake.

"It turns out that Liverpool is the name of a town outside of Syracuse. So this report came up. Liverpool, England. *Not* the Liverpool in upstate New York."

Kalisha pauses. She wants to give the next statement as much drama as she can: "It turns out Miller spent two years as a Spanish teacher in Liverpool, England."

Tierney looks confused.

"Lemme get this straight. Mike Miller..."

Kalisha immediately interrupts.

"Miller was using an alias. Who the hell knows why? He was probably pushing pills and weed there, too, and wanted to live under the radar. Let me introduce you to Simon Paxton."

Kalisha hits a computer key and reveals a series of photos of a young man who is clearly Mike Miller—this, despite his bushy mustache and his lime-green sport jacket.

"What the fuck was he? The fifth Beatle?"

"Coulda been. But like I say, he was an American who taught Spanish to grammar school kids in Liverpool. And here's the story, courtesy of the always dependable *Guardian*."

PRISONER GONE MISSING FROM RAX-FORTH LOCK-UP. SUSPECT IN MISSING PERSON CASE IS ABSENT.

District 7 Liverpool police today confirmed that Simon Paxton, under arrest on charges connected to the disappearance and possible homicide of Mercy McCambridge, his fellow schoolmaster at St. Edward Public School, has mysteriously escaped from Raxforth jail. Police admitted that Paxton had not been under careful watch. They further suspect that

Paxton was assisted in his escape by an official within the Raxforth compound.

Sources say Miss McCambridge had previously moved to press character against Paxton, who she claims, after an evening of dancing and drinking with her, broke her jaw with his fists. She stated further that he had thumped her about the neck and back, causing bleeding and severe contusions.

The subsequent week, Mercy McCambridge was reported missing. Two neighbors recounted seeing Paxton that evening in the rear garden of McCambridge's house.

Liverpool justices, detectives, and constabulary have vowed to keep up their efforts to locate both the escaped prisoner and his alleged victim.

While the search for Mercy McCambridge continues, police are also pursuing the whereabouts of Simon Paxton, a man who they term a vicious and dangerous criminal.

"Is there any follow-up?" asks Tierney.

"There is," says Kalisha. She presses some keys on her computer.

"They found Mercy McCambridge's body in the nearby Mersey River."

Then she presses a few more keys. Tierney sees a document on the screen.

<u>New York City Police Department, Borough of Queens</u>

Kalisha does the interpreting for him.

"Well, the next day...well...right over here in the good old USA...at the good old 113th Precinct in Queens, the police blotter reports that an intoxicated and unruly male passenger aboard a London to New York Delta flight was questioned upon arrival at JFK airport."

Finally, she reads exactly what is written on the screen in the police report.

"'After questioning the man, he was released. The Manhattan resident's name is Michael Miller.'"

MONTH EIGHT

CHAPTER

68

A PIECE OF ADVICE.

If you're eight months pregnant and your best friend calls you totally at the last minute, and she begs you, literally begs you, to babysit her four-year-old twins, say that you can't because... "I have to hammer ten-inch nails through both my eyes" ... "I'm scheduled to jump from a diving board into a pool full of lye..."

Or you can ignore my advice, which is exactly what I did. In that case you just say, "Yes. Of course I'll do it."

It's Betsey, of course.

"I have a bit of a medical emergency," she told

me, "and I managed to get a doctor's appointment. And Frankie is going to go with me to the doctor. It's nothing serious, but I need to have something checked out. I know it's last minute...No...before you ask, it's not Jane Craven, nothing to do with the pregnancy, nothing worth carrying on about. I could go alone, but it'd be great if Frankie could come with me."

"How about...I could go with you to the doctor and Frankie could stay with the kids," I say, all the while thinking, *Why didn't Betsey propose that in the first place?*

"No. This way is better. And anyway, Bobby and Juliet think it's a big treat to have you babysit."

"Okay, okay," I tell Betsey. "Just warn Bobby and Juliet that I will *not* be playing the Backward Baby dance game. That I will *not* be doing anything that requires more than five minutes of standing up. And if I go into labor, they will..."

Again, she cuts me off. Sweetly.

"They know how to dial 911. Thank you. Thank you. Thank you, Em. I know what you're feeling. I'm feeling the same way. But I don't know what I'd do..."

Now it's my turn to interrupt.

"Bets, you know how I am. I've got to ask. What's going on? If the doctor's visit is nothing important, then why is Frank going with you? And why won't you tell me anything about it? Come on, best bud."

Then she says those famous two words, the two words that almost always seem to end up being a lie.

"Trust me."

"I do trust you. Okay. Okay. So I'll shut up right here. Anyway, I have to hang up right this second."

"Right this second, Emily?"

"Right this second. You see, if I hang up right now, I'll have enough time to pee at least three times before the Uber gets here."

And the Uber gets here. And I get to Betsey's place.

Juliet and Bobby act as if Santa Claus has just come down the chimney. Wow. These two kids put the *adore* in the word *adorable*. Just good-looking enough, just chubby enough, just... well, I was going to say that the twins are also just smart enough. But they're not. They are very smart. Perhaps, as my mother used to say, too smart for their own good. They're also charming and extremely funny. When they grow up, they might be the first brother and sister team to do stand-up comedy.

As soon as Betsey and Frankie close the apartment door, Juliet looks at me with her hands on her hips and speaks.

"So, Mommy says you won't play Backward Baby with us." Her little voice is filled with skepticism. "Is Mommy telling the truth?"

"Of course," I say. "Mommies don't lie."

"But how about if we ask you really nicely?" says Bobby.

Please notice he doesn't say "real nice." He says, "really nicely." The proper usage of the adverbs.

"Let's discuss this in a few minutes," I say. "I'll be right back."

When I return from the bathroom, Bobby says that he and Juliet have an announcement.

Juliet begins.

"We both really love you, Emily. And what we want to tell you is that we know you're pregnant. Just like our Mommy. So we're not new to all this."

Bobby takes over.

"So, we understand how uncomfortable you must be," he says.

Then Juliet launches into a spot-on imitation of Betsey. The four-year-old has mastered the slight Pennsylvania accent, Betsey's unique conversational style: a frequent back-and-forth between being very excited and very calm.

"Oh, these friggin' feet. Oh, Frankie. My ankles are sooooo big."

Bobby then slips immediately into an equally impressive imitation of his father.

"Honey, I always listen. You know I do."

I start laughing so hard that my lower stomach and back begin to hurt. But, God, they are funny.

"Now they usually kiss, but we're going to leave that part out. And we're going to ask you what we really want to ask you," says Juliet. Then the question.

"Can we go to the park near IS 227?"

Oh, no. Outside. Walking. Pushing a swing. Making sure the kids aren't abducted.

And what about the person following me?

I couldn't possibly put Bobby and Juliet in that kind of danger.

"You probably know IS 227 better as the Louis Armstrong Middle School," says Bobby.

"Yeah, that's it. I do," I lie. Louis Armstrong's name on a middle school? *Welcome to Queens, New York, Emily. It's more than just a place to catch a plane to Europe.*

"Don't you guys have video games you want to play?" I ask.

I'm hoping they'll forget all about the park. But they don't.

"We don't like video games. We *really* want to play outside," says Juliet.

"Sorry," I say. "Not today."

They are such sweet and clever kids, and they're doing their best to hide their disappointment. It's adorable and heartbreaking at the same time.

Suddenly I want to say what my mother always said to me, the question that always hurt me and drove me crazy.

I hear her voice: *Why can't you be like normal kids?*

But I don't say it. In fact, I'm angry at myself for even thinking it. And there's one thing I promise myself this moment. I will never ever say that sentence to Oscar.

"Pretty please can we go to the park?" says Bobby.

"Pleeease?" says Juliet.

I know it's risky. I know the man who's been following me is still out there.

What I don't know is how I could possibly say no to these two precious puppy-dog faces.

"Okay, fine, we'll go to the park," I say. The kids start yelping and jumping for joy. "But hold on. I've got to sit on the bench. And you've got to do whatever I say. And when it's time to go... Which will be when I need to go to the bathroom... or whenever I say it is, for any reason... you can't argue with me. Deal?"

"Okay," says Bobby. "But don't worry. If you have to do pee-pee, you can always go in the sandbox."

"That's disgusting," I say.

"Yes, it is," says Juliet. "But I've seen some kids do it."

CHAPTER

69

IF YOU'RE WONDERING WHAT I'm thinking as I sit on a park bench and watch Bobby and Juliet run from the slide to tire swings to monkey bars to trapeze...well, I'm wondering how soon we can leave.

And, of course, as always now, I'm wondering if I'm being followed.

Oh, shit. It looks like Bobby and Juliet are about to go into the wooden playhouse. I want to scream: *Get the hell away from that playhouse! Are you two crazy? There might be a madman hiding in there!* But I just say loudly, "Don't go in there!"

Juliet shrugs. Bobby rolls his eyes. But they obey. They do not go into the playhouse.

I watch Bobby and Juliet as if they are cat burglars on a rooftop. They run from the chinning bars to the tire swings to the tip-top of the slide. From the big kid swings (so called because there are no seat belts) to the climbing ropes.

And when I finally turn my eyes away from Juliet and Bobby, I search for dangers elsewhere in this park. I see what I should see: kids playing softball on the grass, kids playing kickball on the grass, the vigilant and not-so-vigilant parents (these days as many men as women).

The stalker could be here. Why not? New geography. New places to hide. Somewhere nearby may be the person who is following… or not. Or maybe. *Keep looking, Emily. You may be wrong. It may be you're imagining it. But, then again, maybe you're right.*

Juliet is gently nudging Bobby out of the way, determined to precede him on the ladder of the slide. To them it's all horseplay, rough fun; to me it's violence and danger. It could lead to a broken wrist or arm, stitches on Juliet's forehead, a big purple lump on Bobby's knee. I get up from the bench and power-walk toward them.

"Hey, you two, you Brown kids. Juliet! Bobby! Cut it out! Stop pushing!"

Two Black moms nearby look at me. Oh, I get it. "Brown kids." I yell, "Bobby Brown and Juliet Brown, you're going to fall and hurt yourselves." I glance toward the women. They've gone back to their conversation. Okay, two new people now think I'm nuts.

Bobby and Juliet stop arguing, and I walk back to my park bench. I see that a man—twenty-five maybe, curly black hair, green Army-style messenger bag, okay, kinda handsome—has sat down on the other end of the bench. He looks up from his phone so quickly that I think he must have been watching me. This guy knows me. Or he doesn't.

"Amazing," he says. "If there's a way to ignore safety rules, a kid will do it."

I smile. The guy keeps talking.

"And imagine what it will be like when your new one comes along." He glances at my pregnant belly.

I feel myself suddenly growing tense. I'm not about to give this stranger one bit of detail. ("No, they're not mine," "I'm just babysitting," "I'm expecting my first.")

"Yes, I can only imagine," I say. I look ahead of me and see that Bobby is pushing Juliet on the tire swing.

"Bye," I say to the cute guy with curly hair. He smiles and goes back to his phone.

"I think we should get going," I say as I walk closer to the children. Of course the litany of "Just a little longer" and "We just got here" is the song both kids sing. I climb the five steps up to the playhouse and the top of the slide. Now I am afraid that I will never get down from up here.

There are just two ways down from the playhouse—five steps or the slide.

"Do the slide, Em. The slide. C'mon!" Bobby shouts.

"No. Don't slide. You're pregnant," says suddenly safety-conscious Juliet.

I go with Juliet's opinion. I carefully navigate the ladder. I'm on the ground.

"I'm thirsty," Bobby says as we walk toward a cluster of trees near the entrance to the park.

I look around for a food truck or a soda machine or a water fountain.

("Do you know how disgusting a New York City water fountain is?" my mother told me one time when I told her I'd drunk from one. "People let their children urinate in them.")

"We'll find something to drink on the way home," I say.

"But I'm thirsty right now," Bobby says. His voice is not selfish or whiny. He's confused by the situation. Why can't he have a drink now?

And suddenly a voice, a man's voice, loud.

"Who's that? I know. I see Emily and Juliet and Bobby."

The voice seems to be coming from behind me. The children look confused. I'm confused. Oh, shit. My stalker? Maybe. No. Maybe. Yes.

I look around me, and I see lots of men and women and children, but I can't figure out where that voice came from. I'm frightened. At least I think I'm frightened.

Then I hear, "Mommy! Daddy!" Bobby is running and yelling as he makes his way to Betsey and Frankie. Juliet joins them. Bobby throws his arms around his mother's legs. Frank bends down and scoops up his daughter.

I hurry to catch up. The four of them look beautiful, wonderful, marvelous. The adorable children. The pretty pregnant mom. The handsome father.

But who's that other woman joining them now? She's pregnant also. Oh, my God. It's me. I'm moving. I'm joining them, but it feels like I'm outside myself, that I'm seeing myself with this family of four.

I see me, another pregnant woman, tired-looking, sad. What's the deal? What's the relationship? Who is she? The pregnant cousin from Iowa? The unmarried pregnant sister? A friend from the neighborhood?

Let me put it another way.

Who am I?

CHAPTER

70

FRANKIE OFFERS TO TAKE the kids for a while.

"You gals, go relax. Get some herbal tea or something," he says. This guy Frankie may be the nicest person I've ever known. He'd be perfect if he stopped using phrases like *you gals*. (But, hey, that should be every man's biggest flaw.)

Bobby and Juliet seem to be delighted with their father's proposition. Apparently two energetic little kids would rather run around like crazy, eat ice cream, and drink Coca-Cola with an energetic dad than spend time with two very off-balance, very pregnant women.

"See you later," Bobby and Juliet each yell.

"Yeah," says Frankie. "Don't pick up too many guys."

Betsey responds with the traditional middle-finger communication. Her husband responds with mock sarcasm, "Betsey, please, not in front of the children."

For me, this little verbal exchange simply extends the charm of the beautiful, happy Brown family unit. These four folks—soon to be five—seem to have cornered the market on good marriage vibes. Sure they have their challenges—both parents have tough jobs, their finances aren't always as sturdy as they'd like—but they love hanging out with one another, and I try hard to bury (or at least, disguise) my envy.

"How'd the kids behave?" Betsey asks as we walk to the edge of the park.

"They were a perfect little lady and gentleman. I was a perfect nervous wreck. That jungle gym is an accident waiting to happen."

I decide *not* to tell Betsey that a big part of my nervousness had nothing to do with her children at all. It had to do with whoever the hell might be following me.

"They don't call it *jungle gym* anymore," says Betsey. "It's called a *climbing gym* or *climbing bars*."

"Is there something offensive about *jungle gym*?" I ask.

I am trying to do my part in keeping up a conversation with Betsey. But the fact is: I don't care one little bit about the right term for jungle gym.

I am worried. I am just a little bit crazy. Yes, I am trying to keep cool with Betsey, but what I'm really doing is imagining which groundskeeper, softball player, old guy, young guy, fat guy, skinny guy, is following me. I am sure someone is watching. And here's something else I'll share: When I'm not sure someone is following me, then I think I'm just either a dry-drunk or a hormonal catastrophe. It is still very difficult not to be the witty, fun-loving boozer that I once was.

"I'm really not sure," Betsey says.

Right. We were talking about the jungle gym.

"I mean, what's wrong with the phrase *jungle gym*?" Betsey continues.

My clever response is "Yeah." The conversation is disintegrating, and I hold myself responsible.

We are outside the park now. We walk on the sidewalk. I inspect the surroundings. There's something soothing about the simplicity of the neighborhood: auto repair places, stores selling electric power tools, a small Pakistani grocer, a big medical supply store, its window filled with walkers, shower stools, bedpans. Betsey stops unexpectedly. This time we're standing in front of a liquor store. A sign in the window says GIANT SALE. MARSALA. SWEET OR DRY. $12.95/BOTTLE.

"Why are we stopping?" I ask. "Are you all out of Marsala?"

"Listen. I want to tell you why Frankie and I went to the doctor."

"You don't need to tell me. Your choice. I don't want to pry."

"No. It's not prying. I should have told you. But I'm so stupid and superstitious and..." Betsey pauses. Then she takes a deep breath and says, "It was *not* a doctor's appointment for me. We were going to see a doctor for Frank."

Oh, shit, no. I'm guilty. It's my fault. I put a curse on them. I should never have thought about how happy and beautiful and wonderful and lucky Betsey and Frankie were. I should never... "Frankie felt this lump on the right side of his neck, just below his ear. And it wasn't going away. So because he's stupid, and because he's a man, and because he's one of New York's bravest, he kept putting off going to a doctor. So finally I made an appointment...and it became obvious that he was scared as shit. So I went with him. He asked me to. So we went..."

Betsey is now crying.

Oh, shit. Oh, no.

I put my hand on her shoulder. Betsey pats her belly as she speaks.

"I don't know why I'm crying. We went for a biopsy today. And everything is fine. Turns out it's just some sort of cyst. The spinal surgeon said that the biopsy fixed the problem. So I don't know why I'm crying. I'm sorry, Emily."

I hug her. "Yeah, I don't know why, either. But it doesn't matter. Anyway, sometimes crying can bring you happiness," I say.

Then I add, "Or so I've heard. I wouldn't know anything about happiness from personal experience."

"Stop it," Betsey says. She gives me a playful, gentle shove. "Respect yourself, Emily. Please start respecting yourself."

We continue to walk. I watch a ConEd worker who is watching another ConEd worker who is watching another ConEd worker remove a manhole cover. Then I stare at two teenage boys, one of whom is pointing at Betsey and me, as if there's something hilarious about two absurdly pregnant women tottering along an industrial street in Queens.

Then Betsey says, "Okay. I want to talk to you about something else."

I say, "Sure. But I reserve the right not to answer if it's going to upset either one of us."

She smiles and speaks.

"I've got to ask you, Emily. Since we're talking about life and happiness and all that sort of thing. Why in hell did you get married?"

"No reason. I've told you this. A fling."

God, I wish she hadn't brought up this subject.

"Stop calling it a fling," Betsey says. "Stop lying to me."

She's just a few inches away from being really angry. So, of course, since I am never really in control, I react with anger as well.

"Try seeing the world through *my* eyes sometime. Try seeing the way I live my life. I don't have a handsome firefighter husband and two adorable kids and a job that helps save people's lives," I tell her.

"You know what you're doing, Emily. You're

accusing me of being happy. And that's not fighting fair."

She looks away from me. She stops walking. So I stop walking.

"Listen," I say. "I call it a fling because that's what it was. It was ... a foolish, crazy Las Vegas wedding that ended the very next day. I can only guess ... Maybe ... Maybe because for a few hours I actually loved the guy."

"You know why I'm interested," Betsey says.

"Of course I know. You think it's important to find out who the father is. And I've got to be honest, I don't really care," I say. "But I've got to take a big breath and get on with this. I don't know who Oscar's dad is."

I think Betsey has given up. So I decide to talk about something else.

"I do have something to share with you. But you've got to promise not to be angry with me or laugh at me or tell me I'm crazy."

"That's a lot to promise," Betsey says.

"I know. So? Promise? Come on."

"Of course I promise. What's going on?"

"There's ... there's something awful going on." I pause. Then I say, as casually as I can, "I think someone's been following me."

"What do you mean 'following you'?"

I want to say: What's not to understand? But I've got to try staying calm. I can't go on being angry at every little thing.

Betsey and I begin walking again.

"Here's what I mean. When I'm out on the street…sometimes I'll catch a glimpse of some guy behind me, keeping up with me, stopping when I stop. Sometimes I think he's calling my name or at least saying my name. It's making me sick. I'm so frightened. I'm throwing up all the time. It's probably affecting Oscar. I'm sure of it."

Now I force us to stop. Then I start to sob. Really sob. Shoulder-shaking, hands-on-my-eyes sobbing. Then Betsey moves in and we do our pregnant best to hug each other.

"We may tip over," I say, laughing while I'm crying.

Betsey stands back.

"Why didn't you tell me about this before?" Betsey asks.

"Because I'm not absolutely sure. Sometimes I think it's just my imagination."

"Damn it. Maybe it's *not* your imagination. What's wrong with you? I'm here for you. I want to help. Will you let me?"

I give that simple, tearful-schoolgirl kind of quick nod.

"We need to go to the police."

"What are *they* going to do, Bets?" I say. "They'll probably just think I'm some hormonal crazy pregnant lady. There's no way they'll take me seriously."

"No, listen. I have a friend from high school who became a detective with the NYPD. We'll go to *him*."

Betsey can probably see the skepticism etched across my face.

"Emily, Joel Tierney is a good guy. Really."

Wait. Did Betsey just say the detective she knows is named...Joel Tierney?

The same man I met at Ted's a few months ago?

The same man who came back to my apartment? The same man who I... "I know Joel and I trust him," Betsey says. "So come on. What do you say?"

I should tell my best friend that I *also* know Joel Tierney. That he and I know each other... as well as two people can.

But instead I say, "Maybe."

CHAPTER

71

BOTH OF US ARE heavily pregnant and exhausted.

"Bets, we're both about to fall down and go to sleep. Go back to Frankie and the kids. Call them and find out where to meet them. I'll get back home on my own," I say.

"No. I'm going to see that you get home okay," Betsey says.

"I'll take an Uber," I say.

"Good. Then I'll take one with you," she says.

"I'm fine," I say.

"No, you're very clearly not."

Betsey wins the argument. I call a car. And Betsey accompanies this very nervous, very nauseated, very frightened woman home.

"Are you still having trouble with your wacky neighbor?" Betsey asks as we enter the elevator of my building.

"Absolutely," I say. "As if I don't have enough to worry about. Someday I'm going to step into the hallway and crazy Dr. Micelli is going to be standing there with a butcher knife."

The elevator stops at my floor.

"Want me to get out first and check the hall?" Betsey asks. I'm not sure that she's being serious. Whatever her intent, for a moment I honestly think that this is a great suggestion, but I say, "No thanks," with a fake *don't be silly* tone to my voice.

We enter. The lights to my apartment—hall overhead, living room overhead, chandelier in the longish hallway leading to the bedrooms—are all on.

"Do you rich people always leave so many lights on?" she asks.

"Yeah. Usually," I say, but that's not really true. Usually the lights are off. Usually I use the master switch. The control is right inside the entranceway.

I turn to Betsey and say, "You need the bathroom?"

She nods and says, "Very much so."

"You can use the one just down the hall. I'll use the bathroom in my bedroom."

When I return, I'm slightly more comfortable, but my brain remains a bit fuzzy from wondering about all the burning lights.

Maybe I did leave them on. I was rushing out to Betsey's to babysit the kids. The Uber was waiting. Of course I left them on. But I'm not sure. Maybe. My world is filled with maybes.

I survey the living room as I wait for Betsey.

A silver-framed photo—not large, not small—is facedown on the piano.

I, of course, know exactly what the photo is inside: a family snapshot of Liz, Lionel, and me at a dinner in honor of their thirtieth anniversary, taken at the 21 Club six years ago. I remember that drunken night well.

What I don't remember is the framed photo collapsed downward on the piano.

And hang on. Didn't I come home a few weeks ago to find two *other* photos lying facedown on the piano, the day my poster had been taken down and *other* lights were left on?

But that's how everything is looking to me these days.

Hell! Am I supposed to remember how everything was when I left this morning for Betsey's? I think not. I don't remember sitting on the sofa last night, but the plate on the coffee table is littered with cracker crumbs and bits of dried cheese.

Betsey enters.

"God! This is such a great space," says Betsey. "I wish I'd accepted more of your invitations."

"That's okay," I say. "I totally get it. I'm childless and jobless. You've got work, the kids, Frankie…"

"Well, still. I really envy you, Emily."

But I know she doesn't envy me at all.

"Nothing to envy," I say. "Nothing at all." Then I say, "Should we order some food? I can get us delivery from Russ & Daughters or Eli Zabar. Either one will only take twenty minutes."

"No, thanks," she says. "But if you have decaf, you can make us pregnant folks some coffee." She follows me into the kitchen.

"Making coffee is the most cooking I've done all month," I tell her.

While I look for coffee, Betsey does what she always does, almost compulsively. She has a habit—only slightly annoying—of touching everything she sees. In a store she will pick up a handbag she has no intention of buying. In a restaurant she'll pick up the tiny flower vase on the table, a pack of matches, a wine list that she has no intention of reading.

As I try to remember where exactly I keep the coffee beans and where exactly I keep the coffee grinder and where exactly I keep the coffeemaker, Betsey examines a half-empty bag of Mallomars, an electric pepper mill, a bowl of cold half-eaten oatmeal. I am still trying to locate the coffee items.

"Emily, how come there are two beer cans on the counter?" Betsey says, walking toward the black granite area near the refrigerator.

Betsey shakes both cans. Michelob Ultra.

"They're empty," she says.

I'm as genuinely surprised to see them as she is.

"They're not mine," I say. "When I fall off the wagon it will be with chilled Bombay gin and a pound of Beluga."

"I never thought they were yours," says Betsey. Clearly she knows I'm telling the truth. Why must I keep reminding myself that Betsey is on my side?

"I don't know where they came from," I say. "Maybe someone…and maybe it's the same someone who put my parents' anniversary photo facedown on the piano."

"Someone did what?" Betsey asks.

I go to the house phone near the kitchen service entrance.

"Was anyone in my apartment today, Leon?" I ask the doorman.

When he tells me no I suggest that maybe one of the maintenance guys let himself in. But he tells me no again.

"I'm a real New Yorker," says Betsey. "I'm usually pretty good about letting things slide. But this is pretty worrying, Emily. Especially after you said someone might be—"

"I know," I say, cutting her off. "I know, I know, I know."

The beer cans. The piano photos. The scary man following me.

I discover that I have begun to tear up. I quickly turn away from Betsey, but it's too late. She sees that I'm crying.

"Sit down, Emily," Betsey says. "I'll get us some water. It's gonna be fine."

Very calmly I say, "No. It isn't. It's all too

much for me. All I care about is my baby. My Oscar. If someone is going to hurt me, they're going to hurt Oscar. If someone is going to kill me, they're . . ."

I look at the doorway to my former office, the room I've so carefully planned for Oscar. The door to the baby's room is slightly ajar. Damn it. I know that I always keep that door closed. I want it perfect, pure, pristine for the baby. I stand up as quickly as I can and walk the few steps to the nursery. Betsey is right behind me.

"Oh, my God," I say.

There's a messy pile of clothing and bedding in the middle of the floor—the crib mattress, the crib linens, the exquisite moon-and-star mobile that hung over the crib, the beautiful red and blue quilt with the big sun that I'd hung on the wall.

Betsey tries to put her arms around me and turn away from the awful pile, the pile that looks to me like a bonfire waiting to burst into flames.

I see a piece of notebook paper on top of the mound of cloth. A quick scrawl, big and bold. So big that I can read it without bending down to touch it.

NO BABY HERE. NO BABY HERE.

Betsey takes charge. She snatches the piece of paper from the top of the heap. She glances at the words and says, "This is fucking incredible."

"Sit down, Emily. Sit down," she says as she walks me to the white wicker rocker, the rocker where I always imagine holding my baby, nursing my baby. Once I'm settled in the rocking chair I watch as Betsey takes her phone from the vest pocket of her jean jacket.

"Hello," I hear her say. "This is Betsey Brown. I need to talk to Detective Joel Tierney."

"No. Don't," I say. "We...I...we'll figure this out. We don't need Tierney."

Betsey shakes her head. Her face is almost contorted with confusion.

"Emily. This is fucking serious."

A pause. Then she speaks calmly and soberly into the phone.

"Joel, it's Betsey. I'm with my friend Emily Atkinson, at her apartment, and, well, we've got what I'd call a pretty serious problem."

CHAPTER

72

JOEL TIERNEY RECOGNIZES ME. I'm sure of it. The moment I open the door.

He proves it by being cute, evasive, and provocative. All at the same time.

Then Betsey makes the superfluous intros.

"Detective Joel Tierney, this is my friend Emily Atkinson."

"Hi, Emily. Nice to meet you. Sorry it's under these circumstances."

Nice to meet me?

Okay, that's apparently the closest Tierney is going to acknowledge that we once spent a night together.

Well. Har-dee-har-har. Maybe that sort of

thing passes for humor in detective land. But it just causes my nausea and dry mouth and headache to increase about a thousand percent.

My former one-night stand steps into the apartment.

If I didn't know that Betsey was the nicest person on the planet earth, I could almost imagine she's teasing me, that she knows plenty more about Joel Tierney and me. Yes, that's a plot, a complicated plot. But it is certainly possible that it's Tierney who's been following me. It's Betsey who's been keeping him informed of my whereabouts. It's Betsey...what the hell is wrong with me? I've got to stop it. I've got to stop being me.

Tierney says, "Let's take a look at everything, Ms. Atkinson."

And, goddamnit, I begin sobbing again. "This is so fucking awful."

"I know it is," he says.

I reach for his hand, but he does not take it. He's not being cold. He's simply being professional. Betsey puts an arm around me. Then we head to the kitchen, where Betsey immediately points out the two empty beer cans.

As far as I can tell, Tierney is not particularly

interested in the beer cans. He doesn't even move close to the counter where they sit.

"I'll bag these and get them over to Forensics. Maybe they'll be able to pull a print or some DNA. But first I'm going to finishing looking around," he says. "Make sure the apartment's empty and you two are safe."

First Betsey nods. Then I nod, and in an instant, I'm feeling at peace with this guy.

I whisper, "Thank you."

"Now, Bets," says Joel, "you texted me after our call that the real shocker is in the baby's room."

Text? When did Betsey have time to text him? We were together since the moment we walked in. What else did she tell Joel? Okay, she did use the bathroom. But...I don't know.

I point to the open door that leads to Oscar's room.

"You don't have to go in there," says Tierney. "If I've got questions I can..."

"No. It's okay. I've seen it. I own it."

I'm really trying to act like the grown-up I should be. And, as you might have already guessed, that doesn't quite work out. The moment we enter the room, the moment I see that pile of baby items, I scream, "Oh, fucking unbelievable!"

"It's okay, Em. It's going to be okay," says Betsey in her soothing, quiet way. She puts her arm around me again. I push her away and stand back.

Now I actually begin screaming at Betsey.

"And you didn't even tell him about the silver picture frame! And why not? Why are you keeping from him that my parents' anniversary photo was moved?"

"Ms. Atkinson, I know you've had quite a shock, so let's try to remain calm," says Tierney.

But I can't stop yelling. I continue my tirade against Betsey.

"And don't tell me that you forgot. You didn't forget. Betsey Brown never forgets anything. You didn't tell him on purpose. You don't want this solved."

And then, as if I suddenly got an injection of some mystical magical peace serum, I am no longer angry. I'm ashamed of the awful words that I've been screaming. I throw my arms around Betsey and apologize.

"We will take care of this, ma'am," says Tierney.

Now he's the one I'm furious with. I seem to have no control over the angry me and the quiet me.

The words in my brain at this time, however, do not move to my lips, but I know that if they did they'd all be big and angry and ugly.

I want to say, *Don't patronize me. Don't bullshit me with kindness. You asshole. You slept with me.*

Instead I simply nod and revert to my usual string of "Yes. Yes. Yes. Thank you."

"Let's get out of this room," Betsey says.

"No, I've got to stay," I answer.

"Are you sure?" Betsey asks.

"Ms. Atkinson is right," Tierney says. "You've always got to stay ahead of the invaders, at least emotionally ahead of them."

Invaders. I wish he hadn't used that word. I think I hate it because it's so precise—*I feel like I've been invaded, violated.* That's exactly what people say. But it's true.

Tierney punches some tabs on his phone. Then he looks at Betsey and me and speaks.

"My partner, Detective Scofield, is going to join us shortly. She'll have some questions and get a statement. Meanwhile…"

Tierney then aims his phone at the pile in the center of the room. He begins taking photos. Quickly. Lots of photos. Then he takes photos of other parts of the room—the crib, the walls, the beautiful mobile, the beautiful mobile.

But now I'm groggy, and I know that if I had any food inside, I'd be throwing up. I tell Betsey that I've got to use the bathroom, that I've got to sit down. She leads me to the small bathroom between the living room and kitchen.

When I exit the bathroom Betsey Brown and Joel Tierney are seated at the kitchen table. Betsey stands and asks if I want something to drink. I shake my head.

Then she says, "Anything for you, Detective?"

I say, "Unfortunately someone drank our last two beers." Both Betsey and Tierney look at me like I escaped from a mental institution.

Then I quickly add, "It's funny. What I just said was meant to be funny."

I can't say that a sparkle invades Tierney's eyes, but I do think that I see a tiny curl of a smile on his face.

"No. I'm good," he says, and I could also swear that Tierney looks at me when he says, "I'm good."

Okay, maybe that's just my stupid mind seeing a stupid double meaning in everything. Who knows? I'm not really functioning on full battery power. It's a miracle that I'm functioning at all.

Betsey fills a glass with water from the tap and joins us at the table.

"Look," Tierney says. "I want to talk to you both. And I need to say—assure you, really— that I am going to find out who pulled this shit. What happened here is horrible, and we'll do everything we can to find out who's behind it."

Tierney has segued into his reassuring, comforting, serious, paternal voice. It doesn't piss me off, but I'm not falling for it. Tierney keeps talking.

"This isn't the first time something like this has happened in New York. And I'm afraid it won't be the last time. But it'll be the last time for this guy."

A little cop tough talk never hurt a situation, I guess. But Betsey can answer cop tough talk with nurse tough talk.

"So, okay, you've got a plan? What is it?"

Tierney explodes. "Stop!" he says. "Just stop it."

And she does. Clearly angry. Now silent.

I look at Betsey. Then I look down at the floor. I'm too tired to cry. I'm even too tired to be scared.

"This is going to get solved," Tierney says. Then he looks right at me. "You are going to be safe, Emily."

I just want to pee. I want to sleep. I want to have a big shot of bourbon with a little bit of Coca-Cola floating on top.

Tierney's phone buzzes. He looks at it.

"Scofield will be here in two minutes. I'm going to wait for her downstairs. Then we'll be up here again. Like I said, Detective Scofield will have some questions and take a statement."

He stands. As soon as he leaves the room, I speak.

"What do you think, Betsey?" I ask.

She sighs.

"I think Joel is a good, smart person," she says. "What do you think, Em?"

"Yeah. He's a good, smart person...when he's not being an asshole."

CHAPTER

73

IT PAYS TO HAVE connections.

I'm experiencing that truth right now. Thanks to Betsey, two NYPD homicide investigators, Detective Tierney and Detective Scofield, have dropped everything to come to my apartment to check out a break-in.

My job seems extremely simple: I just keep saying the phrase, "Do whatever you want" over and over.

"I'm going to take some more photos of the baby's room," says Scofield.

"Do whatever you want."

"I'm going to need a statement. Okay?"

"Do whatever you want."

Everything matters. And nothing matters. I'm in that weird physical world beyond tired. I'm in the world of aching back and incurably dry mouth and hammering headache.

Tierney pulls on latex gloves and drops the two empty beer cans into two plastic evidence bags.

Scofield says, "I want to see the child's room."

First she called it the *baby's room*. Now the *child's room*. Oscar is growing up before he's even born.

I suddenly feel panicky.

"You won't touch anything in there, will you?"

"I won't, unless I think I have to. But I won't disturb anything without telling you."

I do not want to see the pile, the baby items that I had accumulated with so much love and hope and joy.

"Yeah, okay. Go ahead," I say. "Do whatever…" and I don't even bother finishing the sentence.

I don't time how long Scofield is in the nursery, but it's not that long. Tierney, meanwhile, inspects the photos on the piano more closely. He places the overturned anniversary picture in another plastic evidence bag.

When Scofield comes back out she simply says, "As described. I understand why you're so upset, Ms. Atkinson."

I nod.

"Is this an okay time to ask you some questions?"

I nod again.

"Detective Tierney has briefed me on what's happened. So I won't take up much more of your time," says Scofield.

"We've got all night, and then some," says Betsey, impatient, just short of rude.

Now it's Scofield's turn to nod. Then she speaks.

Her questions are simple and to the point. How well do you know the doorman who was on duty when you returned home? Were there any other people in the lobby when you returned home? Anyone else on the elevator?

When she asks, "Do you know your neighbors?" I answer, "Not very well. There is some crabby old lady next door. But we hardly ever speak." I'm too exhausted to share any further details. A quick glance and blink of an eye from Betsey tell me that she agrees with my decision to keep quiet about Mariana Micelli—no need to get her riled up and make her even madder at me than she already is. I've got enough to worry about without throwing fuel on that fire. At least not throwing it on that fire *yet*.

When my brief interview with Detective Scofield ends, she thanks me.

"Thank you both," I say to her and Tierney, who gives me a knowing nod.

"You're welcome, Ms. Atkinson. We'll be in touch."

The detectives leave. Betsey dials her phone and places it to her ear.

"Frankie. Hi, sweetie. Would you hate it if I had an overnight at Emily's? Things are rough here. You got my text, right? No, no, everything's fine. It's just that she needs me."

Oh, hell. I think I want to be alone.

"No. Go home," I say. Loud enough for Frank to hear me on the other end.

"I don't think she should be alone."

"Betsey, you are talking about me like I am not here. I'm perfectly okay."

"So you don't want me to stay?"

"Do whatever you want."

CHAPTER

74

OUR BIG GIRLS' SLEEPOVER is neither a giddy party nor a heartbreaking soap opera. Here's what's really nice about good friends: You can keep adjusting your emotional temperature toward them. Hour by hour, sometimes even minute by minute.

"Where do you keep your vacuum cleaner?" Betsey asks.

"I should know the answer to that question, shouldn't I?" I say.

Betsey laughs. The first time in many hours.

"I think it's in the walk-in closet in the guest room. If it's not there . . . well, I'll help you look."

"I'll find it," she says. And she does.

Apparently, the guest room closet also housed an electric floor polisher, a long-handled brush that Betsey identified as a cordless scrubber, twenty-some-odd items of soaps and powder and cleansers and liquid cleansers, and, as Betsey says, "every Swiffer product ever made." I don't remember buying any of it.

"I'm going to vacuum and straighten up the baby's room," Betsey says. Her voice is soft, tentative. I appreciate that she doesn't want to upset me.

"You don't have to do it with me, Em. Unless you want to."

"I'm not sure," I say. "I know you don't need me. But I guess I should help. But then again..."

Betsey shrugs. "You'll go back in the room when you're ready."

I nod, and decide to follow Betsey as she wheels the vacuum down the hallway, through the kitchen and into the baby's room.

When we get to the door of the room—the baby's room—I say, "I'm ready."

I see now that much of the floor is sprinkled with tiny pieces of gold dust from a gift-packaged stuffed dinosaur. I bought the giant stuffed animal from Mary Arnold Toys, where I used to hang out as a child. For Oscar it would be the first of a million gifts—from video games to ski poles to Paul Smith sweaters—that I'd be giving him for the rest of his life...well, the rest of my life.

"Here. Plug this in," says Betsey. The whir of the vacuum cleaner erupts, and suddenly the carpet is becoming perfectly clean. I cannot say that my terror and sadness are disappearing along with the glitter, but there is something soul-satisfying about a return to an immaculately clean and normal baby's room.

Even though the floor has not been completely vacuumed, Betsey suddenly turns off the machine.

"Where's your phone, Emily?" she asks.

"In my hoodie. In the kitchen."

"I think I hear it ringing. That Drake song. 'Toosie Slide.'"

By the time I get to the kitchen the ringing has stopped. There's no message.

Betsey appears. "Who was it?"

I look at the screen. NO CALLER ID.

"It's probably just a spammer," says Betsey. "Or someone who..."

Betsey trails off. It seems she wants to say more.

"Someone who *what*, Betsey?"

"Someone who's intentionally blocking their number. Someone who wants to keep their identity a secret."

I have to imagine Betsey and I are thinking the same thing. But before we can share it, my phone starts blaring Drake again.

Again the screen reads NO CALLER ID.

This time I quickly answer it. After I say hello, I hear the familiar cut-off of a hang-up.

Drake's song begins again almost immediately. Again NO CALLER ID. Again I answer, only to be hung up on.

"Somebody's fucking with us...or with me," I say. "Enough of that."

I hold the phone away from me like it's some dangerous and diseased animal, which is exactly what it's become.

"Let me see it," says Betsey. She takes the phone. It rings again. Betsey puts it on speaker, answers, and immediately surrenders to her instincts.

"Just stop it, asshole!" she yells into the phone. Then the call ends.

A second later, my Drake ringtone plays.

I grab the phone from Betsey and fling it with all my strength against the kitchen floor.

Even though I just saw the phone break, we hear *another* ring. Not a song. An actual old-fashioned ringing. A sound I hear almost never. At first, I don't even recognize it. Then I do.

"That's the landline," I say. The cordless phone is sitting on the kitchen counter, not far from where the two beer cans were found.

What biological impulse overcomes Betsey and me? Why do we both reach to hold our bellies, to protect our babies at precisely the same time?

It keeps ringing. Incessant. Ominous.

In a fit of rage, I march over and yank the landline from the wall.

"I guess we won," says Betsey.

I walk toward her. I rub my eyes with my hands.

"I don't think so, Bets. Not for a minute."

CHAPTER

75

The Present

BETSEY IS TRYING TO walk, talk, and steer her wheelie suitcase.

Either the phone or the wheelie could escape her grip at any moment. She walks carefully but she very much wants to walk quickly. This very pregnant and very tired woman is now dealing with the usual crowd and mess in the American Airlines terminal of Newark airport.

She realizes, of course, that she could become the star of a classic *accident waiting to happen* scenario.

She talks to her husband on the phone.

"Listen. I got what I wanted in Vegas, but two nights with Auntie Mama is rough on any person, let alone a pregnant person," she tells Frankie. "I watched her drink about four gallons of whiskey sours last night, while my only nourishment was five maraschino cherries."

"Just be sure to take a taxi home, Bets," Frankie says.

"We'll see," she answers.

"Damn, babe. Don't cheap out on yourself now. There's a baby inside you, and you've just been on a six-hour flight that you shouldn't have been on. If your ob-gyn knew you were even flying…"

"Okay. First of all, it was a five-hour flight… Anyway, I'll spring for a cab. I'm beat."

"Good. I love you."

They hang up, and Betsey immediately calls Joel Tierney.

"Are you going to be in your office for the next hour or so?" Betsey asks.

"If you're coming by to bug me about Emily's disappearance, forget it."

Kalisha—her eyes practically hypnotized by the page headlined MIKE MILLER. LIVERPOOL—waves her hands in the air. She is signaling Tierney not to tell Betsey about the Mike Miller breakthrough. Tierney nods vigorously. He doesn't say a word about it.

Tierney continues, "We've got a sort-of-maybe-could-be-possible piece of info. But we can't share it yet."

Betsey exits the terminal and looks for a cab. She has almost grown used to the constant agony of an aching back and a throbbing head.

"Look. You can be a jerk about this, Joel. So don't loop me in. But I've got something important that I need to tell you," says Betsey. "I'm coming by."

"Give me a preview," he says.

"The only preview is that, of course, it has to do with Emily. Oh, and it has to do with the fact that I've been doing the job that you and your partner are supposed to be doing."

Tierney just says, "Oh, for Christ's sake," and then hangs up.

CHAPTER

76

FORTY-FIVE MINUTES LATER BETSEY is sitting with both
Tierney and Scofield in Tierney's office. Betsey's feet (swollen ankles included) rest on an
overturned wastepaper basket. She is suffering
from scorching heartburn, and she knows she
won't be able to douse the heartburn by drinking the station house's weak decaf coffee.

There is no trace of human warmth in the
air. This is very apparent when Betsey says,
"You think I can have a little more milk in this
fabulous coffee?"

Tierney says, "I got it."

As Betsey stirs her coffee, Kalisha, losing
patience, says, "I heard you have something

you wanted to share with us. Perhaps you can start the sharing."

Betsey pauses for a moment, then says, "I've been to Vegas, and I made a killing."

Tierney shows no reaction to Betsey's statement. Kalisha's face is a combination of confused and pissed off.

"You want to explain that a little, ma'am?" asks Kalisha.

"I always had a hunch about who the father of Emily's baby was. And now I'm confident my hunch was right."

"Don't keep the news to yourself, lady," Kalisha says.

"I had to go to Vegas to find out," says Betsey.

"Vegas? Damn," says Tierney. "Don't hold back."

"It's your friendly neighborhood bartender, Ted Burrows. Who, for your information, is also Emily's ex-husband."

Tierney stands up quickly.

"With all due respect, Betsey, that's bullshit," says Tierney.

"I want to hear more," Kalisha says. "Go on."

"Thank you. It's not bullshit at all," says Betsey. "I went to Las Vegas. I found the chapel where Emily and Ted were married in one of those quickie ceremonies. I spoke to the guy who officiated. I saw the marriage certificate."

She takes her phone from her bag. She hits a few buttons.

"Emily said they got it annulled the next day, before they flew home. But take a look. A marriage certificate. Right there. Even if they got it annulled, this proves they were at least married. That's big."

She thrusts the phone toward Tierney and Scofield. Kalisha is actually smiling. Tierney is vaguely startled.

"Maybe you're surprised, Detective Tierney," says Kalisha. "But not me. Not at all. My instincts always told me that Ted Burrows was a creep and a liar. Smooth and sweet and full of shit."

"Listen, Detective—and you listen, too, Betsey. Even if it's true. Even if it's true, what the hell does that matter? Just because they were married doesn't mean he's the father," says Tierney.

Kalisha jumps in, saying, "Well, we're still a lot closer than we were five minutes ago. That's what I have to say."

Tierney presses Betsey for more information about the trip to Vegas. But there isn't much else to say.

Betsey's delivered her message. Now she just wants to wrap it up and get home.

"I went to Las Vegas. I had a hunch. I had to do it. I woke up one morning and my husband was coming in from his shift. And I asked him what he thought about my going to Vegas," says Betsey.

Kalisha speaks.

"And your husband was cool with it?"

"No, not at all. But he knew there was no stopping me."

"That is wicked. I am proud of you," says Kalisha. "You went with your instinct. I went no place with mine." Then Kalisha looks at her partner and says, "Isn't that right, Detective?"

Kalisha knows she is headed into dangerous territory—criticizing her partner. She's angry and frustrated. She's relieved that Tierney responds calmly.

"I really did think that Ted was one of the good ones," Tierney says. "He never seemed sneaky. Just an open and honest guy. So when you said he sounded like a big liar...well, I just thought you were wrong."

Neither Kalisha nor Betsey says anything.

After a moment, Kalisha says, "Well, that could be the problem, sir. With all due respect. Sometimes you ought to listen. You might find out that other people can occasionally be right about things."

CHAPTER

77

THE DETECTIVES TELL TED Burrows that they want to interview him about Emily Atkinson. Ted seems unfazed by the word *interview*.

"Good deal," he says. "Interview away."

Ted offers them a beverage, which they decline. Then he tells a server to "keep both your eyes on the bar." He explains to the detectives that "It's late afternoon, not much of a crowd yet." Then Ted suggests that they "conduct the interview in my office."

A few minutes later Tierney and Kalisha and Ted move into a very small room at the rear of Ted's Bar. Kalisha believes this office is actually a storage closet with a sawed-down barstool serving as a desk. Cases of Gordon's gin and Buffalo Trace bourbon are stacked next to an even taller stack of New Amsterdam vodka.

"You know, when you two guys came in and said you needed to talk to me, I thought two different things. One, that you had good news about Emily. Or two, you had the worst possible news," says Ted. Then he suddenly turns serious and solemn. He speaks quietly: "So what is it? Good news or bad news?"

Kalisha says, "You can be the judge of that."

Then Tierney talks. His voice is stern. His words come fast.

"I don't want to bullshit around, Burrows. For the sake of time and efficiency, let's get to the point."

"Whatever you say, Detective," says Ted.

"That's right. Whatever I say."

Kalisha is alarmed by her partner's increasingly aggressive tone. She tries to turn down the temperature on the confrontation.

"We're going to have a few questions," she says. "The questions are based on information that we have regarding…"

Tierney interrupts.

"Here's the first question, maybe the only

question: Did you and Emily Atkinson get married at the Lucky Little Wedding Chapel in Las Vegas, Nevada?"

Ted looks away. He seems to have become fixated on the nearby towers of liquor. Then he looks up at the ceiling. His eyes flicker quickly. Now he seems to be studying the big, dusty ceiling fan.

"What the hell is going on with Emily?" Ted says, his voice a combination of weeping and pleading and fright.

"Answer the question, man," says Tierney.

"Yes. Yes. And it's not like I've ever denied this. And it's not like you brought a big piece of fucking news with you. Yes, we got drunk. We went to Vegas. We were going to play the craps tables, see a big show, do the town. But, like I said, we got drunk. We got drunk and we got married."

"And then?" Tierney asks.

"And then the next day...before we flew home, we sobered up and stopped at the courthouse and twenty minutes later the whole thing was annulled."

"You're so full of crap," says Kalisha.

"What? What crap? The wedding? I told

you, yes, Emily and I got married. The annulment? I told you, yes, Emily and I got that, too. Why would I lie to you about this?"

Kalisha sizes up Burrows, lets the silence sit for a moment, and then continues.

"Okay, Mr. Burrows, let's say you're telling us the straight truth. Wedding was a lark sort of thing. Right?"

"Right," says Ted.

"You know, what happens in Las Vegas stays there, that sort of thing," says Kalisha.

"Right again," says Ted.

"That all means nothing. But one thing does mean something. And here's what that is. Here is what we need to know. Married. Divorced. Whatever. *Are you the father of Emily Atkinson's baby?*"

Ted smiles, then says, "Like you said...what happens in Vegas—"

Tierney suddenly stands and shouts, "Cut the shit! Emily is missing! She is nine months pregnant!"

Ted twists his head quickly. His eyes are watery. But it's not from fear. It's not from emotional pain.

"I want her to be safe," he says. "I want her

to come home. I want to make her a peach daiquiri. I want to . . . I want it to be good."

Ted immediately pushes his hands against
his eyes. It almost seems that he's trying to push
the tears back where they came from.

"But I am not the father of that baby. And
the reason I'm sure of that is that Emily told
me I wasn't. I asked her a thousand times, and
a thousand times she told me that she knew
who the father was, and it wasn't me, and she
wouldn't tell me who it was . . ."

A long pause. The tears that Ted was fighting a few seconds ago have gone away. He
stands, defiant now.

"Feels like you're through with me."

"Thanks for your help," says Kalisha.

Tierney says nothing. The sneer on his face
says everything.

Apparently, Ted feels the need to say, "Look.
It's the truth. I am not the father here."

The detectives say nothing.

"No, I'm absolutely not the father. But you
know what?"

"What?" asks Kalisha.

"I really wish I was."

CHAPTER

78

WHAT'S THE ADDRESS ON Mike Miller?" Tierney asks Kalisha as they leave from their interview with Ted.

"One thirty-six West 74th Street."

"Let's head up there right now," says Tierney. He is clearly bursting with energy.

"We can't get inside. I checked an hour ago with ADA Wakerman. She won't have a search warrant signed by a judge for us for at least another two or three hours."

"Fuck that," says Tierney.

"I'm with you, Detective. It's just that without a warrant..."

"Watch me, Detective Scofield. Just watch me."

Twenty minutes later, the pair is standing before a multi-unit brownstone between Amsterdam Avenue and Columbus Avenue. The door buzzer to apartment 3B is marked "M. J. Miller."

"I don't know much about this guy," says Kalisha. "But I figured him for a penthouse with a doorman with a fancy bar and a media room."

"Don't judge a crib by its cover," says Tierney. "We might just walk into a museum full of Jasper Johns paintings on the wall and a wine cellar."

Before Tierney can press the buzzer, the big downstairs entrance door opens. An older woman—short, chubby, stern-looking—stands before them. She speaks with a foreign accent. Greek? Turkish? Neither Tierney nor Scofield can identify it.

"You are here visiting?" the woman says curtly. "I am landlady. Why do all my tenants have so many guests? Coming in and out, in and out—"

"We're not exactly *invited* guests," says Tierney. He is intent on sounding tougher than the woman. "I'm Detective Tierney, NYPD. This is Detective Scofield. We need access to Michael Miller's apartment. Do you have a key?"

Clearly the words *detective* and *NYPD* have immediately softened her up.

"But of course I can help you."

Scofield and Tierney's predictions about a glamorous apartment are totally wrong.

They soon find themselves standing in a third-floor studio apartment at the rear of the brownstone. The dark little room is painted a cheap "landlord white." One corner of the room has a dirty reddish-brown club chair, another corner has nothing but a small sink, a half-sized refrigerator, and a microwave.

"So much for a chef's kitchen," says Kalisha.

A twin-size Murphy bed is opened and meticulously made with one white sheet and one thin gray blanket. The Ikea-issue black plastic table holds one short stack of papers, one black coffee mug, one closed Apple laptop, one Montblanc fountain pen, one bottle of blue-black ink. As for wall hangings, none—no *Mona Lisa* repro, no dogs playing poker. Bare walls. This just about ends Tierney and Scofield's real estate tour.

"Why is this place reminding me of a jail cell?" Kalisha says.

Tierney shoots out the tiniest bit of laughter and begins going through the pile of papers. He doesn't rush his inspection, but it becomes pretty clear to him that the papers are mostly monthly receipts showing that Mike Miller is up to date on his ConEd bill, his Visa bill, and—perhaps another avenue for investigation—his membership at a boxing gym on Broadway. Tierney reports to Kalisha what little he's found.

They search the three drawers of the small wooden cabinet next to the bed—two navyblue Lacoste polo shirts, six Paul Stuart white button-down shirts, five neatly ironed handkerchiefs. The top shelf is socks, underwear, a copy of—holy shit—a dog-eared Bible and a few packets of Crown Skinless Skin condoms. Only the best rubbers for Mike Miller.

"I'll check the bathroom," says Tierney.

"I'll get that closet where we came in," says Kalisha. "It looks like the only closet in the place."

Tierney takes in the standard cheap rental fixtures, a white bath towel, and a medicine cabinet filled with nothing but a bottle of Aleve, mouthwash, a container holding three Lunesta sleep tablets, a razor, and a can of Edge shave cream. That's it. The whole deal. The coke, the pills, the heroin, the whole little supermarket of drugs that Miller peddles are obviously kept somewhere else, not in a third-floor walk-up studio with one lock.

"Detective!" comes a shout from Kalisha. Tierney for a moment thinks maybe he's been wrong. Maybe his partner has found a cache of uppers and crack for sale.

It takes Tierney only a few seconds to get back to her.

The closet she's inspecting is small, hardly a walk-in, barely able to contain a few Men's Wearhouse suits and two Men's Wearhouse coats—a raincoat, a woolen topcoat.

"What's up?" Tierney asks.

"Behind you," she says. "Look at the inside of the door."

He snaps his head to the side. A bulletin board hangs against the inside of the door. The board measures about two feet by two feet. It is mostly covered with photographs. One of the photos is easily identifiable as Mike Miller—as a child, a sad-looking six-year-old wearing green shorts and T-shirt that says SEVEN ACRES DAY CAMP. Another is that same little boy, perhaps a year or two older; the boy's arm is extended to the camera. It looks like little Mike Miller is toasting the photographer with a glass of milk.

Beyond these two pictures, all the other photos—ten of them—are candid shots of the same woman.

Emily Atkinson.

Emily walking on Fifth Avenue. Emily leaving her apartment. Emily entering her apartment. Emily in the lobby of the Dazzle building. Emily and a handsome man sitting behind the glass at Madison Square Garden.

In many pictures she's not pregnant. But in a few she clearly is.

"Detective," says Kalisha. "Look at *these*."

A few inches away from the cluster of Emily pictures are two other candid photos of two different women.

One photo is a lovely redhead hailing a taxi.

The other is a lovely blonde alone on a bench in Central Park.

Tierney and Kalisha both move their heads in closer to those two pictures.

"Holy shit," says Tierney. "That's Caitlin Murphy. And that's Nina Powell."

"Holy shit is right," says Kalisha. "One dead woman...and two missing."

Something catches Tierney's eye.

"What's that down there?" he says.

At the bottom of the closet, in the back, there's a small box. Kalisha, gloves on her hands, pulls it out so they can look inside. She removes the top of the box and they find... Caitlin's driver's license. Nina's driver's license.

And a bloody knife.

"Trophies," says Kalisha.

"And a murder weapon," says Tierney.

"Let's hope it's not too late for Emily."

MONTH NINE

CHAPTER

79

ALL I WANT TO DO is hide, get away, be alone.

I have a place where I can do just that—my parents' house. Or, as I should say, my *late* parents' house.

Or, to be even more accurate, *my* house.

It turns out my aunt Dolly had nothing to worry about. They may have treated me terribly in life, but my parents were exceedingly generous to me in death. They had earmarked some of their artwork to be donated to the Metropolitan Museum of Art, the Guggenheim, and others. But most of their collection and massive fortune—including their multiple homes and investment portfolio—now belongs to yours truly.

I've always hated lawyers, contracts, fine print. All that stuff. It gives me a headache just thinking about it. Luckily, the process was pretty seamless. A few mind-numbingly boring calls over the past few months with Henry Kleinhenz, my parents' longtime lawyer. A small stack of papers that needed my John Hancock.

That was it. The deeds were transferred into my name. The money showed up in my accounts. Enough that I never need to work another day in my life. Enough that I can spend all my time and energy raising my precious little Oscar.

Right now I'm on my way to Sharon, Connecticut. The last time I visited the town was for Liz and Lionel's funeral. The last time I visited the house... was when I was a junior in college. God! How my folks loved that place. They could not get enough of it. For me, well, it was lonely, unexciting, boring.

But right now, that house—*my* house— might save my life.

I can no longer keep trying to escape the stalker who may be following me. Every corner I turn, every restaurant where I eat, holds the promise of terror. What's more, the two detectives, Tierney and Scofield, don't believe me. My shrink says she believes me. But for God's sake, she's my shrink. She has to act as if I'm telling the truth. Does my best friend, Saint Betsey of Queens, believe me? Sometimes yes, sometimes no. And I just don't want to deal with it anymore.

It's been a few months since I was last behind the wheel, driving to my parents' funeral. As I cruise north on the Taconic State Parkway, I can hear empty bottles and beer cans rattling on the car's rear floor. Another time? Another place? I think so. Or at least I hope so.

The decision to come here was so last minute that I didn't tell anyone about my escape. I tell myself that I don't want friends worrying. But, face it, Emily, chances are that they've all got bigger problems than the crazy fears of a pregnant lady. The detectives have real crimes to solve. Dr. Craven has patients crowding her waiting room. And Betsey? I've never had a friend this brave and true, but she's pregnant, too. Nine months. Ready to pop, as so many people are so fond of saying. She has kids... and a tough job... and a husband. She doesn't need me on her worry list.

I get it. I understand it. I am alone.

I'm also driving alone, which may not be the

wisest decision I've ever made—even in a life-time of many questionable decisions.

They say drinking and driving don't mix. Well, I've got a new axiom: Pregnancy and driving don't mix. Particularly if you're in your ninth month. Particularly if you have to stop to urinate at every other rest stop along the route. Particularly if you have constant leg cramps, no energy, and—I'm not embarrassed to say it—hemorrhoids that feel like someone has pumped acid up my butt. Yes, a horrible image, I know. But at least I'm leaving out lengthy descriptions of the accompanying farting, spotting, and heartburn.

Oscar has pretty much stopped kicking. I'm not alarmed. You see, he's become way more aggressive: now he's squirming. As Dr. Craven puts it, "He's looking for the exit door." That makes me smile, but, as my mind wanders while I drive, I imagine my belly splitting open and finding ten pounds of baby on my lap.

Like they say, don't judge me. I've admitted that I'm mentally a little off my game.

SUNOCO STATION 3 MILES. Was any sign more welcome than that?

In a few minutes I am going through the

same scene that I've already encountered three times on this ride so far.

Me: May I please have the key to the ladies' room?
He: *(laughing)* You're not gonna deliver that baby in there, are you?
Me: *(laughing)* I hope not.

Back in the car I'm on the lookout for the exit where I cut out of New York and into Connecticut.

The baby inside me, my little Oscar, seems equally excited about our arrival. He is squirming and pushing and struggling in his own little world.

I pat my belly.

"We're going to a wonderful safe place, baby Oscar. It's got lots of grass and trees and flowers. And we'll have milk to drink and food to..."

Shit. I forgot to order groceries. I meant to have them delivered, waiting for me up at the house. *Nice going, Emily.*

My ride to my parents' house just got a little longer.

CHAPTER

80

SUPERMARKETS ARE NEVER the fun they promise to be.

They are almost always shockingly bright from the fluorescent bulbs. They usually smell of bad fruit and dead meat. Long refrigerator cases of dismembered chicken and bloody beef. End aisle pyramids of detergents and bleach and tuna fish cans.

For God's sake, Emily. Get over yourself. Just go in there and buy your low-fat yogurt and organic blueberries and whole milk and get to the house and take a nap.

First things first. I use the bathroom in the Stop & Shop, and a few minutes later I'm pushing a shopping cart. My first instinct, however,

is not to look at the banana tree or the Good
Seasons dressing display.

I need to find out if anyone might have followed me at dawn's early light from Manhattan. And am I crazy enough to think I'll find
them in a Stop & Shop on the New York–
Connecticut border?

Okay. There's the mother with a baby pouch
and baby. The bald chubby man arranging
cantaloupes as if they were bowling balls in
an electric dispenser. The man in baggy blue
shorts and a sleeveless Knicks T-shirt. The
man's girlfriend in a pink sleeveless top and
black tights. Of course, I know this is absurd.
It can't be any of these people. I've got to move
on. Except…Everyone in a supermarket in
Dutchess County New York at nine o'clock on
a crisp fall day looks mean and suspicious, as
well as nice and innocent, as well as none of
those things. Nobody's out to get me, or everyone's out to get me.

I've got to pull myself together and start
shopping. I should just go right to the dairy
case for some yogurt, maybe cottage cheese,
maybe a few Kozy Shack chocolate puddings.

I pass a guy, middle age, pleasant-looking,

yellow Ralph Lauren sport shirt. He glances at me when I pass him, and then he returns to his intense study of … of … cottage cheese?

I pick out some yogurts. Strawberry. Two fruit-on-the-bottom. Five low-fat. Four Greek-style.

The yellow-shirt guy is studying the containers of cottage cheese as if he were in a museum studying art. He takes a few seconds out from his work to glance at me again. I think he's going to talk to me. I've had that feeling a million times before, and I'm usually right.

But he doesn't.

No *Looks like you're quite the yogurt fan.*

No *Excuse me, do you know anything about cottage cheese?*

Hell, he's just another guy in the supermarket. Thin. In shape. Good jeans. A little too much hair on his arms.

But I can't help myself from creating a police report in my head.

Of course, I have no reason to believe that he is following me, that he's trailed me on highways upstate, that he's been stalking me in the city. I have nominated him as chief suspect, all based on nothing. He is no more alarming than the guy in the produce section organizing melons or the harried soccer mom ordering at the deli counter.

I want to run. I just want to run. But I'm pregnant, and I'm pushing the damned cart, and I'm sure I'm just making this whole thing up.

But then the guy in the yellow shirt moves even closer.

Now he's looking at those cardboard cylinders that you twist and they ooze out dough that turns into cinnamon buns—he isn't looking at me.

This would not be a good time or a good place for me to throw up.

I bet he's writing a story about shopping. Maybe he's just picking up a few things for the kids. He moves to the end of the refrigerated aisle, and I walk away. He doesn't look at me. At all. I feel off-balance. I start talking to the baby in my belly. "We're okay, Oscar. We're gonna be fine." But then I think that everyone around me has begun to look at me. I'm talking to myself. I'm hyperventilating, sweating. I should have stayed in the city. There at least I could cross the street, slip into a taxi.

I head toward the checkout counter.

More people are looking at me now. They're whispering; I can feel it. Is it because I'm so large? Do they think I'm about to give birth? A woman in a long, bright-red caftan stops her grocery cart near me.

"Why, hello, Emily!" she says brightly.

Did she say that? Did she actually say "Emily," or did she just say "hello"? I don't know. Does she know me, or is she just being friendly? Look at her, the big straw hat, the chunky red Bakelite necklace. I think I know her. But do I really?

I respond, "So great to see you. Hey. I'm in such a rush."

I move on. And why in hell did I ever think that I could hide away up here?

I will get to my parents' house and lock the door and order food and never answer the door and never answer the phone and everything will be just peachy. No guys in yellow shirts. No women in red caftans.

Keep moving, Emily.

The sign says: TEN ITEMS OR LESS. I peer into my shopping cart. Here's my plan. I count all the yogurts as one item. With that as a loophole, I have twelve items. I pity the person who challenges this very nervous, hassled, pregnant woman on her number of items.

Grocery bags in hand, I leave the Stop & Shop. I go outside. I lean on one of those twenty-five-cent electronic horse rides for kids. I rest. I take a breath. The air stinks of old garbage. Not such a good idea. The electronic horse stands in front of an overflowing garbage bin. I see the supermarket exit door swing open.

The man in the yellow shirt comes out.

He has no grocery bags. He's walking quickly. And as he walks he is looking down at a clipboard, making marks on the board with a pencil.

He passes very close to me. He wrinkles his nose. It's the garbage.

He doesn't even see me.

CHAPTER

81

MY PARENTS ALWAYS CALLED IT *our place in the country.*

And now it's mine.

I can slap white paint over green paint. I can get my own splattered Pollocks to replace Liz and Lionel's splattered Pollocks. I can plant anemones where Liz had tulips. I can replace their Victorian carved bed with a low-slung Japanese minimalist bed.

But whatever I do it will always be *their* house.

I pull into the driveway.

A navy-blue Mercedes GLS is parked near the entrance. Maybe the guy who services the pool is rich. Or perhaps the maniac following me...*oh, shit, Emily, stop it.*

Most likely it's Doris, or Florence Packman, the neighbor.

I walk inside. I stand like an awkward twelve-year-old kid in the front hall. I think I should shout, *Mother! Daddy! I'm home!*

I shake my head. I pat my belly. I look around.

Yes. I'm home. In this crazy, beautiful, ridiculous house with mid-century modern furniture all mixed up with a Jim Dine heart painting and a giant Berenice Abbott photograph of a Lower East Side kosher bakery.

Update on my mental condition: I've suddenly stopped being nervous.

I am perhaps a little sad. But this is what I've gone after. Being alone.

I can't help but think about Liz and Lionel; I'm standing in the house they loved way more than they should have. Would I be this emotional if my parents had not had such an untimely death? Who knows? Why ask questions you can't possibly answer?

First, of course, I pee. Then I carry my bag of

groceries into the kitchen. I stand there and look around. It has the look and feel of the massive kitchen on *Downton Abbey* with a slightly modern touch. The room is spotless (God bless Doris). Big copper bowls hang on the wall. A restaurant-sized Wolf oven sits next to a triple-basin sink.

I know that nothing elaborate will be cooked in here by me. Tuna on white bread and chocolate ice cream, but that's about it. Even that may be too complicated for a very pregnant, very tired lady. Bring on the strawberry yogurt. But whatever I do I've got to keep the liquor cabinet locked. Just one of those notes to self.

I am just about to find the energy for unpacking the groceries when I hear a woman's voice. The voice is joyful, loud. It comes from the hallway that leads from the rear driveway to the kitchen.

"Look who's back! It's Emily!"

Who the hell? What the hell?

Then another voice, a different woman.

"Greetings and welcome home," adds the second woman.

I turn around and see Deborah Jacobi and Suzie Hancher, good summertime friends of my late mother's. That explains the Mercedes in the driveway.

Both women carry baskets with huge bunches of flowers. Mrs. Jacobi's basket holds red gladiola. Mrs. Hancher's has pale purple and yellow irises. Both flowers look like they should be at a funeral.

I am not particularly good at names and faces. But even if I hadn't just seen them at the funeral, I could never forget these two. They are not old biddies. They are sharp, tough women. Like my mother, great at bridge, good at golf, truly awful at tennis.

They walk quickly toward me. They are soon on top of me. They are both hugging nine-months-pregnant me as best they can. When they link hands ring-around-the-rosy style they can encircle me.

"I told you Emily could never let go of a place like this," says Mrs. Hancher. She is serious, but not annoying.

"We are gifting you with flowers from your mother's gardens," says Deb Jacobi.

"Deb likes to use words like *gifting*. You know, nouns used as verbs," says Suzie Hancher.

Her tone of voice sounds particularly impatient. *Please go, please.*

"When is the baby due? Yesterday?" says Mrs. Jacobi. She laughs at her own witty line.

Both women seem unable to take their eyes from my belly.

"Soon," I say.

They stay away from the usual natural questions. Is it a boy or a girl? Do you have a name picked out? They also avoid any reference to my mother or father. Nothing like *If only your folks could be here* or *Your mother would be so happy.*

We discuss pregnancy a little bit. They tell me that they always keep an eye on the house. I guess that's good.

They fetch a few vases for the flowers. These two women know more about the house than I do. They get the vases from a cabinet in the butler's pantry. They know which drawer to open to get scissors for cutting the stems. This frightens me a bit. I see the house as a private therapy center. They seem to see it as a happy friends-and-neighbors resort.

They throw out the cut flower stems. They wipe down the wet counters. They know the house so well that they quickly distribute the four floral vases around the place—the family dining room table, the front hall, the living room, the library.

And then they are somehow wise enough to know that I am longing for that moment when I hear, "Well, we better let Emily rest." Deb Jacobi supplies it.

"Are you okay for food?" asks Suzie Hancher as they walk to the kitchen door.

"I'm all yogurted up," I say. "But thank you. Thank you."

"Call if you need anything," Deb says.

"I will," I say. But I know that I won't.

They leave. I have to put my groceries away. But first... Damn. I have to pee again. It hasn't even been five minutes.

CHAPTER

82

DAYS PASS. I'M NOT SURE how many. I am sleeping a lot. An awful lot. Ten, eleven hours, with time off only for a few bathroom breaks.

During the day I sit in a blur of television with Hoda and Kelly and Whoopi and Ellen and Oprah and yogurt. Then once again I sleep through the night.

The doors are locked. The burners on the stove are off. I leave a few lights on downstairs, as well as in my parents' big bedroom on the second floor.

I'm feeling good...I think. So good, I even think I might have been wrong about my stalker. Maybe I was imagining the whole thing.

But then I see a man jogging on the road in front of the house. Then a lightbulb makes a popping sound and goes out. Then the water from the faucet tastes funny.

Today I don't sleep nearly as long as usual. I'm restless during the night. I'm not hungry. What does that matter? I'm shockingly big with Oscar anyway. Where would the food even fit?

I spend some time in my father's library— two thousand volumes, books from Dickens to Updike, books with every word that Winston Churchill ever wrote. I begin picking my way through a 1968 paperback edition of Dr. Spock's *Baby and Child Care*. What's my father doing with this? A nanny or a housekeeper must have left it behind.

I fall asleep, and when I wake up, I think it must be near midnight, even later. But it's only five thirty in the afternoon. I'm terribly thirsty, and, at the same time, of course, I have to pee.

From the bathroom to the kitchen to the refrigerator. An icy can of Diet Pepsi ("I'd stay away from caffeinated, artificially sweetened beverages," I hear Dr. Craven saying). Then another sound, a different sound. Not quite a whistle, not quite a buzz. My first thought: *What's the fastest way out of here?* I check around. The noise is coming from that gargantuan oven. I glance toward the great steel cooker. I want to scream, but I don't.

I see that a very small flame is lighted beneath a very large pot.

I turn it off and lift the cover.

I'm hit with the powerful scent of—it takes me a moment—chicken soup. I look into the pot and see chunks of carrots, big pieces of chicken breast. I scream again. Where did this come from? Did someone break in, chop vegetables, turn on the oven? Even scarier: Did I do this? I start to panic; I don't remember. *I don't remember!*

My heart is racing. I put the cover back on the pot. I check the kitchen door, the storage pantry, the butler's pantry. Everything is still locked, just as I left it. And yet...I glance into the breakfast room. The dark wood table is set. One place. One linen napkin, a soup spoon, a soup bowl, a baguette. I approach the table as if it were a dead body. Slow. Cautious. And then I see a piece of paper. Some writing.

You were sleeping.

Let ourselves in with key yr mother gave us.

Left a huge pot of Suzie's wonderful chicken soup.

Deborah and Suzie

I guess I'm relieved. Well, sort of. What if someone followed Mrs. Jacobi and Mrs. Hancher? Inside? What if he hid? What if he decided to poison the soup?

I've got to stop.

I look up at the kitchen clock. It's not even six o'clock. Yes. I'll go up to my room now. I was kidding myself to think I could escape up here.

I'll drive back to New York City tomorrow.

CHAPTER

83

I LOCK MYSELF INSIDE my room with a bottle of Fresca and a package of Pepperidge Farm Milano cookies.

I slip into my bed, and because I am achingly tired, I wait for the invasion of sleepiness. That doesn't happen. I thrash around, folding and refolding my pillow, massaging my temples, adjusting the sheets.

Nothing works. I stand up. My ankles are alarmingly swollen and hurt like hell.

I walk to the bay window of my bedroom and watch the sky darken over the front gardens and the oak trees. Then I decide to conduct a test. It's important. I am certain that it could save my life.

I unlock my bedroom door and step out into the hallway. The hall chandeliers and hallway lights are all turned off. Check. I return to the bedroom and flip the bedside safety switch, the switch designed to turn on every light in the house. Here goes. The lamps in my bedroom turn bright.

I slowly waddle back into the hallway. The corridor is so bright that Cher could give a concert out here. I rush back into my room and lock the door behind me. Great! The lighting test is working. I pull up the shades. All the outdoor floodlights and spotlights are blazing. No big men. No small deer. I flip the light switch once again. Everything turns dark. I try to sleep. I try to read. I try my labor breathing. Nothing works.

It is now three in the morning. My ankle pain is getting worse. So is my back pain.

I need to take an Ambien. It really has been months since I've swallowed a pill of any kind. But I still have a tiny stash of some old prescriptions. Not like the mini-pharmacy I used to carry around with me in my purse. But close.

Dr. Craven, of course, has forbidden all such medication. "Especially unnecessary sleep medication like Ambien and Lunesta," she said. "They are dependencies that turn into addictions. And you've had problems with that."

Uh, yeah. To say the least.

So, filled with guilt and fear and shame, I take a five-milligram Ambien tablet. Better take ten milligrams, just to be...safe. Is *safe* the right word?

I do not remember falling asleep. But somehow, it happened.

CHAPTER

84

YES, I SLEEP . . . FOR just a few hours. Then I wake. Really wake. My eyes pop open. They think it's morning. I know it isn't. Dawn might be close, but it's still dark outside.

Xanax and Klonopin always worked better. I used to pop that happy pill duet like after-dinner mints. But that was the old days. Now, for Oscar, for me, no way.

So I do what I usually do lately when I have nothing to do. First, I pee. Then I panic.

Suddenly, I am not feeling Oscar inside of me.

No kicking. No squirming. Please, baby,

push down against my bladder. Batter me with discomfort.

I make my way back to bed, and as soon as I slide under the sheet, I am certain that I hear a noise outside. It sounds like a car engine. Then the crackling sound of tires on the gravel driveway on the side of the house.

I struggle to do my most challenging gymnastic trick—getting out of bed. I walk to the bay window and look down on the driveway.

Empty. No car. Nothing.

I reach and flip on the safety lights. I take one step from my bedroom door into the hallway. Out here everything is alive with brightness— intense spotlights and dazzling chandeliers.

The panic continues. Suddenly, a well-lighted place seems even more frightening than a dark and gloomy house. I may not be able to see the invader outside, but the intruder, the killer, the stalker, the maniac, he can see me.

I should call 911.

But what if it's nothing? What if I'm just another crazy person?

I think I hear my mother speaking. *Leave me alone, Mother. I'm on my own.*

But if I'm truly alone, why do I hear her

talking? *If you end up lying on the staircase, Emily, with a knife in your stomach, bleeding out, killing your baby, well... then you'll wish you had called the police.*

In my stomach. In my stomach. A knife in my Oscar.

As if on cue, I feel my baby move. I feel him move a lot. He twists. He turns. I am too frightened to be relieved.

What should I do about the too-well-lighted hallway? I could switch the house back into total darkness. I begin the return trip to my bedroom. No. I change my mind. I should leave the lights on. I'm wrong about light and dark. If he's outside he won't be able to see me. But if he's inside...I shuffle myself and my belly down the hallway. Afraid of falling or coughing or—impossible?—having a baby right here, right now.

A door closes. I hear it.

Yes, I definitely heard it. The sound of a door closing, the latch, the click, another latch, another click.

I am at the head of the staircase. From up here I can see part of the front entrance door. No one is there, but, damn it, the view from where I stand is limited. The stairs are curved and highly polished. Dangerous. The back stairs, the stairs for the help, are narrower. I think it will be safer, surer. Yes, I'll go there.

I turn and begin the walk to the far staircase. A gable in the hallway looks out on the front of the house. I glance out that window. Nothing out there. Driveway still empty.

Made it. I'm standing at the back staircase. The stairs hardly look as inviting as I had imagined them. But I'll concentrate. I'm strong. I think I can handle the journey down those stairs. Yes, they're narrow steps, and they look steep. The risers. That's what they're called. The risers…are steep. I can't even see the downstairs landing over my enormous belly.

Worse, now I can hear footsteps. Hard. Insistent.

These are real.

No, I am *not* a mistaken crazy lady.

The person I am hearing knows I am hearing him. He's not even trying to hide the noise of his shoes. I must get back to my bedroom. Lock the bedroom door. Lock the bathroom door. Lock the bedroom-sitting room door. I turn around to go back to my bedroom.

I walk like a big mechanical toy robot—one leg, other leg, one leg, other—back down the hallway.

Then comes a voice.

"There you are!"

Then comes the person.

I look. I scream.

CHAPTER

85

BETSEY! HOW THE HELL did you find me?"

The screeching of "Oh, my God" and "What the hell?" pierces the air. We pause. We stare. We screech some more.

Then we purposely bump bellies. Yes, we hug. We stand back and look at each other, then we look at each other's bellies, then we hug again. My Oscar and Betsey's Amy bump into each other again and again and again. Tears? Of course.

A question is tucked somewhere inside my brain. Is this a good surprise?

I'm certainly relieved that Betsey is not a maniac with a hunting knife or a madman with a gun. But am I happy? I think I am. I think that I think I am.

"We've been looking for you for over a week!" Betsey says. "Joel and his partner, me, we've all been so worried. Why did you disappear from everyone?"

"That's a long essay question that I'm too tired to answer." Then I ask, "How did you find me?"

"Honestly, it turned out to be not so hard. I told the detectives your late parents were loaded. Joel said he ran their old property records. He called the local cops and asked them to swing by, just to make sure you weren't here. I guess nothing looked suspicious. But then last night in bed, Frankie said to me, 'Hey, has anyone actually looked *inside* Emily's parents' house? I could barely sleep thinking about it. So at around five, I got out of bed, did some googling, and found this address. Almost without even thinking I hopped in the car. I texted Joel where I was going. And then I added that I was better at his job than he was. And here I am."

Betsey hugs me again. My arms instinctively rise to hug her back.

"Look what I brought you," she says as she reaches into one of those Land's End canvas bags. I glance down at the sack bursting with a mess of books and clothing and a laptop. Betsey pulls out a big, icy plastic container.

"I grabbed this from the freezer," she says. "My boeuf bourguignon."

"Yech," I scream in horror. "I hate that." Then I continue with mock disgust. "Call it whatever you want. It's stew. It's stew. It's stew. And I hate any kind of stew. Flabby, stringy, chewy. I hate it. You know that. But I'm still so glad to see you."

She looks thoughtful, her head tipped to one side. Her index finger on her lip.

"I guess I knew you either loved it or hated it," she says. "Guess I got it wrong. I don't know about you, but I'm famished."

Moments later, with her usual mom-like efficiency, she zaps the stew in the microwave, and we move to the table that remains *Architectural Digest*–ready from the day when Deb Jacobi and Suzie Hancher set it for me, for our most unusual boeuf bourguignon breakfast. I add a place setting for Betsey.

I tell her the chicken soup story. She laughs and then looks around the room. The sun is just beginning to rise, filling the space with beautiful morning light.

"So this is the *family* dining room?" she asks. "That's incredible. What's the formal dining room like, the main altar at St. Patrick's Cathedral?"

I smile. I don't want to discuss the grandeur of the house.

"I figured your folks had a fabulous place. But this is amazing. Does your family own any other real estate?"

I look with embarrassment down at my bowl of boeuf bourguignon.

"A beach house in Southampton. And a three-bedroom apartment in Paris," I say.

Betsey leans in and says, "Let me guess. It's on the Avenue Foch with a view of the Eiffel Tower."

"Wrong-o. Yes, it's on Avenue Foch. But no Eiffel Tower view, only a view of the Arc de Triomphe."

Betsey's smile vanishes. She does not look angry. She just looks sad.

"You know, Emily. Sometimes I think I really don't know you at all."

I think I'm going to explode into tears. But I do manage to say what I really want my friend to know.

"Bets, you know me better than anyone in the world," I say.

CHAPTER

86

OUR BREAKFAST IS NOT as lively as our shared meals usually are. And it's not just because we're eating beef stew at sunrise.

I'm beginning to feel something vaguely unhappy about Betsey and me. The rhythm of our friendship has changed. I can feel it. And I suspect that Betsey can feel it also.

"Are you pissed that I barged in on you up here?" she asks. "Even though you had all of us so scared as hell that something happened to you?"

"No, of course, not. I was getting lonely up here." I answer her question alarmingly fast. So fast that she must know that it's a lie.

"You're lying," she says. "You *wanted* to be alone up here."

"No."

"You just said that I know you better than anyone else in the world."

"Oh, c'mon. I meant it," I say. Then I ask, "You didn't by any chance bring a slice of that fabulous cheesecake that you always make."

"Cheesecake? Are you kidding? I have been ludicrously busy. I've been a crazy lady about you. I've been traipsing all over the city looking for you, looking for clues, talking to your old lovers, calling Joel and his partner every ten minutes, yelling at them to work harder. I even flew to Las Vegas to track down a copy of your marriage certificate! So no, Em, I wasn't baking cheesecakes. I was a mess."

"Oh, my God," I say. "I can't believe you did all that. Thanks for worrying. And really, thanks for finding me."

"But dessert is not totally lost. Frankie and the kids made a sort of fruit salad and, I'm not sure, fresh, frozen, canned, anything. Whatever, I grabbed it and took it for a car ride up here," she says.

Then we both become silent. Up until now

our friendship was filled with talk and talk and talk—about pregnancy and people and men and friends and children and...and now there is silence.

I watch her move the boeuf bourguignon around in her bowl.

"It looks like you're not a big fan of the ol' beef stew either," I say.

"Oh, I am. It's just that I've lost my appetite."

"And the reason for that?" I ask. I am slightly frightened for her answer. I believe she's going to tell me something terrible—about the very things we are not talking about—pregnancy and people and... "You know, Em. Being up here, seeing this incredible house and then hearing about the place in Paris and the apartment...well, it's none of my business, and you don't have to tell me anything you don't want to, and, well, I just thought, how you say that I know you better than anyone else. But there is one thing. One thing you haven't told me."

I speak immediately.

"I know exactly what that thing is. You want to know if I know who the father of my baby is." I say the words calmly.

"No. That's not what I was going to ask."

Then she continues. "No. I have a good guess or two about that. What you've never told me is...and maybe it seems overwhelming now because I'm in their house...it's about your parents."

I nod. She doesn't even have to ask the question.

Now I do know what it is. I speak.

"They killed themselves."

Betsey's hand moves to her mouth. She squints her eyes hard.

"Oh, my God," she says. "I never dreamed."

I nod.

She continues. "I always assumed it was an accident—a car, a boat. Maybe an intruder, a burglar, a drug addict. You never said a word about it, and I was always way too afraid to ask. The obit in the *Times* wasn't clear. The paper just said that the Atkinsons had died. No cause of death. I'm sorry, Em. I'm so sorry. I should stop. I should stop talking. Oh, shit. I'm so sorry, Em."

I wonder if Betsey thinks it strange that I'm not crying. I'm calm actually. In fact, I'm vaguely happy that I am finally telling the story to someone other than my therapist.

"It happened up here. Liz and Lionel told absolutely no one about what they were planning—not their lawyers, not their doctors, and certainly they didn't tell their only child.

"Turns out that my mother was very sick. She had cancer. Pancreatic cancer. It just showed up one day. Like an unwanted surprise visitor. She had been perfectly healthy. Tennis. Golf. Running around the galleries. Then one night she started throwing up. Two days later they tell her and my father that she has stage four pancreatic cancer.

"To be honest, I think from the moment they found out they decided to leave this world together. I bet they didn't even discuss it very much. My father kept a pistol in his desk. It was a Ruger SR22. Dad called it 'my second best friend, after your mother.' And he used it. He died with his two best friends."

Betsey looks frozen with sadness. Then she speaks.

"They simply could not live without each other."

I answer, "And they assumed that I *could* live without them. And I could. And I did. And I have. And I will."

I try to explain to Betsey what I've been unable to explain to a lifetime of psychiatrists, a handful of close women friends, even a small group of men friends. Yet with Betsey it all comes out with a surprising smoothness.

I'm not sure she's buying my story. I'm not even sure she believes it. But I can't stop telling her.

I say how I may have been either a foolish decision or a foolish mistake when I was born. It was clear to me, even as a small child, that I could not penetrate Liz and Lionel's very special relationship. They weren't bad parents, I assure Betsey. They just weren't really parents.

First of all, as a couple they were inseparable. Always, always, always together, at art shows, gallery openings, museum galas. But even more so when they were in simpler settings. The three of us at dinner, and they would reach out and touch each other. The three of us on an airplane; the two of them next to each other, me across the aisle. They read the same books. ("Here, you'll love reading this one, Liz.") They disliked the same people. ("Did you hear that Mary and Carl boasting and bragging all night, Lionel?") You hear the cliché about people finishing each other's sentences, but Liz and Lionel actually always did do that. ("I think we should move that table" she'd say, and he'd finish, "to the front hallway.")

They didn't abuse me or hurt me consciously. I just wasn't... well, I just wasn't *them*.

Yes, I was probably a disappointment in other ways—too chubby, too dull, not popular enough, not fashionable enough. But frankly I don't think they even cared enough to care about that. An occasional "You should lose some weight," or "You should study harder." But nothing more passionate than a casual suggestion.

"How did you put up with it?" Betsey asks.

"It was hard, but, you know, it wasn't *that* hard. Like I say, they were never bad parents. They just didn't want to *be* parents. So I did what I had to do. I escaped. Into my head."

"That's quite the trick. How'd you do that?" Betsey asks.

"I created my own world in my mind. I was so good at creating it that it practically became real."

"Like daydreaming?" asks Betsey.

"Oh, it was more than that, a lot better than

daydreaming. It was self-deception. And I made it real by sharing my world with other people."

I see a touch of fright in Betsey's eyes.

I continue.

"I was so good at it that my stories were always believed. Job offers I never received. Awards I'd never been given. I talked about men and women who propositioned me, tried to force themselves on me. I said that I saw celebrities and spoke to them. I stole Jimmy Choo shoes and Tom Ford dresses. I went to Madrid for weekends. I had fun and sex and friendships and escapades that I never had. Everything so much more exciting or frightening than the stupid little lonely life my parents made me live. Almost none of it ever happened. I never stole shoes or dresses. No son of a Greek tycoon ever asked me out. Google never offered me a job. It was all in my head."

"I guess I get it," says Betsey.

"For me these things weren't lies," I say. "You see, it can't be a lie if I really believe it."

I'm suddenly enormously tired. It must be from the release of telling Betsey my secrets. What's more, we both announce that we need to use the bathroom.

Betsey leaves the table first. This gives me the chance to clear the plates. When she returns ("God, what a relief!") I go off.

When we are together again, we are both very quiet, just simple exchanges of "Is everything okay?" and "You're feeling all right, aren't you?"

"Betsey, just to be clear. This isn't a secret. You can tell anyone you want about my parents' suicide," I tell her.

"Oh, it's nobody's business," she says. "I won't."

"You can even tell people about my other craziness—the secret little life that I keep in my head," I add.

"Who would I tell about that?" she asks as she hands me a small bowl of Frankie's soggy fruit salad—chunks of canned pineapple, defrosted strawberries, green grapes with seeds.

"Frankie," I say.

"Frankie?" Betsey says loudly.

"Yes. You could tell Frankie."

"If I did tell him, you know what the first thing is that he'd ask?"

"No, what would he ask?"

She looks at me with a smile that cannot hide the basic seriousness of what she now says.

"He'd say, 'I bet you're right. I mean, I think she's imagining the story about some crazy guy following her.'"

I don't speak.

"That's what *he'd* say," Betsey says. "Not that *I* don't believe you, of course."

Still I don't speak. I'm not sure I know what I believe anymore.

After a few more seconds I say, "How about I make us some herbal tea? I'm too wired to go back to sleep, but we can go into my father's library and relax."

87

I HAVE NOW TOLD Betsey one of my biggest secrets—the tale of my parents' suicide. From there I told her about emptiness of my childhood and how I created an entire world of half-truths and careful fantasies.

I thought that letting the truth escape from its hiding place would calm me down, bring me peace. But it has not. In fact, I am feeling more and more that something is clawing away at the very core of our friendship.

Here we are. With so much in common—the biggest coincidence, of course, that two people who once felt like sisters are each about to have a baby—we should be closer than ever.

I brew our herbal tea. Then we waddle like two fat ducks to my father's private library, the dark wood-paneled room where he kept his red-bound volumes of Dickens and Thackeray. The only piece of art is a rare framed architectural drawing of St. Paul's Cathedral. Taste and money, an unbeatable combination.

Betsey and I sit on opposite ends of a big old burgundy leather sofa. The leather on the sofa is so worn and cracked that to some people it might look like a refugee from a rummage sale. But I know the story: My parents had seen it on a private tour of a castle in Scotland. They had to have it. So they bought it and had it shipped here. Total cost? $26,000. Liz and Lionel, what a pair.

As Betsey runs her hand over the sofa arm and says, "This is a really odd piece of upholstery," I consider telling her the story of its origin. Then I decide not to. I learned long ago that wealthy people should be very careful with stories that underline their wealth. What's logical to me may simply be obnoxious to Betsey.

"Aren't you scared up here alone?" she asks.

"I'm not alone. I've got you," I say.

"No, really. I'm not joking. Aren't you afraid

you'll go into labor or you'll fall down the stairs or . . . I don't know . . . something awful?"

"Well," I say, smiling, "the only bad thing that's happened so far was having to take two bites of your beef stew."

"Boeuf bourguignon," she corrects me.

"Ken-L Ration is more like it," I say.

She laughs a tiny bit then says, "No, seriously, what if one of our babies starts coming?"

"We're not due for two weeks," I answer.

"Yeah. Tell that to the babies."

"There's a perfectly fine hospital right here in Sharon. And there's always the dining room table."

Silence. A long silence. No laughter. No chatter.

"Can I get you more tea?" I ask.

"You know how you feel about my beef?" she says. "That's how I feel about your herbal tea. Mint and licorice and cough medicine all in one cup. No thanks."

More silence. Silence from two friends who can usually do nothing but fill the air with words and laughter and secrets and advice and sarcasm and love.

After a mildly uncomfortable thirty seconds,

Betsey says, "You know, this baby of yours, this Oscar, he should have a father."

"He does have a father," I say. "Did you think I did this without help?"

"Don't be such a goddamn wise guy. You know what I mean." She's angry, and she isn't faking it.

"We've only discussed it a thousand times. And anyway…"

I pause.

"And anyway…"

I hesitate.

"Come on," Betsey says. "Spit it out."

"Anyway, you have a good idea, you said, and…well, to be honest, I know exactly who the father is."

No pause this time. Betsey starts the inquisition immediately.

"You mean that two NYPD detectives and a heavily pregnant surgical nurse have been running around the city—and flying across the country—for the past week trying to figure out who your baby's father is, and you've always known? You've known exactly? Without a doubt?"

I speak softly. "Without a doubt."

"Don't stop there, Emily. Tell. Me. Now. Asshole."

"I don't think it's a good idea to ..."

"Fuck that. Not a good idea?"

I look away. When I look back, Betsey's eyes—I'm not joking—seem to actually light up. She goes at me with her loudest voice.

"Is this part of your craziness you just told me about? Is this one of those fantasies you just made up?"

I resent Betsey's calling them fantasies. But at the moment I'm way too anxious to object.

"Maybe," I say, and I begin to cry. "Maybe. I didn't mean to. I just thought that it was... well, sort of obvious..."

Obvious? Who am I kidding? I remember how I shamelessly accused Keith Hennessey of being the father, when all along I knew he was not. It is so easy to remember all my oddball fantasies. But now is not the time to dwell on my loony compulsions with Betsey.

Very slowly and firmly Betsey says, "Who is the father?"

Equally slowly, but not nearly so firmly, I answer.

"Ted."

Betsey repeats his name over and over. It sounds like a combination of a mystical chant and a football cheer. "Ted. Ted. Ted. Ted."

"Stop it, Betsey. Just stop," I say, more sorrowful than angry.

She ceases saying Ted's name immediately.

"Are you sure it's Ted?" she asks, almost meekly. "You'll be the first to admit that you had a pretty...robust...sex life. A few other guys might be up for the role of Oscar's dad."

"Yes, I'm sure," I say. And now I am really irritated.

It feels like another confidence revealed on my part, and all I'm getting in return is skepticism.

"Oh, for God's sake, Betsey. You know that Ted and I were on-and-off involved. Hell, we even went to Vegas and got married. You know all that. Yes, and for a while we were pretty exclusive. We were sort of playing at being in love. At least, I was playing at it."

Suddenly Betsey looks sympathetic.

"Does Ted know about this?" she asks. "I mean, that he's the father?"

"Of course he does. But it would never work out, him and me. That's why we got an annulment. I don't want him, and honestly I don't need him. Once my precious, beautiful Oscar is born, all I'll need then is a nice, stiff drink."

I think we both probably feel like laughing at that.

Maybe Betsey doesn't. I do.

But we don't.

CHAPTER

88

THAT NIGHT, BETSEY AND I sleep in the same bed. The bed in my room is queen size, with a good firm mattress and a pile of puffy-soft duvets.

But this will be no happy pajama party. No. We are sharing a bed because, I think, each of us is a little too afraid to stay alone. Maybe it's more than that. Maybe we both are feeling that if we *act* like best friends we will once again *be* best friends. Frankly, I'm confused enough and needy enough that I am hoping that will happen.

We lie side by side, and I notice that Betsey's baby belly is higher than mine.

"How much weight have you gained?" I ask.

Not at all reluctant to answer, Betsey quickly says, "As of last night, exactly thirty pounds. What about you?"

"Well, I'm telling the truth here. I never know how much I weigh unless I'm at Jane Craven's office and that nurse of hers gives her cheery, 'Let's hop on the scale and see how baby and mommy are doing.'"

"So," Betsey says. "How're you doing?"

I guess I can't avoid answering.

"Well, sometimes I've gained as much as five or six pounds. And occasionally...occasionally, like twice...I've lost some weight."

"How much have you ever lost when that happens?"

"Well, once it was in my fifth month. And I lost five pounds. And then a little after that, at the end of my second trimester, I lost about six pounds. But, you know, no matter what, I'm either losing too much or gaining too much. My body is not a particularly helpful pal."

Betsey shakes her head back and forth.

"Your body has been through a great deal of living."

Oh, shit. Time for a short-but-sweet Betsey lecture. I try to nip it in the bud.

"I have behaved impeccably these past nine months," I tell her.

"That's what you say. I'd say, good times and bum times," Betsey says.

"This really hurts me, Bets. You've cast me as a kind of slut in a crappy TV movie. I'm not perfect. I know that. I did drugs and I drank until I was falling down. God. You know that. You were the nurse with me in the hospital when they told me I was pregnant. But I decided then and there that I was going to be the best mother I was capable of being."

"Emily, Emily, all I said was that you lived a hard life. You partied. You played."

"But I did other things. Things you and nobody else ever knew about. I work at the Young Adult Institute. I'm a sponsor for another woman in AA. What more do you want from me?"

And, inevitably, I begin to cry.

Betsey reaches over and puts her hand on my shoulder.

"I'm sorry, Bets. I didn't mean to go crazy. It's just that my life hasn't just been romping around with Quinn Church or taking off with Ted Burrows or lining up and polishing off six peach daiquiris. Maybe I'm just jealous."

I know what Betsey's thinking.

What's the truth about me? What's the fiction?

And that's exactly what I'm thinking, too. Then Betsey speaks quietly.

"I'm going to tell you what a shrink once told me. She said to me at our first session: 'I will always assume that you're speaking the truth. We must assume that. If not, we can't go on. It may be the truth as you see it, as you experience it, as you remember it. But it's *our* truth.'"

I nod quickly. I shut my eyes. I listen to Betsey.

"So that's what I'm going to do. That's what you're going to do. I love you. I love Oscar. I am going to believe whatever you tell me. You do volunteer work? I believe you. You work hard at your meetings? I believe you. You think that some lunatic is following you? I believe you. Okay?"

I open my eyes and say, "Thanks for trusting me. But I'm not sure that I trust myself."

CHAPTER

89

EVER SINCE I GOT SOBER, I've had trouble falling asleep. At the first AA meeting when I felt bold enough to speak, I said out loud that insomnia was a terrible problem for me. As soon as I finished speaking, I was embarrassed. I was talking to a group of twenty people, many of whom—because of drugs and drinking—had destroyed their marriages, whose children had not spoken to them in decades. Two of them had been responsible for vehicular manslaughter. Some had been to jail. Many were without jobs. And here I was, complaining because I was having trouble sleeping.

I stammered for a moment before I sat down.

I said, "In the old days, I used to sleep like a baby."

"Just stay away from the pills!" one of the group yelled.

I think of this meeting as I lie next to the snoring Betsey.

She is sleeping peacefully. I envy that terribly.

I fight the urge to take another Ambien. I don't want to push my luck with medication that I know I shouldn't be taking.

I finally do fall asleep. I don't know how. I surely don't remember it happening.

The next thing I hear is Betsey's voice. No, not a dream. I open my eyes and look to the side of me.

"Emily, I'm sorry. I'm so sorry," I hear her say. But I don't know where her voice is coming from.

"What?"

"I'm sorry for waking you. But I'm sick. Something's wrong."

"The baby?" I say, pushing myself up on my elbows and looking for the energy to swing my legs around to the bedside.

"No, not the baby. Me."

I realize she is standing at my bedside.

I look up at her. She's wearing her enormous Philadelphia Eagles T-shirt. One view and I get the story.

Her eyes are red and swollen. Her ears are the same intense shade of red. Her exposed arms are covered with the tiniest possible pimples, in patches of pink.

"Let me see your belly," I say as I begin pulling the T-shirt up and over. I'm relieved that her stretched skin—slightly veiny, a mottle of light-blue and pink—looks normal. But I ask myself a question I'll be asking myself a lot: What the fuck do I know?

"I've got cramps, Emily. Diarrhea, the whole thing," she says. "My back is killing me."

My back is killing me also, but I say nothing. This is about Betsey, not about me.

"Goddamn!" Betsey shouts as she turns and heads toward the bathroom, leaving a fairly disgusting trail behind her.

"I'm on fire!" she yells from the toilet.

"I'm calling 911," I say.

"No!"

Wrong thing to say, I guess.

"I'm fine. I'm fine. This is some sort of reaction to something. An allergy. Maybe the sheets or the pillowcase. What laundry detergent do you use?"

"I have no idea. I want to call for help because of the baby."

"I'm better. I'm better!" she yells.

Then she half-moans and half-groans. "Oh, God. I think I'm going into labor."

I say nothing. You know the expression *frozen with fear*? Yeah, that's the one that's wrapped its arms around me. Then I speak.

"I can't do this. This is not me, Betsey. We've got to get some help here."

She is sitting on the toilet. She bends forward and grabs her head with both hands.

"Help me stand up!" she yells. I reach out and begin pulling at her extended arms.

"My water broke. I know it," she says. "I felt it."

"It was probably urine."

Betsey is suddenly furious. "No, it's not fucking urine! I'm a nurse! Help me walk."

She takes one step and then moves backward in a kind of drunken, shaky comedy step; it looks as if she's slipping. Then she lowers herself quickly back onto the toilet. She reaches down and under herself. A few seconds later when she brings her hand back up, Betsey is holding a pinkish jelly-like substance.

She looks at me. She says, "Oh, my God."

Then she moans and begins to stand. This time, however, she manages to stand up quickly. She doesn't need my help. Instead she seems to be propelled by some magical new energy.

"Emily, I'm in labor."

I know that the following statement is true: I may no longer be frozen with fear, but I also have never been so scared in my life.

"I've got to call 911," I say.

"It's way too late for that. Just listen to me and do what I tell you to do."

A vodka martini would be a huge help right now.

"Get some pillows. Put them in the back of the bathtub for me to lean against."

I grab pillows from my bed, and, after I stand them up in the tub, I help Betsey to sit down in the tub. Then I help Betsey off with her T-shirt.

She closes her eyes and takes a deep breath. She lets out a few soft grunts and a few short moans.

Then she says, "Stay strong. Remember, just do exactly what I tell you to do."

CHAPTER

90

IT'S AWFUL. IT'S SIMPLY awful.

As always, my first instinct is to have fun with everything. Here's a great comedy setup: a naked pregnant lady in a bathtub...Actually, not a good idea at all. This is all just too goddamn serious. It's deadly serious.

Betsey tells me that she and I have just seen the mucus plug.

Tell me that the phrase *mucus plug* doesn't lend itself to humor.

But I remember that I'm not Amy Poehler. And Betsey's not Tina Fey.

"Stay with me, Em. We can do this. It

happens all the time—in farm fields and native villages and back alleys."

I don't say it, but we are not from any of those places. Okay, she's a nurse. Big fucking deal. I'm just a somewhat psycho pregnant lady.

And then time passes. And it passes. And it passes. An hour, two hours, three.

Now the *not calling 911* seems to be a sort of matter of pride. If not pride, a horrid and misguided compulsion.

"Get the canvas bag from the kitchen," she says. "I have a couple of medications in there."

"I wish you had a couple of obstetricians in there," I say. Then I add, "Do I have time to pee?"

"Yes. It's not ready yet...I mean...*she's* not ready yet."

It takes me a few minutes to manage the winding front stairs to the first floor. When I enter the kitchen, I pick up the landline on the counter. But there's no dial tone. Maybe the phone company cut service after my parents died. Or maybe...No. There's no time to think about another explanation. I can't keep a woman in labor waiting. I fetch the canvas bag and deal with the stairs again.

In my bedroom I stop at my nightstand and punch in 911 into my phone, but there's nothing. Ever since I threw my phone in my kitchen when the intruder got in, it hasn't worked right.

"Where are you?" Betsey yells. "I can hear you."

It doesn't matter, because in a moment of panic, I fumble my phone. It slips from my grasp and slides under the bed. I could try to squat down to retrieve it, but that will take precious seconds, maybe minutes, that Betsey and I don't have. It doesn't work anyway.

Now I'm in the bathroom. Betsey's eyes are puffier than earlier. I glance at her arms. The pinkish-red rash on her neck has turned almost crimson.

"I know what's wrong," she says. And now she is crying. "I know what happened."

I manage to kneel at the side of the bathtub, and I truly think for a moment that I will never be able to get up again. Once more the comedy elements keep popping forward.

"It's the fucking strawberries. It has to be.

Frankie put strawberries in that awful fruit salad," she says.

"Allergic?" I ask.

"I am now. I never was, but I am now."

"But you can't suddenly..." I start.

"Yes! Yes, you can. I can. It happens. Don't tell me!"

I've read about this: the anger that overwhelms the woman in delivery. The screaming when she yells at the husband, *You did this! You made this happen, you bastard!*

For once in my life I shut up. My facility with words is not going to get me out of this nightmare madness.

Minutes pass. A half hour passes. Betsey winces and coughs and she turns to me and says, "I'm a goddamn blueberry."

Now, as well as frightened and nervous, I'm confused. If this is the first directive from her commandment to "do what I tell you to do," then I'm about to fail. Betsey, full of discomfort and anxiety, is sensitive enough to realize that I'm not understanding the blueberry reference.

"My cervix," she says. It's beginning to dilate.

The opening is only as big as a little blueberry now. Eventually it'll be..."

I'm totally on edge with this fruit comparison.

"It'll be an orange, a grapefruit, a melon..."

"Stop there."

I've never heard of this comparison before. But why would I? It seems like some bizarre take-off on the Magritte painting of the man with an apple on his face. Only now, in my mind, I'm seeing a vagina with an orange in front of it, next slide, a vagina with a cantaloupe, next slide...I can't imagine what's next. A baby. Please, God, a baby.

"There's something in my bag, a pill bottle with small blue pills. Get me one."

I rummage through the papers and pens and little kids' toys, the Band-Aids and Kindle reader and Tic Tacs. I find a different plastic bottle labeled BENAZEPRIL.

"Benazepril," I say. "You have high blood pressure?"

"When did you get your medical degree?" Betsey says.

"Uh, we are *both* pregnant. And Dr. Craven

prescribed this stuff for my high blood pressure," I say.

Great. A pause for a medication discussion.

"What else do you take?" Betsey says. I think she's struggling to distract herself from her labor pains.

"Well, for a while I took a cup of Grey Goose four times a day. But then I wanted something gentler, so I switched to Stag's Leap chardonnay, as needed for pain."

Betsey has positioned her hands flat against the sides of the tub. She smiles—well, not quite a smile, a grimace, not that I ever really understood what a grimace was.

"Don't make me laugh," she says. "Let's apply that rule to everything about to happen." I'm not sure whether she means that.

I find the plastic bottle of blue pills.

"Good. Give me one," she says.

I hand her a tablet. "Let me get you some water," I say.

"Don't need it," she says.

She takes the pill dry. She throws her head back and swallows.

CHAPTER
91

APPROXIMATELY TWO HOURS LATER (or is it two weeks, two months, or two years later? I don't know. This is agony) Betsey announces—now moaning and trying to inhale and exhale in a formal cadenced way—"I'm an apple or an orange. I've got to start pushing."

Oh, my God. Oh, my God.

I so want to call some backup people. Someone who knows what the hell they're doing. But as I look at the sweaty red-blotched mass of flesh in the bathtub I don't dare make that suggestion.

"Hold my hand!" Betsey shouts.

I take her right hand and gently hold it.

"Not like that," she sternly says. She pulls her hand away and grasps the sides of the tub. She lets out a sound that is some combination of the word *shit* and the sound *oomph*. So it's some loud intonement of "Shoooomp," which, thirty second later, becomes "shoomph," which, sixty seconds later, becomes "Oh, fuck."

"Take a look, Em. I think I'm there," Betsey says.

"You're where?" I say.

"Look down below. I think I'm a grapefruit or a melon or whatever the hell I'm supposed to be at, whatever the hell is supposed to be ten centimeters."

Still on my knees I slide to the foot of the bathtub. Betsey's knees are bent and in the air. Her thighs are slightly spread. I look. Betsey is definitely dilated. But I am not confident that my grapefruit-melon-pineapple evaluation is accurate.

And then I say, with absolute strength, "I think you're ready to do it. What do you think?"

"You must be crazy!" she yells.

"I may be," I say. "But I'm all you've got."

And the sheer authority of my voice seems to infuse me with confidence. Betsey's liquid-y reddish crotch area looks magnificent to me. I think I see a baby's head crowning, although I probably don't. Probably I wouldn't even know.

Apparently, my confidence is contagious. Betsey still gets her words out with an effort, but her voice turns slightly sweeter.

"The de-stresser breaths, Emily. Help me do them," she says. I could swear she is now smiling. "Do you know what the de-stresser breaths are?"

I snap back at her. I'm trying to be patient, not usually my strong suit. "Uh, lady. I was in the same Lamaze class that you were in," I say.

Now she is noticeably smiling. But…If I hoped that this smile might signal a permanent mood change for her, wow, am I ever wrong.

She screams, "This hurts like shit! This sucks! I'm never doing this again!"

"You're ready to push," I say.

"Fuck you," Betsey says. Then she says, "Shit. There's something wrong down there."

I reposition myself for a clear view of Betsey's cervix. This time—not more than a minute later—I see that there is some liquid on the floor of the bathtub.

"I think it's urine. But it's sort of brownish…

and it might be…well, this can happen. You know, it's natural. They told us this in class," I say.

I make the return journey to Betsey's head.

I tell her to start breathing and pushing, breathing and pushing and counting, breathing and pushing and counting and screeching. And she does. And it's feeling so right and healthy and normal and natural that I think for a moment that I, too, am feeling signs of labor. But, of course, I'm not.

After a few minutes, I tell Betsey to rest.

"The next pushing and breathing…you have to feel the air going through you. Think about it, Bets. Through your windpipe, down into your belly, the birth canal, out the vagina."

She rests. She cries. She screams.

"I can't do this anymore," she says.

Now I ignore her. Then I decide, *Goddamnit, I'm not backing down from the job.*

"Bullshit," I say. "Give me two short breaths. Then a big one."

She does. As the big breath comes to an exhale she breathes out with an enormous sound of a cow. A *moo* that seems to last for an hour.

"I remember that from class. Good work," I

say. Emily the coach. Emily the midwife. Emily the doula.

"Look down there again, Em. Something bad is going on," she says. There is a touch of concern—not panic—in her voice.

I move. I look. The first thing I notice—because I can't help but notice it—is a partial view of the baby's head.

But before I can tell Betsey that it's crowning, I see blood. Real blood. The blood is streaked with brown and mucus-y yellow. But blood.

"There's blood. What should I do?" I ask.

"How much is there?"

I panic. How much? A half cup? A few tablespoons? The amount of blood is increasing. Not a flood. But, my God, it's blood.

Betsey gives a big push. Then a breath. Then another push.

I think that I see more blood.

When I look up at Betsey's face, I also see tears in her eyes. I see streams of sweat dripping down her nose, her cheeks, her neck.

"Your eyes look better to me," I say. They do look better. But the baby's not exiting the eye sockets. I guess I am trying to be helpful?

A short breath. Another short breath. A screaming huge push. "I'm really worried about the bleeding," I say, almost at a screaming level myself.

Then she sends me info meant to reassure me.

"It's nothing. That's just the head ripping the skin. They call it nature's episiotomy."

"That's not nothing. Tearing. Ripping. Bleeding," I say.

A short breath. A big push.

My God!

CHAPTER

92

AMY IS IN THE HOUSE!

In the room!

In the world!

Three people crying like babies. Betsey, me, and the baby.

I keep doing what I'm told to do. A perfect warm wet linen towel washes this little bundle of warm skin and glop. The toes. The toes. These ten perfect pink dots. The minuscule nose. I am mesmerized.

Betsey's Amy. Our Amy. My Amy. Our Amy. Our wrinkled little flesh ball of perfection. She is, I think, minuscule. She must be a mistake. I shake with fear and fatigue. But she is perfect. What's more, she's a trouper.

I place Amy on Betsey's breasts. Amy reaches and tugs.

"I think the bleeding has stopped," I say.

"Of course. The medication you gave me. It helped. I carried it with me the past few months. Because you never know. And, Emily, we didn't know."

I smile, and I cry.

The umbilical cord? Betsey told me that neither baby nor mother would feel the slice. Teeth. Knife. Scissors. Don't ask which method I used. I might remember.

"Call Frankie," she says. "Call him."

"I'll have to use your phone—mine's not working. But...Bets...you...how are you?"

"Fine. Great. Tell Frankie. Tell Juliet and Bobby."

I stand on my achy wobbling legs. I watch Betsey hold Amy in the air. My friend is so sure of herself with her baby. They seem to have known each other for years and years. Old friends. Good friends. This Amy baby is irresistible. I want one. I want one. I want one.

And then—oh, good God, this is going to sound insane—I am sure I am having a labor pain. Yes, a sort of cramp that begins somewhere down—way, way down—in my belly.

I glance back to see Betsey sitting up straight in the tub. She holds Amy tightly against her, and she tries to straighten up even more. She pushes her feet against the bottom of the bathtub.

"Stop that!" I yell. "Lie back down. Lie down."

She slides down a bit, and I return to her side. I stand there and look down, and I swear, I know, I'm certain that Amy turns her head and looks at me.

"Say hi to Emily, Amy," Betsey says, almost in a hypnotic state. Then to me, "She knows you. You were the first person in the entire world to actually see her."

I would like to bathe in the comfort of those words. But the pain in my belly seems to be radiating to other places inside of me—chest, butt, legs, everywhere.

"Frankie! Em, you've got to call him! Get me the phone!" Betsey says.

I get myself to the bedroom and grab Betsey's canvas bag. I find her phone on the bottom.

I hand the phone to the crazy lady in the bathtub.

"It's not working," she says. She hands the phone to me. I try to wake it up, but there's nothing.

"The battery is dead," I say. "Where's your charger?"

"I...I don't know if I brought one. I left the house in such a hurry...Frank must be sick with worry."

I feel a labor pain. But then, after a moment of torture, I'm fine—weak, unfocused, but fine. To distract myself, I take a clean white sheet from the linen closet and fold it to fit into the bottom of a rectangular laundry basket. I've just made a sort of wonderful bassinet. Amy's crib!

Then Betsey hands the baby to me. I take her. I hold her. Yes, heaven. Then a rumble inside of me, down deep and up, and I quickly hand the baby back to Betsey.

She takes Amy, but Betsey's face is slightly contorted.

"I think the placenta is here," she says.

My labor pains—at least I think they're labor pains—are so strong now that I must lean forward.

But I still don't tell Betsey about it.

CHAPTER

93

THE ASTONISHING POWER of a newborn. That's the power of Amy.

She has completely hypnotized her mother and her (favorite) aunt in just a few hours. Betsey and I hover over her laundry basket bassinet. We barely move, but when Amy moves in the slightest, we become breathless and wide-eyed. When Amy stops moving, we become petrified.

I know that Betsey is the perfect mother to her twins, Juliet and Bobby. Now I witness her being the perfect mother to a newborn. It's comforting, but I am also running into my own distress.

Damn it. Not now. Not yet. Why is this

happening, this sudden mental and physical pain?

I am feeling a nasty tightening in my lower stomach, just below what I think of as the womb. The sensation sits in that moment between almost-pain and extreme pain. This puts me in a frightening state of anticipation: waiting for my smallish stabs to turn into giant labor pains.

I try to distract myself by saying something I've been thinking as we've been watching the infant. "She's a peanut. Amy is an absolute peanut."

Finally, we both take our eyes from the baby and look at each other.

"Peanut?" says Betsey.

"Yeah, my little peanut."

"My Little Peanut?" Betsey says. "You mean like My Little Pony?"

"I guess. Isn't that adorable?" I answer, but my lower belly feels so twisted that I'm not really sure of what I'm saying.

"You can call her whatever you like—we both owe everything to you," says Betsey.

Then she reaches across the laundry basket holding her newborn. She takes my hand. Then she looks back down again at her daughter. We both smile.

I'd like to ride on the wave of this warmth. I'd like to say thank you. But instead I say, "Bets, I have to tell you something. I'm sorry. This should all be about you and Amy right now. But...I can't deal with...I have to..."

"What is it, Emily?" she says.

"I think I'm going into labor."

Betsey shouts. "Stand up! Stand up right now!"

We both stand up, and Betsey is all business.

"Start walking!" she yells.

"I don't think I can," I say.

"Of course you can. I'll walk with you."

"But we have to watch Amy," I say as I struggle to my feet, "and you have to recover."

"Emily. We're maybe walking ten feet."

She takes my elbow, and we begin to walk to the other side of the room.

"Shit," she says.

"What's the matter?" I say, assuming that "the matter" has something to do with me. But it doesn't. Betsey has a problem.

"I'm bleeding." She has changed into one of the two hundred silk nightgowns that my mother owned. The problem is not bloodstains; the problem is blood.

"Oh, my God," I say as I stop walking. "We've got to do something."

"I'm fine. It'll stop. Don't worry. Keep walking."

We do, but I am a wreck about Betsey's bleeding. At the same time, I feel like a thick belt is tightening around my belly where my waist used to be.

"How are you feeling?" Betsey asks.

"Awful. I think it's labor."

"Let's hope it's not. Oh, and, by the way, if you think I look like a bloody mess, you should see yourself. You've got blood all over you, too. On your nightshirt, on your arms. You even have some on your face."

Betsey licks an index finger and presses it against my chin. "There. Let's get back to the bathroom and get you changed."

We walk the tiny distance back to Amy's bassinet. Betsey and I look down at her. I am momentarily distracted from my own discomfort by the beauty of my little peanut.

God almighty, Amy is wonderful. How could I not be fascinated by the exquisitely tiny-teeny-weeny-tiny-adorable-minuscule little hands that occasionally reach into the air around her pinkish little baby face?

Then Betsey suddenly puts her hands on my lower belly and pushes gently. Miraculously she touches the precise place where the tightness and cramping are coming from.

"Describe the pain," she says. Her tone is serious. She must be taking Dr. Jane Craven lessons.

"Well, it's not exactly *pain* pain," I say.

"Not *pain* pain," she repeats. "You're supposed to be creative. Come up with a real description."

"I can't. It's sort of like menstrual pain. It's sort of like constipa…hell, I don't know."

"Well, fortunately, I do know. They don't sound like labor pains. They're most likely something we call Braxton Hicks contractions."

I don't know why, but Betsey's use of the pronoun *we*, as if there's the medical community and then there's the rest of us ignoramuses, bugs me a little bit.

"It's just your uterus showing off," she says. "I had BH contractions with Juliet and Bobby. But obviously I didn't have them with Amy."

"So, does this mean I'm going to start getting labor pains now?" I ask, standing and wondering what in hell is going to happen. I

just witnessed a birth—close up. It's not neces-
sarily pretty.

"No," she says. "When real labor pains
start, you'll know it. Right now, just lie down
and keep shifting positions. That should help
relieve them."

"What did you say these things...these
contractions...are called?" I ask.

"Braxton Hicks," Betsey says. Having made
her diagnosis, she now returns all her attention,
understandably, to her baby.

"Why don't you get cleaned up?" she says.

"I just want to rest," I say. Betsey nods. We
both are running on empty.

I lay on the bed. The Braxton Hicks contractions continue. I turn my head to look over
at Amy and Betsey. Then I laugh out loud.

"What's so funny?" Betsey asks.

"I'm just thinking. Braxton Hicks. Sounds like
the name of a guy I went out with at Princeton."

CHAPTER

94

I'VE GOT TO FEED the baby."

Betsey and I are stretched out, exhausted, on the bed. Amy is lying quietly in her laundry basket bassinet on the floor beside us.

"Well, unless the little peanut likes low-fat yogurt or beef stew, we have a problem," I say. "I didn't prepare anything to feed a one-hour-old baby."

Betsey sits up in the bed and then leans over and lifts Amy. Betsey cradles the baby in her left arm and then lifts her left breast with her right hand. It looks to me like Betsey is actually pushing her breast into the baby's face, but Amy proves me wrong. Amy only takes about a second to open her mouth—wide, in my totally ignorant opinion—and relax.

"Good Amy, good, good Amy. You are the best latcher I've ever seen," says Betsey.

"'Latcher'?" I ask.

"'Latcher' as in 'latching,' as in the baby *latches* on to the nipple. Most babies have trouble at first." Then Betsey lapses into vaguely nauseating baby talk. "But not Amy—no, no, no. Amy is the best latcher in the world. The best latcher ever..."

I am spellbound by the sight of Amy's tiny cheeks puffing in and out. Betsey is looking down at her.

Peace. Really quite perfect peace. All this... serenity, I guess... after so much chaos and fear.

After all the hours of pushing and praying. A sweaty naked lady in a bathtub. Blood and weeping. A crazy lady like me not knowing anything but trying to do everything. Then a baby. Then my own pain. And fear and worry and... finally. Peace. The perfect picture of a satisfied mommy and a beautiful infant.

Betsey went into labor this morning, and now it's night. Everything has happened so incredibly fast. And I am never really at peace.

Because, as I lie there, I am thinking that the same mad scene is about to happen all over again. With me. I will be the pushing, praying, sweating woman in the bathtub. And the very thought of it makes me want to vomit. I turn away from the Mommy–Amy picture of peace.

I struggle out of bed and go into the bathroom.

I pee. I sit and study this room. The room where the miracle happened is littered with clothing and towels stained with blood. The tile floors are slick with water and urine and feces and splashes of blood.

I can't have it. Oh, no. I don't mean I can't have it here. I can't go through what Betsey went through. I need nurses and doctors and big baskets of flowers. I need medical specialists and priests. I need painkillers and valium and...I stand up. I need to drive us to the hospital or at least to Florence Packman's house and use her phone to call 911.

But before I can do anything, I hear Betsey's voice. It's loud. It's insistent. Not frightened, but certainly filled with concern. "Emily? Please come in here."

I walk quickly into the bedroom.

Betsey is standing at the foot of the bed. Amy is no longer nursing. Betsey holds the baby close to her naked breasts. The baby is— as mothers sometimes say—fussing. Her teeny hands flail in the air. Her teeny mouth puckers, searching, I assume, for Betsey's breast.

"I hear something," she says. "I'm not sure where it's coming from."

I listen. Maybe I'm hearing something, too. Maybe it's a man's voice. Then I hear noise. It's all confusing.

I stand still. I listen some more.

I guess she's right. I do hear something. Not footsteps or a car on the gravel driveway. I got it, wood on wood. A kind of knocking noise.

"Maybe it's Frankie," I say. "Maybe he got worried and came up here when he couldn't get in touch."

"No. Can't be. He'd call the fire department up here and have them come check on us."

Betsey and I both must share the same reflexive instinct: We've got to take care of Amy. Nothing else really matters.

Betsey hands the baby to me to hold. As

soon as Amy is in my arms she starts crying. Loud. Really loud. Yes, people always say that these miniature people can wail like car alarms. But the volume of Amy's screeching still shocks me.

"I'm still bleeding. My bandage is soaked. I have to change it," Betsey says. Amy and I follow her into the bathroom.

Betsey runs some warm water, wets a towel, and dabs the cloth at her bloody episiotomy. Then she tapes a thick piece of gauze over the wound.

"Don't move," I say suddenly.

Amy continues to scream, but Betsey freezes in place.

"The noise stopped," I say. "It must have been a deer or a raccoon..."

"Or a madman or an escaped convict or..." She begins as she slips into a clean nightgown.

"I'll get you a bathrobe," I say.

"No. I don't need one. That doesn't matter. I just want to find out what that noise is."

"But I think it's gone away, and, anyway, maybe you're wrong. Maybe it *is* Frankie," I say.

"Just stop it, Emily. Just stop it. It's not

Frankie. I explained to you why it can't be him."
She's angry. And I'm a little pissed off also.

"Let me know when I'm allowed to have an opinion, to make a suggestion," I say.

Then she says, "Look, Em. This is not the time for us to have a ridiculous argument. I'm sorry."

I nod my head in total understanding, and we suddenly both notice that Amy has stopped crying.

During this odd moment of peace, I flip the switch that turns the house lights on inside and out.

"Don't all these lights make you want to do a Mariah Carey song?" I say.

Ooops. We trade moods again. Betsey is serious now.

"Here's our plan. We see if anyone is around outside..." she says. She pauses for a second, then adds, "Or inside. Then we jump into a car. My car. I know it has gas. I know the keys are inside it. We'll go to the hospital..."

While Betsey is planning a safety escape plan, I'm drowning in my own little bizarro world. I'm asking myself: Why the hell did I ever do this? Why did I ever think that hiding out alone in a big house in the western Connecticut woods was a good idea?

"We must stay together," Betsey says.

I want to say, *Amy doesn't have much choice,* but I keep my witty comment to myself.

"Maybe we should keep the lights off," Betsey says as she holds her baby even tighter against her nightgown.

"Yeah, well. We should have had a committee meeting," I say.

We approach the top of the stairs, and once again my brain is going wherever it wants to go. It's telling me to worry—but not about this horrible situation—but to worry about what will happen if the three of us get out of this alive. People will ridicule me: "What were you thinking?" Cops will ask, "Why were you two alone up here?" *Why did I ever do this? Come on, Emily, get with the problem of the moment.*

We are about to begin our walk down the stairs, and I suddenly turn to Betsey and say, "I'm so sorry. I'm so sorry. Don't you see? It seemed like a good idea at the time. To escape the lunatic who was following me. To just be alone. To get to know myself and the baby inside me. To eat ice cream and frozen pizzas and watch television and . . ."

She looks at me like I'm crazy, and, of course, I might just be. And, of course, the Braxton Hicks contractions are starting again. (Did they ever really end?)

"Emily, stop it," Betsey says sternly.

And now I'm back on earth.

"Okay. Okay. Yes. But, Bets, you know what I think. I'm thinking we should run straight to the car. No messing around," I say.

"We'll see," she says. "We'll play it by ear."

"I hate that phrase. No. Not play it by ear," I hiss. A gentle hiss, but a hiss nonetheless.

Then my brain goes into fifth gear: Who are these two crazy women—one enormously pregnant, one gripping a newborn? We must look like some hilarious 1970s sitcom. Yeah, that's what this is. A silly television show.

Only it's not. Oh, good Christ. How did I let any of this happen?

As if it makes any difference.

CHAPTER

95

BETSEY AND AMY AND I make a safe, quiet, comfortable landing in the front hallway. If you think our flight down the stairs was easy, then I'm not painting the picture correctly. Two exhausted women with a two-hour-old baby, and the possibility of a burglar (that would be okay, maybe), or a fucking lunatic (not so good).

Just like upstairs, all the rooms down here are alive with bright lights. Betsey cradles Amy tightly. I look through the glass panels on either side of the entrance door—just night, just right. No deer or raccoons.

The only cars parked in the driveway are the two that belong to me and Betsey.

And then—oh, shit—we hear a voice, a big voice, a shout. A man's voice. The voice arrives at the same time one of my gut-strangling contractions arises.

Then, from the kitchen, comes: "Anybody home?"

The voice is oddly cheerful. It sounds familiar. But I can't quite place it in this new context, these new surroundings.

I turn to Betsey. *Frankie?* I mouth. I'm too scared to move.

She just shakes her head.

"Hey, somebody answer me," the voice shouts as it gets closer.

And now I do recognize it. It sounds different in a huge, empty house than it does in a crowded, noisy bar.

We hear footsteps getting close. Close. It's closer. Then we see him.

It's Ted Burrows.

From the bar. From Las Vegas. From my ridiculous life.

Yes, Ted.

My friend. My ex-husband. The father of my unborn child.

He looks at us. His face is a combination of confusion and shock.

"What the hell happened to you two?" he asks. His voice is slightly impatient, but he does have his be-nice-to-the-customer voice.

Because Betsey and I must look such a horror, Ted's question is not unreasonable. My brain takes a snapshot of what Ted sees: two fatigue-shattered women, both covered in sweat and splattered with blood, with crazy hair, near naked, one of them with a suddenly wailing infant.

Everything about this encounter is a huge mountain of confusion and exhaustion.

Ted. Why Ted? Why is he here? Is he angry? And another question, why won't Amy stop crying?

Ted looks the way he always looks: too cute for his own good. Faded jeans and a white tennis shirt with an alligator emblem on it. He holds a phone.

"What the hell are you two doing up here?" he asks. But he doesn't step forward to touch us, to hug us, to comfort us. He is statue-still.

Then he snaps a photo of us with his phone and presses a few buttons.

Betsey looks down at her baby for a moment, then says, "The question, if you don't mind, is: What the hell are *you* doing up here?"

"And how did you know this address?" I ask.

Ted answers, "A little bird told me." Then he glances at the huge nutty Calder sculpture in the middle of the hall and laughs. His laughter arrives with a touch of scorn.

"Ted," says Betsey angrily. "Seriously. Why are you here?"

He shrugs his shoulders and says, "Ask my wife." He smiles.

Of course, I have absolutely no idea what he's talking about. I haven't seen this guy in a week or two. What the hell is he up to?

"Go ahead, tell her," he says as he looks at me.

"Tell her what?"

"Come on, Em, sweetie, tell her that I'm here because I love you."

This is both stupid and frightening. Ted is acting like he's drunk. Like he's stoned. Like he's both.

Then he punches away at his phone, clicks it off and slips it into a front pocket of his jeans.

Immediately he practically swaggers the six or seven feet toward Betsey and me. In seconds he is standing right in front of me, almost nose to nose.

"That sculpture. It's very funny," he says to me.

"It's meant to be," I say.

"Like life," he answers.

Then I scream, "Why…are…you…here?"

"Like you don't know?"

I step back from him. He steps forward and stays close to me.

"I'm here because I am following you, Emily. I'm always following you. On the street. In the stores. On the road. In the city. In the country. I've got to keep my eye on you."

Ted. I never thought. My friend, my… ex-husband…Oscar's dad.

I am practically choking from shock.

"Come on, Emily. You saw me. I watched you watching me. You know I've been following you."

"No. Never. I never knew it was you."

And that is the truth. I never knew. I truly didn't think it could be Ted. Yes, I thought it could be Mike Miller or Quinn Church or even

Keith Hennessey. Greg Hayden even claimed that he'd been following me. But Ted, never.

"Come on, Emily. You knew."

"Never. I knew someone was following me, someone who was trying to scare the shit out of me. And succeeding. But you? No, Ted. Why were you doing it? Why?"

I begin to cry. It is part sorrow and part fear.

"I had to keep a close eye on you. And on your damn baby. I couldn't let anything come between me..." He gestures all around the room. "And what's about to be *mine.*"

I take a step backward. I'm still terribly afraid, but I'm also very confused.

"What are you talking about? What's about to be yours?"

"Everything you have, Emily. Your family's real estate. Your parents' priceless art collection. Your multimillion-dollar inheritance. All of it."

Baby Amy stops crying. I could swear that she turns away from Betsey's embrace to watch Ted.

"Okay, shit, you're even nuttier than I thought," I say. "If you think there's any chance in hell I'd ever give you one goddamn penny..."

"Sorry, Em. It's not your decision. If you happen to end up dead...it's the law."

I see that Betsey is glancing nervously at the front door. We both know that we need to get the hell out of here. Fast.

But then Betsey's eyes suddenly grow wide.

Like she's just realized something.

"You're still married to her." She glares at Ted furiously. "You tricked her."

"No, that's impossible," I say. "We got our stupid little Las Vegas marriage annulled the next day. I was there. We went to the courthouse, signed all the forms..."

My voice trails off. My throat feels dry.

I think back to that scorching-hot desert day nine months ago.

I did sign a stack of legal papers, but it was Ted who went inside to submit them.

"No...I don't believe you," I say.

I lock eyes with Betsey. Amy, squirming in her arms, starts crying again. I'm hoping we can use these few seconds of distraction to get to the front door.

To escape.

Ted keeps smiling. "Believe what you want. It won't make any difference."

"Those other two women," says Betsey. "Are you behind that, too? Did you abduct Nina Powell? Did you kill Caitlin Murphy?"

Ted actually starts to chuckle. It's sickening.

"Caitlin Murphy?" I say. "I used to network with a woman named—"

But Ted starts talking over me before I can even think about it. "I had nothing to do with either of them."

He takes a scary step toward me.

"But talk about lucky coincidences," he says. "Young women disappearing, dying. New Yorkers going crazy with fear. It just fit in so nicely. Turned out to be better cover story than we ever could have hoped for."

We?

Every instinct in my body tells me to push this psycho away. To scratch out his eyes. To knee him in the groin. To run.

He's about to kill me.

Maybe Betsey and Amy, too.

Then, a noise. A car in the driveway. The sound of tires against gravel.

The police? Are we saved?

But the smile on Ted's face stays in place.

"Hey, it sounds to me like we have company."

CHAPTER

96

I AM STUNNED. WITH PAIN and cramps and nausea and fear.

And as for my pregnancy, as for giving birth, didn't Betsey just do that? I keep thinking of the quote that my father liked so much, from that old Yankees catcher, "It feels like déjà vu all over again."

Plus, this is a further replay of a few minutes earlier when Ted Burrows surprised us with his banter and bullshit.

And the bombshell that he's still my husband. My legal next of kin.

If I die—and Oscar, with me—he hits the jackpot.

Now someone else has decided to drop in. One thing's for certain, it's not going to be good. It'll be déjà vu all…More noise now. From the kitchen. The fall of the footsteps. The walk through the dining room. The arrival of the stranger.

Holy shit.

"Thank God!" I say. We're saved.

It's Detective Joel Tierney.

He looks rumpled and tired. His cheap suit wrinkled. His puffy eyes puffier.

I sense in a moment—yes, in one poisonous awful moment—that Tierney and Ted are a team. Why? Because Tierney is calm. And Ted is calm. Too calm.

"All right, I'm here, let's get this over with," he says.

"Joel?" yells Betsey. "You, you, you knew about this? All this time?"

I realize she and I have both been betrayed tonight. Me by my spouse, her by an old friend.

"Evening, Detective," says Ted. "I was just bringing the ladies up to speed. I don't think they believe me that my attention has been on Emily the whole time. Tell them who had the genius idea to link the three cases together and keep the NYPD off my scent?"

"Damnit, is that true?" Betsey demands.

Joel lets out a long, slow breath. Unlike the shit-eating grin on Ted's face, his expression is downcast. He looks like he feels guilty. Even a little sad.

But not sad enough to step in and help us. Then he speaks.

"Missing persons, homicides—crime happens every day in New York City. What do you want me say? I was just helping out a friend. Just trying to make a few bucks. Remember all those break-ins at your place, Emily? That was me. Fifty bucks and your doorman let me in."

Ted says, "You should have seen what we did to your bathroom—smashed the shower stall, splashed chicken blood everywhere...it looked like a horror show in there."

Tierney says, "I popped into his bar on a whim one night and we got to talking, and he promised me a big chunk of change if I'd help him out."

I am shaking. But Betsey, with Amy held tightly in one arm, blood streaming down her leg, suddenly rushes the short distance to Tierney and punches him right in the Adam's apple with her free arm.

I hear a gurgle and a gasp and an awful retching noise as he bends forward. Then Betsey lowers her arm and brings her fist full-force into Tierney's stomach. I now hear another gasp coming out of the detective. He lunges at Betsey.

She ends up falling backward into Ted's hands. Amy is about to fall from her grasp so I jump in and grab the wailing baby just in time.

Ted holds Betsey tight in a sort of backward bear hug. She squirms for a bit until he lets her go. Tierney, that sunuvabitch, seems recovered and unruffled.

I hand Amy back to Betsey. I grab my belly. I scream.

"All for my money?! You scum! You're going to kill two women and a baby and an unborn child just for that?"

"Oh, Emmy-em-em," says Ted. "Of course you don't understand. You're just a spoiled rich bitch. But maybe I'll let our baby live. Raise him myself. I'd be a great dad."

Then, like a volcano in my brain, I lose control.

"You fuckers!" I say with venom in my voice and my heart. "He's not *our* baby, he's *my* baby!

He'll never be yours. I'll hold him inside of me. I'll strangle him when he's delivered. I'll kill myself while I'm in labor if I have to."

Ted and Joel share a brief, sinister look.

"That won't be necessary," says Ted as he removes a smallish plastic syringe from the hip pocket of his jeans and uncaps the needle.

He approaches me slowly. Joel approaches Betsey. He says, "The best part is, no one will ever find your bodies, but in a few days we're going to tack on more murder charges to drug-dealing scumbag Mike Miller. Maybe you haven't heard, but he killed Nina and Caitlin, and I think he may have been coming after you next, Emily. You should thank me. I'll make it easy on you. You should have seen what that psycho did to Caitlin, and what was left of Nina when we found her."

No smile, no sneer this time. Just a look of icy determination.

I have been collecting a large wad of mucus and spit in my mouth.

Suddenly I shoot the great gob in his face.

Ted is startled. He recoils.

I grab his hand holding the syringe, twist it hard, and jam the needle down into his thigh.

The plunger doesn't depress, but I'm sure it hurts like hell.

Ted screams and stumbles backward.

"Emily, run!" shouts Betsey.

And I do.

I run out of the hallway and into the corridor that leads to the living room. I can hear Tierney behind me. I can hear Betsey screaming. Amy crying.

I open the side door near the garden. The garden abuts the woods.

I know those woods from my childhood well. I know the brooks where the skunk cabbage grows, I know where the fallen rotted cherry trees lie, I know where the great patches of poison ivy and poison sumac lurk.

I also know that, even though I've kept up a light jogging regimen these past few months, I'm about to have to run harder and faster than I ever have before.

Not only to save *my* life.

But to save my baby's.

CHAPTER

97

OH, SHIT. I'M BAREFOOT.

I've run about a hundred yards and I've already peed myself.

I'm not even sure what time it is.

There is almost no moon, and that means that there is almost no light. It must be around three in the morning. Maybe. Who knows? Not me.

I keep reminding myself that Jane Craven said, *"A woman can run up to and including when she begins labor."* Including when she begins labor? Oh, how I'd love to believe Dr. Craven. But, as I've learned, you can't believe anyone, anyone, anyone. And what if Jane

Craven is hooked up with Ted and Tierney? And what about Betsey?

I've got to stop thinking this. I already have knees that are burning. I have shin splints. And I think I know where I am. There is a willow tree, far bigger than a willow tree around here should be. I know this tree. The willow tree reminds me that I am running near the drainpipe that runs from the tobacco farm a few miles north of here. The drainpipe is meant to pump out the runoff from the tobacco farmer's irrigation system. But my father told me that when the seasonal tobacco harvesters are working, they attach their cabin waste systems to the drain. So the drainage shoots out all sorts of waste, including feces. The smell is hideous. But the willow tree is big and beautiful.

I move to the left. I know it takes me away from the drainpipe. Once, as a teenager, I ran as far as the small section of the Appalachian Trail that passes through here.

But now I just want to escape. I need to save my baby. I need to save myself. In that order. I try to force myself, *will* myself back into an eighteen-year-old college runner. But my hips are spongey with pain, and I hold my belly from below, and I slow down when I have to, and I run on slippery leaves and deer shit and ankle-deep beds of wild watercress.

In all the movies and books and TV shows, the hero ultimately makes it through. But I honestly do not have a chance here. Ted and Tierney will find me. They will kill me. Or they will find me, and they will shoot me full of medication, and I will deliver Oscar into their hands. As I run, I cry. I cannot let my fat ankles and throbbing knees slow me down. I think I know where I am. Ferns so big that they twine around one another. In college—with Lisa or Joey or Sandi or Laurence—we sat and smoked at least four joints and passed around a quart of vodka until we all started making out with one another. When we awoke we eventually found our way back home.

Okay. Right. That's it now. I have to find my way. If not, they will find me, or, even worse, never find me.

I dig in and somewhere, somehow, find the strength to continue. Yes, I know these woods, but I do not know them like an explorer, a trailblazer. How much time has passed? I am lost in the woods and lost in time. Quickly—or so it seems—the woods become a tiny, teeny bit brighter. Hardly the kind of light to help me find where I'm going, but slightly better than a half hour ago when the moon was almost dead and gone.

I see a lifeless campfire. There is a rickety abandoned folding chair. I stand perfectly still and listen for the sounds of footsteps, voices, any sign of humanity. Could I have lost them? Could they have given up? Of course not. I must take advantage of this freedom.

I guess that I have a rough idea of where I am—a few hundred yards from a bramble where the biggest fallen tree in the world rests. I remember what we always said after cross-country practice: "I hurt all over." It seemed like an exaggeration then. But now I do. I hurt in a thousand different places: my neck and my shoulder bones and my toes. And, of course, the cramps. I have no idea if they're Braxton Hicks or the signal of real delivery.

Please, dear God.

All I wanted was to have my baby.

That's all.

Now I'm near naked and running through the filth of rotted leaves and dirt and bugs. My legs are going to explode.

I could sit and rest on the biggest fallen tree in the world, but I cannot rest. I am determined to get away. I have no chance. But, fuck it, I will die trying.

I slip my hands under myself. I pull my belly up as if it were a bag of very heavy laundry. I run, and I run, and I run. And then I run and smash myself into some object—not a tree, not a stone wall. A person? Yes, a person.

I fall to the muddy ground. I have fallen directly on my stomach. Oh, please God, don't hurt Oscar. I have fallen fast and with my full weight on my baby. I start to cry. I hear a man's voice.

"You bitch. You fucking bitch."

He is on the ground next to me. Both our faces are in the mud. There is hardly any light, but barely enough to see his face.

It is Ted.

Honestly, I am not surprised.

And all I wanted to do was have my baby.

CHAPTER

98

I'M ABOUT TO BE MURDERED in the woods.

Ted starts struggling to his feet. I can barely roll over onto my back. I lie back, and I pull my nightshirt up and begin gently massaging my belly. I don't care that I am nearly naked. All I care about is Oscar. I gently rub my skin, my baby, all the while whispering through my tears, "Oscar. My Oscar."

"You couldn't have made this easy for me," Ted says. He is kneeling next to me, his knees planted in the mud.

"Easy?" I yell. "To kill me? To steal my baby? You're crazy!"

I am staring at the sky. No stars. No moon. A fading darkness tinged with a bluish gray.

Then a different voice, a gruff, sharp voice that I recognize immediately.

Detective Joel Tierney.

He is holding a gun.

"Goddamn woods. I hate the goddamn country."

His gun is aimed toward the two of us on the ground. Me lying. Ted kneeling.

"You bastard! If you laid a finger on Betsey or Amy..."

Tierney seems somber, not angry.

"Don't worry about them. They didn't make it very far."

He and Ted share a look.

Now he slightly changes the direction of the gun.

It is clearly and precisely pointed at me.

Ted tries to stand while Tierney extends his pistol with both hands.

Yes, of course, I quake and shiver and cry.

Yes, of course, I hold my belly tight, my Oscar, my baby, my life.

Then comes the gunshot.

I reflexively close my eyes. The gunshot is horribly sharp, terribly loud.

When I open my eyes, I see Joel Tierney freeze, then stagger, then fall to the ground.

I call out weakly, "Betsey?!"

Then I hear, "Don't move, Ted."

Is it a woman's voice? I'm not certain.

It is. Then I see her.

Detective Kalisha Scofield, strong and tough as hell. And she's holding a smoking gun.

"How're you doing, Ms. Atkinson?" she says as she kneels beside me, keeping her eyes and her gun trained on Ted.

I don't answer. I am too overwhelmed, still too frightened.

Finally, I stammer, "Where'd you come from? How'd you know?"

"We went to your apartment a few days ago, looking for you. I found a flash drive in your computer and I read your diary. I'm sorry. But I found out that you and Joel slept together, and since he conveniently never mentioned that to me, I got very suspicious and stopped trusting him."

Then Detective Scofield gestures to Ted with her gun. "He's not the only one who knows how to tail someone. I'd been following him around since this case started. Something just never sat right with me. Tonight I followed him up the turnpike for two hours. I lost him right around the New York–Connecticut border. So I took an educated guess where he might be. And here we are."

Tough. Dedicated. Vigilant. Smart. I am really liking this woman. She pulls out her phone and says, "What the hell am I waiting for, Ms. Atkinson? We gotta get you some help."

Ted moves slightly.

"Stay perfectly still, Mr. Burrows. I could see to it that you end up like your friend. I'll take a *dead* baby daddy over a deadbeat one any day."

As she speaks into her phone, I manage to get myself into a kneeling position. From there I put the palms of my hand on the ground, and miraculously I manage to hoist myself to my feet.

I take a few steps until I'm standing over Ted. His eyes open wide. Scared? Hurt? Angry? I don't give a shit.

I lean over and begin to punch and kick his neck and face and eyes with all the strength that's in me. Detective Scofield pulls me up and away from him. Out of breath, I look down on this man, this devil, this piece of dirt. I'm afraid that I'll start to cry. But I do not. Perhaps I'm just too damned exhausted.

Then Detective Scofield resumes her phone call.

"My name is Detective Kalisha Scofield, NYPD. I am in Sharon, Connecticut. And we have an emergency."

CHAPTER

99

EVERYTHING IS HAPPENING FAST.

Through the kind of GPS magic that I will never understand, the Connecticut State Police, along with the local Sharon Police, find our location in the woods. Fast. I am passing back and forth between dreamy sleepiness and wide-awake fear.

It seems like only minutes before two EMTs are cleaning and disinfecting me. I'm like a doll who was accidentally tossed in a garbage fire. All the while the EMTs are working on me they assure me that Betsey and Amy are "totally fine, ma'am," and that I will be, too, that I will "come through this with flying colors." And I, like an actor in a TV thriller, only keep saying, "What about my baby? My baby." That really is all I care about.

One of the EMTs says, "We hear a heartbeat inside. We can feel the baby moving. Your blood pressure is remarkably good. We need to get you and your friend to a hospital."

And again, in what seems like a flash, I am in the front driveway of my house, the big house on the edge of the woods, the house where I almost died.

Flashing lights on police cars. I hear a siren. As two men start to slide my stretcher into the rear of an ambulance, I catch a glimpse of Betsey on her own stretcher, being led into another ambulance. A woman, a social worker or a doctor I assume, is holding Amy.

"Emily!" Betsey shouts. The EMTs pause while she yells to me. "Emily," she says. "We made it. We made it." We are both sobbing.

Then Betsey tells me, "They're taking us back into the city. Dr. Craven is waiting for both of us. Who would've thought having a baby could be such an adventure?"

"Yeah," I say. "Who would've thought?"

"Gotta go," an EMT says, and Betsey and I

blow each other air kisses. Moments later my ambulance is speeding down the I-95 Thruway. Lights whirl. Sirens wail.

A dark-haired woman sits next to me in the ambulance.

"I'm Cindy. I'm with the Litchfield County EMT. If you need anything, you let me know. And if you feel anything...pain, discomfort... well, you let me know right away. You and your friend have had quite an evening."

I actually feel pretty good.

I know I have some pretty ugly bruises on my legs, some bloody scratches on my...well, on my butt...and...there is a sort of dull persistent pain in the lower section of my belly. Those damn Braxton Hicks contractions. I wish Betsey had never even told me about them. But I stretch my back as best I'm able. That persistent pain stops for a few seconds. Then it comes back. This time it feels even stronger. I try to roll with it. I begin breathing bigger and harder and faster.

"Cindy," I say, grabbing the arm of the EMT. "You've gotta tell this driver to pull over."

"What seems to be the prob..."

"Pull over. Pull over." I have a very good idea what's happening.

Cindy pushes the talk-remote to the driver, and I keep yelling "Pull over!"

"I'm doing my best. This is a six-lane highway," he says.

When I turn my head and look out my tiny sliver of the window I watch a car pass us. Who the hell drives faster than an ambulance? Then I sense—accurately, I'm sure—that my ambulance is skidding. The car turns treacherously to the right. Clearly our car is out of control. Cindy is thrown to the floor, and if I had not been belted in I would have been on top of her. The ambulance continues its turn. I scream, not from the terrifying car ride, but from the agony that has begun churning in my stomach.

Cindy—God bless her ability to stay calm—says, "I know this driver. He's really good." I guess that's reassuring news.

My pain seems to be moving from the top of my head to the soles of my feet, with a major emphasis on my belly.

"It's happening. It's happening," I say.

"Let's try making your breaths a little

longer," Cindy says. "Just breathe in and then hold it for four seconds and then..."

"I can't!" I yell.

"Sure you can," Cindy says. The picture of calmness.

"I cannot wait another second!" I yell. The picture of panic.

I feel a sharp pain in my stomach. Then I feel a sharp turn on the thruway.

The driver skids off the road.

I breathe in, hold it, then out. I scream.

Once again, those belts do their job of holding me down. The ambulance jumps a hill or a bump or a median... Only God knows.

Suddenly the ambulance stops.

I look out the small window. Nothing is moving. I just see dead branches on leafless trees.

Oh, wait. Something *is* moving. Painful, but bearable.

"Almost," Cindy says. Her voice is gentle. Suddenly I begin to relax.

My eyes tear. My stomach aches.

A life begins.

Here's Oscar.

ABOUT THE AUTHORS

James Patterson is the world's bestselling author and most trusted storyteller. He has created many enduring fictional characters and series, including Alex Cross, the Women's Murder Club, Michael Bennett, Maximum Ride, Middle School, and I Funny. Among his notable literary collaborations are *The President Is Missing*, with President Bill Clinton, and the Max Einstein series, produced in partnership with the Albert Einstein Estate. Patterson's writing career is characterized by a single mission: to prove that there is no such thing as a person who "doesn't like to read," only people who haven't found the right book. He's given more than three million books to schoolkids and the military, donated more than seventy million dollars to support education, and endowed more than five thousand college scholarships for teachers. For his prodigious imagination and championship of literacy in America, Patterson was awarded the 2019 National Humanities Medal. The National Book Foundation presented him with the Literarian Award for Outstanding Service to the American Literary Community, and he is also the recipient of an Edgar Award and nine Emmy Awards. He lives in Florida with his family.

Richard DiLallo is a former advertising executive. He lives in Manhattan with his wife.

A NEW STANDALONE THRILLER IN THE BLOCKBUSTER TRADITION OF *THE PRESIDENT IS MISSING*, *THE FIRST LADY*, AND *THE PRESIDENT'S DAUGHTER* — AMERICA HAS ELECTED ITS MOST BRILLIANT PRESIDENT EVER. UNFORTUNATELY, HE'S ALSO A PSYCHOPATH.

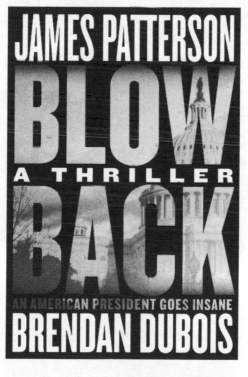

JAMES PATTERSON

BLOW

A THRILLER

BACK

AN AMERICAN PRESIDENT GOES INSANE

BRENDAN DUBOIS

PLEASE TURN THE PAGE FOR A PREVIEW.

THE WHITE HOUSE

ON THE SECOND floor of the White House, where the private family quarters are located, thirty-three-year-old Liam Grey of the Central Intelligence Agency is sitting on an antique couch waiting to see the president. It's nearly seven a.m. as he looks around at the priceless furniture and framed paintings and feels the quiet of the place. These walls have seen the romping and playing of presidential children from Theodore Roosevelt's to JFK's, Jimmy Carter's, and Bill Clinton's, as well as the attentions of numerous first ladies, but not now. This president is the first bachelor chief executive to assume office since James Buchanan—more than a century and a half ago.

As he waits, Liam spends a few moments reflecting on the odd circumstances of his life that led him here. He knows DC well, having grown up in the Southwest & The Wharf neighborhood of the district, and definitely not in the tony Georgetown part. He barely made it through the lousy local schools and luckily caught a track scholarship to BU, where he thrived and joined the Army ROTC, following in the sad footsteps of his older brother, Brian, a captain in the famed 10th Mountain Division who had been killed during his second tour of Afghanistan.

The Army had triggered something in Liam, leading him to military intelligence and a master's degree in foreign service at Georgetown, where he easily slipped into being recruited into the CIA and, from there, its Directorate of Operations. He's bounced back and forth from overseas assignments to Langley, and now he—a kid who used to fish off the wharves in his old DC neighborhood, getting into lots of fights and committing petty thefts after school—is moments away from giving the commander in chief the President's Daily Brief.

The thin black leather binder in his lap contains the morning report—known as the PDB—and he's still surprised that he's the only one here to pass it along to the president. The PDB can run anywhere from ten to fifteen pages and is one of the most closely guarded secrets in Washington, containing a morning overview of the world that is assembled through reports from the CIA, the NSA, the Department of Defense, and lots of other three-letter agencies.

Traditionally it's presented to the president by a high-level administrator in the Agency, accompanied by two or three aides. Three months ago, Liam had been called away from his office to join the director of national intelligence and the acting director of the CIA to accompany them when they presented the PDB. Several weeks later, it had been Liam and his boss, the acting director, and now, he's here alone.

Very strange, off the books, and not the typical way it is done, but President Keegan Barrett is known to like being atypical and off the books. As a former director of the CIA, the president still has friends and allies at the Agency and is known to keep a close eye on the operators that catch his notice.

Like one Liam Grey, apparently.

A door opens to a small office next to this empty living room, and one of President Barrett's aides, a young Black male wearing a lanyard displaying the required White House ID, says, "Mr. Grey? The president will see you now."

"Thank you," he says, and he gets up and takes the half dozen steps that will change everything.

LIKE SOME OTHER presidents before him—Nixon and Trump, for example—President Barrett doesn't like to work from the downstairs Oval Office. The day after his inauguration last year, in a sit-down with editors and reporters from the Washington bureau of the *New York Times,* he had said, "Too much history in that place. It feels like you're in the middle of a museum exhibit. I want to be able to kick back, put my feet on the furniture, and get work done without being interrupted all the goddamn time."

President Barrett is sitting behind an old wooden desk that was supposedly used by President Harding. He gets up from the neatly piled folders and telephone bank and briskly walks over to Liam.

That's when the CIA officer notes he and the president aren't alone in the small, wood-paneled room.

On one of two small blue couches arranged around a wooden coffee table is a woman about Liam's age, sitting still and looking smart. She's wearing a two-piece black suit—slacks and jacket—with an ivory blouse. Her light-olive complexion is framed by black hair that is cut and styled close.

She stares at him with dark-brown eyes, and President Barrett says, "I believe you know each other."

Liam nods, smiles. "Noa Himel. We were in the same training class."

She gets up, offers a hand, and says, "Glad you remembered me. My hair was longer back then."

He takes her grip, firm and warm, and says, "I remembered you outrunning my ass on the obstacle course."

She smiles, sits down. "It's not called that anymore. It's the confidence enhancement course."

With his trademark perfect smile, President Barrett says, "I hate to interrupt this company reunion, but we've got work to do. Liam, take a seat next to Noa."

Liam goes over and does so, catching a slight whiff of her perfume. It's nice. The office is small, with bookcases, a couple of framed Frederic Remington western prints, and not much else. The PDB feels heavy in his lap, and the president says, "Liam, you can put that aside for now. We've got more important things to discuss."

"Yes, sir," he says, now confused, as he puts the leather-bound volume down on the coffee table. The PDB has been nearly sacred since the era of President John F. Kennedy, when it was known as the President's Intelligence Checklist. Since then it has expanded and grown in importance, and it's now considered the most highly classified and important piece of intelligence the president receives on a regular basis. Some presidents wanted the briefings daily, others weekly, and during the last several administrations, it was prepared on a secure computer tablet, but this president—sitting across from him and Noa, wearing dark-gray slacks and a blue Oxford shirt with the collar undone and sleeves rolled up, his skin tanned and thick brown hair carefully trimmed—demanded it go back to paper.

And now he's ignoring it.

Liam thinks maybe he should say something, but...

Liam is CIA but also former Army, and he's in the presence of the commander in chief, so he keeps his mouth shut.

The president says, "Quick question for you both, and one answer apiece. Who are the most dangerous non-state actors we face as a nation? Noa, you're up."

Noa crisply says, "Cyber."

"Go on."

She says, "We've gone beyond the point where hackers and bots can go out and influence an election or steal bank accounts or hold a city's software ransom. They can turn off the power, switch off the internet, and incite people in a country to rise up against a supposed enemy. You can be a First World nation in the morning, but after the cyberattack you can be a Third World nation come sundown."

The president nods. "Exactly. Liam?"

With Noa going before him, he has a few seconds to think it through and says, "Freelance terrorist cells and organizations. They'll preach their ideology or twisted view of their religion while they're killing people and blowing up things, but secretly they're for sale to the highest bidder. They preach a good sermon, but in reality they're nihilists. They'll strike anywhere and anybody for the right price."

"Good answers," the president says. "Which is why I've called you both in here today."

"Sir?" Liam asks. He's not sure where the hell this is going, but his initial impression of his good-looking couch mate, Noa, is positive. She gave a neat, thorough answer to the president's threat question. He has the odd hope that Noa has a similar feeling about his own reply.

The president clasps his hands together and leans over the coffee table.

"After decades of our being the world's punching bag, I've decided this administration isn't going to be reactive anymore," he says. "We're going to be proactive, go after our enemies before they strike. We're no longer going to be the victim. I'm going to set up two CIA teams, one domestic, the other foreign, and you two are going to run them. I'm going to give you the authorization to break things, kill bad guys, and bring back our enemies' heads in a cooler."

NOA HIMEL LETS the president's words sink in for a moment before replying, still wondering what odd circumstances of life have brought her here, her first time meeting the president.

She's originally from Tel Aviv, moving at age five with her family to New York City when her corporate banker mother got a great job offer. Dad is a graphic artist, and she's their only child. After she graduated with a master's degree in international relations from Columbia, her uncle Benny flew in from Israel to congratulate her and recommend that she talk to an old friend of his in Virginia about a job.

That led to two developments: getting employed by the CIA, and confirming the family rumors that Uncle Benny worked for Mossad.

The Agency was still "old boy" in that a lot of managers thought women recruits should go to desk and analysis jobs, but at the time Noa thought, *Screw that shit*—she wasn't spending the rest of her life in a cubicle. She went for the Directorate of Operations and got in, not afraid to ask tough questions along the way.

Like right now.

"Sir…with all due respect, you know we can't operate in the United States," Noa says. "It's against the CIA's charter. Congress and their oversight…they would never allow it."

His eyes flash for a hot second. "You think I don't know that, Noa?"

Noa knows he's quite aware of that, given his background as a former Army general, the secretary of defense, the CIA director, and a two-term congressman from California before he won the White House.

"Sir," she says, "that's what I meant by 'all due respect.' You have the authority to have the Agency conduct overseas operations and missions, but inside the United States…it can't be done."

"Nice observation, Noa, but it *will* be done," he replies. "I've issued a presidential finding regarding the temporary deployment of CIA assets within the United States, and my attorney general has signed off on it. You and Liam have no worries about doing anything illegal. It'll be on the books…though I'll be the one keeping the books, of course."

Noa waits for Liam to speak, but he's keeping his mouth shut and his opinions to himself, usually a wise career move at the CIA. He's dressed well and has a nice-looking face and light-brown hair, but he sits oddly, like he'd rather be standing armed in a desert somewhere. *Besides,* she thinks, *he's former Army, meaning in most circumstances, when receiving an oddball order like this, his instinct will be to salute first and ask no questions.*

But Noa sees things differently. Working in the Agency means both competing in the field and dealing with the bureaucratic infighting that comes with every large organization, but she feels like President Barrett is the proverbial bull in a china shop, asking her to come along for the ride.

A thrill for sure, but to what end? she thinks.

"Sir," she says—thinking if she's going to commit career suicide, why not do it in style?—"don't you think the respective intelligence committees in Congress are going to raise hell over your finding?"

His smile seems to be made of steel. "The Intelligence Authorization Act allows the president to proceed without official notification to Congress if I inform them in a 'timely manner.' That's up for me to define, isn't it? 'Timely manner'?"

Next to her Liam bestirs himself and says, "Absolutely, sir."

Damn Army vet, she thinks.

Barrett seems happy that Liam has spoken and says, "The time of nations and organized terrorist groups fighting other nations in the open is long gone. Now they conceal themselves, depending on our adherence to the rule of law and due process not to respond. Our enemies are activists, now more than ever. We have to be activists in return. Now I want to tell you why I selected you, what I expect of you, and why I decided to brief the two of you together."

He stares at Noa, and she feels uneasy. The president has never married, has borne himself like a "warrior monk," similar to famed Marine general James Mattis. He's totally dedicated to the United States and its defense, yet he has that "thing" that some former presidents had, including JFK, Johnson, and Clinton. When one is in their presence, one takes notice.

Noa also takes notice of an edge to the president's look, like he is sizing her up, and she isn't sure if it's her experience or appearance he is evaluating.

The president says, "In my time at the CIA, I knew where the deadwood was located and that there were open cases involving possible Agency traitors that dragged on for years. But I couldn't do anything about it, due to politics. The director serves at the pleasure of the president, and back then, the president didn't have the nerve to do what had to be done, no matter how many times I briefed her. That stops now. Noa, you're going to have my full authority to clean house at the Agency. I'm going to chop up all the deadwood into very small pieces that will never be found again."

Noa says, "But Director Fenway—"

He snaps, "*Acting* Director Milton Fenway, if you please. No disrespect to your boss, but I've told him what I've planned and he's on board. Don't worry about him."

She thinks she sees Liam give a slight nod to the president. Poor Acting Director Fenway. A few months ago, the president had nominated a smart hard-charger—Hannah Abrams, a former deputy director—who was known at the Agency as a top-notch street woman operating in what was called the "night soil circuit," meaning she took every overseas assignment available, even the worst of the worst. Most in the Directorate of Operations are looking forward to Abrams taking command of the Agency, but her nomination is still being held up in the Senate for some obscure political reason.

Until that logjam is broken, Milton Fenway is the acting director, and he comes from the CIA's Directorate of Science and Technology, meaning he is experienced in various aspects of those technical means of gathering intelligence—SIGINT and ELINT—but not HUMINT, human intelligence. The men and women who work undercover around the world, rightly or wrongly, think they are the tip of the spear for the Agency and have no respect for the man.

The president adds, "There are also safe houses for the Chinese and Russians located across the country. We know where most of them are located. We leave them alone because we don't want to cause a stir or embarrass the Chinese or Russians, or because we don't have the evidence to prosecute them. To hell with that. Those houses are going to be taken out, and the foreign agents within are going to disappear."

Noa is silent for a few seconds.

What did the president just say?

"Disappear"?

NOA THINKS THAT if she doesn't get a good answer right now, she's getting up and leaving.

" 'Disappear'?" she asks. "Sir?"

He smiles. "I don't mean like the Argentine Army did back in their 'Dirty War,' tossing arrestees out of helicopters over the South Atlantic. No, 'disappear' to a facility where they won't have access to the Constitution and American lawyers. They're here illegally, they're conducting war against the United States, and they will be treated accordingly."

He shifts his attention to Liam, and Noa feels a sense of relief, that the force of the man's personality—like the beam of a high-powered searchlight—is now pointed at someone else. She's still processing what's been assigned to her by the president.

Domestic work, she thinks. The legal and institutional handcuffs put on by Barrett's predecessors and Congress have just been slipped off.

One hell of an opportunity.

Sure, she thinks, *an opportunity to really hit hard at some bad actors out there, or an opportunity to be humiliated, arrested, and stripped of my pension if this turns into another Iran–Contra disaster.*

Noa wants to make a difference in the world by being in the Agency, and the president has just given her a golden ticket to do so.

President Barrett is talking a good talk, but will that be enough once the bodies start piling up?

"There are terrorist cells, hackers, and bot farms controlled by the Iranians, Chinese, and Russians, and there are hackers-for-hire across the globe," the president says. "They attack us day and night via cyberspace or in the real world. We don't retaliate appropriately because we don't want to escalate the situation, or because we're not one hundred percent sure of a target, or because we don't want to stoop to their level. That stops today. You're going to get a team together of people from the intelligence and military communities. From there, overseas you'll go. These farms, cells, and other structures…you know what Rome did to Carthage?"

"Yes, sir," Liam says. "Once Rome finally conquered Carthage, they destroyed every building and salted the earth around the ruins so nothing would ever grow there again. And that's exactly what happened."

The president nods. "I want them gone. Gone so

hard that whoever survives won't go back to a computer keyboard or an AK-47 ever again."

Liam says, "If I may, it sounds risky, sir."

"Of course it's risky," he says. "Fortune favors the bold, correct? And it's time for us to be bold. I'll give you both twenty-four hours to pick your teams and then come back here tomorrow. We'll go over your candidates, and then we'll discuss logistics and support. And when it comes to support, you'll have everything you need, with just one phone call or text. As commander in chief, I can get any branch of the military to assist you under any circumstances."

The president leans back into the couch. "I've followed both of your careers over the years. You have the intelligence, toughness, experience, and...well, the perfect background and history of heartbreak to do what must be done. Any questions?"

Dozens of them, Noa thinks, but she doesn't want to speak first.

She feels she's spoken enough, and even though she has misgivings about what's being offered to her, she is also relishing the thought of taking the fight to enemies who have set up camp within the nation's borders.

Let Liam take the lead.

But Liam refuses to do so.

"No, sir," he says. "I'm good."

Noa says, "I'm good as well."

President Barrett nods with satisfaction.

"Get out, get to work, and I'll see you tomorrow. I'll be supplying you both with an initial set of targets, complete with locations and defenses." He adds a chilly smile. "I'll also supply the salt."

A FEW MINUTES after Liam Grey and Noa Himel depart, President Keegan Barrett reviews his schedule for the day when the door to his office opens and Carlton Pope walks in. On the official White House organization chart, he's listed as a "special assistant to the president," which covers a lot of ground, water, and sky—exactly what Barrett wants.

Pope is stocky, heavyset, with a type of blocky body that make Savile Row tailors toss up their respective hands in despair while trying to tailor a suit to fit. His prematurely gray hair is trimmed short, and his nose is round and misshapen, from a long-ago break that never properly healed.

He takes a seat in front of Barrett. Except for the Secret Service, Pope is the only one allowed to come into Barrett's office without knocking first. Even Barrett's chief of staff, Quinn Lawrence, isn't allowed here without a warning phone call.

Pope says, "Well?"

Barrett says, "I think they'll work out. They're young, experienced, and dedicated."

Pope smirks, and Barrett allows him that one look. Years ago, when Barrett was in the Army and on a still-classified mission to Serbia, Barrett had saved this man's career and life, and in the ensuing years, Pope has diligently worked to pay back that debt.

Barrett always relies on the loyalty of others and is glad to pay it back.

He says, "All right, you ignorant peasant, pack that smirk away. Because of bad movies and past history, most people don't realize that the CIA attracts the best and brightest, who'll go to the extremes to perform their mission. It's not the pay that drives them, and it's sure as hell not the publicity. They do it because they're dedicated to the Agency and this country."

Pope says, "All right, I'll take back the smirk. They both seem experienced...and that Noa." He smiles. "A real looker."

"Glad you noticed."

"But sir...this is one hell of a risky venture."

"One that's worth it," he says, feeling reflective. "In my years at the Pentagon, at Langley, and in Congress, I had this...understanding of what threats our nation faces. But to get the right people to listen to you and act...it never could happen. Politics, inertia, bureaucracy. Now that I'm here, that's going to change. I'm finally in a position to make it happen."

"But..."

Barrett glances down at his schedule. If this keeps up, he's going to be late for a coffee-and-Danish visit with the Senate majority leader and his staff downstairs in his private dining room. He needs to keep his relationship with that fool steady for as long as possible, before the hammer falls.

The president says, "I think you're about to ask me, 'But what if they don't work out? Have a change of heart? Decide to go confess all to the *Washington Post*?'"

"That's what I was thinking, yes, sir."

One of the many attributes that Barrett likes about his special assistant is his blunt way of talking and getting things done, and all without any attendant publicity. He's never had his photo in the *Post* or on the various news sites and blogs and prefers to work in the shadows.

Which is part of Pope's unofficial job description.

Barrett says, "If that happens, they'll be replaced. There are twenty-two thousand employees of the CIA. I'm sure we can find two other dedicated individuals."

Pope gets up from his chair. "Replaced or disappeared?"

Barrett says, "Whichever works."

JAMES PATTERSON
RECOMMENDS

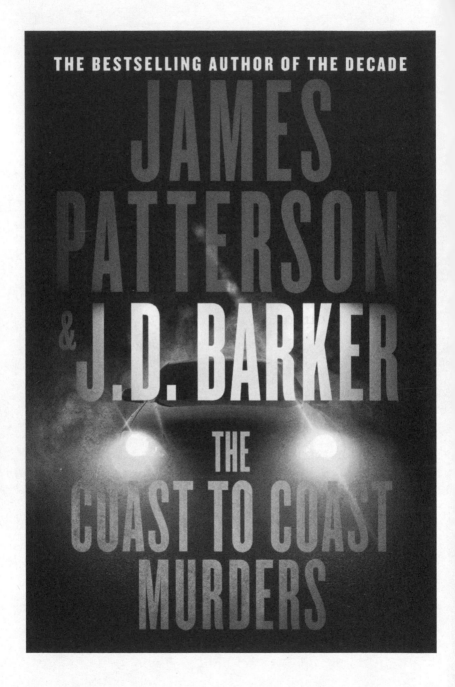

THE BESTSELLING AUTHOR OF THE DECADE

JAMES PATTERSON
& J.D. BARKER

THE COAST TO COAST MURDERS

THE COAST-TO-COAST MURDERS

Nothing brings siblings together more than sharing a terrifying past. Both adopted, and now grown, Michael and Megan Fitzgerald trust each other before anyone else. They've had to. Brought up in a rarefied, experimental environment, they were sheltered from the world's harsh realities, but it also forced secrets upon them.

In Los Angeles, Detective Garrett Dobbs and FBI Agent Jessica Gimble have joined forces to work a murder that seems like a dead cinch until there's another killing. And another. And not just in Los Angeles—the spree spreads across the country. The Fitzgerald family comes to the investigators' attention, but Dobbs and Gimble are at a loss—if one of the four is involved, which Fitzgerald might it be?

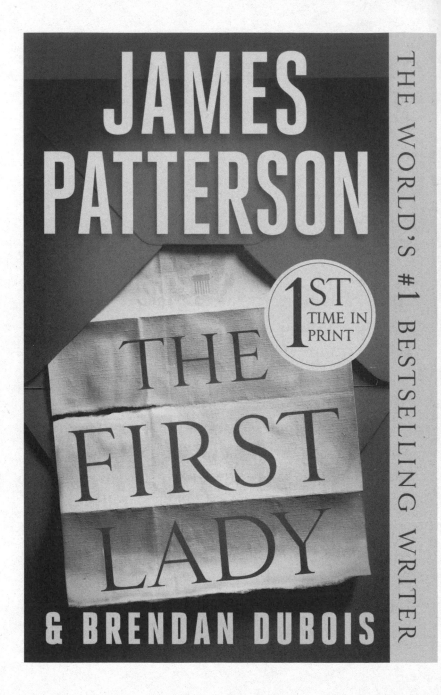

JAMES PATTERSON

THE FIRST LADY

& BRENDAN DUBOIS

THE FIRST LADY

The US government is at the forefront of everyone's mind these days and I've become incredibly fascinated by the idea that one secret can bring it all down. What if that secret is a US president's affair that results in a nightmarish outcome?

Sally Grissom, leader of the Presidential Protection Division, is summoned to a private meeting with the president and his chief of staff to discuss the disappearance of the first lady. What at first seemed an escape to a safe haven turns into a kidnapping when a ransom note arrives along with what could be the first lady's finger.

It's a race against the clock to collect the evidence that all leads to one troubling question: Could the kidnappers be from inside the White House?

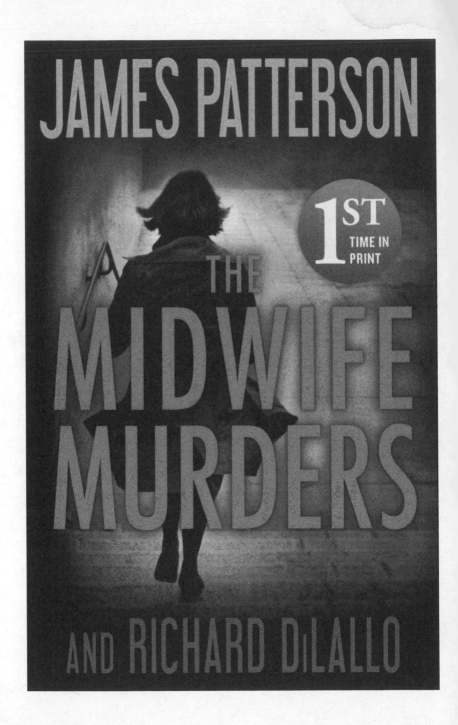

JAMES PATTERSON

1ST
TIME IN
PRINT

THE
MIDWIFE
MURDERS

and RICHARD DiLALLO

THE MIDWIFE MURDERS

I can't imagine a worse crime than one done against a child. But when two kidnappings and a vicious stabbing happen on her watch in a university hospital in Manhattan, her focus abruptly changes. Something has to be done, and senior midwife Lucy is fearless enough to try.

Rumors begin to swirl, with blame falling on everyone from the Russian mafia to an underground adoption network. Fierce single mom Lucy teams up with a skeptical NYPD detective, but I've given her a case where the truth is far more twisted than Lucy could ever have imagined.

THE WORLD'S #1 BESTSELLING WRITER

JAMES PATTERSON

1ST TIME IN PRINT

REVENGE

& ANDREW HOLMES

REVENGE

Former SAS soldier David Shelley was part of the most covert operations team in the special forces. Now settling down to civilian life in London, he has plans for a safer and more stable existence. But the shocking death of a young woman Shelley once helped protect puts those plans on hold.

The police rule the death a suicide but the grieving parents can't accept their beloved Emma would take her own life. They need to find out what really happened, and they turn to their former bodyguard, Shelley, for help.

JAMES PATTERSON
AND BRIAN SITTS
CRIME HAS A NEW ENEMY.
THE NEW YORK TIMES BESTSELLER
THE SHADOW
A THRILLER

THE SHADOW

Only two people know that 1930s society man Lamont Cranston has a secret identity as the Shadow, a crusader for justice. One is his greatest love, Margo Lane, and the other is his fiercest enemy, Shiwan Khan. When Khan ambushes the couple, they must risk everything for the slimmest chance of survival...in the future.

A century and a half later, Lamont awakens in a world both unknown and disturbingly familiar. Most disturbing, Khan's power continues to be felt over the city and its people. No one in this new world understands the dangers of stopping him better than Lamont Cranston. And only the Shadow knows that he's the one person who might succeed before more innocent lives are lost.

For a complete list of books by

JAMES PATTERSON

VISIT
JamesPatterson.com

 Follow James Patterson on Facebook
@JamesPatterson

 Follow James Patterson on Twitter
@JP_Books

 Follow James Patterson on Instagram
@jamespattersonbooks